Praise for

THE ROPE SWING

"Jonathan Corcoran's Appalachian voice—so fierce, so tender—portrays tradition as both weapon and soothing balm. *The Rope Swing* takes us inside quiet revolutions of the soul in mountain towns far from Stonewall: we can never go home again, but we recognize ourselves in these linked stories of love, loss, the economic tyranny of neglect and exploitation, and the lifelong alliance between those who stay and those who leave. *The Rope Swing* establishes a new American writer whose unerring instincts are cause for celebration."

—Jayne Anne Phillips, author of *Quiet Dell*, *Lark and Termite*, and *Black Tickets*

"In this debut book of interconnected stories, Corcoran writes fiercely about the lifelong effects of growing up in a small town on those who leave and those who stay. Corcoran is a remarkably empathetic writer whose subtle portraits capture undeniably tender moments in the lives of his characters. These stories are particularly poignant for anyone who grew up gay in America's desolate places, but Corcoran speaks eloquently to all facets of the human condition."

—*Kirkus Reviews*

"A powerful, moving, and beautifully-written book. Corcoran writes both queer and straight characters with insight and empathy. He is an observant writer who understands people's pain, regrets, heartache, and hope. This much needed, important book explores rural America and queer identity, two subjects rarely portrayed together."

—Carter Sickels, author of *The Evening Hour*

THE ROPE SWING

THE
ROPE SWING

STORIES

JONATHAN CORCORAN

VANDALIA PRESS

MORGANTOWN 2016

Vandalia Press / An imprint of West Virginia University Press

Copyright 2016 Jonathan Corcoran

First edition published 2016 by Vandalia Press

Printed in the United States of America

ISBN:

paper: 978-1-943665-11-2

epub: 978-1-943665-12-9

pdf: 978-1-943665-13-6

Library of Congress Cataloging-in-Publication Data is available
from the Library of Congress

Book and cover design by Than Saffel

To Sam, my love, and to Greg, my incantation

CONTENTS

ACKNOWLEDGMENTS

THIS BOOK wouldn't have been possible without the mentoring I received at the Rutgers-Newark MFA program. I give my enormous gratitude to Alice Elliott Dark, Tayari Jones, and Akhil Sharma. I will forever be indebted to Jayne Anne Phillips who first wowed me with her words and then pushed me to my writerly limits. I wouldn't be writing if I hadn't received encouragement from the good people at Brown: CDBL, Molly, and Meredith. I am humbled by the time and attention given to my work by my colleagues, readers, and friends: Roberto, Hirsh, Joanne, Patrick, Melissa, Anna, and Chris (to name but a few). Special and eternal thanks to Abby Freeland and all the talented folks at WVU Press, who believed in this collection. To Carter Sickels and Marie Manilla, who breathed a new spirit into this book. I am beyond grateful to the ones who have kept me steady over the years: Sara, Emily, Kat, Shawn, Sherry, Nachshon, Britt, and Krissy. To the entire Shulman-Klugman clan, who adopted me as one of their own. To Diana, for finding someone at just the right moment. To my Mandy and my Morgan.

And finally, I must thank you, Sam, for the support, love, and life that you give to me every day.

APPALACHIAN SWAN SONG

WHERE IS *Sheriff Bayless going? And why is he driving so fast?*

We had forgotten how much we loved our mountains in the summertime. It was the beginning of June, and the weather was right—the warming sun returning and the late-falling snow gone for good. Rivers of meltwater sprinted down the cliff faces, came alive, sang their birthing songs. We took once again to the fields, the ponds, and the creeks. We took off our shoes. We spread our toes through the soggy grass. We cocked our heads back and let the light settle onto our skin as our children played with sticks and rocks and dandelions.

We were calm and happy, and we assumed all was well in the world—which in our minds extended only as far as we could see, to the young leaves of the maples and sycamores along our town's streets, to the sharp waves of pine along the twin peaks of the Shavers and Onekanna mountains. What we saw was that the treetops were motionless in the morning. There was no wind. There was certainly no wind of change. We took the still air as a sign from God to relax, to begin the process of shedding the long, cold winter. We delighted in the return of the robins.

The Saturday newspaper arrived early as usual, delivered by twelve-year-old boys on bicycles, who rose at their mothers' prodding before the dawn. None of us paid much attention to the paper, unless we were looking for yard sales or apartments to rent, or, if we were lucky, when our children made the honor roll. We heard the important local news from our neighbors: old women who listened to scanners, memorized police codes, and picked up the phone faster than the paper could print words. Stories became bigger, more real to us that way, delivered with a slant and a backstory and a suggestive drop in tone. All of our stories were like that—beginning as a raindrop falling from the sky, collecting the moisture we breathed into the air. We lived on the wet side of the mountains, and when the rain fell, often and hard upon the pavement, we could see the sky above and the world around reflected on the asphalt. None of our secrets were safe. We knew everyone: every house, every bloodline, and every downfall.

The editor of the newspaper was a woman we hated. She was always reminding us that she was the first female editor in the history of our state, that she was the first editor of our paper to interview a sitting president, that she was the first editor to print in color. We hated her because she was also the first editor who made it a habit of putting pictures of our wrecked cars across the front page. She called this breaking news; we called it the end of decency.

She must have known we didn't pay much attention to her paper. She must have wanted us to see the headline that Saturday when the spring began its shift to summer. Bold letters spread across all six columns, a headline so big that we couldn't help but look: "THE END OF THE LINE, THE END OF AN ERA." It was the day of the last passenger train on the West Virginia–Western Maryland Railroad. Our town was the terminus, the last dot on the map. The railroad had come here when coal and timber were king, funneling our resources out to the big cities on the Eastern Seaboard. The day the railroad was built—some hundred years ago—was the official birth of our town, though people had been living in our mountains since before the Civil War, and the Indians had been hunting here for a millennium. Everyone knew somebody who had an Indian grandmother—at least that's what we told ourselves.

Our resources were abundant, and because of this, we'd all known our share of millionaires, even if only through pictures in the newspaper or roadside plaques commemorating one baron or another. The millionaires left their marks all over: on the elegant architecture of the Presbyterian College buildings, on the polished marble interior of the courthouse, and on the half-dozen mansions resting on the half-dozen hills that towered over our downtown. The millionaires, the owners of our coal mines and our sawmills, gave us modest bonuses at Christmas—made our fathers feel more like men. We never really saw the millionaires in the town. We didn't eat at the same restaurants. We suspected they didn't know any of our names, but they did, of course. With time, their children married our children. Surnames muddled. The legacies of coal and sawdust and politicians passed through our blood and our breast milk, and the stories of our mountains ennobled even the least of us. We thought we were special.

We put the newspaper aside that morning. We thought little of the significance of a town without a train. The day—with the perfect morning sun, and the fresh air, clear as water—required our presence. Years of sitting quietly on our front porches watching thunderstorms roll through the sky had taught us something important about living in the moment, even if that's not what we called it.

We didn't feel guilty. We didn't feel foolish. We took our cues from nature. The birds sang and twitted underneath the cover of fresh leaves, so we, too, laughed under the shade of trees. There were family reunions and barbecues out at Steward's Park, children's birthday parties at the soccer field, and a gathering of Civil War reenactors up on Beverly Mountain, toting muskets and wearing old uniforms of blue and gray. Our parents were nostalgic, telling stories of the riverside parties of their youth. Our fathers bragged about the biggest bucks they'd chased through the woods—they still had the antlers to prove it, hanging over our garage doors and mounted proudly on our tree houses. The children ran and jumped and dreamed of glimpses of the far away—the view from the top of the fire tower on Onekanna Ridge.

Downtown, the G. C. Murphy's was half-buzzing with young mothers wandering the cramped aisles for discounted sheets and lawn furniture. We all knew—had heard from our parents and grandparents—that Murphy's had been busier before, back when the downtown streets had been filled with pedestrians. Back when going to Murphy's was a choice, when three different department stores filled out the big brick buildings that lined our Main Street. The seventies had come and burned through our businesses. The eighties began bleakly, with empty storefronts and boarded up windows, though we felt the contraction less out here than in some other places across the country. The mountains that hugged our town, the rising peaks that made our roads narrow and curve wildly, always shielded us. Because of this, whole movements barely touched us—disco and free love were things to be laughed at, even if we had secretly wished to taste them.

We were mountain people. The mountains were in our voices and on our worn clothes. We were as sturdy as our old oak trees, everlasting, never changing. We were survivors and subsisters. We thought we had internalized the lessons of our great-grandparents who had lived through wars and the Depression. We thought those lessons existed in our blood, swam through our veins. We didn't think it possible that we could become complacent. We thought our skin was as hard as limestone, while our hearts were as soft as coal dust.

We were proud of what remained, our homes that we painted each year, our cars that our neighbors fixed for free—six or seven men gathering under a Sunday sky, tinkering over an open engine. We believed in our little shops that sold necessities and a flourish or two—even if we eschewed them for the big-box stores that descended on our town like a plague. We watched the news on our televisions—oil crises, more wars, hostages—and it was as if Washington, New York, and even Pittsburgh belonged to another country. We sympathized, of course, but we didn't always believe everything we heard. We fancied ourselves prosperous and crafty, and questioned why someone couldn't just get by—gas prices rising or otherwise. We had fruit trees in our front yards and beanstalks growing along trellises in the back. We knew how to skin a deer and how to gut a trout. We gave our children pocketknives and their first guns, and when they used these tools correctly and responsibly, we smiled with pride. Even our daughters could wield a bow and arrow. We thought we were special, and because of this, we thought we were safe.

There were never more than a few thousand people within the borders of our small world at any given time, but we felt our outsized importance. There were the millionaires, of course. Three governors, four senators, a four-star general, and a poet of some consequence had also called our hamlet home. It never sank in that those people, those names, belonged to the past— or that the past of all peoples carried some greatness. Because of our history, which we treated like the present, and because of the gilded, old buildings—even with their cracked marble and faded gold leaf—we never questioned the fact that most of us rarely left the town, save for the occasional trip to the mall, a place only three towns over but more than an hour's drive. We were the last stop on the railroad, and the only town of note in the surrounding five counties. We told our children that we were God's chosen people—Appalachian Israelites—even if we didn't go to church very often. We thought we were given a secret, living out here. We thought that the code to unlocking that secret was fossilized in a piece of falling rock. Living here was both a gift and a test, and one day the secret to life would fall from a mountain face and land in front of our shoes. One of us would rise up again, like Christ himself, and save the world from itself.

***

The wind was picking up by the afternoon—a hint of the thunderstorm the weatherman said was blowing our way. We were packing up our picnics as the sun began its westward descent. The sky was still clear. The children out on Yokum Run were sitting in Mr. Winter's big field of a yard, under the shade of a leaning cherry tree. The tree could have been as old as Mr. Winter himself.

Mr. Winter was a senile man who never left his house. He had done great things once, had been a prosperous man who had his hands in half the town's businesses. At least that's what we were told by those who had known him from before. We didn't inquire further. We preferred to fill in the blanks ourselves—construct his story from the rare glimpse of a sagging face that we saw through his tiny kitchen window—the only window of his home not covered with heavy curtains.

His grass had grown almost as high as the neighbors' split-rail fence. Those same neighbors complained that they'd seen a dozen copperheads slithering in and out of his yard. They forbid their children from playing anywhere near Mr. Winter's home, but their admonishments didn't stop anyone. The children had taken over the field as their hideout, ducking behind the grass when their parents called them home for dinner. On that Saturday afternoon, they were throwing half-ripe cherries onto the pavement, watching as speeding cars zipped around the corner of the road, flattening the fruit. The hot sun baked the smashed cherries onto the road, and then the children threw gravel and more cherries onto the pavement before running back to the safety of the grass and the shade of the cherry tree. They called the mixture Yankee pie and dared each other to eat it.

Their parents were on their front porches drinking iced tea, or off to the grocery store shopping for dinner, or drinking a beer on the back porch, watching the creek flow muddier than usual from the last of the melted snow. The muddy creek gave the whole road the smell of something strangely fresh and oddly fetid—like a spring rain and rotting fish. And then, as the hot wind blew east and the scent of the smashed cherries began to float in, everyone on Yokum Run thought about their mothers' and grandmothers' pies that would come later in the season.

The cherries and apples that grew in our yards were too sour for anything but pie.

Sheriff Bayless, who lived at the dead-end of Yokum Run, was driving, on his way to the train station. He was headed to the farewell ceremony, the one in honor of the last passenger train headed out to Maryland. He was running late, which was out of character for a man who had for three decades fathomed himself the guardian of our townspeople. He was an attractive man, with bristly, silver hair and a tight jaw. He'd never married. He was the type who would tip his hat at our grandmothers. He would wink at all of our young daughters, and then wink again as they blushed. He had a firm handshake that our town's men secretly emulated. He was our protector, and we trusted him. He made us believe in the law.

When he hit the children's pie concoction, his tires skidded, and his sheriff's cruiser spun out across the road into Mr. Winter's yard. With a quick punch of the brakes, the car came to a halt in the high grass. Sheriff Bayless jumped out from the door of his car in his full sheriff's uniform and chased the kids in circles, as they ducked in and out of the sharp blades of grass.

He finally got hold of one of the kids by the round collar of her cotton T-shirt. The others had run off, jumped across the creek and into the woods, leaving poor Emily Weese to bear the brunt of the sheriff's screaming.

"You kids these days have no sense of consequences," he yelled, his mouth inches from her face. She set to crying and the tears streamed through the dirt on her cheeks, leaving visible a clean trail of sun-kissed skin. Bayless looked at her and thought of his poor, dead sister, a woman who'd once protected him from the darker parts of the world. His grip loosened.

"Consider this a warning," he said, and then his voice softened. "A very important warning."

The sheriff huffed back to his car, now another fifteen minutes behind schedule. He was pulling back onto the road, leaving a path of flattened grass in his wake, when the front door of Mr. Winter's house swung open. A gaunt man in gray slacks and a loose sweater hobbled out to the edge of his porch. "Bayless," he croaked, "will you drive me to the station?"

The children emerged from the woods and from their hiding places. They peeked around the corner of the house to watch Bayless tip his hat to the old man, whose arms dangled awkward and loose at his sides. They had expected a corpse, though none of the children could be sure that wasn't what they were seeing.

"By all means, Mr. Winter," Bayless said, pushing open his passenger door.

Mr. Winter closed the front door to his home—the creaking like the sealing of a sarcophagus—and inched down the sidewalk to the sheriff's car.

***

The older set remembered the train as a symbol of the town's glory. When they grew up, the train made ten departures a day. The train had ferried governors, famous actors, and even two presidents who came in different years to serve as grand marshals for the feature parade of the Festival of the Trees. We still laughed about the presidents' Secret Service men, dressed in black suits; how they'd patrolled the parade route down Main Street and stood sentry atop our buildings, as if one of us could have ever been capable of such a violence.

With the train, we could get to the big rail towns in Maryland

and connect to Washington; from there, we could go to New York, to Boston. People dressed in suits and ties and fancy shawls for the ride. There was a sense of old-world gentility that surrounded the depot—from the conductor's black hat, to the attendants' white-gloved hands. None of us ever wore gloves, except for those of us who worked in the factories and the sawmills. And these gloves were never white.

The truth was that almost none of us used the train anymore. By that final voyage in June, the train came only once a day, except for Sunday, the Lord's Day. Even if we could have afforded to ride it, we thought of the train as a relic, even more so because our grandparents said it was a privilege. Our grandparents took us to the depot to remind us of how things were, of how things could be for us, if we only had the sense to want such a life. We associated the train with politicians and the president of the bank. We weren't jealous of those who could afford to take it. It was just that by that last trip in June, we had ceased really considering the train at all. It had become like a part of the land, another worn mountain peak whose name we didn't know. We were more concerned about cars and the promise of the big highway that would make our lives easier. With the new highway, the long drive to the mall would be cut in half.

For us, the train was just a thing that sometimes blocked the roads. It was just a hunk of metal that whistled loudly in the afternoon. Still, when we stayed up past midnight on a lazy summer night, sitting alone on our back porches, we sometimes heard the whistle blowing, even when it shouldn't have been blowing at all. We were good Christians, but we saw the ghosts of our ancestors when we heard that whistle. We saw our great-grandfathers playing the fiddle in the city park. We saw our great-grandmothers plucking pungent ramps from their back-yards. When we heard that whistle, we could smell those ramps and we were hungry. We said prayers aloud in the darkness that we would one day see our great-grandparents again.

By the afternoon on the day of the last train, some three dozen people had gathered on the town square that centered around the brick and wood depot. We expected more to turn out, given the headline in the morning paper; but then again, who of us ever paid any attention to the paper? We watched as the train sat idling—its six cars and the hulking, black steam engine, the company's logo painted in yellow letters across the side.

They were the faces we had always known. Funny Pauly, the town's faithful florist, was much younger then. He was telling jokes, and we were all laughing—laughing at him, laughing with him. He was *funny*, we knew, in a light green shirt and a darker green tie the color of a rose stem, but he was also harmless. The bank president was chatting with the mayor about the lumber companies that were losing contracts to overseas businesses. "There was nothing to be done about it," the mayor said. "Open your eyes. The future is not in those trees. The future is down that road. The future is there. The future is somewhere else altogether." We didn't love the mayor or his views, but he was a man of his word. If we wanted something done—to fix a clogged storm drain or to expedite our husbands' disability pay—he would make the call and the check would come. So we tolerated him, too, because we needed him. We needed him more, we thought, than we needed a rickety steam engine.

The principal of the high school stood quietly with his young, pretty wife, who held their infant child in her arms. They had only lived in our town for a year, and they told stories of all the cities they'd visited—New York, San Francisco, Paris. Everyone wanted to be their friends. Everyone thought that by knowing the principal, their children would get better grades or a better position on the basketball team, even though the principal never remembered any of our names.

And there was Hank, the pawnbroker, a man whose shop was as old, dusty, and disorganized as the town itself, standing off from the crowd smoking a cigarette. Nobody wanted to know Hank, though we all did. We all knew someone who had snuck into the back door of his shop in a time of trouble. His crowd wasn't the kind that would come to this type of event, but we understood. We knew how to read the lines of a man's face. Many of us didn't speak to Hank, but we knew that he belonged here. We understood that the train belonged to him, just as it belonged to all of us.

The train had been scheduled to leave for half an hour, but the mayor said that they were waiting for one last guest to arrive. It wasn't long before Sheriff Bayless pulled up and parked in the lot of the bank, adjacent to the train station. Clumps of grass from Mr. Winter's yard poked out of the sheriff's front bumper. Mr. Winter walked out first, and those who could remember his face from before shuddered—a man whose face now showed a vision of the future.

Bayless got out and walked around his car to the back passenger door. He opened it and offered a hand to the woman inside. It was Mrs. Robert Jennings, the widow of the late governor. She wore a prim, gray suit that matched the color of her hair. Her white pumps shined in the sun, as did her bowed, white hat. We cleared the path when she walked by. We knew that she was a society woman, had been born to important parents in Washington or Virginia. Still, she always waved to us and said hello. We treated her as a dear old acquaintance. When we thought ourselves important, we considered her a friend.

Mrs. Jennings settled next to Hank the pawnbroker. He shook her hand, and some of us cringed imagining all the junk Hank's hands had touched in his shop—but she was as graceful as ever. She leaned over and whispered something into Hank's ear that set him to beaming. Mr. Winter quickly staggered to her side. Hank leaned in to tell them both something like a joke. The first lady blushed before laughing. Mr. Winter, looking confused and distant, took the good lady's hand.

Her kindness was why we couldn't help but love Mrs. Jennings, even though she had more money than most of us would earn in a lifetime. She wasn't from our town, but when the governor retired here, she took to us like everyone's favorite grandmother. She ate in our restaurants, and she attended our churches (she said she liked to hear the word of God spoken in many voices). She came to our cakewalks and our festivals and made our small-town events successful, even joyous. She showed up at every parade, at every ribbon cutting. Our grandmothers told us to wash our dirty faces and emulate her. She was the model of a real woman, they said, without any airs about her. Her clothes, her hat, her perfectly controlled smile were all natural, the sign of a woman who kept love and God as constants in her life. She remembered our names, even the least of us.

She lived in the biggest house at the entrance of the town, at the confluence of two major state roads, one that went east all the way to Virginia, and one that went north to Maryland. It was an odd place for such a grand house—with a gas station across one street and a rusty diner across the other. But that was part of the home's charm, her charm. The house—all four stories of it, with white clapboard and forest-green shutters—announced to anyone who came to the town that the people here had a history. We believed that her house was the thread that held the town together—through change, through recessions, through wars, through highways that threatened to bypass us altogether. We all slowed down when we drove by her house. We never stopped noticing its beauty.

After the governor died, Mrs. Jennings had taken the train frequently. We never knew exactly where she went or who she was visiting, but she would always wave to anyone milling around the station as the train pulled away. She always smiled so genuinely, even after his death. We thought she would take that last train. The town's most prominent citizens (the few who had the money) had bought tickets. They had organized caravans to drive the whole way to Maryland, to meet the train, and then drive them back home—this was the end, after all. They wanted to be able to tell their children and their grandchildren that they had been there, as if it were some monumental sporting event—the seventh game of the World Series or a Super Bowl that went into overtime.

We thought that Mrs. Jennings would take the train, and we feared that she would never come back. We wondered how she could persist in the town without the reassurance of the train. She was too important to be confined to our world, and we imagined that the train was what kept her here. Every time she left, to Washington or wherever it was that she went, we imagined she met with all the famous politicians over tea and fancy steak dinners. We thought there was something tangible to such meetings, as if by sharing a meal with the remarkable, she captured just a little bit of their essence, their importance, and brought it back with her. She planted that essence in her garden. It was that essence that made the windows of her big, beautiful house catch the sun in such a perfect way. She shared that essence with all of us. Most of us couldn't have cared less about the train, but Mrs. Jennings was indispensible. She made us special.

The train whistle sounded, and then the wind began to howl. A few of us, on hearing such a beautiful confluence, considered ourselves lucky that God had shined so brightly on our town. Professor Benedum, a man who pronounced words like no one we knew, was standing alone, his hands in the pockets of his brown corduroy trousers. Professor Benedum taught us the Greeks and their poetry. He likely had some historical analogy for a day like this—Charon's boat crossing the river Styx, maybe.

The mayor boarded the train with the bank president. The principal got on, but his wife stayed behind, forcing the hands of her infant to wave good-bye. We were all surprised when Hank, the rough pawnbroker, took a seat across the aisle from the mayor. They seemed engrossed in deep conversation, and it was then that we began to understand how many of us had grown up together, had shared childhoods on baseball diamonds and in church pews. All those divisions that had occurred since our youth—the separation of the rich from the poor, the educated from the laborer—for a moment we wondered if those divisions wouldn't all just disappear as the train went off into the distance.

The train was less than a quarter full. We suspected other passengers would board along the way, but we couldn't know for sure. We wondered what this train had meant to the other people who had lived in the other small towns along the route. We felt an urge to know them—those people from towns less prosperous, less storied than our own—towns we knew only as discolored old signs, the painted letters of their names chipping off of the warped wood. We began to feel lonely as we realized that we had for so long neglected a bond with these people, our neighbors. We had been connected, after all, by a railroad track—and not just any railroad track. It was our track, laid by our ancestors. We had laid that track with hopeful hands.

The sky became dark as the wind pushed storm clouds over the downtown. We held our breath and waited for Mrs. Jennings to climb the train's steps, but she did not move. She watched solemnly, with her right arm locked regally into that of Mr. Winter, Sheriff Bayless hovering close behind. The sheriff did not watch the train. He watched only Mrs. Jennings.

A murmur began amongst the crowd. Maybe Mrs. Jennings didn't have a ride home on one of the caravans, hadn't wanted to bother someone with the logistics of a one-way train? The principal's wife rushed with her baby in her arm to the window of the train where her husband sat. Surely Mrs. Jennings could share his ride home? The principal nodded his head. His wife then walked over to Mrs. Jennings, who kissed the baby on the cheek. The principal's wife pleaded with Mrs. Jennings, but Mrs. Jennings wouldn't hear it—she would not be taking the train today. The mayor stepped off the train to approach Mrs. Jennings, to offer his own seat, but then a clap of thunder broke. The mayor ran back inside. The remaining crowd hurried under the cover of the depot to shield themselves from the rain that began as a trickle but quickly grew into a downpour.

Sheriff Bayless rushed across the street to his car and brought back an umbrella for Mrs. Jennings, who stood resolutely with Mr. Winter. Bayless was begging her to go and stand under the awning of the depot, pointing to the sky and the periodic bolts of lightning. But she shook her head. Bayless held the umbrella over her and Mr. Winter, even as the rain came down onto his uniform and dripped off the brim of his hat.

The conductor pulled up the stepladder and closed the door. He waved good-bye with his gentleman gloves. The crowd cheered as the train sounded its horn, as billows of smoke puffed from the engine. The train began its slow chug down the tracks, growing smaller and smaller as it crawled away from the depot and the buildings of the town. The long chain of connected cars—which had seemed to stretch halfway across the downtown while parked—now seemed like little tin toys in the distance.

The crowd thinned. Some remained under the awning of the depot, but more and more dashed off to their cars to drive away. Alone in the square, in the rain, were Mr. Winter and Mrs. Jennings, Sheriff Bayless still holding his umbrella over their heads. They watched as the train tracked through the rail yard, over the bridge, across the river, and off toward the mountains. Mrs. Jennings was smiling, though it was a type of smile we couldn't place. She seemed to be looking not at the train but at something in the haze-covered peaks of the Onekannas.

When the train disappeared, so too did the storm. Then the sun was back out again, shining on the empty downtown. Sheriff Bayless, Mr. Winter, Mrs. Jennings—and all of us at home on our porches or in our cars—looked out toward the mountains, thinking we might see a rainbow. But when we craned our necks, there was only the empty, blue sky, solemn and crisp after the passing storm. There were no clouds, just the ball of the sun heading slowly toward the brim of the forested peaks of Onekanna Ridge.

Sheriff Bayless closed his umbrella and walked Mrs. Jennings back to the car, Mr. Winter following behind. Mrs. Jennings stopped and looked back once, to the rail yard. She adjusted the skirt of her suit, and then she got into the sheriff's cruiser. Bayless closed the door behind her. Mr. Winter took the front. They drove away. The town was quiet. The trees on the mountains were green and bright. The air was fresh, with just the slightest hint of acrid smoke—the last breath of the steam engine clinging to our noses.

***

We came home from our barbecues and our parties. We saw the newspaper once again, the picture of our train. The few who had gone to the depot called us and reported the scene. Mrs. Jennings, they said, had cried as the train pulled away, though they wouldn't swear on it. It had been raining, and the sky had gone nearly black.

Don't you understand, the old women asked us. *There is no new highway. There is no train. We are alone out here in the mountains. We are alone, like the pioneers.*

We hung up our phones and laughed at our dramatic neighbors. We opened all of our windows and breathed in the wet summer night. We threw the newspaper in the garbage before we went to bed, the sounds of the creek and the wild wind lulling us to sleep.

THE ROPE SWING

THE DRIVE to the river takes Christopher along the old highway. He passes vacant gas stations at the edge of town, then seemingly idle farmland with lonely rolls of hay, and, finally, miles of unfettered green forest. The old highway consists of two small lanes that rise and fall with the contours of the mountains—steep grades of sudden change, marked by big yellow signs that indicate the climb or descent of the road with a percentage point. The road at times angles sharply and frighteningly around steep cliffs. When he looks out his window, he sees that beyond the tiny gravel shoulder, the land falls precipitously away: a hillside of boulders, some half-buried by moss and wild grass. On the other side of the road, the worn mountain face towers upward. Poplar, pine, and sycamore somehow find patches of soil on these steep surfaces. Christopher, though, trusts in the roots of these trees. He does not worry about them losing their grip on the soil and falling onto his car as he drives past. He trusts mostly in the simplicity of such a life, in which the main concern is against leaning too far in one direction.

The new highway, on the other hand, just two miles to the east but out of sight, has four level lanes paved into the bombed-out heart of the mountains. The ledges that frame both sides of that highway bear the jagged marks of explosives—artificial striations slicing across the once-impenetrable rock. Miles of metal netting hug the bodies of the carved cliffs to prevent the crumbling limestone from dropping down onto the passing drivers. The falling rocks gather in big piles at the bottom of the nets, stretching the metal at the base out toward the road: a reminder, Christopher thinks, of both safety and sadness; one thing created, the other destroyed. And the seeming impermanence, too, the constant erosion of what seems so solid.

Last spring Christopher's geology teacher said that he could find evidence of the prehistoric world in those crumbling rocks. Fossils. Impressions. Living things weighed down and immortalized by mud and silt. Aquatic beings, from when the world had been more ocean than not. But no one stops to notice, the teacher said. People just drive right by, unaware of the treasures literally spilling out onto the shoulder of the road.

People can't get to the river from the new highway. They can get to the mall in a half hour or to DC in three. This, to Christopher, is a small comfort. It means that the river will always be a secret of sorts. As time passes and the old highway is used a little less each day, he imagines that his slice of river, the spot he shares with his friend, Greg, will become forgotten by all but himself. He imagines growing old and building a cabin down at the riverbank with a deck that hangs over the water. There are two chairs on the deck: one for himself and one for Greg. Nights of peace and no one around for miles. An unthinkable touch of the hand, rendered acceptable by the privacy of the forest.

Just as soon as he imagines this life, he wills himself to forget it. The more time he spends at the river with Greg, the more he feels himself floating away from the things he understands. This is both exhilarating and painful. A moment of bliss, and then an evening of aching. He is a split self: his visible body and his hidden blood. The guilt pounds in his gut, especially when his mother lingers at his bedroom door to say good night; he's a year away from adulthood, and she no longer kisses his forehead.

Imprisoned rocks, metal nets rusting toward disintegration, a once-booming rail yard town that no longer has any trains. Extinct creatures swimming toward immortality. A mother hovering a second too long at his door in the darkness. He leaves behind all of these images as he rides down from a mountain peak into the narrow valley below. He thinks only of what he must say to his friend—the words that he's been rehearsing since the summer began. Will he be able to utter the words aloud? He tells himself—just as he did yesterday and the day before—that today will be different. Today he will leave that other version of himself behind. Today he will let his blood flow freely. He inhales the crisp air of the mountains. He feels the burn of the sun on his hands that rest on the steering wheel. Coming down the hill, he lifts his foot off of the pedal and coasts.

He rolls downward, and as the road levels out, Greg's car comes into sight: the sagging bumper, the dented body, Greg himself splayed across the trunk, basking in the sun. A figure that even from fifty feet makes his throat tighten. He tries to speak the words—the ones he has practiced alone in his car— but only his friend's name comes out. "Greg," he says, like an enchantment. And again: "Greg."

He eases in behind Greg's car, which is parked in a bend in the road, along a wide, gravel-strewn shoulder meant for big trucks to stop and check their brakes. But few trucks come here now, thanks to the new highway. They are safe, then, the two boys. They are alone. His tense body loosens.

Greg slides off of the trunk and walks up to Christopher's window—his blonde hair is matted to his skull, damp with a fresh summer sweat. "I thought you weren't going to make it," he says, and by his heaving chest, it's clear that he's frustrated. "I've been waiting for over an hour."

"I'm so sorry," Christopher says, and then Greg's face softens. Christopher could stop there. He could say nothing else and all would be forgotten. But he continues anyway, because he needs to talk, he needs to press forward with any intelligible sentence. He feels that his time is running out. The summer will slip away, and as school begins again, this secret life at the river will have burnt up and fallen like the turning autumn leaves. The freedom their bodies feel here, at the river, could never be possible in the halls of the high school. "Something's wrong. It's my mother again. She was in one of her moods this morning. I didn't want to leave her alone in the house. I was afraid to leave her. I was afraid to stay."

Christopher knows that Greg understands this. It's their river ritual to speak of such things. Then the water washes over them and rinses their skin of all the unpleasant residue. It's like a daily baptism, like going to the altar at church and being born again, reset to zero, over and over.

"It's fine," Greg says and looks down the road. "At least your mother speaks to you. I'm just happy to be here, and not there."

"I drove as fast as I could," Christopher says.

"I know," Greg says. "Let it go. Let's catch the sun while we still can."

***

THE ROPE SWING

Christopher grabs a towel and his swimming trunks from the passenger seat of his car. He takes them and walks with Greg down the steep path from the road into the forest. The walk, along the trampled dirt, underneath the dense canopy of the trees, frees him from all the chaos, the remaining conflict in Christopher's mind. Behind is the town, his mother, the road. At a certain point the whirring of passing cars stops. At a certain point he can no longer see the road at all. For a while, he cannot see the river either: only the green leaves above, and the tan, dry leaves on the ground below.

The sunlight pierces through the forest in spots, almost cinematically, so that what normally seems invisible—individual beams of hot white light—appears suddenly tangible. Christopher reaches out to touch that white light, beating down on a bush of rhododendron. The sounds of trickling water become audible, and then the trickle becomes a rush—the current beating over smooth rocks. As the sound of the water grows louder, Christopher sees the thinning edge of the forest and then the sparkling river itself. This, to Christopher, has begun to feel like home.

"She's coming to the show tonight," Christopher says as they walk down the path along the river's edge.

"Are you nervous?" Greg asks.

"Yes and no. I guess I find myself caring less every day. Or I wish I could care less. I don't know. I'm just going to pretend she's not there. How do you do it? I mean, with the two of you the way you are."

"I don't do anything. There's nothing to do anymore. You just keep moving. You just stop thinking."

Christopher falls back and watches his friend walk ahead. He looks for Greg to shrug his shoulders, to tense his neck—a gesture to indicate a fear of the unknown. But his friend marches forward, shoulders straight, unhindered by his reality.

"I think she's afraid of me," Christopher says. "She's afraid of whatever it is she thinks I'm becoming."

Greg stops walking, turns his head toward Christopher: "And what are you becoming?"

He hesitates only a moment: "I don't know." The words are as true and blue tinted as the summer sky above.

***

They hadn't really known each other before the show, though they were the same age and attended the same high school. Christopher came to the theater like an asylum seeker—a last act of survival, a way to make it through his final years as a teenager with some kind of hiding place—from the kids at school, from his mother. He thought of the old brick building as a cathedral—a place with history and safety and dark crevices for praying to a God that often felt more like an enemy.

Their conversations began in those dark spaces, backstage while they ran lines—Christopher, the Tin Man, and Greg, the Lion—the roles, like their lives, in search of one missing element. Soon they were standing next to each other during vocal warm-ups. Soon they were goofing off in the costume closet. One day Greg asked Christopher to come with him to the river before rehearsal.

The way their friendship developed felt like a dream—the movements blurred, the reality of the situation questionable. It had been so long since Christopher had made a new friend; he had so few to begin with. And here they were now, every single day before the show, stalling at the river, reaching for a feeling that couldn't yet be acted on.

"Do you know where this river flows?" Christopher asks his friend as they walk along the bank, opposite the current. "All this time, and I've never really thought about it."

"The water comes down from the mountains—it actually starts right up there," Greg says, pointing up at a mountain peak off in the distance. "It joins with a bunch of streams—this is what you see here—and then it flows down the valley until it meets its sister river—the one that goes through our town. The rivers meet up, they join as one, and then they flow down south—the Ohio, the Mississippi—until the water we're swimming in goes through New Orleans and out into the Gulf of Mexico—the Atlantic Ocean, really."

"I've never been to the ocean."

They walk along, Christopher leading. He's afraid to look Greg in the eyes. He's afraid that he'll cower into himself again, like every other day, and then say nothing at all when he really wants to say everything—to speak his body and his heart into existence.

Christopher pauses when he notices something attached to the big sycamore tree that leans over the water. "What's that?" he asks.

They step closer, and Christopher sees that tied to a high branch is a long, corded rope. The rope hangs out long and limp, the end dangling just a few feet above the river's surface. A low breeze pushes the rope back and forward over the river— the hempen fabric glowing golden as it touches the edge of the sunlight, then the dull tan of dried mud as it slips into the shade of the tree.

"It's a swing," Greg says excitedly. "Someone's put up a rope swing."

Christopher has no desire to test the rope's weight. He senses something menacing about its hanging there, barely disturbed in the breeze, wanting only a body. "It wasn't here yesterday. That means someone's been out here, either early this morning or last night. Do you think they're out here now?"

Christopher searches around for evidence of teenage mischief. He looks for a beer can, a smoked-out joint, or the cut line of a fishing pole. He's convinced that the intruder must be someone they know, one or more of the boys from school, no doubt, that he'd tried to forget about over the past few months.

"What are you so afraid of?" Greg asks. "Besides, if anyone were here, there'd be a car parked back up at the road."

Of course this is logical, but the presence of the rope persists. Christopher pulls his arms into his chest, and sits down on a damp log. He feels the moisture soaking through his pants onto his skin. Greg sits next to him.

"I ran into someone from school this morning," Greg says. "Matt Boone, of all people."

"I hate that guy," Christopher says.

"I was at the gas station. He was sitting in his truck at the edge of the parking lot. Waiting for someone, I suppose. Or fucking around with nothing to do, like they all do. I was filling up my tank."

"You just have to walk away," Christopher says, his throat tightening—the images of what's to come causing his pulse to quicken.

"I made the mistake of looking in his direction. Do you know what he did? He pointed a gun at me. He had a goddamn shotgun in the cab of his truck, and he pointed it at me and pretended to shoot. And then he just laughed."

"Greg, I can't go back there."

Christopher watches the rope swing gently over the water. And suddenly, he's no longer in the forest, but inside a classroom, with the teacher's back turned. First the gestures. Then the words. The situation escalating. The rising fear of harm—bodily harm—forcing him back into the most instinctual form of a human, thoughts only of self-preservation.

"It's going to be alright," Greg says, but his words don't resonate. He grabs Christopher's hand and squeezes it. "We'll make it through the year. We have each other now."

Christopher allows himself to feel his friend's touch for only a second before pulling away. He turns his gaze away from his friend and out toward the river.

"I'm seventeen and I've only swam in rivers," Christopher says. "Everyone says how easy it is in the ocean, how in the salt water your body just floats. If I could just ride this river all the way down . . ."

***

They sit on the log, listening to the calling birds and flowing water until Christopher has calmed his nerves. He looks around. There are no beer cans. There is no evidence of seventeen-year-old boys hiding in the bushes waiting to sabotage them.

"We're really alone," Greg says. "I promise. Can we enjoy ourselves a little bit?"

Christopher looks down at the sun-reflecting river, through the shadowy forest, trying to imagine how many secrets have been imparted under the protection of these trees.

Greg drapes his towel over the roots of the big sycamore tree. He takes off his shirt and begins to strip off his jean shorts. Christopher quickly turns his head, his cheeks reddening.

"Do you want me to hide?" Greg asks, laughing. "Haven't you seen me do this a hundred times?"

Christopher turns back around. He forces a smile—the easiest smile he can manage. "I'm sorry," he says. "I know I'm weird."

He pretends not to watch as Greg lowers his shorts and underwear. He pretends not to notice his friend's strong legs as he pulls on his swimming trunks. Christopher looks to the river but sees only, in his peripheral vision, Greg's large birthmark, round and chestnut brown, at the spot where his back meets his buttocks.

Christopher knows this is his signal also, to participate in the show that's not supposed to be a show. How many times had they played at this? He pulls down his jeans first, because he's never grown used to walking around without a shirt. He's never grown comfortable with the dark hair sprouting on his chest. He doesn't dare look at Greg, to check to see if Greg is looking at him. He wills it, Greg's vision on his body, but he also knows that to catch Greg in that moment would be to open the floodgates. If Christopher saw Greg staring back, he would have to let Greg in.

Christopher takes off his shirt. Just as he pulls the cotton fabric over his head, he sees a vision of Greg running down the bank, pummeling his way into the water.

"It's freezing," Greg shouts. He grabs the rope swing and drags it back to the shore. He begins to climb up the slanted trunk of the sycamore tree.

"Don't you think that's a little dangerous?" Christopher asks. "What if the water's not deep enough? What if you hurt yourself on the rocks?"

"The water's plenty deep. I won't hit the rocks."

Greg pulls the rope taut, testing its ability to hold his body. Before Christopher has time to dissuade him any further, Greg jumps from the tree. He shoots out over the water, and as he flies, clinging to the rope, a wild sound issues from his mouth—a joyous yowl, a primal scream, an explosion of self. As the rope passes the center of its pendulum, Greg lets go and floats through the air, arms extended. The flying form and the creature howl make Christopher jealous of his friend's courage. They also make him want to run and jump into the river, to find his friend and dance with him, to join together and hold him in the weightlessness of the cold current.

Greg drops from the rope and sinks, leaving a splash and a spray of fast, white bubbles. Then the bubbles are gone. He does not rise.

"Greg?" Christopher calls. "Greg?"

Christopher scans the surface of the water for the shadow of his friend's body. His stomach is a brick. His jaw clenches. "Please, come up! You're scaring me." His eyes begin to well with water. He wants to save his friend, but his body is frozen in place. "I'm so sorry," he murmurs—a summer's worth of unspoken words weighing down his speech.

But of course Greg surfaces—laughing first and then coughing, spitting water. "Now you jump," he says. "What are you afraid of?"

Christopher wipes his eyes in embarrassment, hoping his friend doesn't notice. He looks at the rope swinging in small, tight circles over the current. He sees the mottled trunk of the sycamore tree, Greg treading water. His gentle smile, his warm, brown eyes.

Most of all, he knows that when one jumps, one must also fall. He fears that if he breaks the surface, he might never find the air again.

"Someday," Christopher says. "But not today."

"Your choice," Greg says, "but summer's almost over. If you wait much longer, the water will be too cold."

PAULY'S GIRL

PAULY INSISTED that his body be sent directly to the cremato-rium—none of that funeral-home business with preachers and the smell of a hundred years of death rising from the carpet. He wanted a memorial service at the college auditorium. He didn't care that it had seats for five hundred. If he only filled up twenty, he said, that would be just fine. Of course, he knew all along that the seats would be filled.

The day before he died, sitting in the hospice bed, Pauly looked into a hand mirror as tears flowed down his cheeks. On the nightstand and all along the walls of the room were flow-ers—dozens of vases of elaborate and colorful bouquets, yellow carnations and silken tulips, the scents so sweet and sickening that they could only suggest that his time had come. He turned to Moira, who had been in a chair at his side every night for the past three weeks. "My hair is gone and my scalp is ugly," he said to her. "I mean it. Look at my skin. Take this all in, dear. I am to be burned and there will be no evidence of this version of me. Only you will know."

Moira grabbed the mirror from him and looked at her own reflection: wiry gray hair and a skinny, mean face. She nodded. "I'll do exactly as you tell me, darling."

Moira held his hand while he fell into an easy sleep. He reminded her of a plaster figure, his pained face frozen in despair like a Munch painting. Four months ago the doctors had diagnosed him with lung cancer. He was sixty years old and had smoked for forty-five. Would she miss the dramatic flip of his wrist, the cigarette ashes flying haphazardly through the air?

Moira began to understand that there were certain questions that only a death could answer. She kept a careful and consistent vigil, though her own body ached in anticipation of these answers. The nurses told her that she should go, that they would call her at any hour if his condition worsened. Moira said nothing to the overly kind women, and shook her head. She couldn't say that she had never married, that there were no children to call for comfort. She couldn't say that last year she had buried both of her parents—her father dying so quickly after her mother, their hearts inseparable. The nurses would know nonetheless, in the same way that anyone in their small town could recall all of the relevant details about a person, just at the sight of a face or the mention of a surname. Their gestures, in the lonely hospice room, sprang from etiquette.

One of the young aides doing her rounds walked into the room. She petted Pauly's forehead, and then turned and leaned to Moira. She whispered: "I really don't think he'll be long."

This was an honest statement, and the prospect of his going sent a hopeful feeling surging through Moira's body. The feeling was enough to keep her awake through the night.

Just before the sun rose, a rustle in the bed attracted her attention. She saw the quick jerk of Pauly's body and reached for him. "Hold on my darling," she said and took his hand. He squeezed her fingers tightly. She heard the last bits of his life escape from his mouth with a *puff*, and then his grip loosened.

She kissed him on the forehead. "You were the most lovely thing, you. Now what happens to me?"

***

The service happened on a Saturday afternoon, one week after his death, exactly to his specifications. "Think of their evenings," he'd said to her from his deathbed. "Let us not take any more of their time than necessary."

The college auditorium filled to near capacity—bodies filled even the back seats of the balcony rows. People entered the auditorium and wandered down the aisles, their heads hung low out of respect for this man that they'd loved so much. They had come prepared to grieve, or at least feigned that pretension, but the atmosphere quickly became more like a town fair than a memorial service. Who else could bring this many people together, if not Pauly? Long-forgotten acquaintances reconnected and the volume rose. Greetings and smiles led to laughter and knee slapping. *Oh, that Pauly,* they said.

He had been the town's florist for more than forty years—his entire adult life. He had arranged for the inaugurations of ten mayors, thousands of funerals, forty-some proms, and even a presidential townhall address. He was *Pauly with a P* with a flamboyant bow tie and *just the right touch so your wifey will love it!* The townspeople had expected lilies lining the carpets, animal statues fashioned from black-eyed Susans, edible blossoms pinned to the programs. Moira watched from her seat on the stage as they waited in anticipation. Would rose petals fall from above like confetti?

When the crowd had settled, she ascended to the podium and tapped the microphone twice. The lights were bright, but she could still see all the faces—the men cleaned and shaven, the women wearing their finest earrings. The little blue-collar town had transformed—even their Sunday best wouldn't do. This was an adventure, a historical marker, and they leaned forward and waited for the show to begin.

"This won't be a long memorial," Moira started. "Pauly asked me to keep it short. I'll begin by saying that he was the best and most loyal friend I ever had. And, as many of you know from your visits to the flower shop, he was rarely seen in public without a smile. In typical Pauly fashion, he asked that he have the last word tonight. So I will read to you from a letter."

She took a deep breath and prepared to deliver the speech. She had rehearsed it a dozen times in the past week. He had wanted a show—a performance—and that was what he would get. Channeling an image of his big, jovial body, she began with a voice much louder and animated than her usual plain-spoken tenor. "Hello from the other side. It's quite bright over here." He had actually written *pause for laughter*, and the audience erupted as if on cue. "You've all been my faithful customers and friends, and I'm sorry that I won't be able to arrange for your children's graduations and your grandparents' sixtieth wedding anniversaries. But I'm dead now, so give me a break."

Pause for laughter. Make sure *you wait until they have finished.*

"I don't have much to say except that I've had a wonderful life, in no small part because of you. Remember to be nice to one another, to keep on smiling, and to love your friends. More importantly, do not forget your mother's birthday."

One more pause. That's all. I promise.

"Now let's address the elephant in the room. No, there will not be any flowers. Did you actually think I'd trust someone else on my big day? Farewell my friends, and enjoy the ride. Do stop to smell the roses once in a while."

A tentative applause burst forth and snowballed into a standing ovation. Moira watched some of the older women stop clapping only to wipe away tears. Pauly had meant so much to these women, Moira knew. A ten-minute visit to his shop would often turn into an hour. How many lives, how many marriages had Pauly saved from behind the counter of his shop? With his sleight of hand—his ability to distract from the worst with a laugh and a bouquet, or the perfect comment about the haircut that a husband didn't even notice—he gave the town a brief respite from the drudgery of the everyday.

With the push of a button, she turned on a looped slideshow with pictures from his life set to Janis Joplin's "Bye Bye Baby." Moira stepped off the stage and sat down in the front row. As Pauly had no surviving family members, she assumed the role of grieving wife, receiving the hands of those who came to sign the guestbook. "Think of it, darling," he had said from the hospice bed. "You'll be the fashionable widow. It's the best role a body could ask for."

***

In an unexpected turn of events, Moira found herself the inheritor of Pauly's entire estate. The house, the money, the store—all hers. He had never told her of his plans, or even that he'd drawn up a will. She'd not dared to approach the subject of money on his sickbed. It had taken her two weeks just to work up the courage to ask if he was afraid of death. "The curtain must be drawn, darling," he'd said with a wink.

She received a call from his lawyer. He quoted big numbers, bigger than anything she'd ever known or imagined for herself. She had long ago stopped dreaming of any kind of a break. "Not bad for someone your age," the lawyer said. "You shouldn't have a worry for a long, long time."

She signed the papers. She quit her paralegal job. Twenty years and done. Just like that. The partners at the firm all signed a card, and one of the secretaries baked her a cake. "Make sure to come visit us," the young, pretty receptionist said.

"Sure, sweetie," Moira replied. She felt a sudden wave of grief wash over her as she realized that she would never come back, that she had nothing to say to these people. Twenty years. Twenty years and nothing to say. She had given all of her love, all of her life really, to Pauly. She had to steady herself against the receptionist's desk to keep from falling.

She walked out the door of the office and thought of how much she wanted to call him and make light of the situation. She would have called the receptionist a bimbo. She would have said the cake was dry and tasted like fiber. He would have laughed so loud that she'd have to hold the phone away from her ear. She did not call him. She walked through the parking lot. She got into her car and put her head against the sun-warmed steering wheel. "Fuck you, Pauly. I'm not ready for this."

***

She moved to Pauly's house one week after the memorial service, leaving her little apartment downtown and most of its contents nearly untouched. She paid the rent for another month and didn't say a word about the house to her landlord. She had a nagging suspicion that she might need to return there from time to time, but not for grotesque thoughts of Pauly reanimating. No, she held onto the apartment because of a motion sickness, a feeling in her gut that life was moving too fast; she'd been swept up by the spiral arm of a hurricane and plunged into some unknown surreality. Ten years in an apartment, twenty years at a job, sixty years of life—never had she felt so dizzy.

She packed two suitcases with clothes, toiletries, a few romance novels, and his ashes in a plastic box that weighed more than she expected. She drove away from the little town, down the curvy road to Pauly's house (she couldn't yet say *her* house). He lived in the country, in the same home in which he'd grown up and never left. It was a real antique with a sloping wooden porch and a big green pasture. He'd given up on the cows that his parents had once raised, but everything else on the property remained exactly as it had always been.

As she pulled into the driveway, she remembered how her mother used to drive her out to play with him. Little Moira would run across the front yard to the leaning apple tree and swing from its branches. Her mother had joked loudly to Pauly's parents, "Those two will be married someday," and, in fact, he had proposed to her twice. Both times had been underneath that same ancient tree. The first time she was eight years old, and he had carved her a moist, fragrant ring from the fruit of an apple. She'd accepted with a kiss on his cheek. The second time, she had become a woman, twenty-two years old, sitting in the tree's shade on a picnic blanket. "You know that I could never love you that way," he said, while holding her hand. "But I could love you in a different way. We could be together forever. Picture it."

She said no that day. Forty years later, though, she wondered if a part of her hadn't really accepted the offer. A part of her had become resigned, if not on that exact day, then during the ensuing weeks and years, to be only his. There had been lovers, of course. Affairs and flings. But what man in the town would ever try to take away Pauly's girl? And if one of those men had tried the impossible, would she have even let him?

She walked inside the house for the first time since he'd died.

She took the box of his ashes into the kitchen. She reached into a cabinet over the sink and pulled out the gaudiest vase that she could find: antique ceramic, glazed white and blue, with a pattern of painted daffodils. She opened the box and carefully funneled his ashes into the vase, making sure that no bits of him escaped onto the counter. She grabbed a white saucer from the cabinet to use as a lid. She set the vase on the mantel of the fireplace.

She had brought him home.

***

Each time that Moira stepped through the doorway of the house she was overtaken by the smell of old things: old leather, old books, old wood. She had never lived in a place that carried so many physical reminders of the past. She imagined how Pauly must have constantly worked to fight these reminders, scrubbing at the floors with bleach and filling the halls with scented candles. Or maybe he secretly loved the smells of the earthy wood, thinking that they would wipe away a day's worth of working with flowers.

She walked through the hallways and became reacquainted with the nooks that she knew instinctively but now, as the proprietor, must know differently, more intimately. When Pauly was alive, she would have grabbed the wooden mallard that sat on the coffee table and put him on top of the television. She'd loved how easily she could disrupt his sense of order, and doing so had become a ritual of hers; but now, alone, she was afraid to touch anything. She thought, perhaps, that she understood him more now. Maybe he too had been afraid in this house—afraid of the loneliness, afraid of the possibility of change.

The bookshelves and furniture needed dusting, but not from a week's worth of neglect. The dust seemed as thick and ancient as the house itself. It became gradually clear to her: This was not her house. This was not Pauly's house. This was *their* house: his parents, or whoever had first christened it.

So she walked up and down the stairs, tried to own the floors by treading. When this wore her out, she chose a bedroom—the small guest bedroom—as her own. She took off her shoes and sat on the bed, though she didn't get under the quilt. The quilt smelled, too, of a patchwork of timeworn visitors. She closed her eyes and put her face into the pillow.

She slept for fourteen hours.

***

Moira left the house only once in three days, and only then to pick up groceries. She had thrown everything out of the refrigerator. She didn't care if the jam was good for another year; that jam didn't belong to her. In this way, she had claimed dominion over an appliance.

She acted less savagely with the cookware. She made pasta and carefully observed the places from which she'd taken each pot, bowl, and spoon so that she could put everything back just so. To disturb someone's pots seemed an unforgivable crime, a real spiritual conundrum. She imagined all of the meals that Pauly's mother had made and then imagined Pauly's mother in the metal of the pans, her spirit released with the flame of the range top. She shuddered.

Moira tiptoed throughout the house, offering condolences to the objects that she impacted—the dining-room table that she always seemed to knock with her hip, the dark blue curtains that she accidentally pulled down from the rod as she tried to let in the sunlight. She had no one to call, no boss with whom she could trade snide observations (that was, after all, what had got her promoted from secretary to paralegal). She began to wonder if this would now be the shape of her life.

She lay down on the sofa in the living room and closed her eyes. She tried to remember the house on a good day. A summer dinner party. She and Pauly in their early thirties. Barry Shaw, Pauly's weekend lover who drove in from Pittsburgh. Ronnie Lipscomb, one of the only men who had ever made her feel electric.

There had been jugs of cheap wine. Records playing. Dancing. Pauly, in a drunken flourish, had strung a wreath of intertwined violets like a bacchanalian offering around her head. The nearest neighbor was a mile down the road. They could have run naked through the fields, if they'd wanted.

Ronnie had chased her out into the yard—chased, like a child. She had run laughing, barefoot through the damp evening grass. He'd pushed her back against the wooden slats of the barn wall, the chipped white paint sticking to her skin and falling to the ground. "I'll take you far away from this, baby," he'd said. "We'll go places that you never even dreamed."

She remembered her heart feeling like it might explode, and then the feeling of it dropping as she anticipated her own words. "I could never leave Pauly."

She opened her eyes and sat upright on the couch. Out the living room window she could see that same barn, the remnants of a thirty-year-old paint job. She had loved Pauly in a way that she could never love another man. That was fine, she knew. And a choice. And could a life with any other man really have been any better? She wondered if widows dreamed of casual sex.

***

She had been ignoring the ringing, not wanting to explain to yet another stranger that he had, in fact, passed. She had planned on changing the number. It was boredom, a week's worth of fretting, that finally compelled her to pick up the phone.

The voice on the other end was a man's. His words were terse and agitated. He said that his delivery guy had tried the flower shop each week for three weeks straight, and that while Pauly was a valued, lifelong customer, this was the final warning.

She'd thought about the shop almost every day. It hadn't occurred to her that a business had so many working parts. It hadn't occurred to her that these parts would keep moving after someone's death.

She explained the situation, and to her surprise, the tense, gruff voice settled down to a whimper: "He was a good fellow, that Pauly."

She promised the man to be there on Monday morning for the next delivery.

***

On Monday, she parked her car in the sleepy downtown and walked toward the flower shop. A woman older than herself stopped her on the sidewalk. Moira didn't recognize her. "I'm so sorry for your loss," the woman said with a creaky voice.

"Thank you," Moira replied.

The woman put a hand on Moira's shoulder. "I know what it's like to lose the man you love," the woman whispered.

"I've got to be going," Moira replied, with a defensive tilt of her head.

The store sat on the corner of the busiest intersection of the downtown. It occupied the entire first floor of a three-story brick building. There were two tall, display windows along the front, split by a glass door. The possessive form of his name was written in a florid, red cursive across the center of the left window. Baskets of bougainvillea hung from the ceilings against the windows.

Moira looked through the windows. Everything seemed calm—nothing out of place, the floors shining in the morning sun. She slid the key into the front door and pushed it open.

Something had turned—the shop smelled both fragrant and rancid, like a compost heap. She put a hand over her mouth and nose. She found the light switch and flipped it. The hanging baskets of bougainvillea were still pink and silken. The mottled leaves of the philodendron plant, though a little wilted, still crept down from the shelf behind the counter.

She approached the coolers that ran the length of the side wall. The glass was fogged over, dripping with beads of water, and she couldn't see inside. When she opened one of the doors to inspect the flowers, the smell of deep decay came rushing out and made her turn her head. She felt the urge to vomit. Tulips bent disgustingly downward. The petals of daisies were withered or had fallen away. A brown juice covered the white floor of the units and had begun to show the first patches of mold. Pauly hadn't said a word to her about this—that the refrigerators would need to be emptied, that the shelf life of a flower was shorter than his stay in the hospice. There was a week's worth of cleanup, and the deliveryman would arrive in an hour. Her head felt heavy.

She closed the door to the cooler and walked through the showroom into the windowless, back office. She closed the office door behind her, which reduced the overwhelming smell only a little. Stacks of account books and catalogs lined the walls. Boxes of receipts sat piled and dusty on the desk. She sifted through the papers in a frenzy. Where were the instructions? "The only thing you need to have to run a flower shop is taste," Pauly had once said to her. She now wondered if he'd meant it as a cruel joke, planning years ahead for this very moment when she would throw her hands up in frustration.

***

The deliveryman arrived, and Moira asked him to leave everything on the sidewalk. There were twelve Styrofoam boxes that he stacked against the brick exterior of the shop. "So my boss told me old Pauly finally passed," the man said. "Were you his . . . wife?" The last part sounded forced. There wasn't a person in the world who really believed that Pauly would have a wife.

"Just a friend," she said. "And I guess I'm running the place now."

"It's a tough business, you know," the man said. "It's not easy to sell flowers. It's a personality game. The customers have to like you just as much as the product. You are the product now."

***

For the first three months, the store broke even. It seemed that every other customer came in only to conjure up Pauly's ghost. Out of courtesy, Moira supposed, they occasionally bought a bouquet of flowers. She learned more about Pauly and about the townspeople in those three months than she had in a lifetime. The stories came in unfiltered—life, death, and deception on full display. Moira never did much more than nod her head as these people spoke. It turned out that Pauly hadn't been as much of an exaggerator as she thought.

By month six, the store was digging itself into a hole. She was throwing out more flowers than she was selling—the smell of rotting flowers sticking to her clothes. She began to resent the smell of flowers altogether—there wasn't a single blossom that didn't cause her to wince. She bought unscented soap and showered twice every day, in the mornings and just after she came home from work.

She became increasingly gruff with the customers. Likewise, she became increasingly angry with Pauly—dead or not. Hadn't he known her? Hadn't he known what this store would do to her? Whenever someone mentioned his name, she had to force herself to smile. What she wanted to do was break a vase.

His birthday came and the mailman brought dozens of cards for him from far away, from people whose names she couldn't place. She opened all the cards and read the updates, the rehashing of old anecdotes of how they'd all met Pauly. There were stories of floral conventions, of wild beach parties, of chance meetings on vacations to places Moira never remembered Pauly going. Not a single one of these people showed any indication that Pauly had died. To them, it seemed, Pauly was immortal.

She was sitting during lunch at the sales counter in the store, eating a sandwich and reading over the cards when the phone rang. "Pauly's," she answered—only half-focused.

"I knew he wouldn't answer." It was the voice of an older man.

"I'm sorry, this is Moira speaking. If you weren't aware—"

"Moira, I know. It's Barry Shaw—you remember me, I'm sure. Pauly's on-again, off-again. You're running the shop now?"

She nearly dropped the phone. She hadn't heard his name mentioned in a decade, not since Pauly had finally broken it off for good.

"Yes—Barry, I didn't know if you—yes, he left it for me in his will. I had no idea he was going to do that. How did you find out about him? Where are you these days?"

"He called me before it happened—said he had one week left. He wouldn't let me come visit, or tell me where he was. I had to call the newspaper. They sent me the copy with his obituary."

"Barry, I'm so sorry," and for the first time in a long time, she felt genuine sympathy.

"I'm going to come down this weekend. I'd like to visit the grave."

"He was cremated, darling. I've got his ashes at the old house. That's where I'm living now." And then she added, "If you want to see his ghost, I'm sure we could find that, too. His ghost is everywhere in this town."

***

Moira carried over two lawn chairs and placed them beneath the apple tree. It was spring and the leaves were an ephemeral green, the bright new buds fresh and unweathered. "Sit, darling," she said. "It's so nice to have company."

His face was long, and his skin drooped at his cheekbones, sunken—perhaps he had false teeth. He was older than Pauly, she remembered. He could be seventy now. The youth she had once seen in him, the wild verve that had once drawn in Pauly, had left the man's body. What remained of his hair were scattered white wisps.

"What do you do with your days?" he asked.

"To be honest, I'm lonely," she said. "I don't have a friend in the world."

"And the business?"

"The old biddies at the flower shop can't stand me. I was a novelty at first, but now I can see what they're thinking. They wish that I was the one who had gone down with cancer."

Barry leaned forward and untied his laces. He pulled off his shoes and then his socks. His feet were jagged veins wrapped in ghost-white skin.

"I was always jealous of you," he said, leaning his head back to catch the late afternoon sun. "I always thought that you were the reason he wouldn't let me get close."

"You know that's not true."

"It is and it isn't. He loved you so much. He loved you in a way that he could never love me. Do you know that we continued to speak on the phone? Once a year, every year, on his birthday. We would say good-bye and then I'd think of him for the next 364 days."

The robins had returned and were flitting all across the yard, on and off the branches of the apple tree. The birds called and puffed their orange-red breasts, the bright feathers a hint of the tiger lilies that would soon shoot up in her yard.

"I blame him, sometimes," she said. "I blame him for making me old, setting me up to be lonely. Forgive me for sounding selfish."

"Oh, come off it. He was selfish—we both know it. But not entirely. He gave us something. We all made a pact. We weren't helpless in this arrangement."

The wind howled in pulses, silencing the birds' chirrups with each gust. Heavy clouds were blowing in the distance, rising up the sides of the mountains, but overhead the sky was an azure blue. It looked like the rain had skipped over them.

"No, we weren't helpless," she said. "I just never thought of what would happen when he was gone. I never thought about death. I supposed that's what he gave me. He was a good distraction."

She scanned the grass and reached an arm over the edge of her chair. She grabbed a rotting apple that had survived the winter packed under the snow. The skin of the apple broke at her touch, revealing the browned, yellow pulp beneath. She lifted the fruit to her nose. It had rotted, but it still smelled alive, more apple than not.

"Moira," Barry said. "Do you ever think of Ronnie Lipscomb?"

"Of course," she replied.

"Do you think he's happy now?"

"I don't know. When he left town, I never heard from him again."

Truthfully, since Pauly had gone she thought of her old lover more than ever. At night, alone in the house, she often wrapped herself in his memory, wallowing under the covers thinking of how easy it had been to give up her body. It was oddly fulfilling, to live off the specter of what once had made her quiver. She wondered, of course . . . but she had also grown tired. At times the impression of touch seemed preferable to the real thing.

"Were you happy when Pauly was alive?" Barry asked.

"I think so."

"Then you can't regret it."

She was still holding the rotten apple. She loosened her grip and let it fall to the ground.

"My world has narrowed, dear," she said.

She thought she could see what was to come. The apples would continue to grow and fall to the ground. The flowers would bloom, would be cut and sold. One day—and she wondered if it wouldn't be so long from now—she would be the last one to utter Pauly's name. She'd call out to him as she approached the darkness. And when she passed, they would both be forgotten.

"It's perspective, Moira," he said. "What do they say? *The forest for the trees*. I always hated that phrase."

"I thought I had such a life," she said. "But now . . ."

She couldn't end the sentence.

"He went quickly?" Barry asked.

"He took exactly as much time as he wanted."

She looked at Barry's face—his tired jaw, his cracked lips, and his eyes as moist as the morning lawn. And yet he seemed so happy with the sun beating down on his forehead, his feet naked in the grass. He seemed content. "What's the secret, Barry?"

He let out a quick laugh. "Tell me: Why do you run the flower shop? Why do you stay in this house?"

She shifted her weight in the chair. She couldn't respond.

He bent across the side of his chair and grabbed one of Moira's hands. "You know what Pauly told me once? He said all the beautiful flowers die; but the trees, they live forever. Let it go, dear. Let it all go."

***

They had a quiet dinner inside, a single glass of wine. As the sun began to set, Barry said that he should be going. "The road to Pittsburgh is long. And my eyes, I'd say they've grown quite short."

"Won't you stay?" she asked. "Stay for a day or two. Stay for a couple of weeks. It's a big house."

"No, no," he said. "That's not what you need. Come see me later, when this has all settled down. I've got a beautiful place of my own, you know. The city's less lonely than you'd think."

They walked onto the porch and hugged good-bye. Then he was in his car. She waved as he drove down the road, off toward the town, toward the highway.

She walked down to the lawn and surveyed the world as they'd both seen it—the wild limbs of the leaning apple tree, the golden-brown evening sky, the black silhouettes of the mountains. The trunk and the branches of the tree had bent over the years, under the weight of the heavy fruit. One of the biggest branches had grown down from the canopy of the leaves, all the way to the ground and straight along the grass. But then, there was the thing she hadn't noticed before: the end of that same branch had begun growing up again, at a right angle, the wood bending toward the sky.

Moira went back inside the house and returned with the vase of Pauly's ashes. She walked over to the apple tree and leaned her body against the trunk. She let her cheek touch the rough bark. She took a deep breath.

She tilted the vase and gave it a thrust, imagining that the particles would spread with the wind and blanket the grass. Instead, the mass of him fell in a clump, like dark brown sugar. She used the tip of her shoe to rub him into the earth.

THROUGH THE STILL HOURS

It's Saturday. I wake up early, and after having a cup of coffee alone in the kitchen, I cook and bring him breakfast in bed. French toast and eggs. This, in my head, seems the simplest way to make romance. It's our fourth anniversary—four years since we met each other in that parking lot. I think I might catch him off guard this morning, before he has time to think of all the ways to keep me at arm's length. Food, I reason, is something that still motivates us to make nice with each other. The promise of taste and smell and drink still stirs something inside of us in the most primal ways. Sad, I know, for someone not yet thirty years of age to act fifty, but this is where I'm at—where we're at.

At first, in the bedroom, it seems I might trick him into submission. He awakens with a smile—his ash-blonde hair a mess from the static of the pillow. I think, this is how it should be, two lovers naked, all proverbial walls down. I kiss him on the neck and use the stubble on my chin to trace patterns on his back. His pale, white skin turns red in abstract hearts and figure eights. His initial complacency, his unmoving body, surprises me, given the defensive posturing that usually greets my attempts at sex. His lack of a defense is enough to arouse me, and I try not to overthink things. I let the smell of his night sweat pull me into his body. "I want to make love to you all day long," I say. "And then I want to make love to you some more, until the sun sets and rises again."

I wonder if I really mean these words. I try not to think about how making love, in the few times that it ever happens with us anymore, has become an almost selfish act, driven more by basic needs and less by a desire to revel in the other's pleasure. It's a letting of blood for us. A release of tension. But I don't dwell on the usual way of things. I convince myself that anniversaries can act as a reset button. In bed, as I'm blowing hot air onto his neck, he's the Gerry of day one, with a lust-inducing shyness, his falsely innocent eyes beckoning.

But this doesn't last. As he awakens and recognizes my intent, his smile melts away. His eyes harden. It's as if I've stirred him from the most sexual dream, only for him to realize that the man who's been fucking him in the clouds is not the man in his bed—is not me. "I'm tired, love. Maybe later?" He finishes with a peck of a kiss, quick and dry. He sits up and sticks his fork into the eggs. He eats with zeal.

***

How we found each other goes something like this: four years ago, we message each other on one of those websites whose sexually punny names I prefer not to pronounce aloud. We settle on a spot in the next town over for the sake of discretion. We decide to meet just off the highway in a McDonald's parking lot. I remember seeing his face for the first time. I think of that electric sensation when I'm alone in the shower.

On that first day, we are two anonymous Internet profiles taking a chance on explicit pictures from the chest down. His car is just as he said it would be: a 1991 silver Toyota hatchback with a belt of rust along the bottom. He rolls down the window, wanting to speak, but scared. Before he can say a word, I utter, "Yes. It's me."

He leans over the gearshift and throws open the passenger door. It groans. I make him take his car, because I don't want to run the risk of anyone recognizing me, even here, twenty miles from home. I'm no fool—I know that people talk. Some people drive twenty miles to do their shopping, looking for a change of scenery. Others drive that far because they're tired of being seen. Like the preacher said at church when I was growing up, "Someone's always watching you." God, or that old woman who lives next door.

In his car, the smells wafting from the vents of the fast-food restaurant mix with the scent of his cologne. This combination—salty, florid, cheap—makes him seem younger than the age that was on his online profile. We take one long, deep look at each other, and then we both lock our vision straight ahead through the windshield. His face burns into my mind in that look, exists still in my memory: frightened blue eyes, nervous lips. I prefer that face. Even his blonde hair, back then, seemed to suggest *soiled*. In my dreams, I see that face, and he says, "I'm holding back, but only for a moment."

In the car that evening, he says, "Where are we going?"

"I don't care." My heart beats too quickly. My hands clench down on the sides of the vinyl seats. "Just drive."

So we do. We drive down back roads, past rolling farms at the edge of mountains. We drive past abandoned gas stations, the victims of four-lane highways. He knows the roads by heart, as we all do, because that's where our fathers took us on joy-rides to tell the dirty stories of their youth. My instinct is to recount these stories, to tell him where my father brawled with drunken men. To tell him where my father took an easy girl under a tree and asserted himself. I bite my lip, though, and say nothing. Somehow these stories feel too shocking, as if I'm not actually driving down a back road with a stranger intent on doing things that seem too embarrassing to speak of.

Gerry steals sideways glances when he takes sharp turns. I notice, then look away. We fumble. We shimmy in our seats. We become braver, in fits and starts, make eye contact, breathe heavily to fill the silence. He moves his lips, but no words come out. He put his hand onto mine, after switching gears. He waits for me to meet him halfway, to curl my fingers into his own. It's such a teenage gesture, but for us, there's a newness to it.

"Are you a murderer?" I say, only half-joking, when his skin touches mine. "Why haven't I seen you around town? I've seen everyone."

"I'm from the next county over," he says, naming the town. It's a place I know well, not much more than a pit stop on the way down from the mountain. He looks the part, with his Sunday best on: the checkered shirt, the khaki pants, and the schoolboy cut. He sang in the church choir no doubt, bringing old women to tears with his honey baritone and startled eyes. I judge him for these things, as if being from my town of eight thousand is any better than being from his town of five hundred.

"I just moved here for work," he says.

"You look, well, normal," I say. "What do you do?"

"High-school teacher."

"Are you out?"

"Define out."

"Do people know that you're into men?"

"They suspect. I don't talk about it. Why does anybody need to know?"

We drive for miles, lay down the basics, or at least as much as we feel safe revealing to a stranger who suddenly knows too many of our secrets. It's fall and everything is red—the dropping leaves, the setting sun, the fire of our cigarettes, blazing brighter as they catch the wind from the cracked windows. I see the blood in the back of my eyes with each throat-clenching heartbeat.

We pull over onto a secluded lookout: a meandering river and hay bales in the fields below. We are far from any named town: existence incognito out here. We watch the day disappear. The sky fades like a rotting peach. We sit in silence and pass a flask of whiskey to cut the tension.

At a farmhouse in the distance, a porch light shines like a nightlight or a warning. I understand this darkness. I revel in the feeling of it. One can't avoid it growing up underneath the mountains. The darkness never fails to frighten and to thrill me, to conjure ghosts and campfire stories. We get out of the car and lay back on the warm hood. Thousands of stars circle slowly above, clustered and thick, hanging over the nonforms of trees along the hillsides, the black on blacker horizon.

"Do you do this often?" I ask.

"More than I'd like," he says, his voice quiet but sultry. His admission, which I can also claim as my own, both shames and turns me on. We're pushed by the world to dark spaces, filthy bathrooms, and secret lookouts. We feel dirty always, but then at a certain point, when we become familiar with these dark terrains, we begin to like the feeling. We claim the dark spaces and the secret corridors as our own. These acts become at first an outlet, and then an addiction: an instant erection upon pulling into a highway rest stop.

Because of all this, we know what's coming without prompting. We knew what was coming before we sent the first message online. We get back into the car. We touch lips. We feel the contours of the other's body and delight in the mystery of what exists under our clothing. We recline our seats.

But just as we're beginning, the headlights of a vehicle break the darkness. It's a half mile down the road, lumbering toward us.

"What if someone catches us?" he says.

I don't stop, though. I can't stop. The fear of getting caught is also part of the game, part of the turn-on.

"And what if?" I say, challenging him with my hand as I squeeze his inner thigh.

"Don't you . . . aren't you . . .? Oh, fuck it."

The headlights grow brighter and closer. I kiss him deeply. My hands stop touching and start pushing, forcing their way, fueled by some exhibitionist tendency. I dare the night to interfere, to trespass on this scene.

And then the lights arrive. The truck slows to a halt just outside our car. Bright white pierces the glass, blinding us. Gerry pushes me off of him, looks to the steam on the windows. His shoulders shrink inward. We are guilty and scared. I roll down the window—decipher the face of an old man in a dented pickup. The brim of his ball cap hangs down to the edge of his eyes. He nods his head at us, firm and quick. His face is clean shaven. He looks nervously over his shoulder. Clears his throat. "You boys be careful out here," he says and drives off.

We don't finish what we started. Gerry drives me back to my car, through the night, in silence.

I watch Gerry finish his breakfast. He smiles as he eats. He tells me the food is good, raises his fork, nods his head with approval. When he finishes, he hands me his plate. I get up to walk to the kitchen.

"Happy anniversary," he calls after me.

I take his dish to the sink. I drink a glass of water. I look out the kitchen window. I see the solitary willow tree that takes up a full half of our fenced-in backyard. The willow's thin branches flutter with the breeze, caress the grass like fingers. I imagine my body as the grass. I want to be touched.

I come back to the bedroom to get dressed. Gerry plays on his laptop, as I put on jeans. When I look at him, my neck tenses. I breathe in. The air feels thick.

"Ariana just texted," he says, not looking up from his computer. "She said she really wants margaritas before we go out tonight. We have tequila, but would you mind going to pick up the mixers?"

"You know I didn't want to do this tonight," I say. I want to hit him. I want to grab him by the wrists and squeeze so hard that I leave a bruise. "I still don't understand why we can't celebrate by ourselves. It's our anniversary—not theirs."

"Because what we have is so special," he says, in his high, whiny voice. "I want them to know what we have."

I don't respond. I walk into the living room and put my shoes on. I grab my car keys. He yells good-bye as I walk out the front door.

***

I drive to Walmart, and as I pull into the parking lot, I think maybe I should find a secluded place in the back lot to finish alone what I had attempted to start with Gerry. But the back of the lot is too busy. Saturdays are always madness here, with every last troll and ogre lining up to do their weekend shopping. I decide to save my solo joy for a later time. I clench my teeth and walk inside.

I'm treated to a vision of every person I don't care to see. We all know each other—by face or name. If not, we could surmise enough, by the type of clothes we wear, by the way we carry ourselves. I left the house in a hurry, throwing on whatever I could find, but here, I'm a snobbish prince. I hold my head low, so as not to attract any unneeded attention.

I stop into the bathroom before I begin shopping. In the bathroom, as I'm in the middle of pissing, a wrinkly old man with a high-school letterman jacket begins to jerk his dick at me two urinals down. He swings it around like he's offering me gold or a diamond or both. His all-knowing glance sizes me up, perhaps by my clothes or the way I return his eye contact. He thinks: queer, horny queer, likes to suck queer, takes-whatever-he-can-get queer. That's the standard around here, be it in a bathroom or on the Internet. When I refuse his ilk, I'm never sure if they're going to burst into tears or pummel me.

I've stopped trying to make sense of it. It happens once a week at least. The same old men you hear trash-talking outside the redneck bars—faggot this, faggot that. Gerry doesn't believe me when I tell him this—doesn't trust my face when I emerge red and angry from a piss at the movie theater. It's because he doesn't look at people—at least not directly. He's head-forward everywhere, bulldozing through air—all *excuse me* and *pardon me*. Knows his place.

Before Gerry and I started dating, I'd never kissed the same man more than once. Half of the men I met—on the Internet, in the stalls of bathrooms like this—didn't even kiss me on the mouth. I thought that was the way life worked: a series of shady encounters with men I'd never see again. Gerry gave me something I'd never felt before. It was love, I thought, or something like it.

In the restroom, with the Walmart radio blaring upbeat country music designed to push this week's camouflage coat, my eyes settle not on the old man's dick but on the golden band on his left ring finger. Though I'm not attracted to this man, I feel myself getting hard. I smile. I laugh. I proffer him a look at my penis. "Relationships are tough, huh? I'm sorry I can't help you out."

And what does he say, in response to my gesture at civility? "Fuck you, faggot."

I leave the bathroom and continue on with my shopping, unfazed.

***

I return home with the mixers, and Gerry avoids me for the duration of the day. He lesson-plans for school and then putzes around on the Internet while I read a book. He pulls me aside before our friends arrive. "This means a lot to them," he says. "We're the only gay couple they know."

"And we're the new paradigm," I say. "We're the hope for the future."

"You can be a real dick," he says. "Don't be that way tonight. Be happy. For me."

That's the end of our conversation until evening comes and our friends arrive, couple by couple, taking seats in our living room. There's Ariana and Chris, and Karen and Michael—two pretty and talkative women who Gerry met through teaching, and their blissfully silent husbands, who are really just quiet because they're unsure of what to say to us: the nice little homos that mix such delectable drinks. There's no harm in their silence. I take no offense. It's as awkward for me as it is for them.

It's just another Saturday, slightly altered subjects: the politics du jour and the strange old man who showed up this week outside the grocery store and greets customers with cat noises. He meows if he likes you, hisses if he doesn't. Gerry receives purrs, while I receive claws. I think there must be something in that, some larger comment about the quality of my soul, but I can't quite put my finger on it.

Gerry and I sit on opposite sides of the living room in two hardback chairs. The two couples sit on the loveseat and the big sofa, hands on knees, and close enough to advertise that they still feel something for each other.

We sit and the chatter rolls on. Karen regales us with the politically incorrect things that her high-school students say. Ariana talks about taking a trip to Pittsburgh to go shopping for some "real" clothes. As they blather on, the room grows darkly golden with the sunset. The light always disappears sooner than expected here: the end-of-summer shrinking sun falling behind the mountains, gnawing at my psyche. A breeze blows against the trees and rocks the neighbors' wind chimes as if to say *take cover*! So I close the windows and the curtains. I switch on lamps and light tapers in brass holders on the coffee table. Our shadow figures gesture on the walls, and I wonder, how is it that the shadows seem more animated than we do?

"I always feel so comfortable here, guys," Ariana says. "You have the coziest apartment in town."

Once, I would have been flattered. Once, I would have proudly agreed with her. I remember back when Gerry and I first moved in together. We tried to create beauty and warmth in the way that we draped a curtain just so, in how we painted the walls of the living room an inviting burnt orange. We thought we were so smart in that choice, building our refuge. We wrapped ourselves in blankets on Sunday mornings and held each other until the dusk. I look back on the conversations we had, back when we thought that the burnt-orange walls were a symbol of our life to come, not a marker of stasis. "Imagine," I said then, "a world—this very world, same place, same town—where two men could go walking down the street arm and arm and the neighbors would just smile and wave." And then we'd hold each other some more, and think that maybe that future was a real possibility. We watched the television, the promise of a president. Obama, we thought, a man who would change everything. Childish optimism, I know, to think that the outside world would somehow find its way here, to our small world. But in those moments, there was a forward movement with us: a connection through hope and a sharing of secrets.

And at some point after those moments had played out, something quiet happened. After all our secrets were revealed, our fantasies confessed aloud, we began to pretend that we were just like everyone else. We played at husband and wife, though we knew it was forbidden for people like us. Or maybe we just didn't understand the game, or the rules. Or maybe, most importantly, we tried to be something that we weren't. We became like apes wearing human costumes. We could play the part, and though we were different at the core, we were close enough in kind to fool the onlookers.

Ariana moves her gaze from Gerry to me. She extends her arm and her margarita glass for emphasis. "I'll fucking kill the both of you if you ever break up."

***

We drink until we're all sure of our insobriety. Then we prepare to head off to the bar to go dancing, the second leg of our Saturday night group anniversary celebration. Gerry collects everyone's margarita glasses, and as he takes mine, he kisses me on the cheek. I feel like shivering, but I catch a warning in his eye. I reach out and touch his arm. I feel disgusted with myself for playing at this game.

"You guys are just adorable," Karen says, as if on cue, another hint of what will be an evening of excessive drunken flattery. And I know that he loves this idea: that we're the porcelain figurines missing from their otherwise perfect shadowboxes. He throws an extra shimmy into his hip as he walks. He spouts sassy one-liners stolen from bad reality television. Of course, he won't touch me once we leave the safety of our apartment.

As we walk out the door, I imagine what it would be like to fuck him, right in front of their faces. To show them what a dick looks like going into an ass. To show them that we're capable of lust and aggression and messiness. I picture tying my sweater right around his mouth, jerking his head back as I push into him. Would they remain seated? Would they drop their cocktails?

And what would Gerry do if I grabbed him by the balls and squeezed? Would he moan in pleasure? Would he call my name?

No. I think he would slap my face.

***

We approach the steps of our destination, which is just a short walk from our apartment. The bar is called "The Commander's Pub," and it sits on a residential street, off the main drag of the quiet downtown. It's an old Victorian house with a big wraparound porch where we escape the crowds and smoke cigarettes. The neighbors complain about the hippies and write to the newspaper about the strange music that blasts until two in the morning. It's our sanctuary, and sometimes I wish I could climb up the old wooden stairs and claim one of the Commander's extra bedrooms as my own.

We hear a trumpet and drums as we walk up to the screen door. It's salsa night. Ariana turns to us. "Chris and I've been practicing at home. We've been watching videos online. I think he's finally ready to spin me."

Gerry and I used to dance alone with the blinds pulled. We taught ourselves salsa and swing. I led him with strong arms, and he followed, turning once, twice, dipping low. I would pick him up and toss him around my body and under my legs, as I'd seen on television. We're different, the two of us. His body is light, feather-like. Skin and bones, but not fragile. Easy to push around. Easy to hold.

"I can't wait to see, honey," Gerry says to Ariana.

There's something about the way he speaks to her that makes me want to run away. I'm embarrassed to be a part of this. Sometimes I feel he's like a talking doll with a cord in his back. A jester. Their toy.

The owner of the bar, the namesake, the Commander himself, greets us as we walk inside. He's the town's favorite eccentric, with his bald head and white beard down to his hips. He hugs the girls and shakes the boys' hands. Karen stands on her tiptoes and whispers something into his ear.

"Esmé," the Commander says to his pretty, young wife standing behind the bar. "Drinks on the house for Cliff and Gerry."

She pours us two whiskeys on the rocks—our regular drink. "What's the occasion?"

"Our anniversary," Gerry whispers and winks. The words roll from his mouth so easily that I feel guilty. "Four years."

"Congratulations," she says. "Drink up, lovebirds."

Gerry forces a toast, clanks his glass against mine and bottoms out the whiskey. I can't even bring myself to sip—I just swish it in a circle.

"I'll have another," he says.

I know this is the beginning of many more drinks for him, which means when we go home he'll crawl into the bed and fall asleep in minutes. I used to try to kiss him after nights like these. I would kiss his neck and touch his back, and he'd say he was too tired. He'd roll over, mumbling about how there'd be time in the morning. When the morning came, he'd say he was too hungover.

A half-dozen couples have started dancing in front of the band. We watch the band for a moment: a trumpeter, drummer, and a piano player. Gerry is tapping his feet and his fingers to the rhythm. I lean over to his ear and whisper: "If you love me, then dance with me."

He looks shocked, then angry, then hurt. "You know we can't do that here," he says.

I recognize all the faces: the same ones who have been coming to this bar for years. Every one of them knows about us, though I can't think of a single person who has ever brought it up without prompting. They never ask questions—as if that would be some sort of transgression. They don't need qualifications. Or really, they don't want to know the details. We're just us: Gerry and Cliff, those boys, two names that go together.

***

A few drinks in, and our friends are all out on the dance floor. We sit alone, Gerry looks away, and I look at him.

"We haven't fucked in a month," I say. "Happy anniversary."

"Why are you acting like this?" he asks, and then turns away.

We sip the whiskeys and watch the dancing couples: carefree, ridiculous, completely wrong but right. I swallow the last of my drink, and feel an anger-fueled intoxication streaming through me.

"Just fucking dance with me," I say. I reach for his hand, but he pulls away. He reaches for his cigarettes, takes his glass, and heads to the porch.

I follow him out the door. From the porch, the music bends into something different, creates a tunnel-like dream world. There's the life inside and the quiet reality of the streets just down the steps.

Gerry sits in a rusty metal chair around the corner, out of the light, almost invisible. I go to him. I get down on my knees so that we're face to face.

"I'm sorry," I say. "But what do you expect me to do?"

He seems to consider my words, as he looks into my eyes. His face fades in and out of the shadows, picks up a bit of fire from the cherry of his cigarette. "Why don't we dance together, Cliff? Why don't we hold hands? Do you need me to explain it to you? Do you need me to tell you, step by step, about what happens to men like us in towns like this? Are we really going to go over this right now?" His eyes look like glaciers: reflective and uninviting. "If you don't want to be with me," he says, "then go."

"I can only try so much," I say. "This isn't my fault."

"It's no one's fault," he says. "No. It's everyone's fault."

He's crying now. I want to comfort him, but I can't. We've done this one too many times. I walk off the porch and leave.

***

I weave through the side streets to avoid the main drag. The night is mostly quiet, but with sudden bursts of sound. Yips and yells, and tire squeals that smash the stillness unexpectedly and send chills through my body. The sounds fade just long enough to surprise again when they return.

I walk by the rows of old houses. Brick and clapboard. The lights are mostly off, but television screens flicker blue and white and beckon. The windows sit framed by low-hanging sycamore and maple trees. I want to be home. I want to go into my bedroom and curl under the blankets, pull them over my head, and seal off the world. But I continue to walk along because the home I'm thinking of is not the home in which I live. I'm not sure where that home is.

As I'm walking, I sometimes stop and close my eyes—the sidewalk curves, familiar as a recurring dream. I imagine Gerry taking my arm, and I jump a little, surprised by the vividness of this thought. In my mind, he holds me tightly and leans his head on my shoulder as we walk. People smile when they see us. And then their smiles make us want to take off our clothes. Then we're making love on the streets, and the audience is cheering.

I walk past the homes of the people I've known all of my life. I can assign names to most doors. I meander down sidewalks and look at the moon, and try to imagine what life would be like there, on the bright side, when a shadow is always a shadow, never shifting with the position of the sun.

I take a turn and pick up the pace. Now I'm rushing through the main street of the downtown, past the rough-and-tumble pool halls that I'm afraid to enter. The handful of gruff men who smoke outside these places utter prophecies in my direction: *broken neck, fuck your pussy*. Some of them blow kisses and lick their lips. They call me with two fingers: *here queer*. But this only fuels me. I smile back at them, with teeth. I watch them retreat, then, their heads going down, like dogs backing off from a fight.

I walk past all there is to see in the downtown, which isn't much more than the same old buildings that have been here for a hundred years. Half of them are boarded up and empty. I walk across a swinging footbridge over the town's shallow, dirty river. The river seems so much more enchanting here and now, as it reflects the moonlight and the lamplight from the windows of an adjacent apartment building. I cross the river and leave the downtown, heading back toward my apartment. I look at my watch and realize I've been walking for over an hour. I wonder if Gerry is home now. I wonder if we will apologize to each other and then cuddle, sexlessly, until we fall asleep. Or more likely, we'll say nothing at all, and then in the morning, we'll say even less.

I'm only two blocks from home. I don't see the truck at first. I hear it, sense its presence—air moving different than the wind. I turn around, watch as it drives toward me, a dark form with no headlights turned on. It appears as a living, moving thing under the street lamps: an animate beast of sorts, with instincts, on the hunt. I don't see the driver. Instead, I see the fluorescent reflection of the streetlights in the windshield.

The truck slows down as it nears me, and I look straight ahead, to show that I have a destination. The confidence that I showed to the men earlier is gone, though, and I fear that the driver can sense it. The truck rolls along beside me. I pick up the pace, expecting the worst—though I'm ready for it, prepared to be beaten, can already feel my face against the ground, head stomped by a steel-toed boot, teeth loosened. The thought doesn't bother me—almost delights me, in fact. I can already feel the sidewalk, cold and comforting, like when you have the flu and you collapse onto the bathroom floor. I wonder if I will call out to my lover, as the attacker calls out to me, "Dirty faggot."

The truck drives away, though, and in that moment, lucidity returns. I finger my cell phone in my pocket. Should I call the police? Should I call Gerry to come meet me? I'm only a block from home now. I can see our porch light just down the street. I could run, and that seems smart, but I don't. I have the urge to test fate, or maybe just experience a thrill—anything but home, anything but Gerry.

The truck returns, as I expect. The same pattern—slowing down as if to escort me. The passenger window is rolled down. I see the man's shadow of a face—sad, hard-leather skin. This villain has a backstory, I think, full of broken hearts. His own heart included.

"What do you want with me?" I ask.

I think the man smiles, though in the obscured light I cannot tell. There is some movement in the truck. I can hear the shifting of the man's weight, and his breathing.

"Do you wanna go for a ride?" he asks.

We have stopped moving: two parallel souls in the dark night. There are stars out, and televisions flickering. There are people dancing in bars, and the thought enters my mind that there are children writing wishes in diaries by the light of the moon shining through their bedroom windows.

I wonder if Gerry can see us—if he has hitched a ride home, feeling lonely and raw, and now sits at the kitchen window, watching for moving shadows, my body hulking through the dark streetscape.

I take one step toward the man and pause, waiting for his reaction. He leans across the seat and opens the door. "You don't have to be afraid," he says.

And in this man's voice, in his face, in the darkness of the night, and the still-intact body I inhabit, I know I can trust him, this man who wanders alone through the still hours of the earliest morning, looking for people like me, offering comfort in a familiar phrase: "You have nothing to fear."

"Where are we going?" I ask.

"Wherever you want," he says, as if he were sucking in the words, not speaking them.

He is me four years ago. He is Gerry four years ago. His aged face is unimportant. What matters is the tone of his voice.

"I know a few places," I say, and get into his truck, settling into the seat as if I've always belonged there.

As he drives off, without asking any directions, a surge of feeling emanates from my gut and into my throat. And it's in that feeling that I know this is both exactly where I should and shouldn't be.

FELICITATIONS

ANNETTE MOTIONED to the empty chair. "Have a seat, Mrs. Burton."

Annette hated that the office had no windows. To give such news under a bath of fluorescent light felt like asking someone to drink her coffee without milk—a dose of bitter and sterile efficiency with none of the niceties.

"Mrs. Burton. Your husband—"

"Call me Hattie."

"Hattie."

"He couldn't get off work. The mill's shorthanded, as it is."

Hattie was a young woman—her records said Caucasian, twenty-four, no family history of cancer or genetic disorders. Occupation: gas-station clerk. No drug or alcohol use during pregnancy. She had quit smoking last year. None of this was surprising, given the diagnosis.

"The results of the amniocentesis came back—"

"I knew it was bad. You people always make a body wait for bad news."

Annette reached to adjust the ruffles on her shirt. She was always reaching for something when the tests returned positive—that extra second to calibrate her thoughts, that quick moment to steel herself against the possibility of a patient's breakdown. It was Annette's third meeting with the woman: first, to tell her that the doctor had discovered that she carried a gene that could put her baby at risk; second, to confirm, against all the odds, that her husband carried the same one. And now, this.

"It's what we feared. Your baby has spinal muscular atrophy. SMA."

It was a serious condition, passed on genetically. It could be debilitating—muscle wasting, respiratory failure, joint deformities. It was a painful disease; affected children often didn't live beyond a few years. She had seen it play out, the infant shedding tears of agony and then the mother shedding her own, as she dropped the dirt onto the shoebox-sized coffin.

Annette scanned the woman—her plump fingers, her ruddy face, her wide-open eyes—for a hint of how to proceed. She'd treated many women like her before—the first timers with their sun-red cheeks, ready to spread out on their five acres up the valley. Many of them didn't have a college education, but they'd had the type of education that mattered in these instances. She would have seen this type of pain before—in the rocky soil of her homestead, in the faces of the animals.

"There are choices," Annette said. She handed the woman a pamphlet and a copy of the test results. The woman took the papers mechanically, eyes locked on Annette.

"Are you telling me that I'm going to have to abort my baby?"

"I'm only telling you that you're going to have to do a lot of thinking. There are options. You'll have to learn about the possibilities, about the risks, talk about it with your husband, and then you'll have to decide for yourself. But you should know, you're eighteen weeks in. To make sure that certain options remain available to you, we'll need to speak on Monday at the latest."

***

Annette came home and threw her briefcase onto the floor, kicked her heels toward the shoe rack, and collapsed on the couch. She was the only genetic counselor for a hundred miles, and the women came from ten counties to see her. Sometimes she gave happy news, sometimes she encouraged caution, and sometimes, on a day like this, she wished that all babies were born in a laboratory, that there was never such a thing as a womb.

Home, with the alabaster white walls and the uneven oak floors, was her comfort. She was forty, and she'd paid off the mortgage last year. She had done it all on her own, without help from her father, the bank president; without her mother, who had been born to a line of money so old that no one knew where it had come from in the first place. And she had done it all without the help of a man—a husband—though life had recently thrown her a curveball in that arena.

The curveball pushed open the front door. "Knock, knock," he said.

"I'm so tired, Jimmy. What are you carrying?"

He was a handsome man, taller than most, with brown hair and eyes. He smiled with big, white teeth and had deep dimples in his cheeks. He was wearing blue scrubs and carried two green-tinted bottles, one in each hand.

"Our evening beverage. White wine for me and grape juice for you."

He was the new radiologist—Jaime Vasquez. He spoke with a hint of his native Mexico, which Annette considered a welcome respite from the mountain twang that filled the corridors of the hospital. He was a rare bird around town—reasonably young, single, and gainfully employed in a field that didn't require him to cut wood, dig for coal, or stock a shelf with cheap goods that nobody really needed. When he first arrived at the hospital, Annette had surprised herself by chasing him down, taking him to dinner, and then dragging him home. She hadn't dated anyone seriously in half a decade. And yet here they were, three months later and he let himself in through the front door.

"I can have a glass of wine," she said. "I hate grape juice."

She of all people knew the odds. Oh, she knew them well, which was why she'd allowed herself to be so careless. A woman her age, in her condition, had about a 5 percent chance of conceiving during any cycle. She'd been off the pill since her sex life dried up. She'd been off the pill for longer than she liked to admit. And then came Jimmy, a foolish night, the life that was growing inside of her.

"Can we talk about it tonight?" he asked.

"I'm not ready," she said. "Can't we just watch bad TV and maybe have sex and then fall asleep? I've got a caseload from hell this week. Another SMA diagnosis. I've seen too many of those for one lifetime."

He put the wine and the juice down on the coffee table, and squeezed onto the couch, where she was splayed across all three cushions. He lifted up her feet and began to rub them.

"What did she decide to do?" he asked.

"Nothing. I never ask them to make a decision that soon. I'll see her again on Monday."

There was nothing wrong with this man. Absolutely nothing. She might even learn to love him—his patience, his half-formed jokes. But he was an intrusion. Not necessarily bad, maybe even good, but he was an intrusion still. He was the one who had broken the predictable flow of her days with impromptu trips to the river, the picnics on top of the lonely fire tower up Onekanna Ridge. He was the one who had given her a choice, one that she thought had long ago been decided. A choice that she might never be able to make again.

"We'll do whatever you want tonight, *mi amor*," he said.

She leaned over and buried her head into his chest. She inhaled.

"You're not like the other men around this town."

"Why do you say that? Because I speak to you in Spanish?"

"No, baby. It's your sweat. You work all day and you still come home smelling like roses."

***

It was only ten o'clock, but he was already upstairs in bed snoring. Ever since she'd broken the news to him two weeks ago, he'd begged to sleep over. Some nights she relented; others, she sent him packing to his apartment across town.

"Think about it," he had said. "This could be a blessing. This could be the thing you didn't know you wanted."

It was his presence—she wasn't herself when he was in the room. She filtered her thoughts. She spoke in a voice that she used with no one else. She had said, "OK. I'll think about it," but when she tried, she could hear only static, the cars driving outside of her window, a whirring.

She had worked so long, so hard, to build a life that she loved, that was comfortable—and he had knocked that life into a seven-ten split. She couldn't identify this chaos, whether it was invigorating or maddening. So she ran from him when she could, in order to breathe and to think.

She was sitting in the dining room, at a table that rarely saw use. There were so many spaces like this in her old Victorian home—places to retreat, to close the doors. There were three bedrooms—the master, where Jimmy snored blissfully, and the two guest rooms, where old childhood friends and distant relatives slept when visiting from far away. Her guests looked around the big house with the vacant rooms, at the dining-room table with six chairs. Sometimes they said it outright. Sometimes they implied it with an awkward smile. Why did she decide to come back, to this place, to this town, where she knew the odds were against her?

She spent every day talking about odds—telling a woman that her time was almost up, telling a mother that there was hope in percentages, that the invisible, damaged part of her self, that recessive X or that hidden gene that carried so much weight, might not connect, might not make its way to the life she hoped to foster. But it had never been about odds for Annette. What she wanted to say was that she had been happy here once and knew she could be happy again. That her family mattered to her, even if she had never started one of her own. That she did want to love someone, but love had never stopped her from living life the way she wanted.

She enjoyed spending time with Jimmy. Sometimes she thought she might even end up marrying him. But this child—the rapidly growing cells inside of her—she wasn't sure that it made any sense. And she wanted time to figure it all out. That was really the root of her problem. Time kept passing, and the morning sickness just kept getting worse.

***

Late Saturday morning, she and Jimmy drove out, as

promised, to have lunch with her parents. Mr. and Mrs. Carlisle lived in a big house out in the woods—the fancy woods, that was, with private roads named after indigenous trees. The house had caused her a lot of grief growing up. She had been the rich girl, vested into a predetermined social order during her adolescence. The stone house, with its pool, quietly landscaped yard, and balconies off all the bedrooms, loomed even over the not-so-modest homes of her neighbors, those of the doctors and lawyers and developers. It sat perched on the peak of a hill at the end of Poplar Lane, with a view of the dusty downtown and the tree-covered mountains that guarded on all sides. It was a fitting abode for her father, the bank president, the man who signed off on every loan and blessed every dollar that circulated among the townspeople; he was the king on his mountain.

"Not a word about it," Annette said as she walked up the front steps with Jimmy. "No hints. No Freudian slips."

Her parents were waiting inside, in the glass sitting room with a pitcher of mimosas. Her father's antique Victrola provided a soundtrack of some obscure 1920s' big band. Much to her father's disappointment, she had never much cared for his musical tastes.

"You're late, darling," her mother said, rising from her chair. She wore a thin figure, though not unhealthily so. She was more of a heron than a skeleton, with a craning neck and a devilish chin. Her hair was as white as an eggshell and had been so since Annette was a teenager.

"Five minutes, Mom."

"And that's five minutes too many, dear."

Her mother crossed the room and put a hand on each of Annette's arms. She squeezed them and pursed her lips. "You look good. Something different." She ran a finger through her daughter's hair. "Are you taking vitamins?"

The father remained seated, legs crossed, holding his champagne flute in one hand and the morning paper in the other. "They say the hospital's on a hiring spree, Jimmy. What do you make of this? Are they overreaching? Give that old boy a few cranks, yes?"

Jimmy latched onto the handle of the Victrola. He spoke as his arm pumped at the crank. "People are getting older around here. Somebody's got to take care of them, no?"

Annette's father chortled. "Exactly how many somebodies does it take to wheel a dead man to his grave?"

Mrs. Carlisle took her daughter by the hand. "We'll leave them to talk business. Let's grab the provisions."

They walked into the kitchen, and Annette plopped herself onto the marble counter. The room was as spotless as always—the stone and metal glowing in the afternoon sunlight, nary a crumb or a dirty dish. Her mother kept fresh-cut flowers in a vase in the big center window—today they were orange and black tiger lilies, cut from the edge of the lawn. The lilies sprang up year after year, climbing higher and higher, their blazing fire and black buds opening to signal that summer had arrived.

"Must you?" her mother said, with her head half inside the refrigerator.

"Old habits, mother dearest," she responded, though she did not get down from the counter.

Her mother pulled the silver tray from the refrigerator and sat it on the center of the kitchen island. There were pineapples and mangos and grapes and kiwi, chopped and sliced and arranged like a piece of art. There was enough for a party of ten. "You haven't called in two weeks. You have us worried sick. Is it the good doctor? He's very handsome, you know. Are you too busy for your family? I think I was right about him. I won't say it again, but you know you have my blessing. And I speak for your father, as well."

Annette scanned the room—she thought of all the lessons she had learned and forgotten: the ratio of flour to butter for a perfect pie crust, how to slice the Christmas ham. Annette rarely cooked these days and never baked. What was it her mother had always said to her about cakes? *When the toothpick comes out clean . . .*

"We've been busy. Work, life. Nothing out of the ordinary. You know. Did you hear that Jessie Shannon married Buddy Cooper? I went to the wedding. It was nice. Tasteful. Jimmy joined me. He caused quite the stir."

"Oh?"

"It's just—it's just that look that everyone is giving me. That shit-eating grin, those stupid eyes."

"Language, dear."

"Like I've won the lottery. Like he's a prize. Maybe I'm the prize? Why do people have to talk about relationships like you're coming into some good fortune? I like him. I do. But come on."

Her mother was gathering the utensils—tiny forks and little ceramic plates with stenciled blue flowers and golden rims. "You remember these plates? Your grandmother bought them in London. They'll be yours, of course."

"Not today, Mom," she said. "We've already gone over the instructions."

"As you wish, dear. But there won't be anyone to ask when it happens."

The *instructions* had become her mother's *cause du jour*.

"Be a doll and carry these," her mother said.

They walked back to the sitting room, sat the tray on the coffee table. Annette took a seat on the couch next to Jimmy. The two men were still deep in discussion about the hospital, about whether a small facility could survive in a world where the distance between highways seemed to shrink every day, where the big stores with the big names bulldozed over the smaller ones, leaving behind parking lots where there'd once been histories.

Her father said, "It's about choices. You run a company to serve the customers, and if you do it well, you'll make a dollar in the process. If you serve your customers well, they will reward you with loyalty. They'll weather the storm with you and they'll celebrate your achievements."

"But you forget that I'm not a businessman," Jimmy said. "I'm just a doctor."

"You're wrong, Jimmy. You're in the business of medicine and the business of hospitals should concern you. Annette, too."

Her mother proffered her champagne concoction to Annette and Jimmy.

"Just a small glass," Annette said. "I'm hoping to get to the gym later." She grabbed the flute and took a slow, delicate sip.

"We have an announcement, honey," Mrs. Carlisle said. "We've made some vacation plans. We're going to do something a little different this year. We're thinking Argentina. We used to love to dance so much, you know. Won't that be great?"

"Argentina?" Annette asked. "What about our trip to Nantucket?"

"Well, we're getting older, dear. There are so many places we want to see. We thought that maybe you could keep the rental.

It's already paid. Maybe you and Jimmy could go up together? A nice break from the ordinary?"

Annette sat her champagne flute down. She put a hand on Jimmy's thigh and squeezed. "We'll add that to our list of things we need to talk about. Right, honey?"

He looked at Annette with his big, scared eyes and didn't say a word.

***

Lunch ended with promises that Jimmy would ask the hospital CEO to temper his hiring spree. "Business sense, Jimmy," Mr. Carlisle said. "That's our next project."

They walked down the steps and the parents waved good-bye from the door. Mrs. Carlisle raised a finger—"One thing!"—and then hurried down after them. "You go on, Jimmy," Mrs. Carlisle said.

Jimmy walked to the car, and Mr. Carlisle shouted so-longs, disappearing back into the cavernous home. The two women were alone.

"Honey, sweetie," Mrs. Carlisle started. She spoke in a low voice, through the start of a smile. "You've always been a happy girl."

"Mom—"

"Hush. I just want to say that I think you are so smart and so strong." With a hand, she grabbed the tips of Annette's fingers. "And that I've always been so proud of you."

"Mom, what's this about?"

"Nothing at all, dear. I love you. You know that, right?"

"Of course."

"Now go home with your handsome doctor. That one's a keeper."

Her mother turned and flitted up the stairs, humming a tune that Annette didn't recognize. Her bird body bounced with the lightness of a teenager.

***

They pulled out of the driveway, cruised past the houses of her childhood friends, most long gone to Pittsburgh or Washington or for the warmer climes of the Virginia and Carolina coasts. They drove to the end of Poplar Lane, down Sycamore to Spruce, past the gates of the private community. "Can you take the back roads home?" Annette asked.

"Sure. May I ask why?"

"I want to talk."

They drove in near silence, just the purr of the engine and the wind cutting against the shield, past the Odd Fellows Lodge, along the riverbanks where the young kids fished and camped and swam. Such activities had been forbidden to a younger Annette, her parents always speaking ominously about chemicals and pollution and sewage. She had snuck away anyway, swimming in defiance of the big house on the hill, buoyed by the thrill of hanging with the teens whose names meant trouble.

They drove past the country church, where their maid's daughter, a girl only a year older than Annette, had married one of the Burkham boys. Annette's father had shown up to the wedding in a slick suit, the only man, save for the groom, wearing a tie.

"How much do you know about me?" Annette asked.

Jimmy kept his eyes on the road—the back roads curved and shifted jaggedly along the edge of the riverbank. "Enough to know that you're a good person, that you're a smart woman, that you're someone who makes me happy."

"You sound like my mother."

They drove up a hill, onto the narrow road of the flood control, the pipes and grass and concrete that kept the town safe from summer rains and rising rivers.

"You've just moved here. We've just met. Why are you so sure about all of this?"

She clutched at the door's armrest. She had a vision of the car flipping over the edge of the hill, their bodies sinking to the muddy bottom of the river.

"I'm not so sure," he said. "But I'm not scared, either. I've spent the past decade—hell, more than that—focusing on my career. I'm getting older. I thought maybe this was a sign, a chance to be something more than myself." And then a pause. "What do you want, Annette?"

He never lied, his voice as earnest as a cornstalk. He spoke what he felt, and somehow those feelings always came off so pure. She couldn't fault a man for being like that, but if there had been just a touch of deception or a hint of hubris, it would have been easier.

"Children don't magically fix things," she said, and the words felt right. "Miracles aren't made out of eggs and sperm."

"No, but doing nothing doesn't get a person anywhere."

As they descended the hill, a vision of her world emerged. The brick buildings of the downtown, the metal cross of St. Bartholomew's Cathedral, the bell tower of the courthouse. They drove past the hospital, along the edge of the downtown, past the rail yard that had died and was against all odds showing new signs of life. They said that next year the old rusted trains, which had once carried passengers and timber, would instead carry tourists up and down Onekanna Ridge—sightseeing trips past the waterfalls and the abandoned coal towns that had been forgotten and rendered inaccessible with the death of the train.

"What I'm doing isn't nothing," she said. "What we're doing isn't nothing. I'm living my life, for God's sake. I'm living my life, and that is something. It's everything, in fact. I don't need a kid to fix anything. There's nothing broken with me."

He pulled the car over into the parking lot of the train depot. It was empty and the sun was setting. There were sprays of purple and blue wildflowers blooming along the edge of the tracks, a solitary Pullman car with a fresh coat of black paint.

"It sounds like you've made up your mind," he said.

"I think I made up my mind a long time ago," she said. "This was an accident. I think I was doing just fine before this happened. I don't need this. I don't want this."

He looked like he was about to cry, but she couldn't tell for sure. All of his faces—his grimaces, his smiles, the moments when he made no face at all—she couldn't read him yet. Everything about him was still so new.

"Do you still have room in your life for me?"

She banged her fists against the dashboard. "God, men are so stupid. Do you think we need a baby to be together?"

"No."

She glared at him, her pulse beating red and black at the back of her vision.

"Are you going to be miserable if we don't have a baby together?"

"No."

"Then there's your answer." She rolled down the window and pushed her head out for air—her nose caught the scent of the hot, dry grass. "I don't know where we'll end up. But for the time being, we're not going to be parents. OK?"

"OK."

"Good. Now take me home."

***

It was Monday, only a few days since their last appointment together, and Hattie was waiting in the same chair in Annette's office at the hospital. The fluorescent light was as ghostly as ever. The clock ticked toward five, and Annette's computer buzzed in the background. It was her last appointment of the day.

"Hattie, have you decided what you are going to do?"

"Yes."

Annette allowed her patients to speak on their own terms. She had learned not to interrupt them, not to fill the quiet. The silence was part of the process, the grieving or the healing or, in the best of worlds when the test came back negative, the coming to terms with both joy and fear—the bliss of a dream realized and the recognition that this life, this change, was a permanent responsibility.

"I'm not going to keep him," Hattie said.

"I'm so sorry. That's a hard decision to make."

The woman's face scrunched up and then her cheeks were wet with tears. Annette always thought people looked so much younger when they cried.

"We're going to try again. You said there was a chance, right?"

"Yes. But you know we confirmed that you and your husband are both carriers. Every time that the two of you try to conceive, there's a 25 percent chance that your baby will have the condition. But that means there's a 75 percent chance that your baby will be healthy. It's a risk every time. And it's up to you how long you want to keep trying. It can be a painful process, but it can also be a rewarding one."

Annette reached over to her desk and grabbed a few tissues from a box. "Take these," she said.

"I've always wanted a baby. It feels so wrong to do this. But I want a healthy baby. I want one that's going to be able to live a good life. I couldn't bear to see my baby in pain." The woman wiped her nose. "Tell me. What would you have done?"

Her professors had cautioned her about revealing personal information. Don't touch them, don't tell them what you're thinking. It might seem cold, they had said, but it was important to keep the focus on the patient, on the matter at hand.

"I never had kids. I never had to make your choice. And it doesn't matter what I would have done. You have to make the choices that make sense for you. When and if motherhood finds you, I know you'll be just fine."

Hattie stood up. She shoved the ball of wet tissues into her leather purse. "It seems so cruel that God would do this to a woman. That he would give her a womb, these feelings, and then make it so hard."

In a less clinical world, Annette would have given the woman a hug. Instead, she lifted a hand and motioned toward the exit. "Your case worker will be in touch about your options."

CORPOREAL

It was Friday evening. Jillian arrived home after an uneventful day at school and a quiet afternoon at the library. She was seventeen and aside from the few quirky friends who sat next to her at lunch and in class, she considered herself a loner. She walked through the front door, into their narrow, dimly lit house, past bags of never-worn clothes, past piles of books and bills stacked high along the wall and along the railing of the staircase. Her mother always left the bank at four, and a mound of dumplings was already arranged on the kitchen table. These were her mother's favorite—the ones with nearly translucent skin covering shrimp and bamboo shoots. It was their Friday night ritual, a time when Jillian didn't have to forage through the freezer for something to microwave. She liked the taste of the dumplings, she supposed, but mostly she thought about their briny aroma, which triggered a sense of familiarity.

Her mother said a few words to her in rapid succession. "What did you learn? Did you get your biology test back? Father Williams called and wants you to help with the food pantry on Sunday." After all of the necessary information had been imparted—knowledge learned, good grades upheld—they ate in silence, as the two of them did so often. They kept their attention on the plates in front of them, on the ticking clock, or somewhere else altogether.

After dinner, Jillian washed the dishes and then went to the piano in the living room to practice a Chopin nocturne for a recital the following weekend. She liked to play the piano, but the music her mother wanted her to play always put her in a foul mood. There was something frustratingly fathomless about classical piano—something too deep to decipher. She liked complicated questions, but Chopin, Beethoven, and even Mozart seemed to lead to only more questions.

She wanted to play John Lennon or Joni Mitchell. She could place the emotions of these songs. They were the songs she heard at her father's apartment on the weekends, scratching from the speaker of his old record player. They were the songs that her mother had once listened to when they all lived together. Her parents had divorced, and the record player and all the music that Jillian loved so much went with her father, while she stayed behind in the silence with her mother. She was only nine when it happened, and her mother had worked ever since to purge his presence from their home.

The phone began to ring, and Jillian stopped playing the piano out of courtesy. From her seat on the bench, she watched her mother hesitate in the hallway, pacing the floor and glaring at the receiver. They had no answering machine or voicemail, and so every time the phone rang her mother ceased whatever she had been doing, held captive by questions of nervous import: of whether the person on the other end of the line had any business calling at all, of whether picking up the phone would lead to a trap of sorts—a bill collector, a chatty aunt, a jilted ex-boyfriend, a nosey neighbor. She knew that her mom had issues with patience. As a result, Jillian learned to sit quietly for hours—reading a book, staring out of her bedroom window, or watching the people come and go at the library. Her home was charged enough by her mother's frantic energy. Jillian would fade, then, into the floorboards.

Her mother, Sue, was born in China. She had taken a journey from the mainland to Taiwan, then to the Philippines, and somehow, finally, to their small town in West Virginia. All of this had been related only hazily to Jillian, in separate anecdotes told months apart so that she forgot most of what had been said before and how it all intertwined. Her mother said that the mountains in West Virginia reminded her of home, though she could only remember the Chinese mountains as impressions. She never pressed her mother about any of this, sensing that this was a topic meant only to be narrated, not inquired about.

It was because of China, Jillian had decided long ago, that her mother sometimes acted differently than her friends' parents. In fact, she attributed most of her mother's quirks to China: the nervous pacing, the clutter that consumed every free corner of their house, the shouting to herself in the kitchen, and, of course, the string of boyfriends who came home and treated Jillian like a daughter in need of a father. She had a father, though, and so she quietly resented these men for their condescension. It was the one true bone of contention between the two of them: Jillian had never forgiven her mother for tossing her father out. She'd never told her as much, but she tried to make it plain with a tough, stony face.

She shot her mother that stony gaze now, and Sue finally picked up the phone after what seemed like dozens of rings. When the voice on the other end had spoken, Jillian watched her mother's face turn as white as the snow on the ground out-side. Her mother said, "How did it happen?" She said, "Yes, I will come." She hung up the phone, a yellowed thing mounted on the wall, as old or older than Jillian herself. She turned to Jillian and said, "Your father has shot himself."

She watched as her mother began to sift rapidly through the piles of papers and books that lined all sides of the walls. She sifted through one pile after another, frantically discarding a mess of loose envelopes and magazines onto the floor. She turned to her daughter and said, "I'm sorry. He's dead. We both knew that this was going to happen."

Jillian was only seventeen, but she considered herself obser-vant. She thought that they should both be crying in a mo-ment like this. It occurred to her that she had always been right about her suspicions, that what one saw in movies and read in books might be a false impression of what a human actually felt. She was sad, she supposed, at the thought that her father no longer existed; but more so, she was curious, because his eventual lack of existence had never seemed a possibility. She wondered how her father would react if the roles were reversed. What would he say upon hearing of his daughter's death? She could think of nothing.

"I have to go to the hospital," Sue said, and then, after she had collected her car keys and put on her shoes, "Of course you cannot come with me. You are too young for this. You will be OK alone? You can call your Aunt Linda if you need someone, though I suspect she will be a wreck."

Jillian did not want to call her Aunt Linda. She was not con-cerned about being left alone, and she did not need to be com-forted. There was one thing, however, that weighed inside her unexpectedly. It was not a sadness, exactly. She looked at her mother, the one person who might have the answer. "Why did he do it?"

Sue stopped fidgeting. She took a deep breath and shook her head. "Oh, Jillian! Why wouldn't he do it?"

And then Sue was out the door, and Jillian, not satisfied with her mother's response, was left with the first deep pang that she'd felt that evening. It felt something like loneliness, and she began to wonder if she'd ever really known her father at all.

***

Jillian knew her window of time was short, that her mother would only linger so long at his body, and that soon someone would be sent to clean up the mess in his apartment.

She and her mother lived along the river, across from the town's old black school. Her street consisted of a long row of two-story clapboard houses, shadowed by the brick and block shells of old factories aged with soot and lack of use. On Sundays after church, people would walk through the neighborhood and remark on the old days: of the once-booming economy, of the black baseball team that had won the black state championship. These people would cross the rope bridge from the more affluent part of town and feed the ducks with their grandchildren. On Friday nights, like tonight, the old men would sneak across the bridge on their way to the bars.

Her father's apartment was only a few minutes' walk through the quiet alleyways that led to the downtown. He lived on the main drag in a big apartment building sandwiched between two rival pool halls. The residents of the apartments hung out the windows and yelled to those entering and leaving the bars below. There were no children in the building, as far as she knew, as the place had a reputation for drugs and violence.

Jillian's mother forbade her to go there alone. The courts had already told the father that until he got his act together—until he could put aside the pills and the alcohol, and get a job—he was not to see Jillian without the supervision of her mother. Still, it was a small town and she would sometimes run into him on the way to the library or the grocery store. He would sneak in a hug, a five-dollar bill, and a few words. She thought of him sometimes as more of a doting uncle, a man who showered her with trinkets and gifts to win her affection and make up for the lack of time that they spent together. Once he snuck in a set of keys and said, "If it ever gets too bad with her—and I know how she is—just come find me."

The small amount of time that they spent with each other didn't really bother Jillian. She enjoyed their brief moments and saw them as a respite from the chaos of living alone with her mother. Jillian fancied herself, despite their limited time together, her father's daughter. He too was a quiet man, more concerned about seeing than being seen. When they had lived together, back when he had been able to hold a job at the foundry, the space beneath their Christmas tree had been stacked with neatly wrapped, nearly uniform rectangles: books by the dozen. He would not say much about himself or his past. She would not talk about her day at school. Instead, they would discuss writers, stories, and characters. At first there had been picture books, children's tales; then they were talking about humanity and its pitfalls, as he leafed through texts with calloused fingers, looking for meaningful passages. Through these conversations, as the layers of their knowledge blended over the years, she began to think that she understood him, at least a little. When he said that the absurdity evoked by reading Samuel Beckett seemed not so absurd when one really considered it, he nearly jumped from the couch with excitement. She spent that week sitting in silence at her windowsill, watching the people come and go in their messy patterns.

The men outside the bars catcalled at her as she walked toward her father's building, just as she knew they would. She did not respond to their whistles. She was not bothered by their words—*China doll, Queen of the Orient.* She viewed them as specimens to be dissected. She wondered what motivated them, what could make a man feel so assured.

Early in childhood she had become aware that people noticed her for simply existing: the daughter of a white man and a Chinese woman. Her long black hair not quite her mother's. Her big round eyes, not quite her father's. She grappled with questions of beauty: *Am I beautiful because I'm different from what they know? Am I just their fantasy?* And when the word entered her vocabulary one night when reading an anthology of philosophers that her father had passed along, she asked herself, *Am I corporeal? What makes a body a body?* She had lit a candle that night, closed her eyes, and imagined that her consciousness floated away into the distance.

She was dressed in tight, dark jeans, a white blouse, and a pair of low heels. This was a type of beauty that she could articulate in words. She knew if she dressed smartly, people excused what they thought was her shyness, thinking that a girl who took care of herself probably had something interesting going on in her head. This was how she got through school without saying much. It was why the teachers still smiled at her in the hallways, though she only answered their questions when called upon. It was why the men yelled down from their windows and from the doorways of the bars but would never actually touch her.

She didn't consider herself shy. She liked to first ignore people, and then, when they assumed a certain level of safety—had stopped considering her—she would look them directly in the eyes and hold her gaze firm, until they had to turn away. She did this to her teachers, to her fellow students, and now, to the drunk men who snubbed out their cigarettes and retreated into the dark interiors of the bars. It pleased her that she could make a grown man cower.

At the entryway to her father's building, she put the key into the lock and pushed the door forward. People peered out of their doors along the hallway, disturbed by the events of the evening. The place smelled acidic, like sweat and cat pee. An old woman in a white floral nightie wheeled an oxygen tank from her apartment into the hall and blocked Jillian's path. "Didn't you hear what happened? That old junkie upstairs shot himself. The whole building's going to hell."

Jillian tried to push forward, but the woman would not budge. The lonely, distressed woman wanted to continue their conversation. The effect of her sour face and the oxygen tank made her seem older than her voice would suggest. Jillian wondered if it was emphysema that ailed her—meaning the woman literally had holes in her lungs, just as her father had a hole in his head.

"Who are you coming to see, girl? Don't tell me that you're here to buy drugs. He's dead, and the neighbors won't be selling a thing tonight. The police have been swarming this place all evening. What's a girl like you got to do with drugs anyway? Don't you know any better? Who are your parents?"

Jillian stared back at the woman. She thought, I'm going to visit a ghost. But she didn't believe in ghosts.

"He was my father," Jillian said. "Did you know him very well?"

"Oh heaven forbid," the woman replied, shaking her head. This was too much. She retreated into her apartment, jerking the oxygen tank a little too roughly. She slammed the door shut. From behind the door, the woman uttered: "Good night, and God save your soul, little girl."

Her father lived on the second floor, at the end of a long and dingy hallway. The overhead lights shone a ghoulish yellow and flickered with bursts of sudden brightness. The carpeted walkway appeared tan and stained, though it was hard to judge any color in the strange light. Jillian looked at the skin on her hand: it seemed green and rotten. It was as if she was entering the realm of the dead. She was decomposing with every step.

She saw the yellow police tape across his door: CAUTION. Over the peephole was the number of his apartment: 213. It had been more than a month since she had seen him. Her mother had refused to take her, said that he was off the wagon in a big, big way. Jillian began to realize, looking at his door, that her mother knew more about her father than she let on. What was it about his voice on the telephone that signaled danger?

When Jillian saw her father here on Christmas, on their birthdays, or on their scheduled visits, everything had seemed so ordered. Now she questioned how much of that had been arranged by her mother. They would drink tea and talk about books; before an hour had passed, her mother would stand from her seat in the corner of the apartment and announce that they had better move on. Her father never argued with his ex-wife over the short visits. He lifted the needle from the record player, and the music stopped.

She removed the yellow tape carefully from one side. She would replace it when she left so that no one would know anyone had been there. She felt heat rising in her face. What if there were pieces of brain matter on the carpet? What if there were a note hidden in his bedside drawer? Would it be addressed to Jillian, her mother, a secret lover?

She considered the warning on the tape: CAUTION. A part of her knew that she shouldn't go into the apartment, that what she would see might haunt her forever. Still, an inner voice said that she would regret not looking. In fact, she feared that if she did not go inside, what she imagined would grow into something darker than what actually existed. This unknown would become a beast of sorts, filling the blank spaces of her mind. She would see blood, or she would imagine it. Staring at the yellow tape, doused in the yellow light so that it appeared almost white or colorless, she decided that the reality, in whatever form, would be preferable to her imagination. Further, as every minute passed, she could feel that singular question growing. *Why did he do it?* had morphed into something more primal: *Who was her father?* And by further extension, *Who was she?*

Jillian unlocked the door and turned the knob.

The lights were still on. The apartment was as she remembered: the musty smell, the buzzing of the fluorescent lights. She entered into the sparse and windowless living room, with the old barn-and-farm upholstered sofa, his wooden rocking chair, the record player, and the television. On the coffee table sat the travel mug that she had given him for his previous birthday, when he had started working again. She thought he might need something for the drive in the morning. Though his job did not last—he missed too many shifts—she felt a small amount of comfort upon seeing that he used the object anyway.

Jillian did not see any blood in the living room, and she decided that she did not yet want to see his blood. She realized she had never been in the apartment without him, and she began to feel like an intruder. She sat down on the worn couch and picked up his mug. She put it to her lips and drank. The mixture was cold and bitter: day-old coffee with some liquor in it, probably whiskey. Though she did not like the taste, she willed herself not to spit it out. She drank more of it. She drank from the mug slowly and deliberately until there was nothing left. As she sat on the couch and the liquid settled into her stomach, the burning in her face changed from one of nervousness to one of the sublimely at ease. She began to imagine herself as her father. She felt that with the liquor inside of her, there was a part of him that must inhabit her, too.

She turned on the television with a remote control that she found on the coffee table, but there was only gray and white fuzz. She flipped the channels, but none registered. He did not pay for cable. She scanned the room for a DVD player or a VCR. She rose from the couch and opened the door of the television stand. Inside, there were a few of his old vinyls and a smattering of ancient dust. With a finger, she traced her name across the fake wood: Jillian. And then she traced his name beside her own. She wanted the ones who would clean this mess to know that he hadn't been entirely alone.

So he didn't watch television. He would have spent his time reading books or listening to the sounds of his records or the neighbors filtering in from the hallway. Did he find joy in that solitude? Did he invent stories about the voices he heard? She thought, maybe he listened to the radio. There was a radio in the kitchen, she remembered. And then it occurred to her: she had seen no blood yet. He must have shot himself in the kitchen. The record player was empty. Had he shot himself in silence?

She took one last glance around the room, at the paneled walls, at the popcorn ceiling. She feared that once she saw the blood she would have to run. She must take this all into her mind, sear it into her thoughts like a photograph.

She walked two steps into the kitchen, and there it was: blood on the side of the wall, just over the small Formica table, but only a stain, rounded at the edges, like a rusty watercolor painting on the chipped white paint, more brown than red. The landlord must have dispatched someone before she arrived, because there was no other evidence of him—no piece of him scattered on the linoleum.

On the table was a half-eaten loaf of bread, a pack of cigarettes, and a lighter. She grabbed the cigarettes and lighter and stuffed them into the front pocket of her jeans. She inspected the wall, pressing her fingertips gently against the wash of dried blood. She then looked at her fingers, but no blood had rubbed off. The blood had found a permanent home, and someone would come in and paint over it with white, until one day another person chipped away the layers and he would be gone. He would be forgotten.

She assumed there would be a hole, but she did not see one. She looked at the wall, at the ceiling, on the floor—but there was only more dust, and bits of hard bread crumbs underneath the table. *Where had the bullet gone? Had it lodged in his brain? Would they remove it before they put him into the casket? Would he even have a casket? What would he have wanted? What did he want in life?* The questions spun through her head and stirred thoughts and memories that she hadn't allowed herself to consider.

She saw the clock. She had been gone for more than an hour. Her mother would be worried. She felt that she had seen enough. She could not yet make sense of any of it, but she latched onto the idea that the kitchen was important in all of this. She would go home and sit in her own kitchen and think.

She would think about kitchens and what people did in them. She would think about fluorescent lighting and how fluorescent shadows were different. She would think about what it meant to live alone, almost as a ghost, without a television, without the radio turned on.

She left the apartment in a rush. She didn't want to confront any new surprises, to take in any new mysteries. As she was reattaching the yellow caution tape, a man called to her, and she almost screamed. "Jillian," he said. "You're his daughter, right?"

She turned around. The voice belonged to the neighbor across the hall. She had seen his face maybe once or twice before. He had cracked his door so that only half of his body showed. He had scrubby brown hair and an uneven mustache. He was a short man, but wide. He wore gray sweatpants and a stained gray T-shirt, though the two grays were not the same. There was desperation in the way he gripped the door and tilted his head a little too forward.

"He talked about you a lot," the man said. "He said you were very bright and curious. And beautiful."

Jillian didn't know how to respond to him. Her mind was filled with images—permutations of blood and guns.

"Won't you come in for a minute?" the man asked.

Jillian considered the offer. Here was a man who knew her father in this world, in this building of outcasts. He would say things her mother could not or would not. She knew she would not ask her mother any more questions about her father.

At the same time, Jillian knew it was getting late. If she stayed too long, her mother, on this night in particular, would be tempted to call her friends' parents, her teachers, or even the police. So she declined. "I'm sorry," she said. "My mother is waiting for me."

She hurried down the hallway, down the stairs, and out the front door. She did not look back. On her way home, she lit one of her father's cigarettes. She let the smoke sit in her mouth. She did not take it into her lungs. She wanted to taste him.

***

"Where have you been?" her mother asked, standing in the landing of their home.

"I needed to take a walk. I needed to clear my head."

Her mother's shoulders dropped an inch. "Oh. That makes sense, I suppose." She was too overwhelmed to ask her daughter any probing questions. Jillian felt relief.

She walked past her mother and into the kitchen, where the smell of the dumplings she had eaten earlier persisted. She sat down at the table, and her mother put on a pot of water for tea.

"It was a mess," her mother said. "He was a mess. There won't be a real funeral. He was doomed, Jillian. There was nothing any of us could have done to save him. His sister was there. She looked at me like it was my fault. Can you believe that? She says they're going to have a memorial next weekend. They're going to cremate him. No one has the money for a coffin, and I wasn't about to volunteer my savings."

Jillian did not look at her mother; she barely listened to her. She looked at the table and imagined her father sitting across from her. She pictured him reading the newspaper holding a cup of coffee in the travel mug she had bought him. He would roll his eyes at her mother's rant. He might even wink. She laughed.

"Am I being insensitive? Is something funny? Oh, I know he was your father. I know that you had certain affections for him. He left us because he had to leave us, dear. He left us because he would have brought us all down with him."

They sat in silence, waiting for the water to boil. Jillian wondered if her mother ever drank whiskey. She wondered if at the hospital her aunt had suggested her mother drink a glass of wine to calm her nerves. She wondered if a glass of wine would actually calm her mother, or make her more anxious.

When the water boiled, her mother poured them each a cup of tea. Jillian raised the cup to her mouth. She sipped its warm, herbal contents. "I would like to go to mass this weekend," she said, without qualifying her desire.

"Oh? Well, I suppose if that's how you want to deal with this. Fine. I don't think I'll be going. But do tell the father what has happened. He will want to know."

Jillian and her mother finished their tea, and then they said goodnight. Jillian slipped into her bed and, in her head, repeated her father's name over and over, hoping that she might dream of him drinking whiskey and smoking cigarettes. She wanted to dream of him talking to his neighbor about the absurdity of the world.

***

Jillian woke on Saturday morning having dreamed nothing at all. There were phone calls and visits by relatives and old family friends—many of whom she had never before met. She was glad that they came, that they required the attention of her mother, and that likewise, her mother deflected the attention from Jillian. They brought food and flowers. There was conversation through the sunset, and even laughter.

When the guests left, a great, heavy silence filled the house. The chatter had erased his presence, but now, in the quiet night, his ghost returned. Her mother scrubbed at the dishes that her guests had left behind, her hands pushing harder and harder into the soiled plates, her eyes focus downward into the sink. Jillian retreated to her bedroom and tried to clear her mind—to think of nothing, to make her mind an empty screen of blackness. She fell asleep to a vision of him smiling, holding the gun to his temple.

On Sunday morning, she showered and dressed and walked the few blocks to the cathedral. She took a seat near the back and looked up to the cavernous ceilings, the gilded arches and secret chambers. While the choir sang, she thought of how her father had always held a deep contempt for Catholics. "They want to dumb you down," he would say. "They don't care if you understand one bit of what they're saying. They actively hope that you don't read or think anything for yourself. How many years did they only do things in Latin? You get what I'm saying."

Jillian herself felt ambivalent about Catholics. She liked watching the churchgoers go through the rituals. She liked watching old women and men get down on their knees. She watched people's faces for signs of resonance with the father's words. It seemed to Jillian that people came to mass to get inside their own heads, and when the father gave the homily, they used his words like the swinging watch of the hypnotizer—a way to go deeper, a time to stop perceiving.

After Father Williams had finished and the people had started to clear from the sanctuary, Jillian approached him. She did not say anything. She forced a light smile onto her face, waiting to see if anyone had told him of what happened. In their small town, after all, news had a way of traveling with the wind. People sat at home and listened to the scanner or looked out their windows for flashing lights. It could be a fire, a robbery, a murder, or an old man having a heart attack. It didn't matter. They picked up their phones and called all of their friends and relatives, until the stories developed into stories that bore no resemblance to the originals. Jillian's mother would hear about all of these happenings at the bank, and sometimes, Jillian would hear about them over dinner.

"Jillian, I'm glad to see you," the father said. "Where is your mother? We missed her this morning. Are you going to stick around and help with the pantry?"

This was as she had hoped. She did not want Father Williams to know. She wanted to keep her secret for a while longer. She wanted to work the food pantry without coddling. She wanted to see the down-and-out asking for cans of beans. She wanted to imagine that her father knew these people—and truthfully, he could have been one of them. He, above all the people in her life, would know how people became desperate enough to wait in line for handouts.

Jillian lied to the father and said that her mother was sick with a cold. He said that he would pray for her mother to have a speedy recovery. Jillian, eyes averted, thanked him.

The pantry was run out of the chapel annex. It was a new idea, and this was only the third weekend it had operated. There were a half-dozen people in an assembly line, middle-aged women filling grocery bags full of nonperishables. The Father asked Jillian to work the front table, where she would hand out the food.

"You have a gentle soul," he said. "The people will appreciate a young girl with concern for her fellow humans."

Jillian considered his words: she was not so sure that *concerned* was how she would phrase it. Interested, yes, but concerned seemed something different altogether.

As the pantry was new, few people showed up. The church had more bags of food than people who wanted them. The ones coming up to the table were mostly elderly, some with canes and some with walkers. A blind man approached, led by a nurse. He touched Jillian's hand as she passed him a bag, and then grabbed onto her wrist. His nurse pulled back his hand, apologized, and escorted him away.

Jillian wondered about the people's families, if their families had abandoned them, as her mother had her father? Had their children died? Were the beggars drug users who spent their money foolishly? Or were people in old age just doomed to be alone and helpless?

She was staring out one of the annex windows gazing at the green mountains. She was wondering about all the plights one might succumb to—hunger having never been something she'd really considered. An oddly familiar voice interrupted her thoughts: "Jillian, I didn't know you were Catholic."

It was the man from the apartment building—her father's neighbor. She nodded to him but did not smile.

"I don't think you know my name yet. I'm Michael."

She thought it strange that he didn't go by Mike. Michael seemed too formal, too precise, for this man. But then everything about him seemed somehow askew. Maybe Michael was correct. Maybe he had once been someone else.

His eyes were a blistery red in the daylight. He was at least fifty, if not sixty. He offered his hand, as if to shake with her.

"Would you like a bag of food?" Jillian asked, holding the paper bag out in lieu of her hand.

"Yes, please."

He took the bag but did not leave the table. His eyes and brow twitched as he watched her. He swallowed hard, and she watched how his Adam's apple dipped.

"If you want to talk about your father—anything really—you

know where to find me. I'm always home alone. Every night. Most nights I'm up all night long."

He lingered for a moment longer, and then turned around without saying good-bye. He did not get into a car in the parking lot. He carried the bag over his shoulder, like a satchel, and lumbered down the street back toward her father's apartment building.

***

Her mother always went to bed early on Sunday nights, and this night, with all the turmoil of the weekend, she had disappeared to her room even earlier than usual. Jillian could hear the television still tuned to an old comedy. She could see the shadows flashing under the bedroom door.

Her mother would be deeply asleep. The creaking front door would not startle her. She would think it was the wind or the neighbor going out for a cigarette. Even if she had thought she heard a strange noise, she would never think to check her daughter's room. Jillian never did things out of character.

She waited until midnight. She switched out of her nightshirt and back into jeans and the white blouse she had worn the day before. She wanted to recreate the scene. She brushed her hair and grabbed her father's cigarettes. She looked into her mirror and unbuttoned one more button on her shirt.

Sunday nights were the quietest in the town. The bars closed early. People recovered in solitude for the coming week of work. On her way to the apartment building, she saw no one out walking. A few cars drove by. A pickup truck slowed as it passed her, the driver a gruff man with a beard and a hat. He rolled down his window. "Miss, you need a ride somewhere?" She shook her head, and then he drove off.

There were no men milling about in front of her father's building, no one to catcall at her. She felt a strange pang of emptiness at their absence. She felt that without them, the street seemed too neutral. Without their presence, she did not know how to carry herself.

She unlocked the front door of the building and walked inside. The hallway was quiet, save for the barely audible sounds of a stereo coming from a unit in the back. There was a strong scent of marijuana in the air. She wondered if her father had smoked pot. At first she assumed he had. She had heard that pot dulled the senses. She thought maybe that would answer her mystery, that he was high when he shot himself. But then it occurred to her that one might want to fully feel that final moment—the bullet ripping through the skull and into the brain. That was a sensation that must be interesting, unforgettable if you could stick around to remember it. So maybe he did smoke pot, but most likely, if he was anything like her, he probably wasn't high when he pulled the trigger. He would want to feel the sting. Or the burn. Or the obliteration. Whatever the sense was.

She walked upstairs, down the dank hallway, and once again through the eerie lights. Just as before, she felt her skin transforming—the rules of the underworld. The police tape had been removed from her father's apartment. She walked up to his door, rubbed her fingers across the numbers. She tried the knob, and the door was locked. She would not disturb his space again.

She turned directly around. She took a deep breath, and then she knocked on the neighbor's door. There was some commotion inside. The scrambling of feet, the knocking over of something heavy. Loud cursing. Something rattling in a container.

She saw the peephole go from light to dark, and then Michael opened the door smiling. His eyes were red and glassy, even more so than earlier. His pupils were large and wild. He wore the same gray sweatpants and T-shirt as the previous night. "I didn't expect you so soon," he started, "or else I would have tidied the place up a little."

He spoke to her as her mother had spoken when one of her aunts came to visit unexpectedly. Her mother would run around the house smiling, asking mundane questions while sifting through the large piles of nothing, moving the contents from one stack to the next. Jillian could not tell at first if the man was excited to see her.

His apartment opened into a dingy living room: an old shag carpet, an easy chair with the stuffing coming out of the arms, a wooden coffee table with an orange pill bottle resting on it, and a gray television with an antenna tuned to the local network. He was watching infomercials on mute.

He took her by the arm and led her to the easy chair. "Now would you like anything to drink?"

"Whiskey," she responded without hesitating.

He disappeared into the next room and came out with a small wooden chair. He went back into the room and returned with two coffee mugs and a bottle of whiskey. He took a seat on the wooden chair. He seemed distantly happy as he poured their drinks—distant, she judged, because the largeness of his eyes seemed to indicate that a part of him floated through a reality located someplace else. "I'm sorry. I don't have any ice, and I haven't got any clean drinking glasses. I hope you don't mind drinking out of a mug. A cigarette?"

His voice was surprisingly eloquent. Jillian had always assumed that people living like this—in dirty apartments, existing on the fine line of poverty—could not be all that intelligent. She did not think of her father as the same as this man. She had somehow carved out a space for her father to be the exception. Now she wondered if she was wrong about how life operated. She wondered if this man read many books. She looked around, but she did not see any. She thought once again of her father's fondness for Beckett.

She lifted her mug and took a sip—too deep of a sip. She coughed so hard that she spit some of it onto Michael's leg, leaving a small spray of dark wetness along the thighs of his gray sweatpants. She remembered that the liquor at her father's apartment had been mixed with coffee, making the liquor more palatable.

"Don't worry about it," he said, running his hands over his pants. "You can't ruin anything in here."

She pulled her father's cigarettes out and put one to her lips. She waited for him to light it. She pushed her breasts out and held her chin high. She had seen other women do this. She thought that was what he wanted to see. She thought that was what all old men wanted to see. She found a certain humor in playing this role.

"Oh, of course," he said, and reached awkwardly over her legs into the seams of the easy chair. He brushed her leg as he fished inside the chair and then pulled out a lighter. As he lit her cigarette, she saw that his hand was covered with the dirt and crumbs from the cushion.

She inhaled this time, and coughed again, the smoke running over her whiskey-burnt throat. She was determined to continue. She felt that there was something in this—understanding how to smoke—that she needed to decode. She took another sip of whiskey—a smaller one this time—and after repeating the process a few times, her throat felt numb. Curiously, the inverse seemed to happen with her body. She felt a burning starting from somewhere behind her stomach, and it seemed to spread out to her limbs. She shifted the cigarette around like a wand, felt a certain pleasure and freedom in the loosening of her limbs.

"I have a daughter, you know," he said. "She's not as pretty as you, and she never comes to visit me."

Jillian tried to imagine the woman that would have a relationship with this man. She pictured one of those large women she saw at the grocery store—the ones who reached down to grab a can of soup, and then hung over their carts wheezing for breath. And then she pictured her mother, in bed with this man, making a baby. "Does she look like you?" Jillian asked.

He laughed at her, and grabbed the bottle to refill their mugs. "She is not balding, fat, and ugly, if that's what you are implying."

Jillian smiled, surprising herself at how easy her lips curved. "Who was my father?"

Michael looked at her. Something devilish took hold of his eyes. He put his cigarette down and leaned in close. He grabbed her hand and held it tenderly. "Oh you poor thing. Your father was a good man. A funny man."

She didn't jerk away. She knew that touching her might be what it took for him to get the words out. A small part of her thought that his touch didn't feel so frightening. "Tell me more."

"He liked to read books. He liked to talk to me about them."

"But I already know that," she sighed. "Tell me something I don't know. Tell me a secret that he wouldn't tell his daughter."

Jillian's heart was beating in a way that it hadn't since her father had shot himself. She felt as if she were on the cusp of something very important.

"If he had any secrets," he started, "I don't know if he would have wanted me to tell you."

She felt older suddenly, angry that no one would tell her the things that she most wanted to know. She hated her mother for keeping her father away, for making him such a mystery. "I'm his daughter," she said. "I have a right to his secrets."

Michael took a sip of his whiskey with one hand, his other clutching Jillian's even more firmly. "Do you really want to know?"

"Yes," she begged. "Please tell me."

He let his fingers slip onto her wrist. She did not like this feeling, but she knew that this was the currency—a tit for a tat. Behind the walls of this building—this place that sheltered half the town's outcasts—she understood that the rules of the daylight world did not apply.

"He had a certain penchant for a certain kind of woman."

His words pricked at something in her, and she felt her body, her quickening pulse, pounding for an answer. "More."

He leaned in so close that she could smell his skin—sharp and sweaty, wild. "Give me a kiss—just one kiss—and I will."

He repulsed her—but not enough to cause her face to wrinkle. It wasn't his hideous body, or the pungent smell of his booze-filled sweat. It was the desperation she sensed in his voice. He repulsed her, yet she pitied him. She pitied him because she began to recognize the look in his eye. She wondered if she hadn't seen the same look issuing forth from her father.

She leaned in to kiss him, because she wanted to know. He grabbed the back of her head and pushed his face into hers. He slipped his tongue between her lips. She didn't resist, but neither did she move her own tongue in return. She let him invade, feel around. His tongue brought a taste of rancid food and smoke. He moved his tongue primordially, like a lizard licking from the guts of a wounded animal, greedily lapping her up before something else moved in to steal her. As his tongue dug deeper, his hands slipped down her head and onto her neck. He squeezed her neck as if to massage her, but she felt only the squeezing and none of the pleasure. It seemed as if he would not stop, that she could just sit there and he would do this forever—explore her insides with his tongue. But then she realized that she was not breathing. She tried to breathe through her nose, and she found that she couldn't. Panic washed over her, and she began to pound his thigh with her fists.

He let go. "I never thought—" but then he trailed off, with a dazed look in his eyes. He reached for the bottle of pills, grabbed one, and swallowed it down with whiskey. "Want one?"

She caught her breath. She shook her head.

He closed his eyes. He seemed to be entirely in that other place. She was not sure that he would come back.

Jillian put a hand on his thigh and began to squeeze. Her fingers dug into the fat of his legs—his skin seemed too loose, as if it might come off in chunks, the consistency of thick mud. "Please," she begged.

He leaned back into his chair. His body slumped. He looked at the wall, then at her hand on his leg.

Jillian squeezed his thigh harder. She would do anything to hear about her father. "What if I were your daughter?"

Suddenly and violently, he swung his arm across the coffee table. He knocked the bottle of pills onto the floor—the contents sprinkling blue, white, and orange across the shag carpet. He began to shout. "Don't you get it?"

He stood up and began to pace the room erratically, in strange diagonal lines. His eyes seemed different now—as if on the verge of tears. She could not tell if he was crying, or if it was the drugs. Still, she had not even considered the possibility that a man such as this could be capable of weeping in front of a young girl. The thought of this man crying invaded her mind and caused something to shatter inside her—some invisible scaffolding that had been holding all of her logic together collapsed.

He crossed in front of her and stopped his pacing. "He was just a man, little girl. He was just a lonely old man!"

He took the glass from her hand and slammed it onto the coffee table. There were most certainly tears in his eyes. They streamed down his cheeks. She thought he might hit her.

"Leave now, little girl. Go home to your mother. Forget about all of this. Forget about him. Forget about me."

He grabbed her by the arm and jerked her toward the door. He was surprisingly strong. He pushed her out the door, into the hallway. She turned as if to plead with him, though she could think of nothing to say. "I just want—"

"Just go!" he screamed. "Let an old, lonely man be by himself, just as he should."

His face disappeared behind the door. She heard the bolt shoot across.

It was over now, she knew. She walked quickly down the yellow-lit hallway. She was shaking and, she now realized, a little drunk. She paused at the glass door of the entrance and looked back once more at the inside of her father's apartment building—so dark and lonely. She pushed open the door and stepped out onto the empty street. She lingered on the steps, suddenly feeling very sad and very vulnerable. She was not sure if she knew her father, or even if she wanted to anymore. She wanted to go home into her bed and hide under the covers. She took her father's key from her key ring. She left it carefully on the doorstep and ran through the quiet night toward home.

HANK THE KING

THE LIGHT from the machine flashed over his face like beams of 2 a.m. moonlight breaking through passing clouds. Outside the noon sun was burning, but here, in the windowless back room of the American Legion, the wheels on the screen spun and chirped—happy, beckoning. His eyes followed the wheels like a dog waiting for table scraps. He reached out to touch the glass. It was warm and smooth—as always—and responsive, the sevens and cherries and fruits stopping for his fingers, as if God himself had come down and ordered all the world's movement to cease. In this room, Hank Burkham was God.

Evelyn brought Hank—old Hank the King, as he'd once been known—another diet Coke. He was a man who looked as if the best parts of him had just slipped out of his body, like the air from a balloon: cracked knuckles, water-blue eyes that made people look away, and arms of loose skin that had once encased strong muscles.

Evelyn, on the other hand, looked old but talked young and fast. She ran the back room at the American Legion: spent her time wiping down the greasy surfaces of the half-dozen machines and making chitchat with the customers to keep them going. She didn't need to convince Hank to stay. He was more like a resident than a regular. He slid in another twenty as Evelyn watched over his shoulder with pursed lips. "One of these days, sugar," she said. "We'll strike it big."

If he ever did strike it big, he'd take care of her—he'd buy her a house on the beach, and make sure she never had to work again. She was a woman who had loved Hank once, and because of that, one of the only women of the town's down-and-out with whom he hadn't crossed a certain line. He'd always wanted her—needed her—but as a friend, a reliable presence. He'd had more than enough acquaintances in his lifetime. What he found in Evelyn was someone who saw through his firm handshake, through his cheap jeans that hid his skinny white legs. She saw down to his sad, aging bones. His own wife couldn't even see him like that. Yes, he supposed he loved Evelyn, but with a love like the one he had shared with his now-deceased mother. Because of that love, he would never betray Evelyn by going down that road.

"I'm getting old," he said, running his fingers through his beard and then slicking down a few loose hairs over his balding crown. "I'm an old, old man."

"You always say that. I say quit your whining and embrace it. Me, I'm taking the senior bus to Atlantic City next week. Old? I say, give me the damn discount and bring on the fun. These legs still work."

Thirty-five years was the length of their friendship. They met in one of those rough-housing bars that he'd frequented in his twenties. It was the same year he found his wife, Betty, a woman who'd only gone in the bars to chase him out. He'd always been a man about town, and he'd fooled around for most of his life— especially when he'd been younger and thick chested, a catch for a certain type of late-night woman—but life had gone downhill, slowly, almost imperceptibly, dissipating into a nearly unrecognizable version of itself, not unlike the dying town itself. One day he opened his eyes, it seemed, and the world looked altered. His mother died. His pawnshop had gone out of business. A sore on his right foot had nearly engulfed his whole leg. The doctor said he had diabetes. That had marked the end of his drinking and the beginning of his infatuation with the machines.

His dominion was crumbling: the buildings of the town and his body. He was drawing social security, neck deep in bills, and trying to find what little pleasure was left in the world. He didn't know where to look anymore.

"How's that son of yours?" Evelyn asked. "Still living the big life up in New York?"

"Like a prince," he said, though he hadn't a clue. Betty had burned that child so bad with her caustic love that the minute he turned eighteen he'd run far and fast from the mountains, swearing he'd never come back. Every few Christmases he might turn up, and then they'd all sit down on the couch for a talk that would end with somebody in tears, somebody slamming the front door. "Betty's a wreck without him." That was true, but mostly because she needed somebody to fight. She and Hank barely spoke these days, save a once-a-month blowout when she was bored. Their house had all the liveliness of a crypt.

"I haven't seen that woman in a thousand years," Evelyn said.

"She doesn't leave the house," he said. "She thinks the world's out to get her. She's afraid she'll see somebody she knows. Not a friend in the world anymore."

He slid his last twenty in the machine. He took a long pause, tapped the side of the machine like his old mutt, and then hit the spin button.

"Max bets," he said. "For a last hurrah."

***

Hank left the back room of the Legion empty-handed and tired of talking. He said good-bye to Evelyn and Caroline, the bartender with a voice like a wolf. "See you tomorrow," Caroline said. "Wouldn't be a day without seeing Hank the King."

He got into his white truck with the rusted frame and took the long way home. He drove through the downtown and passed his old pawnshop—now just another vacant storefront, the outline of the old, painted letters still visible on the glass: "Hank the King's: Pawn, Sell, and Trade." Next door was a carpet outlet, also going out of business. The downtown had become a big sea of nothing: the only thing bustling was the dollar store.

He drove slowly and waved from his pickup truck at some of the old-timers, the ones who had frequented his shop back when it had been open. Now, those sad men wandered up and down the streets of the downtown all day, blowing their money at the Legion or the Moonshiner Tavern. If they were more adventurous, or maybe just bored, they'd cash their disability checks, run into the old Green Valley Hotel—the marble lobby cracked and stained—and buy a bag of weed or some pain pills. People would do anything to feel numb.

When he couldn't think of another creative path to cruise, he bought a coffee at the gas station, said hello to a toothless man scratching lottery tickets at the counter. The old man seemed to know Hank, but Hank couldn't place him. Just another face made unrecognizable with the wear of age.

Hank took his coffee back to his truck. He drove and parked his car in front of JB's Pawnshop, thinking he might reminisce about the good old days. JB's was the last pawnman still in business in the town. Back when Hank was still running his own store, there were four different men running such outfits, all seeming to eke out a living one way or another.

JB's was closed for the evening. The lights were off, but Hank could see through the big glass windows to the interior. The place was old-fashioned—paneled walls and display cases made from another era. The merchandise was neatly arranged along the shelves and behind the glass cases. Hank's own store had always been in disarray—the goods stacked and piled up to the ceiling. Still, Hank had always understood his clutter, knew the resting place of every odd trinket, even if that trinket was at the bottom of a big crate filled with useless junk.

JB had been Hank's rival for all those years, and judging from the fact that JB was still going strong, he had obviously been the better businessman. They'd been friendly, not enemies. In reality they'd dealt with a different kind of clientele. JB bought and sold his wares to the kind of people that would have been embarrassed to step onto Hank's dusty, shag carpet. JB sold musical instruments to all the kids who joined the band. Hank kept a locked drawer of wedding rings that came from desperate wives who needed to pay their bills.

The only area of sales they'd every really competed in was guns. JB fancied himself a collector, and would stop by every week or so to see what Hank had acquired. At his peak, Hank probably had almost a hundred locked in the cabinets in his back room. JB would stop by, and the two of them would sit down and break the guns apart, oil them up, and occasionally strike a bargain. When Hank finally went out of business, JB bought him out—nearly every last gun, a good number of them at a discount. The only one Hank wouldn't sell him was his 1887 Winchester Repeater. The gun was given to Hank by his mother, the day his father died. It was slick, a beauty. JB had offered him two grand, but Hank wouldn't relent. "Some things are more valuable than all the money in the world."

***

He pulled up to the curb of his wooden box of a house out on Yokum Run just past three in the afternoon. It was an idyllic spot for a neighborhood, the road cutting through a little valley, with the eponymous creek running shallow behind the houses of the north side of the street. Once, the road had been lined with little bungalows with smoking chimneys and quaint country homes with gardens in the big side yards. The gardens had mostly been removed, the plots divided and subdivided for children who couldn't afford to move on and up. Now, every third residence was a trailer or a doublewide.

The changing character of the street hadn't bothered Hank as much as it had some of the older residents, the ones who claimed that three or four generations of their kin had called Yokum Run home. They'd fallen together, all of them, and he thought this might be a good thing when it came to a lesson about humility. No matter the trailers, no matter the types of cars that parked along the curb, it was still the kind of place where he could leave his front door open night and day.

The front door to his home was open as he got out of his truck, though the curtains were still drawn. He walked inside, and Betty was sitting in her chair at the dinner table smoking a cigarette and drinking a cup of tea. She wore a pair of pilled sweatpants and an oversized T-shirt. Her hair was white and cut short, her face as sour as the apples that grew in their back-yard. It was hard for Hank to reconcile this woman with the one he had met so long ago. Back then, she had worn sharp black skirts and pearly white blouses. Her hair had been long and coal black, as shiny and deceptive as a freshly shed snake.

"Which whore was it today?" Betty asked. "Margot? Cassie?"

"Woman," he said, and walked straight to the living room. He took a seat on his busted-up recliner, which was patched with duct tape to keep the stuffing from bursting from the holes in the fake leather. He turned the television onto the news and scaled up the volume.

"You can't tune me out," she screamed.

He could only pity her so much. She hadn't always been like this, at least not to this extreme. He knew it was partly his fault, if not mostly his fault. He'd screwed around for the better part of their marriage, but hadn't she always had the power to leave? He didn't think of himself as a good man, but he wasn't the worst. When he'd had his pawnshop, he'd helped just about everyone who needed helping, buying up junk at prices that he never should have offered. That was what had done him in: he couldn't say no to a man in need. Or a woman, for that matter. If he'd been better at saying no, he probably never would have married Betty.

"You can fix your own damn supper."

His problem in life was clear-cut. He'd ended up in the wrong place with the wrong person. He was a man who could never make choices, couldn't choose not to be with those other women, couldn't choose to be anything but the kind of father he was (not much of one at all). He'd married a woman who was just as passive. They'd die together, in their cramped, little house, probably one right after another because neither could learn how to go on living alone.

Betty appeared in the doorway to the living room. He remembered his mother before she had died, how her wrinkled face seemed so soft, benign. Here was his wife with her tight, anxious face, a chin so sharp it could cut. "Did you turn your hearing aid off on me?" Her hands pointed and her arms pumped as she spoke, like the drum major of a high-school marching band. "I'm talking to you."

He turned his head toward her, took a deep breath. "You're in one of your moods, I see. I won't bother you." He turned the television off.

"One of my moods? You want to talk about moods? Why don't we talk about the mortgage payment that's overdue? Why don't we talk about how I'm supposed to buy groceries this month? Why don't we talk about how our son hates us so much that he never calls?"

Once he would have matched her, got up in her face and screamed back. He'd have thrown two kitchen chairs for every dish she broke against the wall. Now he felt only fatigue when he listened to her voice. Every word she spoke seemed to bring him closer to a deep sleep.

He got up from his chair. He walked across the living room and pushed past her. "Let it be, Betty. I'm leaving now."

He walked out the front door toward his truck.

"You go on, Hank Burkham," she called after him. "You keep on running until you find what you're looking for."

He started the engine of his truck, made a three-point turn, and headed back the way he'd come.

***

Hank drove once again through the downtown. He passed the old pharmacy, now a Salvation Army, where he had first met Betty. On that first encounter, he'd come in with a black eye and cuts all over his face. It had been a particularly drunk Friday night, a particularly painful Saturday morning. She was the counter lady, young with big, dark, vulnerable eyes. He thought she would be a challenge, that he would teach her to narrow those eyes, to be strong and sure.

She was smitten back then—he now knew—because no man had ever treated her the way she deserved to be treated. There was a dark family history, somewhere in that brain of hers, but she played it off as shyness, as innocence. That first meeting she had rubbed ointment over his bruise and cuts, leaning her thin body over the drugstore counter, probably thinking that was the start of something reciprocal. What she had needed was a strong man, a family man, a sensitive man who would fawn all over her and buy her nice clothes. What she hadn't needed was a Burkham boy. The whole lot of them had always been bad with women, terrible with money, and even worse with kids (his own father included). But that was how life worked. People clamoring for something. Grabbing anything.

Hank drove in circles through the town looking for any sign of life, but the streets were dead. If it had been a decade ago, he would have found other ways to amuse himself. He'd have gone off to the bars, maybe fooled around with some old flame who'd been through another six men since he'd last seen her. He would have gone out and drank until his eyes blurred, and then he would have slept on the cot he kept in the back room of his pawnshop. But the pawnshop was gone, the diabetes had killed the drinking, and as far as he could tell, his equipment down below was no longer up for the task. So he drove.

On days like these, when all Betty wanted to do was fight until she nearly gave herself a stroke, he had taken to going out to Burkham Ridge—a place that, though wide and open, felt more safe than his own four walls. Anyone in the town with a long family history had such a place: an old forgotten peak, a family namesake. They were found on unsigned, dirt roads: plateaus and valleys settled a hundred or more years ago by hardscrabble pioneers who'd claimed the land as their own. Now, the coal and timber companies had bought out most of these places, leveled all the old mountain houses. A few of the old-timers had held out and still owned their land, using them for hunting camps. Rarely, whole clans of three or four generations lined the hollows, everyone eating dinner each night at Grandma's house as they watched the outside world slide away.

Hank's great-grandfather, Ezekiel Burkham, had sold his property to one of the timber outfits like most everybody else. Whatever money he'd gotten for the land, which probably wasn't much, had been squandered before Hank was born. The company had agreed, however, to leave deeded access to the old family cemetery where four generations of Burkhams lay in neat rows, where Hank and Betty would someday in the not-too-distant future take up residence themselves.

The road to Burkham Ridge was off of the old highway, about six miles outside of the city line. The gravel road wound up and around, all the way to the top, a couple thousand feet above the town. It was a forgotten world of big old trees and vines and deer. Whatever timbering the company did, if they did any timbering at all anymore, wasn't visible from the road. The land appeared as unspoiled as the fresh mountain water that cascaded over the rocks. Hank stopped his truck along the road and filled up a jug of that water. He knew of no other taste so pure.

Near the top, Hank pulled alongside an even smaller, grass-covered trail, with deep, mud-packed tire tracks. It was a short road, but a slow, bumpy drive. At the end of the trail, the place of the old Burkham homestead came into view. The forest thinned, the footprint of the old house now covered by a field of high grass and wildflowers. The sun shone down in rays—the thick, white kind that a person could reach out and touch. It was like a secret opening up out of the darkness.

At the edge of the old property, the boundary marked by the forest, was the little family cemetery, a twelve-by-twelve square, surrounded by a wrought-iron fence, the gate rusted permanently open. Hank parked where the trail stopped. He reached behind the seat of his truck to where he kept the Winchester Repeater that his mother had given him. When his father died, Hank was only twelve years old. Hank's father was given the gun by his own father.

He grabbed the gun, clutching it like a talisman, and walked to the cemetery. He thought that if he brought that gun to the place where his parents were buried, it might help conjure their ghosts.

At the gate of the cemetery, he took off his shoes and socks and unbuttoned his shirt. He kneeled next to his mother's tombstone. Etched onto the marble were the words she'd designated from her deathbed: "She loved her family like she loved God." He ran his fingers over those words, then lay down on the mossy ground, his face to the sky and the gun resting in his arm. His white chest hair reflected the sunlight. "Mama," he said, "I feel like life's over, and I'm not even dead yet."

The ground was hard against his back. An ant crawled over his left arm. He flicked it off. He thought he felt a rumble from the ground—probably a reverberation from a coal truck down the mountain—but he pretended that it was his mother communicating through the earth. "You were the only woman who ever really knew me and still loved me," he said. "How were you so good?"

He'd thought a lot lately about pulling the trigger of that shotgun. If he'd had the courage, he would have done it. Betty would have been better off without him. Nobody would miss him, except maybe Evelyn. He doubted his son would even show up for the funeral.

But when he thought about doing it, he was afraid that hell waited for him or, worse, that there would be only darkness. He'd always been scared of being alone, even if he'd never admitted it. He'd always needed people. He'd needed people so badly that Betty, just one woman, had never been enough.

"Oh Mother," he called, "save my soul."

He lay there for hours, waiting for a sign from God, or even just for the wind to blow the treetops a certain way. He dozed in and out of sleep until the sunset, when the birds began to liven and feed. He got back into his truck. He drove down the mountain in moonlight and shadows.

***

In the morning, Betty's mood had returned to the standard. She ignored Hank, made him breakfast, and then ignored him some more.

He ate breakfast in his chair in the living room. He heard the phone ring, and he could tell by the way Betty's voice perked up, it was their son on the other end. His son never asked to speak to Hank, though, so he just listened to Betty talk.

The conversation went sour fast. "No, I can't help you. I'm sorry. What do you want me to do? We're not like most families. You know I'd give you my last dime, but your father's gone and blown that, too. Why don't you explain the situation to *your father*."

Betty walked out into the living room and pushed the cordless phone into Hank's face. When he held it to his ear, there was only a dial tone.

"He hung up," Hank said.

"What did you expect?" Betty retorted.

She jerked the phone from his hand and marched back to her half of the house.

***

Hank snuck out of the house around eleven. He wanted to go play the machines, to get away from Betty, really, just to talk about nothing with Evelyn. But he couldn't go to the Legion today. He hardly had enough money for a pack of cigarettes. All he had was a tank of gas, so he drove in loops around the downtown, once again, but the sky was too overcast, made him feel depressed; the old, crumbling buildings, rising up from the cracked sidewalks looked like giant versions of the headstones on Burkham Ridge.

He could drive up to Burkham Ridge again, but then he couldn't stand the thought of sitting at his mother's grave and explaining for the thousandth time his empty pockets and failed marriage. He felt helpless, like an infant. What would his mother say to him? *I lived through the Depression. I somehow managed to raise five kids even after your father went and kicked the bucket on me. My hands were calloused, but I held you kids tight anyway.*

He took the main road to the south side of town, where the middle class lived on streets with gas lamps. He parked in front of the house of his old rival JB.

JB answered the door and his eyes went wide. "Well, I'll be damned. I'm seeing a ghost." He shook Hank's hand vigorously. "Where the hell have you been hiding?"

Hank walked in, said hello to JB's wife, and then took a seat in the living room. "I'm here on business," Hank said.

"Oh? I thought you were done with that kind of thing."

"Me, too," Hank said. "But I think I've got something you want."

They chatted for a few minutes before Hank led JB to the truck.

***

He came home with a fat, white envelope.

"Here," he said. "This should help with the bills."

Betty looked quizzically at him. She opened the flap of the envelope and ran her fingers over the contents. She counted more than a thousand dollars in cash. "What the hell have you done? Where'd you get this?"

He shook his head. "Just take it. Why do you need to know?"

"I don't trust you," she said. "Tell me where you got this."

He put his hands in his jean pockets. He looked down to the ground. "I sold the old gun," he said. "I paid a visit to JB"

Betty looked at him like he was a stranger.

"It's all there," he said. "I only took enough to get me through the week. Give half to our son. You take the rest and hide it."

Before she could say anything, he turned around and walked out the door to his truck. Betty was standing in the doorway as he drove off. She looked like a different woman, standing there with that envelope. It was like she was almost sad to see him go.

***

He had six twenties in his wallet. He figured he'd play half today and half tomorrow.

He sat down at his favorite machine, the one on which he'd won five hundred a couple years ago. He slid in the first bill, just as Evelyn came into the room with his diet Coke. She handed him the can, rolled over a chair, and then lit a cigarette.

"Evelyn," he started, "what do you reckon makes a man good?"

She coughed on her cigarette smoke. "Why are you being all serious, Hank? Did someone die?"

He punched at the screen to set the bet, then pulled the lever on the side. He always pulled the lever on the first spin, even though it was old-fashioned. "Woman," he said. "I asked you a question."

The poorly ventilated room became thick with her smoke. At first she looked like she might start laughing, but then she took a serious turn. "Well, some people say a man's only as good as his bloodline. Me, I think it has more to do with integrity. And what I mean by that is that a man ought to be just the man he is."

He nodded his head, then played through the rest of his credits. "When are you going to Atlantic City?" he asked.

"Next week. Took Friday and Saturday off. You going to miss me? Why don't you come? You haven't left this town in a decade."

Hank reached for his wallet and pulled out three twenties. "Here," he said, "you play these for me."

She smiled, took the money from his hand, and walked across the room to fetch her purse. "If I win, we'll split it fifty-fifty. That sound right?"

"Fine by me," he said. "Just make sure you play max bets."

She sat back down in the chair and put a hand on his shoulder. "You know me. I only play max bets."

They sat there for the better part of the afternoon, Evelyn commenting on the ups and downs of his slot pulls. A few more gamblers came, shook his hand, and then wished him luck when their own had run out. Just as Hank was about to call it quits, a few sevens lined up across the center.

"Well, look at that," she said. "That ought to give you enough to play for a while."

He cashed out the receipt, and Evelyn came back with three hundred dollars in increments of twenties. He handed her three of them. "Let's see if we can't do better," he said.

They played for hours, through every last bill. When he left, he didn't feel guilty about a thing.

***

Outside the bar, the sun was setting over the mountains. He looked out toward Burkham Ridge. He thought of his mother.

Maybe he would stop off and buy some flowers for his mom's grave. Maybe he'd buy some more and take them home to Betty. But then he remembered: he reached into his wallet, and it was empty.

He walked across the street and got into his truck. He circled through the town and watched the old men coming and going. He took the long way home.

EXCAVATION

AMY WAS waiting at the back steps, a half hour before midnight, toting a backpack filled with all the supplies for such an expedition—a bottle of water, a digital camera, a flashlight with extra batteries, and a hammer. The last item felt important, for safety or excavation. The town gossip mill swore the school was haunted by the ghosts of the dead teachers and the troubled students who had spent the worst years of their lives trapped within those walls. Amy looked the part of a reluctant burglar, clad in dark jeans and a black T-shirt, her blonde hair pulled up under a Pittsburgh Pirates baseball cap.

The building loomed at the edge of the downtown. Four stories high with an exterior of smooth-cut limestone, the old high school was one of the last relics of a boomtown architecture that the modern world had deemed obsolete. It was a monument to the times, or had been once. Long gone were the leaden glass windows, since replaced by sheets of plywood that bulged with age and wear. The remains of the carved cornice lay scattered along the unkempt lawn, in between patches of weeds growing waist high. If the preservationists—The Coalition for a Town with a History—lost their battle for an injunction, the work crews would soon come in with their wrecking balls to tear down the parts that hadn't already fallen to the ground.

The *thump thump* of feet drew Amy's eyes across the grass to Benny, her partner for this adventure. "Turn off your flashlight," she hissed. "Do you want someone to call the cops on us?"

His light went out and the round of his face emerged from the pale darkness. The white-blue moonlight smoothed his sharp chin. He looked like a ghost of himself, the version that Amy had met as a young child. His dark hair a little lighter, his cheekbones softer.

"The plan is on," he said. "My parents think we're at the late show. I read the plot online, so I think I'll be able to fake it."

They had been friends for most of their lives, and now, within a week's time, they would begin college. He had been accepted to a quaint school in the Northeast, while she would stay put, attending classes at the local school on the hill. It was the only place that had given her the kind of money that would make college possible. The thought of staying made her stomach as heavy as a bag of bricks. She could see only a life on repeat— the same faces, the same drama. She would inherit her parents' house, and then the sorry child she'd birth with the husband she'd settled for would begin the process all over again.

"Come on," she said. "The door's supposed to be unlocked down here."

She shimmied down the stone ledge behind the steps to the entrance of the basement. She pulled on a metal door, her fingers gripping the hole where a knob had once been, and with the groan of metal grinding against metal, they were into the building.

Her flashlight clicked on and shined across the dusty cement floor, onto the rusted hunks of what had been a coal boiler. The basement was in ruins, not much different from the photos she had seen in her history textbooks—the shell of the Parthenon or the rubble of Dresden. She shifted the flashlight over pieces of concrete that had fallen from the ceiling and saw the evidence of prior intruders scattered along the ground. There were beer cans and broken glass, a hypodermic needle next to a used condom. A soiled stuffed lion—the school's mascot—lay face down in a pile of old newspapers.

"This is disgusting," she said, clearing a path through the detritus with her foot. "Maybe we should turn back."

"Let's be bad," he said, "for once in our lives."

Benny's voice seemed to be absorbed by the walls or time. It wasn't exactly a silence that filled the room, but a hollow buzzing of sorts, like the steady whir of a computer tower spinning its disc. The sound reminded her of the one that filled her head these days, the one that came as she imagined Benny departing and her staying put—a slow, sad buzz of a future that she didn't want to contemplate.

"Here's a story for your fancy friends up north," she said. "That time you were stabbed by a meth junkie in a bombed-out old school. How your best friend in the entire world died trying to pry the knife out of the bad man's hands."

"This whole place smells like a mold-infested morgue," he said. "It would be one hell of a shitty place for you to kick the bucket."

Amy didn't want to die here. Not in this crumbling school and certainly not in this town. What had her chemistry teacher said to her? "You should be an educator. I'd hire you. You're funny, you're dark, and you're strangely patient with idiots." All she saw before her were well-trodden paths. What she wanted was an adventure, something different, even if she didn't know what that looked like.

She reached into her backpack and grabbed the camera. She pointed it at Benny and the flash went off, freezing his face against a backdrop of the broken boiler and the crude graffiti that covered the blocked walls. She looked at the screen. "You look like a scared teenager at a heavy-metal concert. Perfect."

They made their way over the cans and bottles, past the remains of an impromptu fire pit, to a set of concrete stairs. They cautiously inched their way up and through a doorway, until they were standing on sagging, wooden floors in the middle of the main hallway. The corridor stretched out on both sides of them for the whole length of the building. The school seemed frozen in time: a worn banner congratulating the '85 state boys' basketball champions; a clock set to 3:35; a single writing desk, chair attached, outside of what was once the principal's office.

Amy was running her fingers over the carved surface of the writing desk, over the memorialized love notes and curse words, when a loud, metallic clang sounded from down the hallway. The sound sent a pain through her molars.

"It was just a pipe," Benny whispered.

"Take my arm," she said.

He latched onto her. His arm was familiar, comfortable. Theirs had never been a relationship of lust, but she did love him in her way. They were the odd kids out—the smart ones, the weird ones—and in their friendship they found a bond that allowed them to claw through adolescence, the ability to thrive, even. Their friendship allowed them to disappear from the other kids' visions, to blend into the fabric of the walls of the new high school that had replaced the dilapidated structure through which they currently walked. She wouldn't admit it to anyone, but she had enjoyed her time in school. With Benny at her side, their life together had been like a long-running inside joke.

As they walked arm in arm down the hallway, Amy looked up at the ceiling, at the torn plaster and to a series of mouth-like holes—the evidence of a burst pipe or the flood from some long-ago storm. It was hard not to imagine her parents walking through these same halls, some twenty-five years ago. It was where they had met and where they had decided to get married. Her father had proposed to her mother on the day of their graduation. Her mother accepted and then they'd settled into a life not unlike the others in their little town—quiet and predictable in the little bungalow they'd bought with their savings, their once-a-year trips over the mountains to the Atlantic Ocean.

"Do you remember how we became friends?" Amy asked.

"Of course," he responded. "Fourth grade. You were sitting behind me and we were coloring in art class. I turned around and asked you for a—"

His words were cut off by the sound of a door banging shut.

"That wasn't a pipe," she whispered.

"Do you want to get out of here?" he asked.

She shook her head and then tugged him forward. "This is our last hurrah. You said you wanted to be bad, right?"

"I said I wanted to be bad, not stupid."

"What's the worst that could happen?"

He elbowed her in the side of the gut. "You tell me. You were always the creative one."

They crept down the hall and Amy stopped to take photos of the spray-painted walls: "THIS PLACE RUINED ME" and "FUCK YOU MR. REYNOLDS" and "GO LIONS!" Amy tried the knob of a classroom door, but it was locked. They walked on and then paused to listen for any sounds of life. There was only the *whoosh* of a passing car, the hushed noise filtering in from outside the building.

They wound their way through open classrooms and utility closets covered in cobwebs, past track-and-field records engraved onto plaques and framed portraits of retired teachers who had probably long since passed. She grabbed one of the smaller plaques from the wall and stuck it into her backpack.

"I can't believe anyone wanted to save this piece of junk," Amy said.

The fight over the building had raged on for more than a year. The preservationists said it was not just an important piece of architecture but the conscience of the community—the story of all the coaches and teachers and counselors who had molded so many lives. Surely they could repurpose the place, they argued. An apartment building, maybe, or a youth center that the town so badly needed. But the preservationists were a small bunch, and the rest of the community had grown tired of the eyesore.

The mayor said that all the development was leaving for the strip malls. Here was a blighted old piece of stone sitting on one of the largest, most centrally located lots in the downtown. Was it any wonder, he asked, that a person wouldn't want to do business next to the shell of a rat-infested building? And what of the bad memories, a man had written in a letter to the editor. The teacher convicted of molesting some half-dozen students. The three teens who had jumped from the roof, taking their lives on a cold, winter night. The past was the past, the man had written, and the future was not in those stone blocks.

"I don't know," Benny started. "I could see why someone wouldn't want to forget the place they'd spent so much time in. It's a living reminder—when you look at this kind of a place, it's hard not to think of all the people who've been in your life."

She hated when he got serious—the way his eyebrows pitched with his voice and his forehead wrinkled up with the point of his words. He looked even dumber with his face half-covered in shadows. "You're just thinking about yourself. When you go up north, you'll forget about me and feel guilty. I know how it works. You want to come back here with a pretty girlfriend in tow and tell her about this sad girl named Amy who used to crack sarcastic jokes during homeroom. You're the kind of person who needs a building to remember."

He let go of her arm. "Funny. I wouldn't have called you sad until this very moment."

Amy marched ahead of him and into the stairwell at the end of the hall. She felt hot and sick and mad, more so at herself than at him. She felt duped, as if the point of her life had been in preparing Benny for something great. He got to leave, while she got to stay behind with the ghost of their friendship.

"You know that pretty girls aren't my type," he yelled after her.

She stopped and turned to him with a finger to her lips. "Shhhh! I swear I heard a door again."

Footsteps echoed through the staircase, and then another door thumped shut. There was no question that someone else was in the building.

"What do you think they're doing?" he asked.

"Probably the same thing we are. Or drugs. That seems highly possible."

"Great. We're walking around the dark with a bunch of inebriated jackasses."

"Maybe we'll get drunk and high with them," she said. "Isn't that what you're supposed to do in college? We can get a head start."

They exited the staircase on the second floor, the floor that housed the gymnasium. She remembered from when she was a little kid and her father had taken her to basketball games before the place was condemned. She used to love going to games with her dad. He'd tell her about all the big plays he'd made when he was on the team, about how her mom had sat on the balcony and cheered for him. "Those were the best days of my life," he'd said to her without irony.

She often wished she were as optimistic as him. He kept on working and kept on smiling and telling his dumb jokes. He was the kind of guy she would have hated if he weren't her father. And she didn't hate him, not even a bit, which surprised her.

"You know what my dad told me when I turned sixteen?" she said. "He told me that he lost his virginity behind the bleachers at the football field. I think it was his way of trying to tell me about sex, about how to be careful. Mom was never good at that stuff. God that was weird."

They tried to walk on quietly, but the floorboards creaked with their every movement. Their flashlights shifted from the floor to the walls, intersecting and crossing like a smaller-scale version of those Hollywood lights she'd always seen at the start of movies.

"There," she pointed. "That's the entrance to the gym."

She reached into her backpack and pulled out the hammer. "Just in case."

"We're here to take pictures," he replied, "not to maim."

The double doors at the gymnasium entrance were missing. They walked through the opening and looked up and around. The room was bathed in starlight—the skylights above existed only in pieces, entire glass panes now gone, the ceiling open to the air. The metal railings of the balcony had been dislodged and hung down precariously, nearly touching the floor. The center of the court was blackened and disintegrating; the rain had dripped down and eaten through the once-polished wood.

"Be careful," Benny said. "I don't think the floor is stable."

They stuck to the periphery of the room where the floor looked sturdiest, flashlights and starlight blending to form double shadows. They approached the bleachers and saw hundreds of yellowed papers littered across the seats. Amy picked one up. Large, bolded letters read "YOU CAN'T ERASE HISTORY." Each paper was identical.

"They really don't want this place gone," she said and then dropped the paper back into the pile.

"Let's sit down," Benny said.

She followed him up to the third row and pushed a mess of the papers off of the seat with her hands. Some of them fell to the next row, and the others fell through the open slats of the bleachers to the floor below. She sat down next to him, and he leaned his head on her shoulder. She turned off her flashlight and lay down the hammer and backpack. The room was quiet, no hint of the intruders they'd heard before.

"I would have fought to save this place," Benny said.

He had always been the sappy one, yet as he spoke, she imagined a parallel world in which she lived to old age with Benny by her side. They'd come and sit on these same bleachers and relive the days of their youth, sharing conversations of everything that had once been but was no longer.

"I hope I don't become too cynical when you go," she said, only half-joking.

He reached over and squeezed her hand. "You're going to be fine without me. You're going to be better than fine. I promise."

"And what about you?" she asked. "Are you ready for the big time?"

She watched him as he contemplated her question. All the years she'd known him, he had been so close to her that he never seemed to change. She always felt surprised when she looked at old photos and saw how their bodies had grown and how the edges of their faces had hardened. She knew that when he came back next—at Christmas or on his summer break—he would be different. And she would be different, too.

"I'm just as scared as you are," he said. "I'm leaving this place, and I doubt I'm coming back. It's frightening to think that everything you've ever known will just keep on spinning without you, like you were never there in the first place."

"That's what you're scared of?" she said. "I'd kill to get out of here. Let them all forget that I ever existed. Hardly anyone knows who I am anyways. You should be happy that you're going."

They sat there in the half darkness, eyes looking out on the collapsing floor, at the starlight shooting in from the night. Through the holes in the skylight came the chirping of crickets and cicadas and the damp night air. And then slowly something else filtered in—something not like the rotting wood, not like the crumbling blocks of the walls.

"Do you smell that?" Benny asked.

She inhaled through her nose, licked her lips. The smell was choking, the taste bitter. She jumped to her feet and grabbed her flashlight and the backpack. "Get up. Run."

They hurried along the edge of the gym and out into the hallway. She could see the smoke billowing out of the staircase that they had used earlier. "The other end," she said. "I think there's another one."

They ran down the hall, the light of their flashlights bouncing with their jolting bodies. There was an opening at the end of the hallway, and sure enough, another stairwell. Amy stepped inside and scanned for smoke. The stairs appeared clear, so she rushed down the steps, turning her head to make sure that Benny was close behind. He was right on her heels, his face contorted in fear.

The first-floor hallway was filled with smoke, and the light of her flashlight could only penetrate a few feet. She pulled her shirt over her nose with a hand and grabbed Benny with the other. "There's no way we're getting out through the basement."

They got on their knees and crawled along the floor until they found the frame of a door. Amy reached up and found the knob. She turned the knob and the door pushed open. They rushed inside and slammed the door shut behind them, the smoke following them, creeping in through the cracks of the doorframe. It was another empty classroom, a table at the front, and a few lonely desks and chairs. The large windows in the room, like all the others at the school, were boarded over.

"What do we do?" she asked.

"What about your hammer?" he said.

"I left it upstairs. Should I go get it?"

"No time."

They ran up to one of the windows to inspect the plywood. The wood had been nailed into the window frame from the inside. Amy dug her fingers behind the edge of the board and tugged. The edge of the decaying wood popped right out, the nail still attached. "Grab the other side," she said.

Together they tugged at the wood until the whole lower half had been loosened. With another yank, the whole board came off the wall and fell to the ground right at the edge of their feet. The window frame had been stuffed with a mound of insulation, and Amy began to pull it out with her hands.

The fiberglass scratched and burned at her skin. Finally, behind the insulation, was another board, this one presumably nailed to the outside of the building. Benny hopped into the window frame and gave a few kicks to the wood with his foot until the board popped out and fell to the ground beneath them. "It's only a few feet down," he said. In a quick second, he was out the window and onto the ground below. Amy jumped up and out behind him, landing hard on the ground with a thud.

Before she could catch her breath, Benny grabbed her hand and they ran together across the grass to hide under a cover of pine trees that marked the edge of the school's property. When they looked back at the building, the whole east wing had bright orange flames shooting up from the windows.

"We've got to call the fire department," he said.

"Are you crazy?" she snapped, but before she could make an argument, the wail of fire engines started up and screeched over from the other end of town. They stood cowering behind the trees as a caravan of fire trucks and police cars and ambulances rolled up to the street in front of the school and then across the lawn in the back, not far from where they were hiding. The firemen hustled out of their trucks and began to unravel their hoses and soon heavy streams of water were shooting onto the old shell of the school, the water losing its fight against the flames.

"We've got to get out of here," she said.

They sat plotting their exit, how they could evade the firemen and police by sneaking off through trees and down the street through the quiet neighborhood that abutted the rear of the school. But as they were nearing the edge of the tree cover, they saw that dozens of people were leaving their houses, stepping down from their porches, and walking down the sidewalk toward the fire. If they snuck out now and tried to run from the scene, they would be noticed—and in their small town, every last body would be able to name the two teens.

"I think it's safer if we stay," Benny said. "We'll wait until the crowd gathers and then we'll walk out onto the grass. They'll be watching the fire. They'll think we're just onlookers."

And the crowd did amass. At first a dozen, then two dozen, and then more bodies than she could count. By the time Amy and Benny exited from their hiding place under the trees, it seemed half the town had come to watch the school burn. There were the men and women who lived down the block, the parents of their old peers from school. There were wide-eyed children hiding under the legs of their mothers. The town's businessmen and women and the mill workers and the clerks of the big-box stores gathered and looked up to the flames and listened as the fire grumbled, the sound of a hundred hooves stampeding against the earth. Elderly couples hobbled across the grass, arm in arm. One old woman appeared to be weeping into the sleeve of her husband's shirt.

Amy and Benny moved forward and stepped into the center of the crowd, anonymous, watching the blaze grow higher and wider. The crowd gawked slack jawed and speechless, faces lit bright by the burning glow. It seemed that not a single person could find a word to eulogize the quickly disappearing school. The fire had spread from the east wing to the west, orange tongues of heat issuing from the dozens of windows, licking against the limestone walls. The flames seemed to dance, to taunt, as the firemen sprayed thousands of gallons of water onto the building. Flames were leaping up the walls to the roof, reaching up toward the sky. A massive cloud of smoke, backlit by the flames and the streetlights, blew with the wind toward the buildings of the downtown.

Amy grabbed Benny's hand and caught his gaze. This would be the last she would see of him until at least December. She saw him as he was and remembered him as he had been. His body had grown and his voice had deepened, but his eyes remained the same. He was looking at her now, wide eyes against the wind, the same way he had when they'd first met.

They held hands and watched as the school crackled and burned. They looked to the smoke-filled sky, where the few wisps of clouds reflected a deep red, the color of pooling blood. They were helpless, all of them. It would be a total loss. There was no stopping this fire.

BROOKLYN, 4 A.M.

HE RISES from his bed, quietly and carefully, so as not to disturb his partner. It's 4 a.m. and sleep won't come again—not after three glasses of wine, not after two melatonin pills, and certainly not with the light of the full moon penetrating through the bedroom curtains.

He walks naked through the dark house, fishing for his robe and pack of cigarettes. He bumps his shin against the open dishwasher in the kitchen and holds back a yelp. He bangs his left big toe on the edge of the dining-room table and digs his fingernails into his palms. Finally, he remembers, he left the robe in a heap on the bathroom floor after taking a shower in an attempt to calm his nerves—his lover then already two hours into dreaming.

He finds the robe. The cigarettes are in the front pocket.

He puts on the robe and a pair of old loafers, and walks up the narrow staircase that leads to his rooftop oasis in the city. At the top of the stairs, he pushes the door open, and there—on this unseasonable January night with no snow, and even more unexpectedly, a warm breeze—sprawls the New York skyline, like a scene from some movie in his childhood. No one told him that to get such a panoramic view, to see Manhattan naked and blinking, you'd have to shoot the film from Brooklyn, Queens, or Jersey. He has learned this and many other pieces of wisdom from a life transplanted to the city. This knowledge—these secrets shared by millions—are a large part of the reason why he stays in New York.

He walks from one end of the wooden deck to the other and peers over the edges of the wrought-iron gate. The windows in most of the brownstones sit dark, reflecting the soft white orb of the moon. A few televisions interrupt this darkness in fits and starts, flashing thirty different shades of blue. He could never sleep with that chaos washing over him now, though he did as a child, watching *Late Nights with John Cremeans* on the Home Shopping Network until his eyelids grew too heavy to follow the showman's constant smile. He doesn't have a television in his apartment, but he thinks often of John Cremeans and his perfect shock of silver hair.

He pushes open the gate and steps out from his manicured enclosure, onto the unadorned portion of the roof, onto the silver-white tar. He sits down in a solitary folding chair a few feet from the edge of the brownstone awning. The view looks southwest, over gentrified Brooklyn, and farther, to Staten Island. He sees the faint, sparkling lights of the Verrazano Narrows and the elevated F-line, the trains rumbling along like toy engines in the distance. He turns his head just a little and there is the Statue of Liberty, majestic torch and crown burning, impressive, even when cast in miniature. He tries to inhale the view, breathing so deeply that he becomes dizzy.

Above, the stars shine more or less brightly, even in the bath of the moonlight. He had never really bothered to look up when he first moved here a decade ago. Everyone had always said the stars were invisible in New York. But there, emblazoned onto the fabric of the blue and orange cosmos, rules Orion—each star of his mythic body as clear as the next.

The light of the moon always reminds him of Shakespeare. He thinks of characters running into the woods for saturnalian delights. And this makes him think of home—a place so different from New York that he sometimes questions the reality of either. Home, a place so isolated that he, like the Shakespearean characters of old, learned to fear the darkness of a new moon, to close the curtains tightly and stay indoors.

With this thought—like a reflex—he lights his cigarette and wonders if he will be doomed to live with this early-morning nostalgia for the rest of his life. His body aches with fatigue, but his mind races with a frightening vigor. He wonders if he made the wrong decision in choosing to run away to New York so many years ago—so long ago, in fact, that the names of the streets and the faces of his childhood are beginning to slip away. Now what he knows of that long-ago place is like a taste memory. He'll catch a smell of wild onion in a restaurant, and then he's on his hands and knees in the woods behind his house, digging for the roots.

His mother said, "Go, if you must, but know what you're doing. Once you go, this place will be lost to you forever. You won't come back." People in the country always spoke like that when they got serious. She didn't lie, and now he thinks of blood ties. He thinks of other ties, too. He has more of the other kind, these days. He looks up at Orion, as the warm January wind blows up under the hem of his robe, and he speaks: "If your spirit is floating out there tonight, please let it come to me. I'm lonely and I'm scared." He hears the crackling sound of water flowing over river rocks. He feels the hand of a shirt-less boy brushing against his neck. He feels the boy's lips on his cheek. And then he remembers the taste of his own tears, briny and warm. He tastes them again, now, as they wet his face. He remembers the boy dangling over the water, and the shape of an innocent rope swing turned into a noose.

Is that a shooting star he sees? Probably not, but he wants to believe that even here, on a rooftop in Brooklyn, he can still see such wonders of light and fire. He wants to believe that all the lives of boys who left this world too early are that shooting light.

He walks back across the rooftop, back through the iron gate, and drops his cigarette into an empty wine bottle. He opens the door and enters the dark house. He walks down the stairs, throws his robe on the bedroom floor, and slips quietly back into bed. He carefully wraps his arms around his lover, his partner, clamoring for a sense of recognition. His partner sleepily obliges—a brief moan, a squeeze of the hand.

After another hour of lying with his eyes open, his heart pulsing so fast that his thoughts seem to work in double time, he begins to let go. The warmth of this man—the one who loves him, the man with his even and calm breathing—lulls him into a deep, blank sleep.

A TOUCH

"He said that he would die if he stayed with me," I say to Darren, probably for the third time since my breakup. I continue to repeat these words, not because I don't believe them or because I need to reiterate them to make them understandable; it's just that my thoughts are single track. We were together eight years, and I thought that life would never shift again.

"And was he wrong?" Darren asks. "Did you think maybe you, too, would die if you stayed with him?"

We're sitting in a wine bar off of Ninth Avenue. It's as cozy a place as there can be in this neighborhood, with soft music playing and a crowd that knows not to raise their voices. The interior of the bar is meant to look like old Europe, with a white-and black-tiled floor and rustic tables with wrought-iron bases. It's a caricature of sorts, like all of Hell's Kitchen, and really, most of New York—people isolating themselves further and further until all the decorations in all the bars and restaurants come to look and feel more like a mood than a place to grab a drink or a salad.

"He got everything," I say. "The friends, the apartment. I'm too old for this kind of game. I'm too old to care, but I do."

I'm thirty-nine, sitting at a window table in a lonely wine bar, drinking the cheapest Malbec. It tastes like Malbec should: heavy and spicy, and alcoholic enough to go straight to my head. My arm keeps brushing up against the velvet curtains. I trace my fingers over the fogged glass of the window and then wipe the moisture onto a cocktail napkin. Fall has come to the city. Leaves drop to the sidewalk and then degenerate into fragments under the feet of hundreds, maybe thousands, of passersby. Fall never lasts long here, and that means that soon it will be winter.

"He said I was damaged goods. Incapable of real love."

"We *are* damaged goods," Darren says. "Fucked in the head, by virtue of our unfortunate birthplace. Our mothers drank too much of that southern water. Cheers."

At least there's Darren. I remember when we first met, twenty years ago, just two weeks after I'd moved to New York. I found a bartending job in Chelsea and was trying to pay my way through college. I could tell that he was like me. We were the runaways, dressing too flamboyantly because we had never before had the chance. Everything was fabulous, every night on the town another drunken dream. He called me "Mountain Boy" and I called him "Kentucky," a reference to our shared former geography. We were careless with our freedom, burned through everything we touched: the money, the booze, the boys we thought we loved the most. But he was always my constant. We formed our own little band of orphans, even though we had living, breathing parents back home. We said we would make our own families, with ties that had nothing to do with blood, and wouldn't we be so much stronger because of it?

"When you were growing up," I say, "did you go swimming in rivers?"

"Why the sudden nostalgia? Don't tell me you have cancer."

"Cancer of the spirit. OK, I'll stop. That was ridiculous."

Through the window I watch the tourists trekking to the theaters, the young boys stumbling toward drinks they'll substitute for dinner, the Hoboken set smashing their overpriced heels into the concrete. Everyone seems to be marching forward, toward a destination. And what is life in the city without a destination, without a party, without someone waiting for you at the door?

"I haven't gone home in fifteen years, Darren. I'm homesick, I'm lonely. Don't you ever get lonely?"

The sun is setting over the Hudson and a warm tangerine light filters through the window, settling onto his face. His brown skin glows almost golden in the light. Though Darren's older than me by a few years, his face appears younger than mine—softer and more at ease. When I look in the mirror, I see a trio of thick worry lines across my forehead. My graying hair recedes farther with every haircut. I want to reach out and touch him, his gentle face, but I don't. I can't. What I really need is for someone to reach out and touch me.

"Of course, I get lonely," he says, "but I doubt I'm the loneliest soul in this city."

What I know is that romance fizzles. I understand the slow burn of love. It is real, and some people survive it. Some don't. I didn't. But the city is that, too, I suppose: a place for survivors. It takes us in and tests us—and then it gives us second chances. It gives us new identities and asks only that we commit ourselves to stay. And so, here I am, obedient to this place, or maybe just aware that there is nowhere else left to go. I'm trying to imagine what one more chance would even look like.

We've been in the wine bar for almost two hours, and Darren's getting antsy, shifting his wait on the stool and punching at his cell phone. "Come on," I say, "I'll set you free for the night."

He gives me that older, wiser look—one eyebrow up, lips set firmly. "Life goes on, my dear. I promise that you will love again."

Just as we're starting to rise, I see a man walk through the front door of the bar with a face that makes my stomach churn. "Wait," I say. I grab Darren's arm, and pull at him to sit back down. I motion with a slight tilt of my head for him to look at the man, who's taking a seat alone at the long, wooden bar.

"What?" Darren whispers. Then Darren sees him and looks away. "Oh, that poor, poor man."

I would know him anywhere. Deep, pink scars cover almost all of his face and his hands—his pulpy, uneven skin visible even in the dimmed light. Skin so far from human that I almost can't bear to look. Skin so damaged that I can't not look.

"Darren," I say, startled by what I see. "Don't you recognize him?"

"How on Earth would I know that man?" Darren asks. "I think I would remember a face like that."

Of course he doesn't remember his face. People always forgot the worst images. I know why, I understand. If we held onto those images, how would we ever get to work in the morning?

"Think back," I whisper. "The boy from Ohio. The one they burned."

Somehow his hair has survived in tact: blonde and wispy, an effortless look. The hair so suggestive of his youth! And he is young, I know from reading the newspapers, from watching the reports on television. He can't be more than twenty-three or -four. But to look at his ruined face, I would think he was a hundred. The pain he must have experienced is etched in his oddly drooping eyes and his offset mouth, now little more than a moving hole, the lips not lips anymore.

I remember sitting in front of my television. It was only a year ago. I was still with my partner then, but he was late at work. The evening news came in with photos of the boy's face—his former, perfect face. The pictures were probably the first they could find—the ones from his senior yearbook. He was smiling, with clear blue eyes, tanned skin, as yet unaware that humans could be capable of a violence so extraordinary.

"Why is he alone?" I ask Darren. "How could anyone leave him alone?"

His attackers followed him out of a bar in his small Ohio town. He had been with his friends, and he left early to go home. The men beat him and forced him into their car. They took him to a field and doused him in gasoline. They lit him on fire. They left him to die. The story was so horrific that I needed to memorize the details to understand any of it. The news reporters fought to maintain their composure onscreen, relating every blow, every drip of blood spilled onto the uniforms of the EMTs as they put his limp body onto the stretcher and assumed the worst. And then, when every last detail had been repeated over and over, it was so familiar, like all the awful stories that had happened to young boys in small towns across America, that at first I couldn't feel much. I could only watch the television and look at the pictures of his once-perfect face. My lover came home that night, and he didn't say a word. He came and sat on the couch and held my hand. We watched and watched until I fell asleep. I woke up and the television had been turned off, a blanket placed over my tense body.

"Maybe he wants to be alone," Darren says. "Don't you think he's been through enough?"

For months I thought of that boy, trying to understand how something so cruel could have happened to a face so innocent. I kept thinking that everything would be all right, though, because he was still alive, against all odds. That meant something. But then, when enough time had passed, they replaced the images of the young smiling boy with those of a body covered in bandages. It was his choice to speak out. They would have left him alone. He invited the cameras into his hospital room and savaged his assailants, behind a mask of white gauze. He must have thought he was being courageous. He must have decided that in order to continue living he would need to speak out. But when I saw him then, like a reanimated mummy, I thought only that it would have been better for him to have died that night, in the dark, damp field. I couldn't attribute his speaking out to some wellspring of bravery. I thought of him as mad, pushed beyond the limits.

"We could have been him," I say, "if we hadn't left our own little shitholes so long ago."

"But we did leave," Darren says. "Now let's leave this man alone."

When the boy turns his head around to face the bartender and I see only his back, he could be any other young man in New York: thin, dressed in jeans and a tight sweater, his blond hair that perfect mess. He could have been me, a decade ago. When he turns around, when he looks over his shoulder and sees me staring at him, I see only a life cut short. I see his eyes glowing behind a mound of damaged skin. I think that no one will ever love him and my heart aches. He'll never find someone again—if he ever knew love in the first place—especially not here, in this city. I wish him back to his small town, where, hiding behind the walls of his distraught mother's home, no one would ever dare challenge him or make him feel unwelcome. The town's collective guilt would shelter him. He could be an enduring symbol there, but here he'll be just another strange face in a city of oddities. No one will ever bother to ask how he came to be such a hideous sight. And he'll be alone. I know this. He'll always be alone.

"I'm going to stay for one more," I say. "I need to clear my head."

"You're crazy," he says, looking over to the boy at the bar. "You're not thinking straight."

"Go on without me. I'll get home."

Darren stands. I rise to see him off. "Thank you for trying to cheer me up."

"Madman." He hugs me tightly. "Don't stay too long, and don't get into trouble. Go home and sleep. That's what you need."

He walks out the door.

I'm alone now, but this time the air doesn't feel so heavy. I settle onto my window seat, flag down the waiter, and order another glass of red. I watch the boy's every movement.

***

I know what I'm doing the second that I walk out the door. I march forward. The boy is in my vision, and I won't let him go.

I follow him down Ninth Avenue, through the throngs of drunken revelers: the girls who've come in from Jersey wearing their short skirts, even in this cold, autumn breeze. I pass the muscled, bearded men, arm in arm, smoking cigarettes and laughing on their way to the gay bars. I see the young men, the boys who look fresh off the bus from the Midwest—their eyes so big, so in awe of this, the most beautiful, ugliest city in the world. I see the excitement on those boys' faces as they see the potential for love in every passing soul. And then I see their fears, as they realize that a life here means that nothing will ever be the same for them. A life here means that a life somewhere else has ended. There's always a deep sadness in that—even if the lives they've left behind didn't seem worth living at all.

Wasn't that why I moved here so long ago? To escape? To breathe anonymity? That, too, must have been the reason that this man—the one with the scarred face—came. To get away from the ones who wanted to hurt him. To try and blend in, as much as possible, amongst nine million individuals. He would have known that people would still look at his skin, but they would only look for a second, before the next creature walked past.

What he doesn't know is how lonely he will be. I follow him because if he's not lonely yet, he will be soon. I think that in following him, maybe he will see my loneliness and run back home to where people will have to love him, because of what he's been through. I keep my distance—a half block back—but I can't let him leave my sight. I feel that I'm now both his protector and his tormentor.

The street smells like roasted lamb and chestnuts from the food carts that line the corners. It's cold with the wind, so I wrap my wool scarf—a gift from my old lover—around my face. I wonder if the boy can feel the cold anymore, if there are any nerve endings left behind his charred flesh. What can he feel, and what does he hope to feel? What does he hope to find, sitting alone at a wine bar? Who does he hope to see on such a cold, windy night? Does he replay the vicious scene in his mind night after night? Does he wish to replicate it in order to understand it?

We walk ten blocks north, to the edge of Hell's Kitchen where the crowds have thinned. He turns left down Fifty-Fourth

Street, and in a moment, I do the same. We're the only bodies on the street. He looks back and sees me. His pink skin looks yellow under the streetlights. He picks up the pace. I'm not thinking anymore, I'm just walking. I'll go wherever he goes, and I don't know exactly why, but I can't leave him. I want to hold his hand and tell him everything that I've learned from my life here. I want to advise him and warn him.

He senses that something is wrong with me. He's alarmed, almost jogging, and then he's running. He turns off the street, climbs up the steps of a bland, brick apartment building, a place where the rent must be cheap enough for a boy from Ohio. Does he work? He fumbles for his keys and opens the door. I'm close to him, at the edge of his building. He walks halfway inside, but doesn't close the door. He's both in and out. I stop at the base of the steps and look up to him.

"Why are you following me?" he yells. "What do you want?"

I don't know what I want, or maybe I just don't want to be alone, but I can't say any of that. This sad boy is being stalked by a man who doesn't know why. A man who has nothing better to do. I take a breath and try to speak to him. I want to caution him about how hard it will be here for a boy without a face. I want to say so many things. I want to be his friend. I try to imagine if I could be his lover. I have almost convinced myself that I could lie next to him in a bed, my arms draped protectively over his ruined chest.

"You're scaring me," he shouts. The words come out garbled from his mouth that looks like no other mouth I've ever seen. He looks like a war victim, a casualty of a chemical massacre.

I open my own mouth, with my lips that have kissed many men before and could continue to kiss many more. I'm going to tell him that I love him and that I'll fight for him and protect him. I close my eyes to summon the words, but when I open them, he slams the door shut. I hear the faint thud of his feet on the stairs of his hallway.

I have said nothing to him. I see no more of him. I will never say anything to him again.

I sit down on the steps. Now we're both alone, I think. Or maybe I'm wrong. Maybe there's a warm body waiting for him in the apartment above. Maybe it's just me out here by myself in the cold.

My head is spinning. Darren sends me a text and asks if I'm OK. I respond that I am, but I know that I'm not. I'm not sure what I'm feeling. Desperation? Insanity? I work up the energy to leave the steps, half-thinking that the young man might have called the cops on me. I walk toward Tenth Avenue and look back to try to see his face in one of the windows, but there is only darkness across his entire building. He's hiding from me, or sleeping, or maybe he just likes the dark. I walk on.

Now I'm walking along the seedier side of the neighborhood, where the cabbies fill up their tanks and the cars rush by on their way to the West Side Highway, sharing conversations about all of the bizarre things they've seen during their night's work. What would they say about me? Would I be the scorned lover, the lonely old man, or both?

I chain-smoke and zigzag up and down the side streets, between Ninth and Tenth, working my way south. I walk past the projects and the schools and then past the nice brick row houses. I look into the parlor-floor window of one of the houses. Two old men sit with books in their living room. They look comfortable, even peaceful. I think of my old lover, who wasn't content with that kind of life. He said that he wanted to feel passion. He said that he would rather die alone than spend the rest of his life with someone who had become at best a friend, at worst a roommate.

What did my mother say when I left for New York? "Life isn't the same there. You won't live like other people do." My mother wasn't wrong. My lover wasn't wrong. I didn't want the life of the two men in the nice row house anymore than my lover did. I don't want that life now, but I don't even know what my options are. When I came to New York, I kissed so many boys that I thought that one person would never be enough. I thought that there was so much love to go around that I would never run out. Now I feel so alone that I don't even know how to figure out what love means.

I walk down Forty-Fourth Street, past the Actor's Studio, toward the wine bar where the night began. I see a man more drunk than not, wearing a faded down jacket. He sees the cigarette in my hand. "Got one to spare?" he asks.

"I'm sorry," I say, and I instantly regret refusing him. I think that I'm so stuck in my ways, so woven into the fabric of this city, that even on this night of all the lonely nights, I'm unable to be anything but a hardened version of myself.

I walk past him, and then I feel a tap on my shoulder. "Just a minute," he calls. This time I stop. I reach into my pocket, prepared to hand him a cigarette, but then he points down to my jeans. "I'll suck your dick for a twenty."

My face is burning. I want to hit him. I want to pummel him to the ground and beat the life out of him. I want to know what violence tastes like. But then I see a shadow—another human walking down the street, so I resist. I throw my entire pack of cigarettes at his face, not out of anger anymore, but out of sadness, a sadness for both of us. I wonder what it would take to be in this man's position, and if I'm really that far from his lot anyway.

I turn away from him, and I'm running. I'm running down Forty-Fourth Street and then I turn back onto crowded Ninth Avenue. I'm running and crying and people are staring at me. People are afraid of me. I stop them in their tracks, and this is what I want. I want to be on the other side. I want to be stared at. I run down the avenue, through stoplights, and cars honk at me. I don't care if anyone sees me like this. I'm running, and running, and I think that this is what it means, in the most literal sense, to run for your life.

***

I could run forever, even without a destination. I don't really know where I'm headed, though I know these streets so well that I could never get lost. I could close my eyes and still find my way out, just by the sounds of the traffic.

As I run, I think of my lover. I think of Darren. I think of my family back home—both mother and father passed now. I think of how I left everything to have a chance at this life. I want to raise my parents from the dead and say that I'm sorry for being so lost.

I would run forever, but my years of life catch up with me. I'm panting as I turn down one last street. I will end here. Maybe I will collapse here. I stop to catch my breath. I hold my head down into my chest. I'm ready to lie down and sleep under a stranger's stoop.

When I look up, though, I'm paralyzed by what I see and what I hear. There are hundreds of bodies gathered in front of an old Jewish temple. Their voices rise up in a beautiful melody that seems so familiar, though I can't place it. The people spill out from the steps of the building, across the sidewalk, and onto the center of the road. There are police barriers at both ends of the block that I hadn't noticed before.

The people hold candles—a sea of yellow flames against the dim streetlight. The temple is a beautiful stone thing with slices of red and blue stained glass in a circle over the door and a silver Star of David in the center of the pitched roof. It's such a serene scene. I'm not sure I belong here. I see mostly women, holding hands. I'm at a rally or a vigil for some awful violent thing that probably happened on a dark street corner. Someone's life was changed forever. I think of the boy from Ohio. I remember the vigils they held for him all across the country, the television zooming in on the tears of the people who didn't even know him.

I'm drawn to this gathering, even though I sense that this is not my fight. I fear they will look at me and turn away, as they see the sweat dripping down my forehead and my hair damp and askew from running. I walk closer to the edge of the crowd. A young woman, singing with the chorus of voices, turns to me and smiles. She is blonde, and so stunningly beautiful—her calm eyes reflecting the candle she holds, the skin of her face lit as if by one of the campfires of my youth. She reaches for my hand, and I give it to her. She squeezes my hand in return, and I know that for the first time in a long time, I'm not alone. The tingle of her touch—so reassuring on this frigid, autumn night—spreads up my arms. I feel even the heat of her candle—of all of their candles—returning life into my face. When the song stops, she turns to me. "We'll get through this together," she says. I smile and we sway to the songs of love and unity until all the candles burn down to their cardboard holders, and the spirit moves us to say that the night's work is done. As we walk away in peaceful silence, I turn and see, all across the pavement, thousands of drops of wax, barely visible in the streetlight.

READING
AND DISCUSSION
QUESTIONS

1. *The Rope Swing* contains ten loosely connected stories large-ly set in the same small town in West Virginia. The author never identifies the name of this town. Do you think this was a conscious choice on the part of the author? How does leaving the town unnamed affect your understanding of the book?

2. The author chose "The Rope Swing" as the title story of the book. In this story, we don't learn what happens to Christopher and Greg. We are instead left with a moment of inaction, as Christopher watches Greg jump from the rope swing into the river below. Near the end of the book in "Brooklyn, 4 a.m.," we find an echo of the earlier story: "He remembers the boy dangling over the water—an in-nocent rope swing turned into a noose." Do you think this memory speaks to something real or metaphorical? What does the rope swing mean to Christopher? What does it mean for the other characters in this book?

3. This book has been praised for its depictions of rural gay characters, a subject that is not often touched on in literature. How do you think the lives of these characters are different than their counterparts in urban centers? Are the concerns of the gay characters in this book any different than those of the straight characters?

4. In the opening story, "Appalachian Swan Song," the narrator speaks with what is known as the first-person plural or the "we voice." Who is this "we" and how does the use of this voice change how you understand the story?

5. Throughout *The Rope Swing*, there is a rich physicality to the language. Buildings and bodies are crumbling, the looming mountains act as both protector and tormentor, and the starry night sky reflects the characters' choices and decisions. How do the descriptions of the landscape shape your understanding of this book? How do you think the landscape of the stories affects the characters and their lives?

6. All but two of the stories are set in West Virginia. Why do you think the author chose to set the last two stories in New York City?

7. In "Pauly's Girl" and "Felicitations," we read about women faced with major and unexpected choices. Moira loses her longtime companion and is left wondering how to reinvent her life. Annette finds herself pregnant at the age of forty with a man she has only known for a few months. Are there similarities in these women's situations and in the decisions they make? Were you surprised by their choices?

8. In "Hank the King," the title character is a philanderer past his prime who can't seem to make peace with his family. Do you sympathize with him? Why or why not?

9. In many of the stories, the slightest amount of physical

contact has the power to alter the course of a character's life. What moments of physical contact did you find particularly interesting or jarring? How did these moments of touch affect the characters and their actions?

10. What motivates Jillian in "Corporeal" to sneak into her dead father's apartment? How would you describe her reaction to her father's death?

11. Many of the characters in the book long for an escape, either from their lives or from the town. If these characters were granted an escape, do you think they would find happiness or peace?

12. If you could ask a question to one character in the book, who would you ask and what would your question be? How do you imagine the character would respond?

13. In "Through the Still Hours," the story ends when Cliff steps into the stranger's truck. What do you think happens to Cliff? What do you think happens to his relationship with Gerry?

14. How does the town change from the first story to the last? If someone asked you to describe this town, what would you say?

15. At the end of the last story, "A Touch," the main character stumbles onto a late-night vigil down a side street in Manhattan. As he's leaving the vigil, he says, "As we walk away in peaceful silence, I turn and see that barely visible in the streetlight are hundreds of drops of wax all across the pavement." What happens to him in this moment? How does this moment affect your understanding of the book?

ABOUT THE AUTHOR

JONATHAN CORCORAN received a BA in literary arts from Brown University and an MFA in fiction writing from Rutgers University-Newark. He was born and raised in a small town in West Virginia and currently resides in Brooklyn, NY. This is his debut book. Learn more at jonathancorcoranwrites.com.

MEET THE HOLY SPIRIT

MEET THE
HOLY SPIRIT

Dr. Jack Hyles

September 25, 1926~February 6, 2001

Pastor
First Baptist Church
Hammond, Indiana
1959~2001

Chancellor—Hyles-Anderson College
1972~2001
Superintendent—Hammond Baptist Schools
1970~2001
Superintendent—City Baptist Schools
1978~2001

Contents

Foreword

One of the most grievous things that one can endure is to be ignored. How grieved, then, must the Holy Spirit be, for to be ignored has been His lot for these many centuries! He, Who is the Indweller of the believer, the Anointer of the anointed, the Power of the pulpit and the Fulness of power for the believer, continues to go about His work with little or no acknowledgment or attention. Few sermons are preached about Him, fewer books are written of Him; yet He quietly continues to offer us leadership, comfort, wisdom, strength, teaching and power.

He must be a wonderful Person to go about His work among us with little or no recognition. Each of us enjoys introducing to our friends someone whom we have met and whose presence has enriched our lives. Years ago I met the Holy Spirit. How rich has been my life since that day! I want you to know Him too. May I introduce the Holy Spirit to you.

About Dr. Jack Hyles

Jack Hyles began preaching at the age of 19 and pastored for over half a century. At the time of his death, First Baptist Church had a membership of over 100,000 with a high year of 20,000 conversions and 10,000 baptisms. For many years the church has been acclaimed to have the "World's Largest Sunday School." During Dr. Hyles' ministry, the property value of the First Baptist Church increased to over $70,000,000.

In an average week, Dr. Hyles counseled over 150 church members, managed two Christian elementary schools, one Christian junior high school, two Christian high schools, and the largest fundamental Baptist Bible college in America along with his regular pastoral duties and sermon preparation.

Dr. Hyles has left his mark on Christianity, and his legacy remains through the books he has written, through the sermons he has preached, and through the lives he has changed. He is the author of 49 books and pamphlets, exceeding over 10 million copies in sales. He preached over 60,000 sermons; many of his sermons are available on tape.

Dr. Hyles' experience covers numerous evangelistic campaigns, Bible conferences, etc. He preached in virtually every state of the Union and in many foreign countries. The annual Pastors' School, started by Dr. Hyles, attracts thousands of preachers from every state and many foreign countries.

Lest anyone should be confused with all that Dr. Hyles accomplished, he did so by spending more than 20 hours a week in prayer and the study of God's Word. He was a firm believer in the surrendered Christian life and the necessity of the Holy Spirit to accomplish much good for God.

1
The Holy Spirit and the Bible

Everything that God has ever done and everything that God will ever do, He has done and will do by His Word. He created the universe by His Word. Again and again in the book of Genesis we find the words, "and God said." **Genesis 1:14, "And God said, Let there be lights in the firmament of the heaven to divide the day from the night; and let them be for signs, and for seasons, and for days, and years." Genesis 1:20, "And God said, Let the waters bring forth abundantly the moving creature that hath life, and fowl that may fly above the earth in the open firmament of heaven." Genesis 1:24, "And God said, Let the earth bring forth the living creature after his kind, cattle, and creeping thing, and beast of the earth after his kind: and it was so." Genesis 1:26, "And God said, Let us make man in our image, after our likeness: and let them have dominion over the fish of the sea, and over the fowl of the air, over the cattle, and over all the earth, and over every creeping thing that creepeth upon the earth." Genesis 1:29, "And God said, Behold, I have given you every herb bearing seed, which is upon the face of all the earth, and every tree, in the which is the fruit of a tree yielding seed; to you it shall be for meat."** You will note that all God did in creation He did by His Word.

When Jesus comes again, He will put down the Antichrist by His Word. **II Thessalonians 2:8, "And then shall that Wicked** be revealed, whom the Lord shall consume with **THE SPIRIT OF HIS MOUTH, and shall destroy with the brightness of his coming.**" Then in **Revelation 19:13** we find that His name is called "The Word of God" when He comes again. **"And he was clothed with a vesture dipped in blood: and his name is called The Word of God."**

Now the Word of God was authored by the Spirit of God. To know the Word properly, one must know the Holy Spirit personally.

1. *The Word of God is eternal.* **Psalm 119:89, "For ever, O LORD, thy word is settled in heaven."** It, along with the Godhead, is eternal. It is eternal in Heaven, which means that the entire Word of God was in Heaven before the world was ever created. The last verse in Revelation was in Heaven before the first verse in Genesis was ever given to man. This forever settles the truth of verbal inspiration. Pseudo-scholars have sat behind desks and stood before chalkboards in our colleges and seminaries and advanced the heresy that God gave the thoughts of His Word to man and that man put them down in his own words. These pseudo-scholars remind us that Paul had his style of writing, etc. They would lead us to believe that each man took the truth and gave it to us in his own style and manner of writing. Let the deceivers be reminded that God did not make His Word to fit a man; God made a man to fit His Word. The Word of God is eternal in the heavens. God made a man like Paul to fit the portion of His Word that He wanted Paul to pen. Hence, God not did make His Word to suit the personality of a man or a human vocabulary, but God made a personality and a man with a certain type vocabulary in order to reveal to us the eternal Word of God that was in Heaven completed before its first word came to earth.

2. *God gave His Word to man.* **II Peter 1:20, 21, "Knowing this first, that no prophecy of the scripture is of any private interpretation. For the prophecy came not in old time by the**

will of man: but holy men of God spake as they were moved by the Holy Ghost." The word "moved" here implies breathing. God breathed His Word to man. The term "Holy Spirit" could easily be stated "Holy Breath." Thus, His Holy Spirit, a Holy Breath, moved upon man and God breathed His book into man. God spoke to Moses and told him to write. He spoke, "In the beginning." Moses wrote, "In the beginning." God spoke, "God created the heaven and the earth." Some man-made scholars shout, "But that's mechanical dictation." No, that's verbal inspiration! The eternal Word of God was given word by word to holy men of old as the Holy Spirit breathed the Word of God into them and upon them. The term "mechanical dictation" is a term invented by the liberals and Bible doubters to cast reflection upon verbal inspiration. It is a term of satire in their attempt to make those who believe in verbal inspiration look unscholarly. This is their attempt to cast a stigma upon the fundamentalist. This is their effort to prove that those who believe in verbal inspiration are shallow.

The fact remains that the Word of God is eternal and forever settled in Heaven and that God gave this Word to man as He breathed upon him, and man wrote it word for word as God gave it!

3. *The Holy Spirit accompanies the Word of God.* **I Peter 1:12, "Unto whom it was revealed, that not unto themselves, but unto us they did minister the things, which are now reported unto you by them that have preached the gospel unto you with the Holy Ghost sent down from heaven; which things the angels desire to look into."** The Bible alone is not the answer. Teaching and preaching the Bible in the power of the Holy Spirit is the answer. There is nothing more wonderful than to preach the Book that the Holy Spirit gave to us and while we preach it have Him speak to the hearts of those who hear it. The Holy Spirit speaks from the outside through His Word and then He speaks from the inside as He confirms His preached Word to the hearer. It is also a wonderful thing to read His Word as the Holy Spirit

accompanies it.

One day I was riding on an airplane. I was amazed as I looked across the aisle and saw a passenger reading my book, *Blue Denim and Lace*. I looked across the aisle and introduced myself, whereupon the reader was so pleased to meet the author of the book and asked me if I would shed light upon its truth. Because I wrote the book, my explanation of the book would give added meaning to the words.

Not only did the Holy Spirit write the Book and not only did He breathe it to holy men of old as they were moved by Him to give it to us, but He is available to teach it to us if we will read it. It is not a math book to be studied analytically, but it is a love story, written from God to man, and confirmed to us by the Holy Spirit as we read it, as we teach it and as we preach it.

4. *The Holy Spirit quickens the Word of God.* **John 6:63, "It is the spirit that quickeneth; the flesh profiteth nothing: the words that I speak unto you, they are spirit, and they are life."** He makes it alive to us. Most of the cults are started by people who read the Bible but do not study it in the presence of the Author. Thank God, the Author is available to teach it to us and to make it live as we learn it, teach it and preach it.

5. *The Holy Spirit teaches the deeper truths of the Word of God.* **I Corinthians 2:9, 10, "But as it is written, Eye hath not seen, nor ear heard, neither have entered into the heart of man, the things which God hath prepared for them that love him. But God hath revealed them unto us by his Spirit: for the Spirit searcheth all things, yea, the deep things of God."** He not only teaches us what He said in the Book, but He teaches us what He meant when He said it. There are so many handfuls of purpose that God has for us as we glean in the Word of God, but this must be done under the leadership and tutorship of the Holy Spirit. There are truths in the Word of God that the eye cannot see and that the ear cannot hear, but He Who breathed the Book to us

through holy men of old can sit beside us as we study it, and He will teach things not on the surface.

Every step that the Christian takes should be a step in obedience to the Holy Spirit. How does the Spirit lead us? First, He gives us a Book of instructions. He never goes contrary to His Book, and we need not seek His will concerning something that is written in the Book. A young lady says, "I'm going to pray and ask the Holy Spirit if I should marry that unsaved man." There is no need to pray. The Holy Spirit has already told you not to marry an unsaved man. It's in the Book! A man says, "I'm going to pray and ask the Holy Spirit whether or not I should tithe." There is no need to pray that prayer. The Holy Spirit has already answered it. It's in the Book! The Bible is basically then a set of instructions given to us by our Guide. To be sure, there are circumstances that are not specifically covered by the Word of God. The Word of God may tell us that we are to spread the Gospel, but it does not tell us in what country or city that we are supposed to live and headquarter as we spread the Gospel. Therefore, we read the Bible to find the leadership of the Holy Spirit and then we seek Him to lead us in every detail that is not specifically laid down in the Word of God.

For guard duty in the Army we had what we called "general orders." These general orders were exactly that — several things that we were supposed to do while on guard duty. The last of these was to call the Corporal of the guard in any case not covered by instructions. This meant that there were some circumstances not covered by the general orders. In such a case we were to call the Corporal of the guard. In the Bible we find our general orders as breathed to us through holy men of old by the Holy Spirit. We are to call upon Him personally in any case not covered by instructions; that is, by the general orders; that is, by the Word of God.

When I was a little boy, my mother used to call me to her knee every night. She would hold the Bible up and say, "Son, this is the Bible. The Bible is the Word of God." Then I had to repeat it three times. She would then tell me that the Bible was about Jesus and that Jesus was the Son of God. Then she would make me repeat that three times. Then she would exhort me always to believe the Bible, and she warned me against those professors, teachers and preachers who would shake my faith in the Word of God.

When I was a poor teenager, she continued this ritual. In fact, every night until I went into the U.S. Army in World War II, I was required to say three times that the Bible is the Word of God and that Jesus is the Son of God, and I was warned against those who would shake my faith in its truths. I was exhorted always to believe that the Bible is the verbally inspired Word of God.

When I was in the paratroopers in World War II, the Bible was my constant companion. Now, for over a third of a century, I have preached its truths. It is the first book I pick up in the morning and the last book I lay down at night. It is God's eternal Word, forever settled in the heavens, brought to me by the Holy Spirit, taught to me by the Holy Spirit. What a book! What a Saviour! What a Teacher!

2

The Holy Spirit and Regeneration

John 3:1-7, "There was a man of the Pharisees, named Nicodemus, a ruler of the Jews: The same came to Jesus by night, and said unto him, Rabbi, we know that thou art a teacher come from God: for no man can do these miracles that thou doest, except God be with him. Jesus answered and said unto him, Verily, verily, I say unto thee, Except a man be born again, he cannot see the kingdom of God. Nicodemus saith unto him, How can a man be born when he is old? can he enter the second time into his mother's womb, and be born? Jesus answered, Verily, verily, I say unto thee, Except a man be born of water and of the Spirit, he cannot enter into the kingdom of God. That which is born of the flesh is flesh; and that which is born of the Spirit is spirit. Marvel not that I said unto thee, Ye must be born again."

Perhaps no term has been used more carelessly and lightly in our generation than the term, "born again." Politicians and statesmen claim to have been born again. They drink alcoholic beverages, participate in sensuous dancing, are interviewed by pornographic magazines and deny the Scripture concerning the woman's place in society. Athletes speak of being born again and, in the next breath, grant an interview with a pornographic magazine. Entertainers talk about being born again, but with their

17

talents, they lure customers into nightclubs where they can drink and live lives that are profane and godless! Singers talk about being born again and then participate in a rock concert which not only defies God but betrays decency. It is time for the believer to take a sane and Scriptural look at the new birth and the relationship that the Holy Spirit has with being born again!

1. *Being born again means being born anew.* **John 3:7.** The word "again" in this verse comes from a Greek word which means, "from the first," or "from the beginning." Actually it means, "the beginning born in you." **Revelation 22:13** tells us Who the Beginning is: **"I am Alpha and Omega, the beginning and the end, the first and the last."** Jesus is the beginning! When a person is born again, the "Beginning" is born in him!

2. *The new birth is not a change of nature.* It is not the old nature changing into a new nature.

3. *The new birth is not the beginning of a new nature.* It is the One Who is the Beginning entering a person. That is why Paul could say, **"Christ in me, the hope of glory."** Being born again is not a new nature being begun; it is the nature of Christ Himself entering into us as we are "born from the Beginning" or "have the Beginning born in us."

4. *Being born again is the coming of a divine nature.* Somebody says, "I am a new man." This does not do an injustice to the Scripture, but it is not exactly accurate. Our actions, to be sure, are different, but what has happened is that the very nature of Christ has entered into us. We have been born from the first!

5. *This means eternity is born in the new convert.* The Bible speaks of eternal life. **John 3:15, "That whosoever believeth in him should not perish, but have eternal life."** The Bible also speaks of everlasting life in **John 3:16, "For God so loved the**

world, that he gave his only begotten Son, that whosoever believeth in him should not perish, but have everlasting life." This eternal life is actually the Eternal One, Who was without beginning and ending, coming into our lives. Eternal means, "without beginning or ending." The "I Am" has joined the "I become"; the Eternal has joined the temporal. That is not that nature which was born at physical birth joining up with a new nature that is born at conversion. It is that nature that was born at physical birth joining up with the eternal nature of Christ! Now, to be sure, that new life is NEW TO US, and as Paul said in **II Corinthians 5:17,** we are new creatures, or better still, a new creation, but that which has entered us is really that Person Who is the beginning and the ending.

Someone may say, "I have a new car." That doesn't mean the new car was made the minute he got in it or paid for it; it already existed, but it was new to him. A family moves into a house and they say, "We have a new house." The truth is, the house didn't come into existence when they moved in; it was simply new to them. Hence, the new nature is new to us, but in reality, it is the eternal nature of Christ Himself living in us. This miracle of His coming into us and regenerating us is performed by the Holy Spirit. **John 3:5, 6, "Jesus answered, Verily, verily, I say unto thee, Except a man be born of water and of the Spirit, he cannot enter into the kingdom of God. That which is born of the flesh is flesh; and that which is born of the Spirit is spirit."**

Light is given to this truth in **Philippians 2:5, "Let this mind be in you, which was also in Christ Jesus."** The key word in this verse is "let." In other words, we are to "allow" the mind of Christ to come into us. Though this occasion changes us, it is not the beginning of the mind of Christ. The only thing new is that His mind has entered into us. That little word "let" is one of the most important words in the Bible. God has so much for us if we will "let" Him do what He wills. **Romans 12:1** explains this, **"I beseech you therefore, brethren, by the mercies of God, that ye present your bodies a living sacrifice, holy, acceptable unto**

God, which is your reasonable service." The word "present" or "yield" carries the same connotation as the word "let." God will do His work in us if we will LET HIM.

6. *The warfare then is really the old nature against Jesus.* Certainly one does not do an injustice to the Scripture when he talks about the old nature fighting the new nature, but in reality, since the new nature is Jesus in us, we are really fighting the Son of God Himself when we "do our own thing," go our own way and go contrary to the will of God. When the Christian observes a lustful television program, it is Jesus Whom he fights. When he listens to rock music, it is Jesus Whom he fights. When he attends the movie or theater, it is Jesus Whom he fights. When he holds bitterness in his heart toward a brother or sister in Christ, it is Jesus Whom he fights.

When one puts his faith in Christ, the Holy Spirit, in response to that faith, brings Him Who was from the beginning into the believer's life. He is not just a new creature, nor is he simply enjoying the creation of a new nature; rather, he is having the Beginning born in him. That Beginning is Jesus. Eternity is joining time. The "I Am" is joining the "I become." The Everlasting is joining the temporal. What a motivation this is for the believer to yield himself to that Christ Who lives in him, as the Holy Spirit has wrought the amazing work of regeneration! This is amplified in **Galatians 2:20, "I am crucified with Christ: nevertheless I live; yet not I, but Christ liveth in me: and the life which I now live in the flesh I live by the faith of the Son of God, who loved me, and gave himself for me."** Notice the words, "I am crucified with Christ." In a mysterious sense, since the Eternal dwells in me, I was IN HIM at Calvary. It would not be improper then to say, "I created with Him, I was tried with Him, I was condemned with Him, I was crucified with Him, I arose with Him." What a truth! What a salvation! What a Saviour!

3
The Reception of the Holy Spirit

I was preaching in a southern state. My message dealt with the fulness of the Holy Spirit and how that we are to meet the conditions and then plead with God constantly for His mighty power. A wonderful preacher followed me and made the statement that we do not have to plead for the fulness of the Holy Spirit but that if we simply claimed that fulness by faith, it could be ours. Though he was sincere, and though I think that he is a Spirit-filled preacher, I was saddened that he would make such an over-simplification of this vital doctrine. He overlooked **Luke 11:13, "If ye then, being evil, know how to give good gifts unto your children: how much more shall your heavenly Father give the Holy Spirit to them that ask him?** In this verse the word "ask" is in the linear or durative which means we are to ask and ask and ask and ask. What a dangerous thing it is to misunderstand the fact that God insists that we pay the price for the fulness of His power — the kind of price that George Fox paid when he was alone with God for two weeks in prayer and fasting for the power of the Spirit, the kind of price that Dwight Moody paid when he pleaded with God for His mighty power, the kind of price that Jacob paid when he wrestled with the angel of God throughout the night, the kind of price that the New Testament church paid during the ten days preceding Pentecost!

I think it is possible that this misunderstanding of simply claiming the Holy Spirit fulness by faith is caused by the omission of a truth which I call "THE RECEPTION OF THE HOLY SPIRIT." Careful attention should be given to the following discourse concerning this doctrine.

First, we must establish the fact that the Holy Spirit does come in at salvation. **Romans 8:9, "But ye are not in the flesh, but in the Spirit, if so be that the Spirit of God dwell in you. Now if any man have not the Spirit of Christ, he is none of his." I Corinthians 6:19, "What? know ye not that your body is the temple of the Holy Ghost which is in you, which ye have of God, and ye are not your own?"**

Though He does come in at salvation, there remains something else for us, and that is THE RECEPTION OF THE HOLY SPIRIT. Do not confuse this with the fulness, the anointing or the indwelling. It is a doctrine all its own. Here are some illustrations.

A man realizes that his mother-in-law is unable to continue housekeeping. He feels that it is his obligation to invite her to live in his house. She comes in to live, but he has a hard time accepting her. He pays her little attention. He does not accept her as a part of the family. Then one day he realizes his error. He comes to her and says, "Please forgive me. I want to accept you as one of the family." Now she had been living in the house for some time, but he had not accepted her yet. There are many believers who are indwelt by the Holy Spirit, but who have not accepted Him and acknowledged His presence and, as it were, His being a member of the family.

A widow with children marries for the second time. Her new husband comes in to live where she and her children have been living. The children do not accept him; perhaps they are bitter; perhaps they are suspicious or perhaps they are jealous. Now they live in the same house with their stepfather, but they have not yet accepted him as such. Then one day they learn to love him and suddenly they accept him as a member of the family. This simple illustration describes millions of Christians who, when they received Christ, became temples of the Holy Spirit. However, they never acknowledge Him; they never speak to Him! They accepted Christ as their Saviour. When Christ came, the Holy Spirit came with Him, and He indwells them, but they have never come to the place where they say, "Holy Spirit, just as I accepted Christ, I accept You. You are a member of the family. I will acknowledge You as such."

Now the Holy Spirit has been there all along to lead, to strengthen and to comfort, but He awaits His acceptance. The stepfather provided for his stepchildren. He may have comforted them, taught them and loved them, but they did not accept him as their own and acknowledge his presence and membership in the family.

Notice **John 7:37-39, "In the last day, that great day of the feast, Jesus stood and cried, saying, If any man thirst, let him come unto me, and drink. He that believeth on me, as the scripture hath said, out of his belly shall flow rivers of living water. (But this spake he of the Spirit, which they that believe on him should receive: for the Holy Ghost was not yet given; because that Jesus was not yet glorified.)"** Now compare that with **John 20:22, "And when he had said this, he breathed on them, and saith unto them, Receive ye the Holy Ghost." John 20:22** is a fulfillment of **John 7:37-39.** In **John 7** our Lord had promised that the Holy Ghost would be available to indwell believers upon the resurrection of Christ. In **John 20:22** our glorified Lord admonished His disciples to receive the Holy Spirit. This verb "receive" is not passive but active. It could be worded, "accept the Holy Spirit" (just as you accepted Christ). You see, Jesus is the Saviour of the world, but we have to accept Him personally for Him to be our personal Saviour. The Holy Spirit indwells believers, but we need to come to a time when we receive Him or accept Him, even as the stepchild received the stepfather and the son-in-law received the mother-in-law.

This explains **Acts 19:1, 2, "And it came to pass, that, while Apollos was at Corinth, Paul having passed through the upper coasts came to Ephesus: and finding certain disciples, He said unto them, Have ye received the Holy Ghost since ye believed? And they said unto him, We have not so much as heard whether there be any Holy Ghost."** These disciples, though they were indwelt by the Holy Spirit, had not heard about Him Who lived in them. This, no doubt, is true in the lives of so many Christians. The One Who indwells us receives no attention, no conversation, no expression of love and, in many cases, no awareness of His presence.

Notice **Galatians 3:2, 14, "This only would I learn of you, RECEIVED YE THE SPIRIT by the works of the law, or by the hearing of faith? That the blessing of Abraham might come on the Gentiles through Jesus Christ; THAT WE MIGHT RECEIVE THE PROMISE OF THE SPIRIT through faith."**

The main purpose of these studies is to acquaint believers with a Person (the Holy Spirit) so that they may ACCEPT Him Who came in at salvation and yet Who is being treated like an unwanted stepfather or an unwanted mother-in-law!

I had been preaching for many years. I knew that the Holy Spirit lived in me. The Bible said so. I even taught the doctrine, but I had never one time spoken a word to the Holy Spirit. Though I realized He lived in my body, and I knew my body was His dwelling place, I had never accepted Him as a person. Yes, He provided; yes, He assured; yes, He comforted; yes, He strengthened; yes, He taught. Though I was aware of these marvelous works in my life, I never accepted Him as a person or received Him as such.

One day I was preaching on a radio broadcast. I was standing behind the pulpit of my small church in east Texas. My coat was half off, my collar was unbuttoned, and my tie was draped around my neck as I was preaching in the early morning hours to a radio audience from behind the pulpit of my empty church building.

That morning I said to my radio audience, "The Holy Spirit lives in you. He hears what you say. He knows what you do. He sees where you go. He knows how you are dressed this morning." I began to tremble. I realized for the first time that He saw me and that He was a person. I finished the broadcast with much difficulty. Tears were streaming down my cheeks as I preached. When I finished the broadcast, I fell to my knees, lifted my voice to God and looked heavenward as I said, "Dear Holy Spirit, forgive me. I have never spoken to You. Doctrinally I knew You lived in me, but I have never accepted You as a person. I have never reckoned that You were part of my life in a practical way. I accept you today."

My life was changed! I have never been the same! I went out to get in the car to drive home for breakfast. I bowed beside the car and said, "Holy Spirit, lead me to know the route that I should take as I drive home." I then included Him in every decision that I had to make. I asked Him to help me when I went shopping. I asked Him to lead me in every area of my life. There has not been one day from that day until this when I have neglected to say a word to the Holy Spirit. To me He is a person. He not only lives in my body, but I accept Him as such. I acknowledge His presence. I talk to Him. I seek His guidance in even the smallest of decisions.

In summary, dear reader, when you accepted Jesus and asked Him to come into your life, He had with Him another member of the Godhead. As Jesus entered, this other member silently entered. Perhaps you did not realize it, or perhaps you realized it and have never taken time to accept this other member for what He really is. The purpose of this manuscript and of these studies is to acquaint you with Him. May we begin by accepting Him. Bow your head now and say, "Holy Spirit, I know You have been living in me. I now accept You." Beloved reader, would you do what this preacher did many years ago in an empty church building after preaching on a radio broadcast? Your life will never be the same. Accept Him now; receive Him now; include Him in everything. Ask Him to help you find the bargains when you go grocery shopping. Ask Him to lead you to the right clothing when you shop for apparel. Ask Him what route to take as you take even the smallest and most insignificant of journeys. Ask Him where to sit on the airplane. Ask Him to help you as you wash the dishes and clean the house. He yearns to be accepted by you.

Yes, He does come in at salvation. **Romans 8:9, "But ye are not in the flesh, but in the Spirit, if so be that the Spirit of God dwell in you. Now if any man have not the Spirit of Christ, he is none of his."**

Yes, we are to plead with God for the fulness of the Holy Spirit. **Ephesians 5:18, "And be not drunk with wine, wherein is excess; but be filled with the Spirit." Luke 11:13, "If ye then, being evil, know how to give good gifts unto your children: how much more shall your heavenly Father give the Holy Spirit to them that ask him?"**

Yet, in between His entering at salvation and His filling us for service, there needs to come a time in our lives when we receive Him or accept Him Who very quietly and without fanfare has been doing His work in us, through us and for us. Without any attention or gratitude He has been strengthening you, comforting you, teaching you, exhorting you, helping you and guiding you. He longs for you to know that He is there. He longs for you to fellowship with Him as a person. This moment could be the dawning of a new day, the beginning of a new era and a day of gladness for the Holy Spirit. He is in you. He is your guide. He is your teacher. He is your comforter. Bow your head now and accept Him as such and tell Him that you will never again live a day without fellowshipping with Him, expressing your love to Him and acknowledging His presence in your life.

4

The Holy Spirit and Christlikeness

In Bethlehem 2,000 years ago a male Child was born. He was conceived by the Holy Spirit. One of His titles was Paraclete (helper). He gave Himself to helping others. When He saw hungry people, He fed them. When He saw sad people, He cheered them. When He saw weary people, He strengthened them. When He saw discouraged people, He encouraged them. When He saw poor little children, He blessed them. When He saw bereaved people, He comforted them.

He never hated anybody. When people cursed Him, He blessed them. When people hated Him, He loved them. When people despitefully used Him, He prayed for them. When one betrayed Him, He called him, "Friend." When people reviled Him, He did not retaliate. He never sought vengeance. His feet never trod a wicked path. His mind never had a wicked thought. His hands never took that which they should not have taken. His tongue never spoke that which was sinful to speak. His heart never entertained an unholy motive. His hands never performed a sinful deed.

It was wonderful. One of those who knew Him best summarized His life by saying He "went about doing good." **Acts 10:38, "How God anointed Jesus of Nazareth with the Holy Ghost and with power: who went about doing good, and**

healing all that were oppressed of the devil; for God was with him." Yes, it was wonderful.

Yet there was something sad about this. You say, "Something sad about this wonderful life of Jesus?" Yes, there was something very sad. The sadness is that His entire life was spent in a small geographical area of no more than 75 miles by 40 miles and in a chronological era of 33 years. America never saw Him. China never saw Him. Southeast Asia never saw Him. The islands of the sea never entertained Him. Europe never saw Him. The other countries of the Middle East never saw Him. People of Russia never saw Him. Only those who lived in that small little country of Palestine and only those who lived during His brief life span on earth saw this wonderful life.

Do others not need to see Him too? Is it fair for most of the world to live and die and never see the life of Jesus? No, it is not. So God conceived a plan. This plan was that there would be a Jesus in every country. His plan included that there be a Jesus in every city of every country. His plan included that there be a Jesus in every city of every country and in every neighborhood of every city and in every home, factory, office, shop and school of every neighborhood. He arranged for each of His people to have access to the same power through which He lived His life. That power was the power of the Holy Spirit. Jesus did not live His life, perform His miracles, preach His sermons nor do His deeds as God. He did them as a Spirit-filled man. **Luke 4:1, "And Jesus being full of the Holy Ghost returned from Jordan, and was led by the Spirit into the wilderness."** That same Holy Spirit has been made available to every Christian so that every one in the world will have opportunity to see the amazing life that Jesus lived. Now every country can see Him, every business can see Him, every office can see Him, every factory can see Him, every home can see Him.

There are so many passages that remind us of our obligation to be Christlike.

We are to represent Christ on earth. The Apostle Paul reminds us that we are here "in Christ's stead." **II Corinthians 5:20, "Now then we are ambassadors for Christ, as though God did beseech you by us: we pray you in Christ's stead, be ye reconciled to God."**

We are to have His mind. **Philippians 2:5, "Let this mind be in you, which was also in Christ Jesus."**

We are to do His work. **John 14:12, "Verily, verily, I say unto you, He that believeth on me, the works that I do shall he do also; and greater works than these shall he do; because I go unto my Father."**

We have been sent by Him, even as He was sent by the Father. **John 20:21, "Then said Jesus to them again, Peace be unto you: as my Father hath sent me, even so send I you."**

We are to attempt to live in His likeness. **Psalm 17:15, "As for me, I will behold thy face in righteousness: I shall be satisfied, when I awake, with thy likeness."**

We are to be exactly as He was as we walk and talk among men. **I John 4:17, "Herein is our love made perfect, that we may have boldness in the day of judgment: because as he is, so are we in this world."**

We are to love as He loved. **John 15:12, "This is my commandment, That ye love one another, as I have loved you."**

We are to do as He did. **John 13:15, "For I have given you an example, that ye should do as I have done to you."**

Our son, David, is now a preacher and a father. For years he rode home from church with me. He would wait until nearly the middle of the afternoon to ride home with Dad after I had counseled with scores of people. Then I would again counsel after the evening service and Dave, through the years, would wait and ride home with Dad. When he was just a little boy, he was promoted into his first Sunday school class where he sat up and listened to a teacher in a classroom situation. Going home one Sunday morning, I asked him what he learned in Sunday school that day.

He said, "I learned about God."

I said, "What did you learn about God?"

He replied, "I learned that God loves me more than anybody loves me."

"What else did you learn about God?" I asked.

"I learned that when I do bad, God spanks me and does He spank me hard!"

"What else did you learn?"

"I learned that after God spanks me, He hugs me and tells me that it hurt . . . Him . . . more than it hurts . . . me . . . Hey, Dad, are you God?"

I hugged my little boy to my breast and said, "No, Son, I'm not God, but I'm glad you think I am, and I hope after you've been in our home for 18 or 20 years that you still get me mixed up with Jesus."

A little boy in our church used to call me Brother God. One day I was preaching Hellfire and brimstone. He looked up to his mother and said, "Mama, ain't God mad today!" One day I went by his house to make a visit. He hollered into the house and said, "Mother, Brother God is here." I noticed his bicycle was broken. I tried to fix it and failed. As I left, his father came home from work. His father saw the broken bicycle and said, "Hey, Son, is your bicycle broken?" whereupon the boy replied, "Yes, Dad."

The father said, "Let me fix it for you."

The son said, "You can't fix it, Daddy."

"Why?" asked the father.

The boy said, "Well, God came by and he couldn't fix it, and if God couldn't fix it, Daddy, you dead sure can't."

One day I tied a little boy's shoe. He was a bus kid. His mother watched as I tied his shoe. As I walked away, he looked up to his mother and said, "Mama, did you see God tie my shoe?"

These are but a few illustrations to remind us that we are to be like Jesus. Cindy, our youngest daughter, used to stand on the hearth of the fireplace when she was a little girl and sing, "To be like Jesus, to be like Jesus, all I ask to be like Him. All through life's journey, through hill and valley, all I ask, to be like Him." Though she didn't always get the words exactly right, often her dad would weep as her little voice would sing clearly, "To be like Jesus, to be like Jesus, all I ask to be like Him. All through life's journey, through hill and valley, all I ask, to be like Him." The entire Christian life can be wrapped up in those words. We are to be like Jesus. He cannot be here in person to forgive now. I have to show people how He forgives. He is not here in person to feed the hungry, to strengthen the weak, to encourage the discouraged, to clothe the cold, to help the widows and orphans, so He says to me and to you, "Show them how I would love. Show them what I would do. Go where I would go. Preach what I would preach. Teach what I would teach. Sing what I would sing. Love as I would love. Forgive as I would forgive. Be kind as I would be kind. Do good as I would do good."

And so I set out to be like Jesus. I tried so hard. I would sing, "Trying to walk in the steps of the Saviour." I would sing, "O, to be like Thee! O to be like Thee, Blessed Redeemer, pure as Thou art; Come in Thy sweetness, come in Thy fullness; Stamp Thine own image deep on my heart." I would sing, "Be like Jesus, this my song, In the home and in the throng; Be like Jesus, all day long! I would be like Jesus." I really tried, but I failed. I found that I would rather be served than serve. I found that I would rather be helped than to help. I found that I would rather receive than to give, to be fed than to feed, to be clothed than to clothe. I found that I would rather hate my enemies than love them. I found it difficult to bless those that cursed me, and I also found that I would rather be cheered than cheer and be comforted than to comfort. Try though I may, I failed. I could not be like Him.

Then one day I came across a verse that transformed my life. **Romans 8:11, "But if the Spirit of him that raised up Jesus from the dead dwell in you, he that raised up Christ from the dead shall also quicken your mortal bodies by his Spirit that dwelleth in you."**

I had always thought that that passage dealt with the

resurrection of the body. I thought that our Lord was saying that if his Spirit dwelt in us, we would be resurrected someday, even as His body was resurrected. Then I became aware that **Romans 8:11** is not talking about our coming physical resurrection but rather the availability of the resurrected life while we are yet in the body. Our Lord is saying that if the Holy Spirit can raise up Jesus from the dead, that same Holy Spirit can raise me up from selfishness and self-centeredness in order that I may live a resurrected life. That resurrected life can be lived only in the power of the Holy Spirit. If the Holy Spirit of God could raise the body of our Lord and Saviour Jesus Christ, that Holy Spirit can raise us to walk in the Spirit and to have daily victory to live a resurrected life.

Bear in mind that it was by the Holy Spirit that Jesus cast out devils. **Matthew 12:28, "But if cast out devils by the Spirit of God, then the kingdom of God is come unto you."** It was by the Holy Spirit that Jesus offered Himself as our substitute. **Hebrews 9:14, "How much more shall the blood of Christ, who through the eternal Spirit offered himself without spot to God, purge your conscience from dead works to serve the living God?"** In the millennial kingdom when our Lord reigns, He will reign by the power of the Holy Spirit. **Isaiah 11:2, "And the spirit of the LORD shall rest upon him, the spirit of wisdom and under-standing, the spirit of counsel and might, the spirit of knowledge and of the fear of the LORD."**

When I was in Rome I went with our party to visit the Vatican City. High on my list of priorities was that amazing Sistine Chapel adorned with Michelangelo's famous painting, "The Last Judgment." The painting covers the entire ceiling and much of the walls. It is an unbelievable work of art.

Now suppose for a minute that we were to go to the Sistine Chapel, and suppose that the Lord Jesus said to me, "Paint another 'Last Judgment' like the one painted by Michelangelo." It matters not how hard I tried; I could not paint a likeness of that masterpiece. I would say, "Lord, try though I may, my painting is as a child's first-grade attempt."

There could be a way, perhaps, that I could paint another "Last Judgment." Suppose God offered to take the spirit of Michelangelo and place that spirit within my body. Could I not then make a replica of his famous painting? To be sure, it would take some time. Day by day, week by week, month by month and even year by year I would add a little bit as did Michelangelo until someday perhaps I could, with Michelangelo's spirit within me, make a replica.

The Lord Jesus came to me and said, "My child, make another life like Mine." I tried, but I failed. I miserably failed. Then one day He said to me, "You could succeed perhaps if I would put My Spirit in you." So He made His Spirit available to me, and by that Spirit I can attempt to paint a likeness of the life of the Son of God.

Yet again I failed. I could not match His masterpiece. I could not completely show this old world how He lives. Then I came across what to me is the most important Scripture in the Bible on this subject. **II Corinthians 3:18, "But we all, with open face beholding as in a glass the glory of the Lord, are changed into the same image from glory to glory, even as by the Spirit of the Lord."**

Notice the words, "are changed into the same image from glory to glory," and notice the words, "even as by the Spirit of the Lord." Then it dawned on me. I AM NOT THE PAINTER! I AM THE CANVAS! THE HOLY SPIRIT IS THE PAINTER! My job is simply to present myself, or to yield to Him. **Romans 12:1, "I beseech you therefore, brethren, by the mercies of God, that ye present your bodies a living sacrifice, holy, acceptable unto God, which is your reasonable service."**

So as I yield to Him, just as a canvas yields to the artist, the Holy Spirit paints from glory to glory a likeness of Christ in my life. Ah, here is the secret: Yield, yield, yield, yield! He does the work that I cannot do.

Yes, I tried to be like Him; I failed. Then in the power of the Holy Spirit I tried to paint His likeness. This helped some, but again I failed. Then I realized that I am not the painter; I am the canvas. I, as canvas, yielded to the master artist, and He, in turn, paints day by day the life of Christ in my yielded flesh.

So every morning I yield to Him, and then I ask Him to let me cross the paths of people whose paths our Lord would cross and whom our Lord would help if He were on earth. I must yield to Him to make me like Jesus, and then I must yield for Him to lead me where Jesus would go, for what value is it to be like Jesus if my path does not cross the path of that one that Jesus would help today?

Several years ago I made several trips to see my dentist. His wife was both his nurse and receptionist. When I would go visit the dentist's office, I would sit in the waiting room and attempt to witness to his wife. She had no interest in the Gospel, and my attempt proved feeble. One morning I arose early, yielded to the Holy Spirit, and asked Him to let me cross the path of that one that Jesus would help if He were on the earth today. On my schedule was a trip to the dentist's office. As I was sitting in the waiting room reading an old magazine, the door opened. An old lady walked in wearing tennis shoes and clothing associated with poverty. She was holding a handkerchief in her hand, and in the handkerchief was a set of false teeth covered with blood. She said through a toothless mouth, "My teeth don't fit! My teeth don't fit! Could the dentist make my teeth fit?"

The dentist's wife said, "Mary, I'm sorry but your guarantee is past."

Mary replied, "But my teeth don't fit and my gums hurt! I've got to have my teeth made to fit."

The dentist's wife again replied, "Mary, I'm sorry, but you should have come earlier."

Mary replied, "I couldn't come earlier. I don't have a car and it's been cold and snowy. This is the first day I could come."

Again the dentist's wife said, "I'm sorry, Mary. Your guarantee period has past."

I looked up, as the Holy Spirit reminded me of the prayer I had prayed that morning. I asked the dentist's wife, "How much would it cost to have a new set of teeth made for Mary?"

She told me that it would cost over $400.

I said, "Then make her a new set and put it on my bill."

The dentist's wife then asked me if I knew Mary. Of course, I replied that I did not. I told her about my prayer that morning, as I yielded to the Holy Spirit and asked Him to let me cross the paths of the ones that Jesus would help if He were on earth.

A few days later I received a call from the dentist's office. It was the wife of the dentist. She said, "Reverend, could I come to your office to see you? I cannot forget your kindness to Mary. I believe I can get saved now." She did come to my office. She did get saved.

May God forgive me for the many times that I have forgotten to ask Him to let my path cross the path of that one that our Lord would help, and may God forgive me for the many times that I have crossed such paths and have forgotten or refused to help.

Someone is saying, "Dr. Hyles, I could not afford that kind of money." Then maybe the following illustration would fit your life better. I was at a supermarket waiting to be checked out. The little lady in front of me was very poor. Her bill came to $4.72, but I noticed that she had only $4.00. She timidly told the clerk that she didn't think she would take the bananas that she had planned to buy. She just was not very hungry for bananas any more.

The clerk was offended and suggested that she make up her mind. With tears in her eyes, the little lady who had only $4 had no other choice but to place the bananas back. After she was checked out and had received several insults from the lady at the check-out counter, I picked up the bananas and added them to my bill. I then followed the little lady who could not afford the bananas. When I came to where she was I said, "Lady, you left something back at the supermarket."

She said, "Oh, I didn't buy those bananas."

I said, "Oh, yes, I saw you buy them."

She began to weep and she said, "Mister, are you giving me those bananas?" Then with a stunned look on her face she said, "You're Reverend Hyles, aren't you? You're the Jesus-man. I've seen you before." It was not difficult to win her to the Saviour.

In Bethlehem 2,000 years ago, a male Child was born. He was conceived by the Holy Spirit. One of His titles was Paraclete (helper). He gave Himself to helping others. When He saw hungry people, He fed them. When He saw cold people, He clothed them. When He saw sad people, He cheered them. When He saw weary people, He strengthened them. When He saw discouraged people, He encouraged them. When He saw poor little children, He blessed them. When He saw bereaved people, He comforted them.

He never hated anybody. When people cursed Him, He blessed them. When people hated Him, He loved them. When people despitefully used Him, He prayed for them. When one betrayed Him, He called him, "Friend." When people reviled Him, He did not retaliate. He never sought vengeance. His feet never trod a wicked path. His mind never had a wicked thought. His hands never took that which they should not have taken. His tongue never spoke that which was sinful to speak. His heart never entertained an unholy motive. His hands never performed a sinful deed.

It was wonderful. One of those who knew Him best summarized His life by saying He "went about doing good." **Acts 10:38, "How God anointed Jesus of Nazareth with the Holy Ghost and with power: who went about doing good, and healing all that were oppressed of the devil; for God was with him."** Yes, it was wonderful.

Yet there was something sad about this in that His life was confined to one area that at most would be 75 miles by 40 miles and to one era of 33 short years. Yet, thanks be to God, His plan makes it possible for every one of His people to be like Jesus and to so yield himself to the master painter, which is the Holy Spirit, that people in every country, state, county, city, township, neighborhood, school, office, business and home can see the life that Jesus lived!

Oh, Holy Spirit of God, may people who cross my path have the privilege and the blessing of seeing Jesus!

5

The Fulness of the Holy Spirit

A pastor requested that I bring my message on "Fresh Oil" to his people. I refused to do so using as an excuse that the sermon was more adapted to preachers rather than to laymen. After the service that night I returned to my room, and the Holy Spirit began to convict me and rebuke me for limiting to preachers the doctrine about Himself. He reminded me that His fulness was for everybody, and He led me to reexamine **Joel 2:28, 29, "And it shall come to pass afterward, that I will pour out my spirit upon all flesh; and your sons and your daughters shall prophesy, your old men shall dream dreams, your young men shall see visions: And also upon the servants and upon the handmaids in those days will I pour out my spirit."** He especially pointed out to me that He would pour out His Spirit on all flesh. That would include our sons and daughters, our old men and young men and even servants and handmaids. I fell to my knees asking His forgiveness and promised Him that I would make the doctrine of His fulness as plain as I could so that young men and old men, sons and daughters, handmaids and servants could understand. This blessed truth is for the busy housewife who goes about her duties. It is for the mother who rocks the world in her lap. It is for the steel worker at the blast furnace. It is for the service station attendant who pumps gas. It is for the maid who cleans rooms at the motel. It is for everybody. So, in simple language, understandable by the layman and the clergy, I approach this vital truth.

First came the light. Then came the firmament. Then God lit the starry host of the nighttime. After that came the fish of the sea and then all the tribes of the animal kingdom. Now God was ready for man. He made man in His own image, and it was marvelous. Man walked in the garden of Eden fellowshipping with his Creator. They walked in splendor. Every tree that grew was pleasant to the eyes. Rivers flowed peaceably through verdant valleys. Every sound was a melody. Every scene was a delight. There was no war to unrest the breast. There was no sickness to cause a fear of death. The leaf never withered; the wind never chilled. No perspiration moistened the brow. No profanity cursed the ear. There was no weariness, no heat and no cold. No blossoms were smitten by a tempest. Man hand not yet learned to sigh or weep. There was no withering frost to chill the rose. There was no shadow of guilt ever known. Choirs of birds serenaded man. It was wonderful!

Yet something was missing. There was no kindred creature on earth with whom man could share this beauty and this wonder. Then there she comes, dressed in all the beauty a human being could possess. Grace was in her step. Heaven was in her eye. Every gesture possessed dignity and love. Perfection was stamped upon her. Perfection was stamped upon her. The sons of God shouted for joy. The morning stars sang together, and Eden was transformed.

How wonderful it was! Man and woman, made for Him, sharing fellowship with God in Edenic splendor. They knew not the definition of sorrow. They had never seen a funeral. There were gardens of perpetual bloom, orchards that surrendered their fruit daily. No child was dying with leukemia. Garlands of flowers covered their path. Brows never furrowed, faces never wrinkled, hands were never palsied, the step was never unsure, shoulders never stooped, breath was never offensive.

All the while the Lord Jesus was with the Father in Heaven. Torches flared as He walked the golden streets. Trumpets announced His every arrival. Demonstrations dogged His heels. Multitudes adored Him; worshippers bowed before Him. Angels ministered to Him. The planets sang His praises. All of the earth's diamonds could not fill His scepter. All of earth's gems could not fill His crown. He was always in the presence of the Father. The sun and the moon obeyed His voice, and the four living creatures sang His praises!

Then one day it happened! There were groans heard in Heaven because something tragic had happened on earth. God's race had fallen. Ruin had blighted His creation. Now the winds howl, the serpents hiss, the brow furrows, the shoulder stoops, the hands tremble, the eyes grow weary, the mind grows dull, the hair turns grey. Sin had blighted the human race.

God's mercy wanted restoration, but God's justice would not allow it until the penalty was paid. The only way the inhabitants of earth could be salvaged for God was for the Lord Jesus Christ to go to earth. This He did. He fled to a virgin's womb. There was no welcome for Him. The only open door to Him was a barn door. He was born in another man's stable, ate at another man's table, rode another man's beast, slept on another man's pillow, cruised in another man's boat and was buried in another man's tomb. He was King of kings, but He had no throne but a cross, He had no crown but a crown of thorns, He had no scepter but a walking stick, He had no royal robe but a borrowed coat from a soldier. He had no subjects but a jeering mob. He was despised and rejected of men. He was a man of sorrows; He was acquainted with grief. He bore our griefs, He carried our sorrows, He was wounded for our transgressions, he was bruised for our iniquities. He was oppressed, He was afflicted, He made His grave with the wicked, He gave His soul an offering for sin and, worst of all, He became sin and stood before the judgment of God bearing the sin of the whole world! He was pronounced guilty by His Father and, on the cross, He paid the penalty for the sins of mankind. He was buried and rose after three days and three nights. Now the message is complete. It is time to send that message out to a lost world. Twelve men are chosen to begin this task.

But there is still a problem! The message is unbelievable! Imagine twelve common men starting out to convince a world of unsaved people that Jesus was born of a virgin! Imagine how that will be received by the natural ear, the natural mind, and the natural heart! Imagine trying to convince a sinful world that Jesus lived for 33 years and never committed one sin! Imagine how difficult it would be to convince the world of the vicarious death and bodily resurrection of the Lord Jesus Christ!

So God made it possible for Someone to accompany these men Who could talk to people from within as these missionaries told the story form without. This One talking from within would be the Holy Spirit. God would make it possible for these preachers and missionaries to be so filled with the Holy Spirit that while they preached the message from without, the Holy Spirit would convince the listeners from within that the message is true.

For example, a preacher who is filled with the Holy Spirit stands in his pulpit and preaches. While he is preaching the truth, a voice talks from within to the congregation saying, "That's right! What the preacher says is true. Jesus was born of a virgin. He did live a sinless life. He did die on the cross to pay the penalty for your sins. He did rise again after three days and three nights. He did ascend back to the Father. He is at the right hand of the Father interceding even now. He is coming again." The preacher keeps preaching. He says that those who accept Christ go to Heaven. From within, the Holy Spirit says, "He's right. He's right. Listen to him. Listen to what he says." Ah, what blessedness it is to preach in the power of the Holy Spirit so that while the words come from the lips of the pastor to the ear of the hearer, the Holy Spirit comes to the heart of the hearer and confirms what the pastor is saying!

Ah, this will transform a Sunday school teacher! The Spirit-filled teacher can stand before his class and teach the Word of

God. What would have been a boring lesson suddenly becomes life-changing because the Holy Spirit is saying to the pupils, "Listen to your teacher. He loves you. That's right. Believe him." This is the need for our Sunday schools.

Imagine a Spirit-filled soloist singing in the public services and as the song is sung and the message is heard by human ears, there is a Voice from within speaking to each member of the congregation saying, "That song is right. Jesus does save. He does comfort. He is your need!" This would transform the music program of our churches. While Spirit-filled choirs sing, a Voice from within speaks to the congregation saying, "That choir is right. Believe them." Their hearts begin to burn. Conviction settles in and decisions follow.

An organist or pianist is playing the offertory on Sunday morning. That organist is filled with the Holy Spirit after having paid the price in fervent prayer and after having met the conditions for His fulness. The organist plays the offertory and as she plays a song like "Sweet Hour of Prayer," a Voice speaks to the hearts of those in the congregation: "That's right. Prayer is sweet and it does call you from a world of care. It is the answer for your life." The Voice continues to say, "You should pray. You should pray often. You should pray before you eat. You should pray before you start the day. You should have seasons of prayer."

The Spirit-filled Christian school teacher stands before his or her class, and as the teacher teaches, the Holy Spirit says to the pupils, "Your teacher is right. Believe what your teacher is saying. Listen carefully." Ah, that will help the deportment and behavior in the classroom.

Imagine a Spirit-filled soul winner knocking at the door of a house. A person comes to the door and suddenly the Holy Spirit speaks from within. The soul winner begins to tell the wonderful story of Christ and from within the heart of the hearer there is this Voice saying, "Believe him. The man is from God. He is telling you the truth. This is the way to Heaven. This is your only hope."

At Pentecost that Voice even spoke different languages so that people who could not understand the language that was used in the preaching could hear the message of Christ and be saved!

Oh, preacher, this is your answer! Sunday school teacher, this will transform your class. Singer, this will give life to your special numbers. Instrumentalists, this will multiply your effectiveness. Christian school teachers, this will help us to produce dedicated young people. Nursery worker, this will help the children even in the nursery. Imagine a nursery worker telling a baby about Jesus; the Holy Spirit can even speak to that little heart. Mothers, this will help you rear your children properly.

The question immediately comes: How may this power be obtained? Of course, there are the obvious steps such as separation from the world, faithfulness to the cause of Christ, hours of studying the Word, obedience to the commands of God and to the will of God, etc., but the main thing is for a Christian to be so sincere that he pays the price in agonizing and pleading and tarrying, begging God for His power. Notice **Luke 11:5-13, "And he said unto them, Which of you shall have a friend, and shall go unto him at midnight, and say unto him, Friend, lend me three loaves; For a friend of mine in his journey is come to me, and I have nothing to set before him? And he from within shall answer and say, Trouble me not: the door is now shut, and my children are with me in bed; I cannot rise and give thee. I say unto you, Though he will not rise and give him, because he is his friend, yet because of his importunity he will rise and give him as many as he needeth. And I say unto you, Ask, and it shall be given you; seek, and ye shall find; knock, and it shall be opened unto you. For every one that asketh receiveth; and he that seeketh findeth; and to him that knocketh it shall be opened. If a son shall ask bread of any of you that is a father, will he give him a stone? or if he ask a fish, will he for a fish give him a serpent? Or if he shall ask an egg, will he offer him a scorpion? If ye then, being evil, know how to give good gifts unto your children: how much more shall your heavenly Father give the Holy Spirit to them that ask**

him? The word "importunity" in verse 8 means "much begging."

This chapter is being written at my desk. On my desk I see the words, "Pray for power." Behind my desk I see the words, "Pray for power." In the Bible that is in my lap I see the words, "Pray for power." On the mirror where I shave I see the words, "Pray for power." On the door leading from my office into the hallway I see the words, "Pray for power." Hundreds of times a day I plead with God for His power. Then, of course, there are seasons of prayer when I go alone with God to plead for the power of God.

I am commanded in the Scripture to be filled with the Spirit. **Ephesians 5:18, "And be not drunk with wine, wherein is excess; but be filled with the Spirit."** Notice that in the same passage about Spirit-fulness, drunkenness is mentioned. It would seem then that it is just as wicked for a person to do God's work without the fulness of the Holy Spirit as it would be to do God's word drunk with wine wherein is excess.

As a child I was very nervous. We were very, very poor. My father was an alcoholic. He left our home when I was a boy. Through a series of events, God called me to preach His Gospel. I was very sincere. When I was 21 years of age, I began to pastor. For one lonely year I pastored with no results. No one walked the aisle for salvation, no one walked the aisle to transfer membership. It was a long, barren year. I decided to find the answer. I went to a library at a Baptist college. I began to read the biographies of great men. I read how Dwight Moody was filled with the Holy Spirit while walking down Wall Street one day. I read how his ministry was changed and how he would preach the old sermons where he at one time had five conversions and then he had fifty! I read how his ministry was transformed, and my heart began to burn from within. I wondered, "Could that be available for me? Could that which Dwight Moody received when he was filled with the Holy Spirit be available for a little Texas preacher?" I continued reading. I read about Savonarola, who went to his pulpit one day and realizing he was powerless, refused to preach until the power of God came upon him. For five hours he sat and waited until the power of God came, and then he was filled with the Holy Spirit as he preached. I read about Christmas Evans, who was riding his horse on his circuit one day and suddenly the power of God came upon him. He knew for the first time in his life that he was filled with the Holy Spirit. I read about Charles G. Finney and his Spirit-filled life. I began to ask God as a young preacher, "Is that for me? Is that for today? Is there actually a power that can come over me where the Holy Spirit can speak to people from within as I speak from without?"

I read about John Wesley, who at three o'clock in the morning on October 3, 1738, after having prayed with a number of preachers for most of the night was filled with the Holy Spirit. His ministry was never the same. I read about George Fox, who went alone for two weeks begging for the power of God, and how his life was transformed. I read about Peter Cartwright, who had been filled with the Holy Spirit and mighty power came upon him. I read of George Whitefield, who on June 20, 1736, was ordained to preach. As he knelt at the altar, Bishop Benson laid his hands on the young preacher and George Whitefield knew then and there that he was filled with the Holy Spirit! I read about George Müeller, who was filled with the Holy Spirit the first time he ever saw Christians on their knees in prayer. I read how Billy Sunday used to preach every sermon with his Bible open to **Isaiah 61:1** and how the Spirit of God came on him. My heart began to burn from within! "Was this for me as well as for them? Was that power that Moody had and Wesley had and Whitefield had and Billy Sunday had available for little Jack Hyles, a poor country preacher in East Texas?"

I began to walk in the woods at night. Night after night I would walk and cry and pray and beg for power. My heart was hungry. I got a Cruden's Concordance and looked up the terms, "Holy Ghost," "Spirit of the Lord," "Spirit of God," etc. I looked up every Scripture in the Bible that had to do with the Holy Spirit. I read in **Judges 6:34** that the Spirit of the Lord came upon Gideon and in **Judges 14:6** how the Spirit of the Lord came upon Samson and in

I Samuel 11:6 how the Spirit of God came upon Saul. I read in **I Samuel 16:13** how the Spirit of the Lord came upon David. I read in **Acts 9:17** where Paul was filled with the Holy Ghost and in **Luke 4:1** where Jesus was full of the Holy Ghost. My heart burned! I needed something. I needed the blessed power of God. I needed the fulness of the Holy Spirit. I didn't understand all the Scriptures. I read in **Luke 3:16** the words, **"...he shall baptize you with the Holy Ghost and with fire."** I read in **Acts 1:4** the mention of the **"promise of the Father."** In **Luke 24:49** I found **"be endued with power from on high."** In **Acts 1:8** I found the words, **"after that the Holy Ghost is come upon you."** In **Acts 2:17** I learned of the pouring out of the Spirit and in **Ephesians 5:18** I found the term, **"filled with the Spirit."**

I was not seeking sinless perfection nor was I trying to name what I wanted God to give me. I had no desire to speak in tongues nor did I even have a desire to have some kind of an experience. I just wanted God to work in the hearts of people while I preached and witnessed. Could it be for me? Yes, it was for Samson, for Gideon, for Torrey, for Moody, for Billy Sunday, for Jonathan Edwards, for Müeller, for Whitefield, for George Fox, for Christmas Evans, for Savonarola, for Peter Cartwright, for John Rice, for Bob Jones, for Lee Roberson, but was it for me? I was just a country preacher. I can recall how my eyes fastened on **Isaiah 40:31** and **Acts 2:4** and **Acts 4:31**. I was hungry!

"I must have results. I must have power." I can recall saying to God, "I'm not going to be a normal preacher. I'm not going to be an average preacher. I'm not going to be a powerless preacher."

Night after night I would walk through the pine thickets of east Texas, up and down the sand hills, begging God for His power. If you had driven down Highway 43 outside Marshall, Texas, on the way to Henderson, Texas, in the wee hours of most any morning, you could have heard me praying, "Where is the Lord God of Elijah?" and begging God to give me power.

I was losing weight. I couldn't eat. What I did eat came back up! My family was worried about me. My deacons got together and said to me, "Pastor, you've got to take care of yourself. You are going to get bad sick."

Then came May 12, 1950. All night I prayed! Just about sunrise I fell to my face in some pine needles and told God I would pay the price, whatever it was, for the power of God! I did not know what I was saying. I did not know what that meant.

In less than four hours, my phone rang in our little country parsonage. The operator said that it was a long distance call for Reverend Jack Hyles. She put the call through and a voice said, "This is Mr. Smith. I work with your dad. Reverend Hyles, your dad just dropped dead with a heart attack." I put the phone down. I could not believe what I had heard. Just a few months before I had preached to my daddy, but I was powerless. He did not get saved. I had witnessed to him, but once again I was powerless and he did not get saved. He had promised me on the first of January, 1950, that in a few months he would come back to east Texas and receive Christ as his Saviour. He never made it. As far as I know, he died under the influence of alcohol without Jesus. We drove to Dallas to the same funeral home that later embalmed President Kennedy when he was killed. On May 13, 1950, Mother's Day afternoon, we had a little service in the chapel. We then followed the hearse about 50 miles south to a little cemetery on the northeast corner of Italy, Texas, where two of my little sisters were buried. Down near the creek was a hole in the ground. They lowered my daddy's body in the grave. Not long after, I returned to that grave and fell on my face and told God I was not going to leave that grave until something happened to me. I don't know how long I stayed. It may have been hours; it may have been days. I lost all consciousness and awareness of time. I did not become sinlessly perfect nor did I talk in another language nor was I completely sanctified, but my ministry was transformed!

To God be the praise, there has not been one single Sunday since that day without conversions in the churches I have pastored. That's been over 31 years now, and though I'm not the preacher I ought to be, I have seen the mighty power of God over and over and over again. Over a quarter of a million people have walked the aisle in the churches I have pastored professing faith in Christ. I am no great preacher. I am no giant of the faith. I just found out there was a way that a person could be filled with the Holy Spirit, enabling Him to speak from within as I preached from without.

One of the great mistakes that Christians make, however, is believing that the fulness of the Spirit is a one-time happening. The truth is that the New Testament church was filled with the Spirit over and over and over again. They were filled with the Spirit in **Acts 2:4, "And they were all filled with the Holy Ghost, and began to speak with other tongues, as the Spirit gave them utterance."** Again they were filled with the Spirit in **Acts 4:31, "And when they had prayed, the place was shaken where they were assembled together; and they were all filled with the Holy Ghost, and they spake the word of God with boldness."**

Several years later I was called to pastor the Miller Road Baptist Church of Garland, Texas. Twenty-one people voted on me — eighteen voted for me, two voted neutral and one voted undecided. The church enjoyed unbelievable growth. What a ministry God gave us, and how blessed was the Holy Spirit's power! The church grew so fast that it was too big for me and I felt that I must resign. On December 31, 1954, I went to my study on New Year's Eve. I went alone with God and told Him the church was too big for me and that I would have to resign and let someone more qualified and capable continue the ministry. I would be content to go to some smaller church and start over again. I wrote out my resignation, laid it on the floor of my study and told God that unless He gave me a new power I would have to read the resignation on January 1, 1955. I did not want to resign, because I loved my people dearly, but there was no other choice. I prayed from 9:00 until 10:00; from 10:00 until 11:00; from 11:00 to 12:00; from 12:00 to 1:00. Sometime past midnight, there was a knock on the door of my study. I went to the door. It was one of my deacons. He was weeping. He said, "Pastor, what's wrong?"

I said, "Why do you ask?"

He said, "The Holy Spirit told me something was wrong with my preacher tonight. I called your house and they did not know where you were, so I thought I would come to the study. What's wrong?"

I showed him the letter of resignation and told him that God was going to have to give me something more than what I had if I stayed. He said, "Pastor, let's pray." We prayed from 1:00 until 2:00; from 2:00 to 3:00; from 3:00 to 4:00; from 4:00 until 5:00 and sometime between 5:00 and 6:00 in the morning the sweet power of God settled upon us, and I knew that God had given me a fresh power, some fresh oil, as spoken of by the Psalmist in **Psalm 92:10, "But my horn shalt thou exalt like the horn of an unicorn: I shall be anointed with fresh oil."** I tore up the letter of resignation. My deacon and I danced for joy and hugged and lifted our hands in holy praises to God. Oh, the sweet years we had after that!

Then in December, 1958, I received a letter from Hammond, Indiana. For months I wrestled with the possibility of becoming Pastor in that Chicagoland church. I did not want to go, but the Holy Spirit led in that direction, and I became Pastor of the First Baptist Church of Hammond in August of 1959. Soon the problems mounted. The church and I were different. It seemed there was no way I could continue pastoring that church.

I was preaching for a week at the Bill Rice Ranch. Every night I wrestled with the calls from other churches to return to Texas. It just seemed that I was not cut out for the First Baptist Church of Hammond. On Friday night I could not sleep. The Holy Spirit kept me awake. About ten o'clock I knelt to pray beside the bed in room 11 of the Widner Inn at the Bill Rice Ranch. I told God I was going to resign the church the next Sunday, but God wrestled me through the night. All night long I pleaded for God to give me something I must have if I were to stay in Hammond. After a night of prayer and a night of wrestling with the Holy Spirit, that "something" came. Again I knew that I was filled with the Holy Spirit in a new and fresh way. Fresh oil had come! The rest of the story is legend. The great First Baptist Church of Hammond was born that night.

It has been over 21 years since that all-night prayer meeting, but I find myself again and again needing a new fulness of fresh oil. That's my only hope. I need that Voice talking to people as I preach. I need Him to speak from the inside as I witness from the outside.

Dear reader, you too need that fulness. Dear music director, you need that power; and so do you, choir director, choir member, Sunday school teacher, bus worker, Christian school teacher, Christian school administrator, instrumentalist, youth worker, and Sunday school worker; and, blessed be God, it is available for you! It's for sons and daughters, for young men and old men, for handmaids and servants. Joel says it is for all flesh! Praise the Lord!

Won't you now bow your head? Promise God several things. Promise Him that you are going to be clean and separate from the world. Promise Him that you are going to live in His Book. Promise Him that you are going to be sure that He gets what is His financially and in every other way. Promise Him that you are going to work hard and be faithful and loyal to Him. Then promise Him that you are going to pray and plead and wrestle with Him. Don't be concerned about having some kind of an experience; just be concerned about the Holy Spirit talking from within as you talk from without. It may be that that power will come upon you the next time you preach or teach or sing. It may be that it will be a gradual thing and that more and more you will be aware of His presence and power as you serve. Don't be concerned about having some kind of a stereotype experience and don't be concerned about getting up and telling what happened to you. Just yield yourself; sanctify yourself; live in His Book; walk with the Saviour; be clean and pure, and pray and pray and pray and pray until as you speak you see people moved by that Voice that speaks from within! When you see this, continue to pray, continue to ask Him for His fulness and continue to love Him and serve Him. Crown Him, honor Him and praise Him until the veil is pulled and we shall see Him as He is!

6

The Holy Spirit — Our Prayer Partner

Romans 8:26-28, "Likewise the Spirit also helpeth our infirmities: for we know not what we should pray for as we ought: but the Spirit itself maketh intercession for us with groanings which cannot be uttered. And he that searcheth the hearts knoweth what is the mind of the Spirit, because he maketh intercession for the saints according to the will of God. And we know that all things work together for good to them that love God, to them who are the called according to his purpose."

Two of the most important things that the young Christian has to learn are (1) how to get things from God, and (2) how to share with others and give to others what God gives.

It should be remembered that in the Bible prayer is asking. Prayer is not praise; it is asking. Prayer is not thanksgiving; it is asking. Prayer is not adoration; it is asking. This discussion will deal with the Holy Spirit, our prayer partner, Who joins with us in our prayer life.

1. *The Holy Spirit intercedes with us.* Romans 8:26, "Likewise the Spirit also helpeth our infirmities: for we know not what we should pray for as we ought: but the Spirit itself

maketh intercession for us with groanings which cannot be uttered." The word "intercession" in verse 26 is not the same word that is translated "intercession" in verse 27. In verse 26 the word means that the Holy Spirit goes WITH us to the Father to help us plead for our needs and, yes, for our wants. There are several aspects: (1) I don't know what I need. (2) The Holy Spirit DOES know what I need. (3) I go to Him, that is, the Holy Spirit, to find my needs. (4) He tells me what my needs are. (5) I make a list of the things He reminds me. (6) I then go to the Father. (7) He goes with me.

After I have been to the Holy Spirit with pen and paper in hand to inquire of Him what my needs are, after He has told me what they are, and after I have made a list of them, I then go to the Father with the needs that the Holy Spirit has given me. Then, praise God, the Holy Spirit goes with me to the Father. He knows the Father better than I, and He knows me perhaps better than the Father, so what better Person could I have go with me to the Father when I present my petitions than the Holy Spirit Who led me in making my petitions.

Now for an illustration. Before I go to the Father, I ask the Holy Spirit what I need. Let's suppose, for example, I go to the Holy Spirit and say, "Holy Spirit, I would like to have a cashmere coat with a mink collar. What do You think?"

The Holy Spirit says, "Now I do think you need a new coat, but you could surely get along without a cashmere coat and you certainly don't need a mink collar." So the Holy Spirit leads me to ask for a coat. I then ask the Holy Spirit, "I would like to have a mink hat." The Holy Spirit reminds me that I perhaps could use a hat, but mink would be too extravagant. I then suggest to the Holy Spirit that He and I go to the Father and ask for a new $500 suit of clothes. The Holy Spirit reminds me that I do need a new suit, but not a $500 suit.

So I make my list: a new coat, a new hat and a new suit. The Holy Spirit has led me. After he has led me and after I have written down what I believe the Holy Spirit wants me to ask the

Father, I ask the Holy Spirit to go with me to the Father. This He does as my petitions are presented to the Heavenly Father, as I pray in and with the Holy Spirit.

Note **Ephesians 2:18, "For through him we both have access by one Spirit unto the Father."** Note the word "both." We find then that we pray TO the Father THROUGH the Son WITH the Spirit. Our access to the Father is through His Son. Our prayer partner when we go to the Father is the Holy Spirit.

Now notice **Matthew 18:19, "Again I say unto you, That if two of you shall agree on earth as touching any thing that they shall ask, it shall be done for them of my Father which is in heaven."** Notice that if two shall agree as touching anything on earth, it shall be done for them. The word "agree" is the word from which we get our word "symphony" or "harmony." When we are in tune with the Holy Spirit or when we harmonize with the Holy Spirit, we can present our petitions to the Father. Not only can we present them to the Father, but the Holy Spirit will accompany us as we appear at the throne of grace.

Now notice **Acts 15:28, "For it seemed good to the Holy Ghost, and to us, to lay upon you no greater burden than these necessary things."** Ah, these are beautiful words: "It seemed good to the Holy Ghost, AND TO US." Notice the agreement there. There was a fellowship between the Holy Spirit and the apostles. They had communed with the Holy Spirit, and there was a harmony between them.

There is another way that the Holy Spirit helps us when we pray. Just as He talks to the sinner as I talk to the sinner, He also talks to the Father as I talk to the Father. He has helped me make up my prayer list. I have taken the prayer list that He has led me to make and brought it before the Father. The Holy Spirit went with me as I went to the Father and now, praise the Lord, He talks to the Father as I talk to the Father. I say, "Father, give me a new coat."

The Holy Spirit says, "Yes, Father, he does need a new coat. He and I have talked about it."

I say, "Father, give me a new hat."

The Holy Spirit says, "Father, I believe he needs a new hat. We have talked about this too."

I ask, "Father, give me a new suit."

The Holy Spirit says, "Father, I do believe he needs a new suit. He and I have talked about this before coming to You."

Notice He is our prayer partner. He prays with us.

In summary and in practicality, let's review. It is time for me to pray; that is, to ask God for some things. I bow to my knees and talk to the Holy Spirit. I tell Him what I think I need. He impresses me concerning my needs. He leads me to make a prayer list of things for which I am to ask the Father. Then I go to the Father in prayer. The dear Holy Spirit accompanies me. He leads me as I talk to the Father and then He talks to the Father with me, reminding the Father that we have talked together before coming to present the petitions.

Then I can claim **Psalm 37:4, "Delight thyself also in the LORD; and he shall give thee the desires of thine heart."** Then I can claim **John 15:7, "If ye abide in me, and my words abide in you, ye shall ask what ye will, and it shall be done unto you."** There is a way that the Christian can walk in the Spirit in such a way that the Lord will almost give him power of attorney. He will almost give the Christian a blank check because as we walk in the Spirit, with the Spirit and through the Spirit, our wants become much like the wants of God, our delights become His delights, our desires become His desires.

2. *The Holy Spirit intercedes for us concerning things for which we do not ask.* See **Romans 8:27.** The word "intercession" here does not imply the Holy Spirit meeting with us to plead. This is the Holy Spirit coming before God for us on our behalf. Here he tells God about the needs for which we forgot to ask. He tells the Father our needs even when we forget them. Suppose, for example, that I prayed to the Father for the aforementioned "coat and suit," but I forgot the hat. I say, "Father, please give me a new

coat and please give a new suit." The Holy Spirit says, "Father, he needs a new hat too." You see, he is interceding FOR me just as He previously interceded WITH me.

There are some things that I need that I do not know that I need. There are some things I forget when I come to the Father. The Holy Spirit knows my needs. Some of these may not be things that I myself would choose, but He knows what they are, and so He intercedes before the Father on my behalf, asking the Father to give me the things that I need. I may want all sunshiny days, but He may know I need a cloudy day. I may want all noontimes, but He may know that I need a midnight. I may want all victories, but He may know that I need a defeat. I may want all smiles, but He may know that I need some tears. This is where **Romans 8:28** comes in. **"And we know that all things work together for good to them that love God, to them who are the called according to his purpose."**

Years ago I was preaching in a big tent in Jacksonville, Florida. After the crowd had dispersed one night, I was kneeling at the altar praying. I thought I was alone. An old preacher walked up beside me and asked if he could pray with me. Of course, I was delighted to have him join me in payer. He prayed aloud: "Dear Lord, I hate baking powder." I could not believe what I heard. Then he prayed, "Dear Lord, I hate flour." I could not believe what I was hearing. Through tears he said, "Dear Lord, I hate baking soda." Then he prayed, "Dear Lord, I hate salt." He continued to list several things that he hated, and the more he prayed the louder he got. Then a smile came across his face as his voice continued heavenward. "But, dear Lord," he said, "put together all those things I hate, stir them up, put them in the oven and cook them, and I sure do love hot biscuits!"

That is the best explanation of **Romans 8:28** that I have ever heard. Thank God that the Holy Spirit knows what I need and makes intercession for me.

Now in review, dear Christian, the next time you come to God in prayer concerning your needs, first talk to the Holy Spirit.

Speak something like this, "Dear Holy Spirit, I have a pen and paper in hand, and I'm on my way to the Father to present my needs. Would You help me make out my prayer list?" Tell Him what you want to ask from the Father. Ask Him what He thinks about it. Then ask Him to impress you about other things for which you should ask. Once you have completed your prayer list, as led by the Holy Spirit, then come to the Heavenly Father, asking the Holy Spirit to appear with you before the throne of grace. Then pray in the Spirit to the Father, trusting the Holy Spirit to help you convince the Father of what you and He have decided to request. Be grateful that the Holy Spirit will work on your behalf. Realize that those things for which you forget to ask, He will not forget to mention to the Father. For those things that you do not even know you need, ask the Holy Spirit to petition the Father if He thinks best.

7

The Anointing of the Holy Spirit

Perhaps no doctrine concerning the Holy Spirit has been more misunderstood than that of the anointing of the Spirit. This doctrine has been associated with the fulness of the Spirit. There is, however, a difference between the two.

There were three different types of anointing in the Old Testament. First was the anointing of the priests. **Leviticus 8:12, "And he poured of the anointing oil upon Aaron's head, and anointed him, to sanctify him."** It is noteworthy that this anointing took place only one time for each priest.

Second, there was the anointing of the kings. **I Samuel 16:13, "Then Samuel took the horn of oil, and anointed him in the midst of his brethren: and the Spirit of the LORD came upon David from that day forward. So Samuel rose up, and went to Ramah."** This anointing was likewise a one-time ritual.

Third, there was the anointing of the prophets. **I Kings 19:16, "And Jehu the son of Nimshi shalt thou anoint to be king over Israel: and Elisha the son of Shaphat of Abel-meholah shalt thou anoint to be prophet in thy room."** Again, it took place only one time for each prophet.

Since our Lord Jesus was priest and king and prophet, then He was anointed. **Luke 4:18, "The Spirit of the Lord is upon me,** because he hath anointed me to preach the gospel to the poor; he hath sent me to heal the brokenhearted, to preach deliverance to the captives, and recovering of sight to the blind, to set at liberty them that are bruised." Acts 4:27, "For of a truth against thy holy child Jesus, whom thou hast anointed, both Herod, and Pontius Pilate, with the Gentiles, and the people of Israel, were gathered together." Acts 10:38, "How God anointed Jesus of Nazareth with the Holy Ghost and with power: who went about doing good, and healing all that were oppressed of the devil; for God was with him." Notice now in Luke 4:18 the words, "The Spirit of the Lord is upon me, because he HATH anointed me." It had already been done. Now compare this one-time anointing to Ephesians 5:18, "And be not drunk with wine, wherein is excess; but be filled with the Spirit." The words, "be filled," here are in the durative or linear which means "be being filled" or "be filled and be filled and be filled and be filled." Notice the fulness of the Holy Spirit is a durative doctrine, whereas the doctrine of the anointing is an aorist or a one-time anointing. That is, one time for each job or each responsibility. Notice the words in Acts 4:27, "hast anointed." Notice the past tense and then in Acts 10:38 we have the word "anointed." Once again, this is the past tense.

Therefore, the anointing of the Holy Spirit was and is like the anointing of a king or a priest or a prophet. When one was chosen to be a priest, he was anointed with oil, symbolic of the Holy Spirit coming upon him and giving him power, wisdom and ability for the task set before him. The same was true when a king was anointed and when a prophet was anointed. This leads us to some conclusions.

1. *The anointing was done upon the accepting of a new responsibility.* When a Christian accepts a new responsibility, he should be anointed by the Holy Spirit for that task. When a pastor is called to a new church or when a Christian is chosen to be a

Sunday school teacher, a choir member, a choir director, a departmental superintendent or an usher, he should be anointed by the Holy Spirit. Any new task to which a child of God is chosen and any new responsibility that God has give to him is so important that the Holy Spirit should anoint him upon the assumption of his new responsibility. Likewise, as the Christian ministers and continues to fulfill the work to which God has called him, he should constantly be being filled with the Spirit. However, the doctrine of being filled should not be mistaken for the doctrine of the anointing.

2. *This anointing was an appropriation; it equipped one for a task.* When God calls, He qualifies, He equips and He prepares. When a Christian is called to a new responsibility, he needs to be equipped. Hence, he needs to be anointed by the Holy Spirit as God appropriates to him what he needs to fulfill his new calling and equips him for that calling.

3. *The Christian simply yields himself to the Spirit for this anointing.* He may, upon being given a new ministry, go alone with God and yield himself and surrender his will and present himself for the anointing of the Holy Spirit. Have you been called to a new task? Is there a new charge given you? Then choose several hours. Get alone with God. Plead with Him to equip you or anoint you for the task to which God has called you. This should be done by a new parent, a new bride, a new groom, a new pastor, a new song director, a new choir director, a new Sunday school teacher, a new bus captain, a new usher, a new choir member, a new deacon and a new evangelist. This anointing will not take the place of the fulness of the Spirit. After the king or the priest or the prophet was anointed by God, he still from time to time was filled with the Holy Spirit as we are admonished by the apostle to be "being filled" with the Spirit.

4. ***This anointing is, in a sense, God giving His mind to the task.*** It is a little private ordination service. It is a private inauguration. It is a private installation service.

I have pastored five churches. At the beginning of each pastorate I have gotten alone with God for hours, and in some cases, for days, and asked God to anoint me and equip me for the task ahead.

A perfect illustration of this truth is shown in the life of a dear preacher friend. He had just assumed a new pastorate. It was his first. He came to the nationwide Pastors' School at First Baptist Church of Hammond, Indiana. His life was transformed. As he and his wife and another couple drove their rented car back to the airport, they came to the Hammond city limit sign and yielded themselves to the Holy Spirit of God to be used of Him to build a great work in Florida. This was anointing time. God did anoint him. This did not take the place of his need to be filled again and again with the Holy Spirit but, in some wonderful way, God equipped him at this little inauguration service beside a road with the Hammond city limit sign as an altar. In a marvelous way God will give His mind to a task as the Christian yields himself for equipping, for anointing and yes, for sanctifying.

This anointing could be called "sanctifying" or "being set apart for a task." The nation of Israel faced an impossible task. Three million people with no food, no water, no homes and no jobs had to march across a dangerous wilderness toward a land they had never seen. God told them to sanctify themselves. **Exodus 19:10, "And the LORD said unto Moses, Go unto the people, and sanctify them to day and to morrow, and let them wash their clothes."**

When this little nation stood before the Jordan River facing the land of heathen nations, each to become their enemy and each larger than theirs, again God told His people to sanctify themselves. **Joshua 3:5, "And Joshua said unto the people, Sanctify yourselves: for to morrow the LORD will do wonders among you."**

When that nation came to Ai, again they had a task before them; again they needed to be sanctified. **Joshua 7:13, "Up, sanctify the people, and say, Sanctify yourselves against to morrow: for thus saith the LORD God of Israel, There is an accursed thing in the midst of thee, O Israel: thou canst not stand before thine enemies, until ye take away the accursed thing from among you."** When those people had endured terrible apostasy under King Ahaz, God raised up another king named Hezekiah. Again God admonished them to sanctify them-selves. **II Chronicles 29:5, "And said unto them, Hear me, ye Levites, sanctify yourselves, and sanctify the house of the LORD God of your fathers, and carry forth the filthiness out of the holy place."**

Another apostasy came under Manasseh and Amon, but God raised up another king named Josiah. Again he told the people that before revival could come they would have to sanctify themselves. **II Chronicles 35:6, "So kill the passover, and sanctify yourselves, and prepare your brethren, that they may do according to the word of the LORD by the hand of Moses."**

Blessed believer, aren't you weary of laboring in the energy of the flesh? Aren't you tired of going through the motions of serving God without having been anointed for the task that is yours? Tiptoe into the woods somewhere. Drive away from civilization for a while. Spend some hours with God. Tell Him that the task is bigger than you and the responsibility is too great for the flesh. Ask Him to anoint you, to sanctify you, to equip you, to inaugurate you for the job ahead. Ask Him for His mind as you serve. Ask Him to appropriate to you what you need.

Have you recently been chosen for a new responsibility? Begin this responsibility by finding a quiet place and having a little private ordination service between you and God. Ask God to lay His hands upon you and to anoint you for the task ahead. Then day by day beg for His power, plead for His fulness and walk in the Spirit.

Remember that the anointing of the priest took place at the

beginning of his ministry, the anointing of the
the beginning of his reign and the anointing of
place at the beginning of his work. Perhaps no
place olive oil on your brow (though this is
order), but at such a time of surrender the hand of God
His Holy Spirit and equip you for a task for which by nature you
are not equipped.

Even now, place a marker in this book, walk or drive to a place
where you can get alone with God. Sanctify yourself; set yourself
apart; yield yourself to the Holy Spirit for His anointing. The rest
is up to Him. Believe that He does it. No doubt, He will!

An old country preacher was heard praying, "Lord, give me the
unction. Lord, give me the unction. Lord, give me the unction."

Someone who overheard the prayer said, "Reverend, what is
the unction?"

The old preacher, through tears, cried, "I don't know what is,
but I know what it ain't."

Perhaps we do not know all that the anointing is, but far too
many of us know "what it ain't."

Lord, give us the unction!

8

The Holy Spirit and
Complete Sanctification

John 17:17, "Sanctify them through thy truth: thy word is truth."

Sanctification means to be set apart for special use. In a spiritual sense, the word "sanctification" means "being set apart for special use for God." Sanctification does not mean sinless perfection or the eradication of the flesh; it simply means to be set apart for the Lord's work. The church pulpit is sanctified; it is set apart for the teaching and the preaching of the Word of God. That does not mean it is a perfect pulpit; it simply means it is given to special use. The chairs in the church choir are sanctified. They may be imperfect chairs, as most church choir chairs are, but they are set apart or sanctified to be used only by those who sing the praises of our Lord.

There are three ways which the believer is sanctified.

1. *He HAS BEEN sanctified.* When one receives Christ as Saviour, he is sanctified in the sense that he is set apart for Heaven. It is all settled. He is God's child. God prepares a place in Heaven for him and he is sanctified or set apart eternally for Heaven.

2. *He IS BEING sanctified.* This means that from day to day the Holy Spirit is conforming him more in the image of the Lord Jesus. As the artist slowly paints on the canvas what is already in his mind, even so the Holy Spirit gradually day by day is setting us apart more and more for the service of Christ. This is not done all at one time but rather from grace to grace. **John 1:16, "And of his fulness have all we received, and grace for grace."** It is done from faith to faith. **Romans 1:17, "For therein is the righteousness of God revealed from faith to faith: as it is written, The just shall live by faith."** It is done from glory to glory. **II Corinthians 3:18, "But we all, with open face beholding as in a glass the glory of the Lord, are changed into the same image from glory to glory, even as by the Spirit of the Lord."** The Word of God teaches us that He has predestinated us to be conformed in the image of His Son. **Romans 8:29, "For whom he did foreknow, he also did predestinate to be conformed to the image of his Son, that he might be the firstborn among many brethren."** This means that someday every believer will be like Jesus. That sanctifying process is a gradual one, from grace to grace, from glory to glory and from faith to faith as we yield ourselves daily to the Holy Spirit and He conforms us more and more to the image of our Saviour.

3. *He SHALL BE sanctified.* The day will come when every believer will be like Jesus and then we will be satisfied to awake in His likeness. **Psalm 17:15, "As for me, I will behold thy face in righteousness: I shall be satisfied, when I awake, with thy likeness."**

Now the question comes, "WHEN will we be completely sanctified and be like Jesus?" In a recent poll most believers expressed that they think that complete sanctification would be at death when the believer gets to Heaven. However, the Scripture does not teach that. Notice **I Thessalonians 5:23, "And the very**

God of peace sanctify you wholly; and I pray God your whole spirit and soul and body BE PRESERVED BLAMELESS UNTO THE COMING OF OUR LORD JESUS CHRIST." Now read I Thessalonians 3:13, **"To the end he may stablish your hearts unblameable in holiness before God, even our Father, AT THE COMING OF OUR LORD JESUS CHRIST WITH ALL HIS SAINTS."** Now read I John 3:2, **"Beloved, now are we the sons of God, and it doth not yet appear what we shall be: but we know that, WHEN HE SHALL APPEAR, WE SHALL BE LIKE HIM; for we shall see him as he is."** Now when will we be like Him? These verses are very plain that we will be like Him WHEN HE SHALL APPEAR, or WHEN HE COMES AGAIN. This means that the believer in Heaven now is NOT like Jesus. To be sure, that believer is free from sin and he is in a body, but he is not in his final glorified body which is like the body of Jesus. Hence, he is not completely sanctified or set apart and will not be until he is like Jesus, and that will be at the appearing of our Lord. Perhaps this is why the saints in Heaven cry, "How long, O Lord, how long?" **Revelation 6:10, "And they cried with a loud voice, saying, How long, O Lord, holy and true, dost thou not judge and avenge our blood on them that dwell on the earth?"**

Many Christians erroneously believe that at death the Christian becomes like Jesus and that he is immediately sanctified and set apart. True, the saints in Heaven do not sin; nevertheless, they are not mature yet. They have not reached their adulthood yet, which means that they continue to grow. Though they do not sin, they enter Heaven at the spiritual maturity with which they left earth. There will be room for more growth in Heaven until the rapture when Jesus comes and we shall then be like Him, for we shall see Him as He is! A Christian who never praises the Lord on earth will not suddenly upon his entrance into Heaven start shouting praises to God. The Christian who was not interested in his Bible on earth will not enjoy Heaven as much as the Christian who loved the Word of God and spent time with it and in it. The

Christian who spent three hours a day watching television and five minutes a day in his Bible will not enjoy Heaven as much at first as the Christian who walked with God. The Christian who spends three hours on Sunday watching the football game and 15 minutes preparing his Sunday school lesson, the one who spends an hour after the service at a hamburger stand and 10 minutes in prayer before he goes to bed, the one who gets up before dawn to go fishing but never gets up before dawn to pray, the one who can spend four hours a week on the golf course and only one hour a week in prayer, the one who can sit up until two o'clock to fellowship but never pray past midnight, the one who can sit in the rain at the ball game but won't drive through the rain to church, and the one who has beer in his ice box, rock music on his stereo, grudges in his heart and God's money in his pocket will certainly not enter into the presence of Christ with the same joy and delight as will the Spirit-filled Christian who walks with God, loves the Book and obeys the commands of Christ.

The Christian in Heaven now is still a minor. He will not become an adult until he receives his glorified body. **Romans 8:23, "And not only they, but ourselves also, which have the firstfruits of the Spirit, even we ourselves groan within ourselves, WAITING FOR THE ADOPTION, TO WIT, THE REDEMPTION OF OUR BODY."** The word "adoption" here means "majority" or "adulthood." It is contrasted with "minority" or "childhood." Now it is plain that this adoption (majority or adulthood) comes when our bodies are redeemed. Our bodies will be redeemed at the coming of Christ FOR HIS OWN. This means that until Christ comes for His own, even the saints in Heaven are not yet adults. Therefore, they still have access to spiritual growth.

The Jewish male child wore a particular type coat which signified that he was a minor. This coat was worn until he became an adult. On the day of his adulthood (majority) he received another coat that signified his adulthood.

One the day that he became an adult, he was taken by his father to the Bema. This was a public place in a conspicuous part of town. He would stand with his son before the citizens of the town and would make several declarations. First he would say, "Thou art my son." He would then say, "Son, inherit my name. Son, inherit my wealth." Then he would remove the coat of childhood (minority) from his son and place on him the coat of adulthood (majority). Now he is an adult and all may see that the day of his adoption has come.

One day I too shall come to the Bema (the judgment seat). **II Corinthians 5:10, "For we must all appear before the judgment seat of Christ; that every one may receive the things done in his body, according to that he hath done, whether it be good or bad."** My Saviour shall appear with me. He shall say to me before the entire universe, "Thou art My son. Son, inherit My name. Son, inherit My wealth," and He shall give me a coat of adulthood; that is, my glorified body. This present coat of childhood shall be removed and then I shall be like Jesus and shall know complete sanctification. Hallelujah! No wonder this body groans and travails for its adoption (redemption). No wonder the saints in Heaven shout, "How long, O Lord, how long?"

This then leads to the conclusion that even saints in Heaven are still minors and will not become adults until Jesus comes. The old is gone, but the new is not yet grown. We await the rapture to be totally like Him and totally sanctified. This behooves the believer to grow in grace so that he will enter Heaven more able to enjoy it and more in the likeness of his Saviour.

The prophet Amos admonished the people to prepare to meet God. **Amos 4:12, "Therefore thus will I do unto thee, O Israel: and because I will do this unto thee, PREPARE TO MEET THY GOD, O ISRAEL."** Now this is interesting. These were not unsaved people; these were God's people. Amos wasn't telling unsaved people to prepare to meet God by being born again. He was telling saved people to prepare to meet God.

Years ago I preached in Jamaica. I shared the platform with Dr. John R. Rice. He flew to Jamaica on Saturday; I joined him on Monday. As I was clearing customs in Jamaica, the customs official welcomed me and asked me what I planned to do while I was there. I told him that I was there to preach. He asked, "Where?" To save my life I could not remember the name of the church. With a suspicious look he asked, "In what town?"

I told him I did not know in which town I was to speak, but that I was to be met at the airport by Dr. John R. Rice and a local pastor or missionary. He became even more suspicious. Then he asked, "What is the name of the pastor?"

Oh, brother! I could not even think of his name! The official became very disturbed. He said, "Sir, don't tell me you are coming to Jamaica to preach without even knowing the name of the pastor of the church or the town."

I said, "Neighbor, that's exactly the story." Suddenly I saw Dr. John Rice. Pointing to Dr. Rice, I told the custom official, "That man knows me. He will verify who I am and will tell you where I am to preach."

The official called Dr. Rice and asked him to identify me. Dr. Rice looked up with a sheepish grin and said, "Sir, I never saw that man before in my life!"

If someone had asked me on the airplane where I was going, I would have said, "To Jamaica." The airplane was going to Jamaica, and I was aboard the airplane, but I was not prepared for Jamaica! There are millions of Christians who are going to Heaven and know it, but they are not prepared to meet God.

Suppose two people go to a football game. One knows the games and its rules; the other does not. They pay the same price for the ticket and sit side by side at the game. Who enjoys the game more? The one who knows the rules, of course, will enjoy it greatly. The one who knows little or nothing about the game will scarcely enjoy it.

Suppose two Christians go to Heaven side by side. One knows the Bible; the other doesn't. Which one will enjoy Heaven more? The one who knows the Bible, of course. The one who has not learned the Rule Book will be in Heaven but will not enjoy it as much as the one who has prepared to meet his God.

I am writing this chapter aboard an airplane flying from Pittsburgh to Chicago. In a few minutes we will land in Chicago. Suppose all of a sudden I removed my pocketknife, opened it and began to cut the seat in front of me. Now where am I going? To Chicago, of course. Suppose that the pilot or co-pilot came back and said, "Sir, I understand you are causing some trouble." Let's suppose I took the knife and cut off the tie of the co-pilot or pilot. Now where am I going? I am going to Chicago, of course. Suppose the steward comes back and says, "Sir, you are going to have to behave yourself," and then I kick him in the shin. Now where am I going? I am going to Chicago, of course, but I am not prepared for Chicago and I will not enjoy Chicago as much as I would have enjoyed it had I behaved myself on the journey. The person who has received Christ as Saviour is going to Heaven, but his enjoyment of Heaven will be determined by his behavior on the journey. He will arrive in Heaven, but he is not prepared to meet his God.

Years ago I was preaching one night in Minneapolis, Minnesota. The next night I was to preach in Phoenix, Arizona. I took only one suit. It was a dark flannel suit. I also wore a heavy overcoat and a winter hat. That was fine for Minneapolis, Minnesota. Then the next day I flew to Phoenix, Arizona. It was 104°. I got off the airplane wearing a flannel suit, heavy winter overcoat and a winter hat. People at the airport looked at me and began to laugh! I realized what I had done. I had arrived in Phoenix, but I was not prepared for Phoenix. Multitudes of God's people will arrive in Heaven, but they will not be prepared.

Many years ago I was asked to come to Tennessee Temple College and preach the dedication message for the Weigle Music Center built in honor of Dr. Charles Weigle, a blessed old evangelist who lived on the campus of Tennessee Temple and who was one of the sweetest and happiest Christians I ever met. Dr. Weigle was approaching the century mark in years. I preached the dedication message and then the great crowd of several thousand went out to the street in front of the Weigle Music Center for the cutting of the ribbon and the dedication prayer. Many dignitaries were there, and it was a time of refreshment and blessing. After the crowd had left, I wanted to talk to Dr. Weigle. I went to his apartment, which was in the back of the new Weigle Music Center. Just before I knocked on his door I heard some noise. I heard the clapping of hands and the squeaking of bed springs. I heard an old voice shout, "Hallelujah! Glory to God! Praise the Lord!" I waited for a while realizing that the old man was up on the bed jumping up and down and singing and shouting praises. I then knocked on the door. When the door opened, there stood Dr. Weigle with bare feet, shirt unbuttoned, hair ruffled and a look of Heaven on his face. I said, "Dr. Weigle, what's going on in here?"

He sweetly replied, "I'm just practicing for Heaven, Dr. Hyles." That is exactly what all of us are supposed to do. We are supposed to be practicing constantly for Heaven!

How can this practicing be done? We should do those things on earth which we will continue to do in Heaven. We should chose friends on earth whom we will know in Heaven. We should realize that we are strangers here. We can praise God; that is something which will be continued in Heaven. We should live in the Word of God because that will also be continued in Heaven. How sad that most of us spend most of our lives doing those things which will not equip us for Heaven!

Not long ago I was in the Philadelphia area. Suddenly I got happy late at night. I got up on the bed and began to praise the Lord. It must have been two o'clock in the morning and I was still praising Him. There was a knock on the door. I shouted, "Who is it?" A voice came from the outside and said, "It's the man from the next room. What's going on in there?"

"I'm praising the Lord," I replied.

He said, "Can't we praise the Lord in the morning and sleep tonight?"

I was just doing a little practicing for Heaven!

This preparation for Heaven can be done only as we yield ourselves to the Holy Spirit, realizing that we have been sanctified at salvation; at the coming of Jesus we shall be totally sanctified, but until then, we are yet minors needing to grow in grace. We need to yield ourselves to the Holy Spirit day by day so that we can grow from glory to glory, from faith to faith and from grace to grace!

9

A Spirit-Controlled,
Mind-Controlled Body

II Corinthians 10:5, "Casting down imaginations, and
every high thing that exalteth itself against the knowledge of
God, and bringing into captivity every thought to the
obedience of Christ."

Man is a threefold creature. For this study we shall call him a
spirit, a mind, and a body. There are six ways that these three can
be arranged. The order of these three in a person's life will
determine what he is. Following are these six arrangements:

1. *First, spirit; second, mind; third, body.* This is the way
that the spiritual man has his priorities. The spirit controls the
mind and the mind controls the body. In other words, the mind
tells the body what to do. This is character. The mind tells the
body when to get up in the morning, when to go to bed at night,
what to eat, how much to eat, when to work, when to quit work. In
other words, the appetites of the body are controlled by the mind.
How sad it is when appetites control the body!

Not only does the mind tell the body what to do, but the spirit
tells the mind what to do. We could go a step farther and say the
spirit tells the mind what to tell the body to do. When the mind is
controlled by the spirit and the body is controlled by the mind,
then the body is controlled by the spirit. When a person's spirit
controls his mind and his mind controls his body, he has learned

something about the priorities in life.

2. ***First, spirit; second, body; third, mind.*** Notice in this arrangement, the spirit is first, so this person is saved, but his body controls his mind. The spirit tells the body what to do, but the body tells the mind what to do. This is a saved person who is spiritual and perhaps sincere, but he is unproductive. He has no schedule. He is not self-disciplined. He has no set prayer time, set Bible study time or set soul-winning time. Since he does not live by schedule, in school he will make bad grades. He will probably have no budget, so he will be in debt. Now his intentions are good. He intends to pay his debts because he knows it is right, but since the body controls the mind, he never gets around to drawing up a budget or setting a schedule. He is usually a heavy eater. Normally he is in a financial mess.

Some of the finest Christians I know have these priorities. They are sincere, they love the Lord, and if they feel an urge, they will pray. They will testify. They have a sincere devotion to Christ. They are spiritual. You will notice that the spirit is on top of the list. How tragic for such devotion to go to waste because of an unscheduled, undisciplined body which is not in subjection to the mind.

3. ***First, body; second, spirit; third, mind.*** Here is a believer. The spirit controls his mind, so he is probably saved, but his body controls his spirit. Because of this, he will no doubt have a religion that is associated with the physical. The beat of the music will be sensuous. He will want religious words set to rock music. This kind of Christian would wear excessive makeup, and to him, the charismatic movement would be appealing. Bear in mind, he is sincere, and he is probably saved, but his religion is flavored by the flesh.

4. ***First, mind; second, spirit; third, body.*** Now we are getting to the dangerous position. The mind is above the spirit and the spirit is above the body. This person is religious as is indicated

by the spirit being above the body but he is usually not willing to accept the revealed Word of God and the fundamentals of the faith. He wants to understand it all, figure it all out. He is religious, for the spirit is over the body. Yet his mind determines his religion. This becomes spiritual idolatry. He has not made with his hands a material god, but he has made his god with his mind. This group would include liberals, cultists, legalists, etc. They will follow the way that seems right to a man. You often find them lodged in theological seminaries trying to disprove the virgin birth, the bodily resurrection or the verbal inspiration of the Scriptures. They are more concerned about figuring God out than they are in believing Him. The tragic thing about this group is that they often rise to places of responsibility in educational institutions and are used by Satan to corrupt the minds of those whom they teach.

5. *First, mind; second, body; third, spirit.* This is good in one sense, because the mind is over the body. It is not good, however, because the body is over the spirit. Since the mind is over the body, this person usually has character. He is often successful. He is a decent citizen. He works hard. He pays his debts. He cares for his body. He may be a doctor, a lawyer or a successful businessman. He is what lazy folks would call an "over-achiever," but he is not saved.

One of the reasons he is not saved is because he has little confidence in those Christians who put their bodies over their minds. He goes to work earlier than the preacher does. He is a success; the preacher is not. He is disciplined; the preacher is not. He is scheduled; the preacher is not. Hence, he does not want what the preacher has because he has no confidence in the preacher as a man. He works harder in his secular work than the preacher does in his spiritual work. He works harder for the temporal than the preacher does for the eternal. Perhaps he will die and spend eternity in Hell because he, though unsaved, had his mind before his body and has little or no confidence in those Christians who have their bodies controlling their minds.

6. *First, body; second, mind; third, spirit.* Here is the most dangerous crowd. They are those who believe that anything goes. "Satisfy the physical appetites first" is their motto. "Eat, drink and be merry" is their dogma. These are they who build the permissive society and who spawn situation ethics. Their mind is above the spirit, so they have little use for God, the Bible, or for that matter, anything that is not temporal. Then because the body controls the mind, they are sensuous and dirty-minded; they yield to the beastly appetites. They make good hippies, love communal life, and are the material from which atheists are made; in general, they ruin society.

Every reader is in one of these six groups. Classify yourself. Are you that one who has a spirit-controlled, mind-controlled body where the spirit tells the mind what to do and the mind tells the body what to do? Or are you in that group where the spirit is first but the body controls the mind? You are saved but have little character. Do you find yourself in the third group where the body is first and then the spirit controls the mind? Do you find yourself looking for a religion that appeals to the senses? Are you in the group where the mind is supreme, where the mind conceives its own religion and its own dogma? Do you find yourself in the group of admirable people who have character and whose body is in subjection to the mind but have never yet yielded to the Lord Jesus Christ and made yourself right with God through His Son? Or are you a part of that crowd whose spirit is controlled by the mind and whose mind is controlled by the body? Be honest with yourself and classify your priorities. Join that disciplined, productive, spiritual group who have a spirit-controlled, mind-controlled body.

10
The Holy Spirit and Growth in Grace

Regardless of the degree of one's spiritual maturity, he is always a minor here. **Romans 8:23, "And not only they, but ourselves also, which have the firstfruits of the Spirit, even we ourselves groan within ourselves, waiting for the adoption, to wit, the redemption of our body."** Notice the word "adoption." It means "majority" or "adulthood." The child of God does not reach spiritual majority or adulthood until his body is redeemed. That time will take place when Jesus comes for us and we receive our glorified bodies. **I John 3:2, "Beloved, now are we the sons of God, and it doth not yet appear what we shall be: but we know that, when he shall appear, we shall be like him; for we shall see him as he is."** Though we cannot grow to full maturity until then, we can, nevertheless, grow as children. As long as we have this body of flesh, we will be known as children of God.

If leaving the flesh at the rapture makes us adults, then the lessening of the flesh and its influence in our lives will enable us to grow to adulthood. This is the reason that the Corinthian church members were babes. **I Corinthians 2:14, "But the natural man receiveth not the things of the Spirit of God: for they are foolishness unto him: neither can he know them, because they are spiritually discerned." I Corinthians 3:1, "And I, brethren,**

could not speak unto you as unto spiritual, but as unto carnal, even as unto babes in Christ." They were carnal. The word "carnal" means "flesh." To the degree that a Christian lives after the flesh he becomes childish. As he lives less after the flesh and more after the Spirit, though he is still a child, he does grow toward adulthood. The sad thing is that this growth is not necessarily progressive. At best, it is gradual. The growth is certainly not inevitable, and it can be reverted. In other words, a Christian can grow in grace and become more mature. He then can become less mature by living more after the flesh. Consequently, the Christian's growth in grace is in exact ratio to his walking after the Spirit and not after the flesh.

This growth in grace is a progressive one. Notice the words in **I John 3:2, "...we shall be like him; FOR we shall see him as he is."** Why shall we be like Him? Because we shall see Him as He is. We shall not see Him as He is in a full sense until the rapture, but until then, the more we can see Him as He is, the more we will be like Him, for seeing Him as He is is what makes us like Him. These words, "for we shall see Him as He is," in **I John 3:2** mean "as he shall be made manifested." The word "manifested" means "unveiled." This is like the unveiling of a statue. Day by day as we walk with God and walk in the Spirit, a little more of Christ is unveiled to us, and as we see more of Him due to this unveiling, we become more like Him. Hence, here is the divine order of growth in grace:

1. We walk with Him.
2. A little more of Him is unveiled.
3. We see Him more as He is.
4. When we see Him, we want to be like Him.
5. We then yield to the Holy Spirit, Who forms us more in the image of Christ.

Notice again, He makes us like Himself TO THE EXTENT THAT WE SEE HIM. We are as an unfinished block seeing more of the finished sculpture thereby desiring to be more like Him. With that desire and yielding, the Holy Spirit responds by making us more like Jesus.

We find then that the secret is to see Him more, for when we see Him, our appetites are whetted to be more like Him, and then the process of growth in grace is put into motion. How then may we see Him more? First and foremost, we must read and know the Word of God. If we would see Him, we must live in His Book. Second, we must walk with Him and talk with Him in prayer. The more time we spend with Him and the more we consequently see Him, the more we will become like Him. Then also, we can see Him as we walk with people who are like Him. As we see Him in others who are like Him, our desire to be like them and like Him is increased. Then, of course, a day-by-day yielding to the Holy Spirit is necessary in order that He may reveal Christ to us as we behold His glory. **II Corinthians 3:18, "Be we all, with open face beholding as in a glass the glory of the Lord, are changed into the same image from glory to glory, even as by the Spirit of the Lord."**

Now as we walk with Christ and fellowship with Him and become more like Him, we then begin to yield the fruit of the Spirit. **Galatians 5:22, 23, "But the fruit of the Spirit is love, joy, peace, longsuffering, gentleness, goodness, faith, Meekness, temperance: against such there is no law."** This fruit is not generated by human effort. It is caused by a constant walk with Christ in the Spirit so that subconsciously we take His traits upon us. One cannot love because he DECIDES to love. He walks with the Author of love, and then gradually, love is transferred to him. One cannot have peace because he decides to have peace; peace is a fruit of the Spirit. As one walks in the Spirit, he then becomes more like Him, and peace is a natural result. Through constant fellowship with Christ, as we walk in the Spirit, He rubs off on us. This process brings forth the fruit of the Spirit.

Notice it is all one fruit. The Apostle does not say, "the FRUITS of the Spirit," but rather, "the FRUIT of the Spirit." One does not work on getting love and then work on getting joy and then work on getting peace, and once he gets those, works on getting longsuffering, gentleness, goodness, faith, etc. He walks with the One Who is the embodiment of this fruit, and as one fruit, these ingredients come to us.

It is an accepted fact that constant dwelling with a person will make us take on his habits, his mannerisms, his gestures and oftentimes this even affects one's looks. Hence, we are not to seek the fruit; we are to seek HIM!

I guess the two people who have influenced me the most in my personality have been my Uncle Harvey Harris and Dr. John R. Rice. In the early days of my life, I got to know my uncle very well. His personality was contagious. The more I was with him, the more of his mannerisms I acquired.

For 22 years I spent much of my life with Dr. John R. Rice. I preached with him, shared motel rooms with him, ate meals with him, prayed with him, fellowshipped with him, and in so doing, acquired many of his mannerisms. Now, I did not TRY to do so; it just happened.

This is true concerning the fruit of the Spirit. We are not to try to obtain the fruit; we are to try to walk with Him Who possesses it in its perfection, and as we walk with Him and yield to His Spirit, the Spirit of God gives us more and more of this fruit. Now we are not to try to be like someone else; we just join their venture and let it happen. It may be that this is the most important part of education. Perhaps the most important thing obtained by formal training is not a collection of facts and the acquiring of certain knowledge, but rather the privilege of having close contact with great people. In so doing, their personalities merge with ours and we are the better for it. This is the reason young people should go to Christian schools where dedicated, Spirit-filled professors and teachers cannot only impart to them great truths but show to them the fruit of these truths in a life. Perhaps if we would spend less time wanting to be like Jesus and more time wanting to be with Him, maybe we would be more like Him. Maybe if we spent less time attempting to walk LIKE Him and more time walking WITH Him, we would then walk more like Him. Oh, yes, to be sure, we should have a desire and yearning to be like Jesus, but being like Him does not come because of a desire or yearning; it comes because we get to know Him better; perhaps by osmosis we become more like Him.

The same is true concerning walking and fellowshippping with the wrong crowd. **Galatians 5:19-21, "Now the works of the flesh are manifest, which are these; Adultery, fornication, uncleanness, lasciviousness, Idolatry, witchcraft, hatred, variance, emulations, wrath, strife, seditions, heresies, Envyings, murders, drunkenness, revellings, and such like: of the which I tell you before, as I have also told you in time past, that they which do such things shall not inherit the kingdom of God."** Most people who begin doing the works of the flesh do not start on such a path by seeking to do so. Rather, they walk with those who possess these qualities and are subconsciously affected by them until they find themselves doing the works of the flesh because of their association with those who embodied these evil deeds.

The Bible says that we are predestinated to be like Jesus. **Romans 8:29, "For whom he did foreknow, he also did predestinate to be conformed to the image of his Son, that he might be the firstborn among many brethren."** Here the word "predestinated" means "determined." The words "to be" in that verse are durative, which means, "to be being." The word "conformed" comes from two words meaning "with form." Put them together and we have, "God had determined for us to BE BEING with the form of His Son." This passage is not speaking at all about salvation; it is simply telling us that God in His foreknowledge wanted to conform us to the image of His Son and to make us like Jesus, and He is doing that now, in that we are to BE BEING like Jesus. So it is the will of God that we BE BEING like Jesus or that we become more like Him daily.

God has also predestinated us to be holy. **Ephesians 1:4, 11, "According as he hath chosen us in him before the foundation of the world, that we should be holy and without blame before** him in love: In whom also we have obtained an inheritance, being predestinated according to the purpose of him who worketh all things after the counsel of his own will." God has determined that we should be holy, or set apart. Note also **Ephesians 1:5, "Having predestinated us unto the adoption of children by Jesus Christ to himself, according to the good pleasure of his will."** The word "adoption" here means "majority" or "adulthood." God has predetermined that someday we will be adults. **Romans 8:23, "And not only they, but ourselves also, which have the firstfruits of the Spirit, even we ourselves groan within ourselves, waiting for the adoption, to wit, the redemption of our body."** Notice that this adoption comes AT THE REDEMPTION OF OUR BODIES. The redemption of our bodies comes at the rapture. So one day we will become adults. The Holy Spirit will see to it. In the meantime, God wants us to be becoming more holy all the time. This is done as we yield to the Holy Spirit.

I can recall my mother telling me when I was a little boy, "Son, I love you, but I loved you even before you were born. I loved you before I knew what you would look like, how big you would be, and what color your eyes and hair would be." Jesus is saying, "A long time before you were born, I knew you would be saved, and I loved you. Even then I determined that someday I would make you like Me and that the Holy Spirit would perform this work." He is saying, "Before you were born, I wanted you to be holy and set apart and live for the praise of God's glory."

Now the Holy Spirit's part in all of this is found in **Romans 8:13, "For if ye live after the flesh, ye shall die: but if ye through the Spirit do mortify the deeds of the body, ye shall live."** Our part is in **Romans 12:1, "I beseech you therefore, brethren, by the mercies of God, that ye present your bodies a living sacrifice, holy, acceptable unto God, which is your reasonable service."** We are to present our bodies or yield our bodies constantly a living sacrifice, holy, acceptable unto God, which is our reasonable service. The word "reasonable" here means "spiritual," which means that EVEN THIS is accomplished by the Holy Spirit.

There is one other thing that God has chosen us to do. **John 15:16, "Ye have not chosen me, but I have chosen you, and ordained you, that ye should go and bring forth fruit, and that your fruit should remain: that whatsoever ye shall ask of the Father in my name, he may give it you."** These words do not teach us that God has chosen some people to go to Heaven and some to go to Hell! Nothing is farther from the truth! They do teach us that God has chosen that each of His children should bring forth fruit. Again, this fruit is brought forth as the Holy Spirit works in our lives.

We can then say that before the foundation of the world, God ordained that those whom He knew would trust Him would have the Holy Spirit to help them to be more and more conformed to His image, that this same Holy Spirit would lead them to win others to Christ, and that this same Holy Spirit would someday present them faultless before the presence of His glory with exceeding joy. **Jude 24, "Now unto him that is able to keep you from falling, and to present you faultless before the presence of his glory with exceeding joy."** Hence, the Holy Spirit will someday make me like Jesus. Until that day, it is the plan of God that I yield to Him more and more so that He can make me more and more like Jesus, until that day when I awake in His likeness.

11
The Gifts of the Spirit

Before our Lord returned to Heaven, He told us that we would do the same works after He left that He did while He was here. **John 14:12, "Verily, verily, I say unto you, He that believeth on me, the works that I do shall he do also; and greater works than these shall he do; because I go unto my Father."** He then gave us what we call the Great Commission. **Matthew 28:19, 20, "Go ye therefore, and teach all nations, baptizing them in the name of the Father, and of the Son, and of the Holy Ghost: Teaching them to observe all things whatsoever I have commanded you: and, lo, I am with you alway, even unto the end of the world. Amen."**

It is obvious then that every believer is to do the work that Jesus did while He was on earth. We are supposed to win folks to Christ, get them baptized, and then we are to teach them how to win folks to Christ and get them baptized. This is our task. Such a task, however, is very involved. If we are going to baptize people, someone has to prepare the baptistery or find a suitable place. Someone needs to get the converts cared for concerning proper clothing for baptism. As we go forward obeying the command of our Lord, someone no doubt will become ill. They need to be cared for. As we increase in numbers, there must be buildings.

This involves finances. Some must take care of the finances. Some must take care of the buildings.

Realizing this, our Lord through His Holy Spirit, gives special gifts to believers in order that the work of evangelizing might be done more efficiently and effectively. Some of these gifts are listed in **I Corinthians 12:8-10, 28, "For to one is given by the Spirit the word of wisdom; to another the word of knowledge by the same Spirit; To another faith by the same Spirit; to another the gifts of healing by the same Spirit; To another the working of miracles; to another prophecy; to another discerning of spirits; to another divers kinds of tongues; to another the interpretation of tongues. And God hath set some in the church, first apostles, secondarily prophets, thirdly teachers, after that miracles, then gifts of healings, helps, governments, diversities of tongues."** These gifts are not given as substitutes for soul winning but rather as aids for soul winning. One of the soul winners, in addition to his winning folks to Christ, is given a gift of helps. Another, in addition to his soul winning, is given the gift of governments. Another, in addition to his soul winning, is given the gift of healing. It should be noted that soul winning is not one of the gifts. Soul winning is a command given to all believers; whereas each Christian is given a gift or different gifts in order that soul winning might be done more effectively.

How sad it is when a Christian feels that his service for God is simply the exercising of his gift! There is no need for the gift if there is not the soul winning.

It must be noted that these gifts are given by grace. It is God Who makes the decision concerning the distribution of the gifts. **I Corinthians 12:11, "But all these worketh that one and the selfsame Spirit, dividing to every man severally AS HE WILL."**

There are those who choose one of these gifts and insist that every Christian is to have a particular gift. Some say that if a person does not have one particular gift, he is not even a Christian.

Others say that the obtaining of one particular gift is an evidence of being filled with the Holy Spirit, but even a casual look at the passages in **I Corinthians 12** reveals to us that one is given one gift, another is given another gift, and another is given another gift. For example, in verse 10 it says, **"To another the working of miracles; to another prophecy; to another discerning of spirits;"** etc. It is obvious then that no one has all the gifts and there is no gift that all have.

The Bible plainly teaches how ridiculous it would be to assume that all would have the same gift. **I Corinthians 12:17, "If the whole body were an eye, where were the hearing? If the whole were hearing, where were the smelling?"** It is also evident that each of us needs the gifts of the rest of us. **I Corinthians 12:14-16, "For the body is not one member, but many. If the foot shall say, Because I am not the hand, I am not of the body; is it therefore not of the body? And if the ear shall say, Because I am not the eye, I am not of the body; is it therefore not of the body?"**

Our Lord established the New Testament church in order that the Gospel of Christ might be propagated more effectively. In a church, somebody plays the organ, somebody leads the choir, somebody cares for the church business, somebody works in the PA room, somebody teaches the Sunday school class, somebody has a special gift to pray for the sick, somebody has exceptional faith, etc. All of these gifts simply oil the machinery so that soul winning might be done more effectively. It is a sad condition when the gifts are substituted for soul winning, leaving in a real sense little need for the gifts.

Many churches are encumbered by multitudes of unnecessary committees who have been delegated responsibility of doing the work of the various gifts. When these duties have been discharged, these committees feel that they have done their work for the Lord, while an unsaved world perishes without the Gospel. There are thousands of churches all over this nation and all around the world who have treasurers, finance committees, deacon boards, music committees, Christian education committees and even committees on committees, and yet there is not one soul winner to be found! These dear saints have been deceived into believing that the using of their gifts is their main service for God. So the well-oiled machinery works beautifully while Hell enlarges herself. It is a sin; it is a shame; it is a crime that hundreds of churches in America do not baptize one convert a year.

We have our choirs, we have our Sunday schools, we have our ladies missionary groups, we even have our mission programs where we hire people to do our soul winning for us in order that we may salve and sooth our consciences. Even preachers feel that their pulpit work is the discharging of their obligation of service for God. Our churches are filled with deacons who never make an effort to tell anybody how to be saved, with musicians who never win a soul to Christ, with committee members chosen because they are wealthy or well-to-do in the community who never lift a hand to obey the great commission. To many of these affluent people, soul winning is left to a few of the old ladies, some of the overly-zealous new Christians and others who are not spiritual enough or learned enough to sit on committees and boards!

A good illustration is that of the fire department. Every fireman is hired for one main purpose, and this is to fight fires. However, in the fire station there are duties that must be performed. Suppose, for example, one fireman is given the duty of sweeping the building. Another is given the duty of cleaning the rest rooms. Another's gift is that of caring for the paper work. Now these duties are not substitutes for fire fighting.

Suppose, for example, that there is a fire alarm. A building is burning! Someone gives the signal to man the trucks. One man says, "I'm sorry; I can't go. My job is to sweep the building, and every time we come back from a fire the building is filthy. The rest of you go ahead and fight fires; I will stay here and sweep."

Another says, "I can't go either. I have noticed that the rest rooms aren't real clean, and I'm supposed to have them clean by noon every day. You fellows go ahead; my job is to clean the rest rooms."

Another says, "I have some papers that must be filled out and mailed this afternoon. It is my job to care for the paper work, you know, and besides, fires are very messy and spectacular. I believe I would rather stay here and do my paper work, and when I finish with that, I'll study the history of the fire department."

"Absurd!" you say. Yes, it is absurd, but no more absurd or ridiculous than for God's people to stay home from the battle administering their gifts when the main job of every believer is that of winning folks to Christ. While the world goes without the Gospel and people are dying and plunging into eternal torments, one stays home to perform miracles; the other stays home to prophesy; another stays home to discern spirits; another stays home to talk in some kind of a tongue; another stays home to pray for the sick; another stays home to care for the church government; another stays home to teach the Bible; another stays home to prepare the baptistery.

Now the gifts are important, but they are important ONLY as they improve our soul-winning work and help us to do the Lord's work more efficiently so we can win more souls to Christ. It must be emphasized again and again that the gifts are not given to some so that they can make it easier for others to go soul winning; the gifts are given to all so that ALL of us can make it easier for ALL OF US to go soul winning and to do it decently and in order.

There are many who choose the most glamorous of the gifts and place them in a position of importance above those gifts that are less exciting. The Apostle reminds us that every gift is necessary. **I Corinthians 12:22, 23, "Nay, much more those members of the body, which seem to be more feeble, are necessary: And those members of the body, which we think to be less honourable, upon these we bestow more abundant honour; and our uncomely parts have more abundant comeliness."**

A perfect illustration of the purpose of the gifts is given in **Mark 16:15-18, "And he said unto them, Go ye into all the**

world, and preach the gospel to every creature. He that believeth and is baptized shall be saved; but he that believeth not shall be damned. And these signs shall follow them that believe; In my name shall they cast out devils; they shall speak with new tongues; They shall take up serpents; and if they drink any deadly thing, it shall not hurt them; they shall lay hands on the sick, and they shall recover." You will notice the command in verse 15, "Go ye into all the world, and preach the gospel to every creature." In verse 17 notice the words, "follow them that believe." In verses 17 and 18 you will notice some of the things that follow those that believe: " In My name shall they cast out devils; they shall speak with new tongues; They shall take up serpents; and if they drink any deadly thing, it shall not hurt them; they shall lay hands on the sick, and they shall recover." The key word here is the word "follow." This, of course, implies that someone is going somewhere. Until one is going, he cannot be followed. Now where were these people going? The answer is in verse 15. "Go ye into all the world, and preach the gospel to every creature." Now, if we do not GO, these things do not FOLLOW. The Scripture does not say, "...these signs shall be with those that believe." It says, "...these signs shall FOLLOW them that believe." Consequently, the promises in verses 17 and 18 are only to those who are soul winning. These things are aids to soul winning. God is not admonishing us to pick up deadly serpents, nor is He admonishing us to go up and down the corridor of the hospital laying our hands on sick folks, nor is He admonishing us to speak glibly in some strange language. He is promising us that when we go and obey the commission, these things will follow us in order that they may help us while we get out the Gospel.

God is saying that, if WHILE WE ARE SOUL WINNING, a serpent bites us, God will intervene. He is saying that if, WHILE WE ARE SOUL WINNING, someone tries to poison us, God will intervene. He is teaching us that WHILE WE ARE SOUL WINNING we may come across someone who cannot understand the language in which we speak. This very thing happened on

Pentecost. There were people there from every nation under Heaven who could not understand the language in which Peter was preaching and with which the people were soul winning. **Acts 2:4-14, "And they were all filled with the Holy Ghost, and began to speak with other tongues, as the Spirit gave them utterance. And there were dwelling at Jerusalem Jews, devout men, out of every nation under heaven. Now when this was noised abroad, the multitude came together, and were confounded, because that every man heard them speak in his own language. And they were all amazed and marvelled, saying one to another, Behold, are not all these which speak Galilæans? And how hear we every man in our own tongue, wherein we were born? Parthians, and Medes, and Elamites, and the dwellers in Mesopotamia, and in Judæa, and Cappadocia, in Pontus, and Asia, Phrygia, and Pamphylia, in Egypt, and in the parts of Libya about Cyrene, and strangers of Rome, Jews and proselytes, Cretes and Arabians, we do hear them speak in our tongues the wonderful works of God. And they were all amazed, and were in doubt, saying one to another, What meaneth this? Others mocking said, These men are full of new wine. But Peter, standing up with the eleven, lifted up his voice, and said unto them, Ye men of Judæa, and all ye that dwell at Jerusalem, be this known unto you, and hearken to my words."** Notice that this gift of tongues was an aid to soul winning. It was not an end in itself to make the Christian feel better or for self-edification for the saints. It was what all the gifts are for; it was to make soul winning easier.

One Sunday morning here at the First Baptist Church of Hammond a man came to the platform during the invitation time and said, "Pastor, we have a Chinese lady here that we believe would get saved if someone could speak Chinese to her." I stopped the service and asked if anyone could speak Chinese. No one could. I told the soul winner that I was very sorry that no one in the crowd could speak Chinese. The invitation was finished, the names were read, the converts were baptized and the service was dismissed. This soul winner, who is a very fine, refined young man, came up to me after the benediction with his face as white as a ghost. He said, "Pastor, you won't believe what happened! I took the Chinese lady to the back of the auditorium, sat down beside her on a pew and told her, 'I'm going to tell you how to be saved in English even though you can't understand me.' The lady had a puzzled look on her face, pointed to her ears, and shook her head from side to side in a negative fashion." When the soul winner started talking about the plan of salvation, suddenly she brightened up, shook her head up and down affirmatively, pointed to her ears and grinned. She was understanding! God was giving her the ability to understand what the soul winner said! When the soul winner asked her to bow her head, she did! When he asked her to receive Christ, she did! As soon as she received Christ, the man talked further, but she then shook her head from side to side in a negative fashion, pointed to her ears and frowned. She no longer could understand! Now this has never happened to me, but I know the man to whom it happened, and he was as surprised as I was and as the lady was. He did not seek the gift, but God miraculously allowed that lady to understand him as he was speaking. On one other occasion the same thing happened with a Vietnamese. This is exactly what happened on Pentecost.

How tragic and how pitiful it is that so many have taken the gifts and played with them as toys and even formed movements emphasizing the gifts! When you are around these people, you can hardly start a conversation without their bringing up one of the gifts. Usually it is one of the more glamorous ones. For example, did you ever have anyone come up to you and say, "Have you been baptized by the Holy Ghost as evidenced by the gift of helps?" Of course not. Did anybody ever ask you, "Do you believe in the gifts — especially the gift of government?" Of course not. They are interested only in some kind of a movement that emphasizes one or two or three of these gifts at the expense of the others, and all the while people are perishing and plunging toward a Christless eternity without the Gospel!

Now practically, beloved Christian, let us face the issue in summary. Each of us is to give himself to soul winning. Bow your head now and promise God that you are going to obey the commission of our Lord, that you are going to start telling folks how to be saved and leading folks to Christ. Then, in your local New Testament church be faithful and busy. Do not seek a certain gift, but ask God to show you where to serve, and as He gives you a place of service, He will give you the gift to fulfill that place of service, but do not accept any place of service unless it will aid in the carrying out of the great commission — that of soul winning, baptizing and teaching, training and growing Christians to be mature so they can go soul winning, as we all together obey the command that God has given us as each of us uses what gifts God gives to us to aid all of us in pointing people from an eternity without Christ to the glories of salvation and eternal life.

There is a beautiful story in Genesis 24. Notice verses 1-4, **"And Abraham was old, and well stricken in age: and the LORD had blessed Abraham in all things. And Abraham said unto his eldest servant of his house, that ruled over all that he had, Put, I pray thee, thy hand under my thigh: And I will make thee swear by the LORD, the God of heaven, and the God of the earth, that thou shalt not take a wife unto my son of the daughters of the Canaanites, among whom I dwell: But thou shalt go unto my country, and to my kindred, and take a wife unto my son Isaac."**

In verse 2 Abraham is a beautiful type of God the Father. In verse 2 his servant is a beautiful type of the Holy Spirit. In verse 3 the wife, which was to be Rebekah, is a beautiful symbol of the bride of Christ, His believers. In verse 3 the son is a beautiful type of the Lord Jesus. The son in this case was Isaac. In verse 4 the country was a beautiful type of the world.

Abraham (representing God the Father) sent his servant (representing the Holy Spirit) back to his country (representing the world) to seek a bride (representing believers) for his son Isaac (representing Jesus). Here we have a beautiful picture of God the

Father sending the Holy Spirit to the world to choose a bride for the Lord Jesus. The Holy Spirit does this as redeemed people are filled by this selfsame Holy Spirit and go throughout the world proclaiming the Gospel of salvation through faith in Christ.

Now notice that the one main supreme task of the servant was to get a bride for his master's son. The one supreme task for the church and for the believer is to be busy in getting a bride for the Lord Jesus. In other words, our job is soul winning!

Now concerning the gifts, notice **Genesis 24:22, "And it came to pass, as the camels had done drinking, that the man took a golden earring of half a shekel weight, and two bracelets for her hands of ten shekels weight of gold."** The servant gave gifts to Rebekah, but the gifts were ONLY AIDS in helping to secure the bride. Abraham did not tell his servant to go into the far country and give out earrings and bracelets. Suppose when the servant returned to Abraham this would have happened: Abraham asked him if he got the bride. The servant said, "No, but I gave her the earrings and the bracelets." He would not have been a good servant. His job was to get the bride. The gifts were only to make it easier to get the bride.

Our Father has sent us into this world to get a bride for His Son. In an effort to help us get the bride, he has given to each of us gifts that He has chosen. These gifts are not to be used as ends in themselves but rather as helps in getting the bride. Soul winning is the main business. The gifts are to make soul winning more productive in order that we may present our souls as trophies at the feet of our Saviour at the marriage of the Lamb when the Bridegroom receives His bride.

The same thing is true concerning the FRUIT OF THE SPIRIT. Just as the gifts of the Spirit are aids in getting the bride, so is the fruit of the Spirit a manner of behavior that we are to have as we win souls. Bear in mind, the purpose of it all is to get the bride! If the servant had gone to the far country with an unkind disposition or with a sullen, discouraged or hateful manner, he would not have been successful in getting Rebekah to come to

Isaac. No doubt he was kind. No doubt he had love, joy, peace, longsuffering, gentleness, kindness, etc. However, he was not commanded to go into the far country and be kind. He was commanded to go into the far country to get the bride. Being kind was simply the manner and behavior that he was to have as he went about his mission.

The Holy Spirit is that servant. He goes into the far country working through believers. As we are used by Him in the securing of the bride for our Saviour, that is, soul winning, He gives us His fruit. Notice the singular. These are not fruits, but one fruit! This fruit is in **Galatians 5:22, 23, "But the fruit of the Spirit is love, joy, peace, longsuffering, gentleness, goodness, faith, Meekness, temperance: against such there is no law."** In other words, as we go soul winning, we are supposed to have love. As we go soul winning, we are supposed to have joy. As we go soul winning, we are supposed to have peace, longsuffering, gentleness, goodness, faith, meekness and temperance. Again this, like the gifts of the Spirit, is an aid to soul winning. A loving soul winner is a better soul winner. A happy soul winner is a better soul winner. A peaceful soul winner is a better soul winner. A patient soul winner is a better soul winner. A gentle soul winner is a better soul winner, etc.

Suppose this happened when the servant returned from the far country: Abraham asked, "Did you get the bride for Isaac?"

The servant said, "No, but I had love."

Abraham said, "But I did not send you into the far country to have love; I sent you into the far country to get a bride, and love was a tool in the securing of that bride!" Abraham asked again, "Did you get the bride?"

"No, but I had joy. I shouted, praised the Lord and rolled in the aisles while I was there!"

Abraham said, "But I didn't send you to the far country to shout and praise the Lord and roll in the aisles. I sent you to get the bride."

One day every believer shall face his Lord. The Lord shall ask,

"Where are the souls?"

Many believers will say, "I had love."

The Lord will say, "I didn't send you into the world to love. I sent you in to the world to win people to Christ, and you can win folks better with love."

Many believers will say, "But I had joy. I shouted, talked in tongues, joined the charismatic movement, and hollered, 'Hallelujah' in a fundamental Baptist church."

Then the Master shall say, "I didn't send you into the world to shout or roll in the aisle or be happy. I sent you into the world to obey Me. Happiness will help you obey me better, and obeying Me will help you to be happier. I sent you to get a bride."

Suppose a father sends his son to the grocery store to get some bread and milk. As he leaves, the father says, "Son, don't forget now to behave yourself while you are gone. I want you to be a good boy."

After a while the boy returns. The father ask, "Did you get the bread and milk?"

The boy says, "No, I didn't get the bread and milk, but I had love. I hugged the butcher, kissed the baker, walked up and down the aisles of the grocery store saying, 'I love you, I love you, I love you.' "

The father asks, "But did you get the bread and milk?"

The son replies, "No, but I had joy. I shouted in the dairy department, and I hollered 'Praise the Lord' as I walked in the store. Everybody in that store said I was the happiest boy who had ever been there."

The father asks, "But did you get the bread and milk?"

"No, Dad, but I had peace. I stopped two fights, prevented another, wore a peace symbol, carried a peace flag and sang, 'Peace in the Valley,' all the time I was in the store."

The dad asks, "But did you get the bread and milk?"

"No," replies the boy, "but I had longsuffering. There were two lines waiting to get checked out. One line had 4 people; one had 47, and I got in the long line. I waited for an hour to get checked out, and all the time I quoted the Scripture, **'And let us not be weary in well doing: for in due season we shall reap, if we faint not.'** In fact, everybody was talking about how patient I was."

The father asks, "Son, did you get the bread and milk?"

"No, but I was gentle. I helped an old lady pick up some groceries that she dropped. I helped an old man across the street. I kissed a little baby on the brow. Everybody was talking about my gentleness."

The father asks, "But son, did you get the bread and milk?"

"No, Dad, I didn't," he said, "but I was good. I read my Bible all the way, and I prayed while I was coming back home. I didn't smoke or drink or curse or go with the wrong crowd to the grocery store. Daddy, they said I was one of the best boys who ever went to that store."

The father asks, "Did you get the bread and milk?"

"No," replies the son, "but I had faith. I believed all the time I was going that I would get there, and I believed all the time I was coming back that I would get back. I believed the Word of God, and I had faith in God, and I knew God would take care of me."

The father asks, "But, son, did you get the bread and milk?"

"No, Dad, I didn't get the bread and milk, but I was meek. In fact, I told people how great God was and how little I am. I didn't boast. I even stopped a fellow in the store and confessed my sins, and I asked one of the stock boys to pray for me because I felt unworthy to be there."

The father asks, "But, son, did you get the bread and milk?"

"No," says the son, "but I had temperance. Dad, I didn't take a drink all the time I was gone. I was offered a bottle of whiskey; I was offered a martini, a bloody Mary, a screwdriver and a bottle of beer, but, Dad, I didn't drink a one. Not only that, I was temperate in everything I did while I was on my way to the store, while I was at the store, and while I came back."

"But," asks the father, "did you get the bread and the milk?"

"No," says the son, "I did not get the bread and the milk."

The father says, "Son, you have not been faithful. I did not send you to the store to love; I sent you to get the bread and milk and be loving as you did. I did not send you to the store to have joy; I sent you to the store to get bread and milk and be happy as you did. I did not send you to the store to promote peace; I sent you to the store to get bread and milk, and I wanted you to be peaceful as you did. I did not send you to the store to have patience and longsuffering; I sent you to the store to get bread and milk, but I wanted you to be patient and longsuffering as you did. I did not send you to the store to be gentle; I sent you to the store to get bread and milk, but I wanted you to be gentle as you purchased your merchandise. I did not send you to the store to be good; I sent you to the store to get bread and milk, and I wanted you to be good as you shopped. I did not send you to the store to have faith; I sent you to the store to get bread and milk, but I wanted you to have faith as you went. I did not send you to the store to have meekness; I sent you to the store to get bread and milk, but I wanted you to be meek as you went. I did not send you to the store to be temperate; I sent you to the store to get bread and milk, and I wanted you to be temperate as you went. Son, you are not a good son. You have the fruit, but you did not obey my command."

One day we shall stand before God. The command of our Lord is clear and plain. We are to do the works that Jesus did. **John 14:12, "Verily, verily, I say unto you, He that believeth on me, the works that I do shall he do also; and greater works than these shall he do; because I go unto my Father."** Jesus came to seek and to save the lost. **Luke 19:10** says **"For the Son of man is come to seek and to save that which was lost."** We are commanded to go into all the world and preach the Gospel to every creature. **Mark 16:15, "And he said unto them, Go ye into all the world, and preach the gospel to every creature."** We are commanded to go into the world and teach all nations. **Matthew 28:19, "Go ye therefore, and teach all nations, baptizing them in the name of the Father, and of the Son, and of the Holy**

Ghost." However, as we go, God has said, "I want to make it an effective ministry and an effective endeavor, so I'm going to give gifts to My people so that the soul-winning job may be more efficient and more effective, and I'm going to give you the fruit of the Spirit so that you may be loving, happy, peaceful, gentle and patient as you go."

How sad we will be if we face our Lord having played with the gifts as toys and having used the fruit without obeying the simple and yet direct command of our Lord! It is our job to obey the command given to every one of us and then to receive the gifts given to each one of us severally as the Lord wills and to ask the Holy Spirit to go with us, imparting to us the fruit of the Spirit, so that we may efficiently and graciously bring back the bride so that one day we can lay the trophies of the souls that we have won at the feet of Jesus and hear Him say, "Well done."

12
The Quiet Work of the Holy Spirit

Sometimes we preachers do an injustice to our hearers. We love to share with our congregations the unusual stories. We love to tell of the startling conversions and the spectacular experiences.

One day I was visiting on the north side of Hammond. A tall man came to the door. I told him who I was. He said that he had company. The truth is, he had 13 people in his living room. I told him, "My name is Jack Hyles," and immediately he began to mock and make fun. He looked at his guests and sarcastically said, "Hey, folks, here's old Hyles, the biggest fake in town."

I told him I wished he hadn't said that. He said, "Oh, Hyles, everybody in town knows you are a fake."

I said, "Sir, I wish you wouldn't call me a fake. I am sincere from the crown of my head to the soles of my feet."

He said, "Hey, folks, old Hyles is a fake!"

Suddenly I said, "Sir, you'll be sorry if you say that one more time."

He said, "What are you going to do, Hyles, if I say it one more time?"

I said, "I'm going to pray for God to kill you." (I had never done anything like that in my life! I was shocked to hear myself say it! I could not believe what I was hearing!)

He then looked at his guests and said, "Folks, old Hyles is threatening me." Then again he said, "You're a fake, Hyles!"

Very quietly I put my hand on his head and began to pray something like this: "Dear Lord, Thou the God of Abraham, Isaac and Jacob, Thou the God Who made the sun to stand still for Joshua, the God Who parted the Red Sea for Moses, the God Who created the entire universe, I pray that in Jesus' name, right now, You would . . ."

"Hold it, Hyles! Hold it!" he interrupted.

I kept on praying. "Dear Lord, I pray You'll . . ."

Then the man said, "You ain't no fake. Hyles, you ain't no fake. You ain't no fake."

This is the kind of story we love to tell. It is the only one like it in my life, but it did happen, and this is the kind we love to tell.

Years ago in Garland, Texas, a very fashionable lady visited our services. Her married daughter was saved, and other members of her family had come to Christ, but she gave no sign of any desire to receive Christ as Saviour. I prayed for her and witnessed to her. She came to our services over and over and over again. Finally one Sunday night during the invitation, I tiptoed back while every head was bowed and said to her, "Wouldn't you like to be a Christian?"

She said, "Yes, I would, but I don't feel anything."

I said, "Come down the aisle. Let's kneel and pray at the altar."

She said, "I would, but I don't feel anything. When I get saved, I want to feel it."

I told her she didn't have to feel it, but she had to put her faith in Christ and that faith would be counted for her righteousness. She chuckled and said, "But I don't feel anything, and I'm not going to walk down the aisle until I feel it. When I get saved, I want to feel it."

Suddenly I looked up at her and said, "If I guaranteed you a feeling, would you come down the aisle?"

She glibly responded that she would. I said, "Then come on."

We went to the altar. She knelt and made the sign of the cross, and then I prayed something like this: "Dear God, I pray that You would give this lady a feeling. I pray You would help her to trust You and know that she is saved, but I pray in Jesus' name You would help her to be saved tonight." Then I said, "You pray."

"But," she said, "I don't feel anything."

I said, "Pray anyway!"

She said, "What should I pray?"

I said, "Pray, 'Lord, be merciful to me a sinner, and save my soul.' "

She prayed just about these words: "Dear Lord, I don't feel anything and this is silly, but the Preacher said pray, so here goes! Dear Lord . . . be merciful . . . to me . . . Lord, I'm beginning to feel it . . . a sinner, and save my soul. Lord, I feel it now! I feel it! I feel it! I feel it! Lord, I feel it!"

This is the kind of story we like to tell, and this is the kind of experience that we use for illustrations in our sermons. Perhaps we do our audiences an injustice, for the usual work of the Spirit is a quiet one. The illustrations used above are the exceptions to the rule rather than the rule. They are the unusual, not the usual! The usual is a very quiet working of the Spirit of God that brings about salvation or some blessing of victory for the child of God.

Notice the name, "Holy Spirit." The word "Holy" means "sanctifying." The word "Spirit" comes from the Greek word which means "wind" or "blown wind" or "breath." Put the two together and you get "sanctifying breath," or "blown apart" (from the world, from some sin, or from some temptation).

The question then comes, "How does a person get 'blown' by the Spirit?" The answer is that he yields. **Galatians 5:17, 18, "For the flesh lusteth against the Spirit, and the Spirit against the**

flesh: and these are contrary the one to the other: so that ye cannot do the things that ye would. But if ye be led of the Spirit, ye are not under the law."

This is how a person gets saved: He is going against the wind. He yields, and the Holy Breath or the Holy Wind brings him to God through Christ.

This is the way a person lives a Spirit-filled life: He yields to the Holy Spirit, and the Holy Breath of God blows him and thereby moves him as He wills.

There are three enemies of the Christian: the world, the flesh and the Devil, but the Holy Breath, or Holy Spirit, is blowing the other way. When we yield to Him, He quietly, as a soft wind, controls our lives. Of course, the key word is YIELD!

It is true that sometimes the Holy Spirit blows like a tornado, hurricane or a mighty gale, but normally He blows very quietly and goes about His work of directing the affairs of our lives in a very quiet, unobtrusive manner.

A seed is planted in the ground. It is not seen, but it is doing its work. There is no fanfare, no noise and nothing visible, but one day soon a little plant opens the earth and pushes its way out. This is the way the Holy Spirit works in His normal ministry. A seed is planted and then one day we begin to notice its fruit.

A germ enters the body. The germ is not seen and the person does not immediately have symptoms of an illness or disease. This does not, however, mean that the germ is not working. The germ goes about its work in a quiet way; then come the chills, the headache, the fever, the sore throat, etc. The Holy Spirit works much the same way in His normal operation.

A prescription is given for medicine to fight the germ. The medicine is taken. There is no immediate sign that it has helped, but it does its work as quietly as did the germ. The medicine fights the infection and then, after some hours or maybe even days, the patient feels better. Notice that he felt quite the same when he first took the medicine, but by faith he took it.

When a person comes to Christ and yields to Him by faith, he may or may not feel differently. The main thing is: Did he trust the finished work of the Saviour? The Holy Spirit quietly enters. If you ask the person if the Holy Spirit is within him, he may say, "I don't know." (If he does answer in the affirmative, it is simply because somebody has told him or he has read it in the Bible and believed it.) Then soon evidences of the Holy Spirit begin to appear. There is a desire to read the Bible, a desire to pray, a lessening desire for things of the world. What has happened? The Holy Spirit was doing His quiet work.

When a couple first hears the news that a baby is coming, it is exciting and thrilling. However, the wife was expecting weeks before they found out about it. The evidence and manifestation came later.

This is not to say that instantaneous, overwhelming demonstrations of the Holy spirit can never happen. Quite to the contrary! Some marvelous instantaneous victories have dotted the ministry of this preacher, but for every one like that, there have been hundreds of sweet, calm conversions and decisions whose genuineness has been proven by the fruit that they bore in subsequent days, weeks and years.

In the matter of salvation there are often startling, Saul-of-Tarsus-like conversions, whereas most conversions are more like Matthew, who simply left all and followed Jesus.

Over a quarter of a century ago as I went soul wining one night in Garland, Texas, I made two visits. The first visit was very spectacular. The man received Christ. When he did, he jumped up, hugged his wife, shouted, hugged the children, clapped his hands, jumped up on the sofa and had a real spell! My, what a time we had! I left the place praising God for His wonderful power. I then drove across town and visited another man. He came to the door. I told him who I was. He said, "Sit down." But he didn't sit down! He stood up leaning against the door. (I did not know until later that he had a bad back." He was as matter of fact as a person could be. In fact, he was a bit abrupt and nearly rude at times.

I said, "Sir, do you know if you died tonight you would go to

Heaven?"

He replied, "No!"

I said, "Would you like to know?"

He replied, "Yes!"

I said, "If I showed you how you could know, would you do what the Bible says?"

He replied, "Yes!"

I told him the plan of salvation as best I could and showed him in the Bible the wonderful story of Christ. Then I asked him, "Do you realize that you are a sinner? "

Abruptly he replied, "Yes!"

I asked, "Do you know that if you died tonight, you would go to Hell?"

Without any emotion at all he replied, "Yes!"

I then asked, "Do you realize Jesus Christ came to the earth as the virgin-born Son of God, lived a perfect life, fulfilled the law, went to the cross, bore your sins in His body, was buried and rose again after three days and three nights?"

He abruptly said, "Yes."

I then asked, "Do you believe that if you would receive Him as your Saviour by faith now, that He would make you His child?"

He said, "Yes!"

All of this transpired in the coldest, most unemotional manner that you can imagine. I said, "Could we kneel and pray? "

He said, "You kneel. I have a bad back." He leaned against he door. I prayed. I asked him to pray.

He said as coldly as anybody could ever say in a prayer, "Lord, be merciful to me a sinner and save my soul. Amen."

I felt nothing but doubt, and so I said, "Sir, were you sincere?"

He replied coldly, "Yes."

I asked, "Where would you go if you died now?"

Matter-of-factly he replied, "Heaven."

I said, "How do you know?"

He looked at me through stern-looking eyes and said, "The Bible says it, doesn't it?"

I said, "Yes, and if you're sincere, you got it."

I walked away from the house filled with doubt about his sincerity. The first man who shouted came to church the next Sunday and was baptized. He lasted about four weeks. The last man, whom I doubted, has now for 25 years been a faithful, loyal servant of God.

The same is true concerning healing. I keep a little bottle of olive oil in my office, and I pray for the sick when they come and seek to be anointed. Some marvelous answers to prayer have taken place. At least three ladies have been healed of brain tumors immediately. (At least the next x-rays showed so.) One little boy was healed from a hole in his heart. There have been many other wonderful, miraculous demonstrations of God's power in the human body. I do not know how many young couples have come to my office who have been told by doctors that they could not have children and whom I have anointed with oil and prayed for, only to find within a few weeks or months that God was going to give them their own baby. These are the kind we all enjoy and the kind we like to have. However, the usual healing is a very quiet one. It may be that the Holy Spirit enters the body and there is no visible change or no immediate evidence of healing, but like the medicine that fights the germ, like the seed that pushes its way toward the daylight, the Holy Spirit continues to do His job.

The same is true concerning the fulness of the Holy Spirit. All of us like to read about Moody's marvelous filling when he was walking down Wall Street in New York City one day and was overcome by the power of God. He rushed to a friend's home and asked to be alone with God. God's power was so mighty upon him that he had to ask God to withhold Himself, and he was never the same.

We like the startling experiences such as that of Christmas Evans, who was riding his horse on his circuit one day when suddenly he was knocked off the horse by the power of the Holy Spirit. He fell to his knees and was then and there filled for the first time with the Holy Spirit!

We love to read of those amazing experiences like that of John Wesley, who on October 3, 1738, at 3:00 a.m. in a prayer meeting with many pastors, was filled with the Holy Spirit for the first time. We love to read about George Fox, who went alone, fasted and prayed for two weeks and came back with the mighty power of God upon him; or that of George Whitefield, who was filled with the Holy Spirit on June 20, 1736, when he was being ordained and Bishop Benson laid his hands on the young preacher.

These experiences are wonderful, but the truth is, many people are filled with the Holy Spirit and know it who have had a much quieter experience than Moody, Evans, Wesley, Fox and Whitefield. There was Billy Sunday, who always preached his sermons with his Bible open to **Isaiah 61:1, "The Spirit of the LORD God is upon me; because the LORD hath anointed me to preach good tidings unto the meek; he hath sent me to bind up the brokenhearted, to proclaim liberty to the captives, and the opening of the prison to them that are bound."** John Rice, Bob Jones, Sr. and countless thousands of others have known the fulness of the Holy Spirit because they kept pleading and begging for God's power. Quietly, but definitely that power came and they knew the mighty power of the fulness of the Holy Spirit.

In my life, it was much more spectacular than that. I fell on the grave of my drunkard father and told God I would not leave until something happened to me. I do not know how long I was there, but I knew that for the first time in my life, the power of God came upon me and I was filled with the Holy Spirit. I have many friends who are filled with the Holy Spirit who did not have such a startling experience as I had, but they have pleaded with Him, met His conditions and claimed His power, and God has seen fit to give them Spirit-filled lives and ministries.

How then can a person without a startling experience know that he is filled? The truth is that the startling experience does not give evidence that one is filled, nor for that matter, does it give evidence that one is saved. The evidence is seen later in soul winning, preaching and teaching, as God works in the hearts of men as they serve Him.

Many people, especially young preachers, spend too much time wanting an experience and pleading to God for that experience when they should be pleading to God for power. I'll be happy to bypass the experience in order to see hundreds of sinners come to Christ. Far better it is to have the sinners saved without the startling experience than to have the experience and not have the evidence of the fulness of power!

This author would suggest that every believer read the Scriptures in the Bible that deal with the power of the Holy Spirit. Then several times a day yield to Him. Then many times a day pray for the power of God. Then I would suggest that there be seasons of prayer, sometimes at night, sometimes an hour, sometimes 30 minutes, sometimes a few hours, but definite seasons of prayer when the Christian begs for the power of the Holy Spirit. Then if the power begins to come, don't go around announcing it! It will be obvious. You don't have to speak of it!

After I was filled with the Holy Spirit on the grave of my father, I waited its proof through my ministry, not just through a spectacular, emotional experience. Oh, but blessed be God, the evidence has come, and through these years the mighty power of God has rested upon the ministry of this simple servant of God.

Beloved reader, do not seek the emotion. Accept it with joy when it comes, but do not seek it. Seek the power of God for soul winning and for the changing of the lives of men, women, boys and girls. If God wants to give it to you in a spectacular fashion with a light from Heaven or the rushing mighty wind, splendid; but if God wants to do to you like He did to Billy Sunday, John Rice, Bob Jones, Sr. and others, just thank God for the evidence of His power and that He has given you His fulness.

Remember, the Holy Spirit sometimes comes as a rushing mighty wind, a tornadic blast or a hurricane, but usually He comes with a soft breeze. Whichever way it is, let us thank Him that He has made available to us a miraculous power that can be used by mortals like you and me to change the eternal destinies of human souls and lives!

13

The Holy Spirit
and Divine Appointments

One of the most wonderful things about walking in the Spirit is that He makes appointments for us in a miraculous way so that the Spirit-filled Christian will cross the paths of those who need help and salvation. I am sure that in Acts 8 Philip had some doubts when the Holy Spirit told him to leave the great meetings he was having in Samaria when he was preaching to great crows and go to the desert. However, Philip being sensitive to the leadership of the Holy Spirit, obeyed and there God had made a prior appointment for him to talk to an Ethiopian eunuch. **Acts 8:29, "Then the Spirit said unto Philip, Go near, and join thyself to this chariot."** The word "join" in this verse implies "glue" or "cement." God had previously appointed that Philip be "glued" to this man who needed the Saviour. Wonderful and many are such appointments when a person walks in the Spirit!

Recently in a sermon that I was preaching at the First Baptist Church of Hammond, I stopped and made the statement with a loud voice, "Suicide is not the answer!" Later, in another state a man was in the act of committed suicide when he heard that statement from that sermon on a tape recorder. His life was spared! God planned it so!

Years ago a man in Fort Worth, Texas, was driving to work. While on the freeway that morning this unsaved man turned on his radio and heard me preaching. The man in his natural state was offended by my preaching and turned off the radio. The next morning he was curious to know what I was preaching about, so again he turned on his radio to the station on which I was preaching. Again he was offended. He cursed and turned off his radio. The third morning he went through the same procedure, but as he reached down to turn off the radio, I said, "Hold it, fellow, driving down the freeway, don't touch that radio!" He was so startled that he pulled his hand away from the dial. Then I said, "Now pull the car over beside the freeway and park." He did. Then I said, "Get out of the car." He did. I then said, "Now get on your knees and ask Christ to come into your heart." He did. I knew nothing about the story, but the last Sunday that I was pastoring in Garland, Texas, this man made a special trip to Miller Road Baptist Church to tell me this amazing story and to thank me for being faithful to follow the leadership of the Holy Spirit. Several years later I was in Fort Worth, Texas, preaching. This same man came up to me and told me that he was now pastoring a Baptist church. Wonderful are the appointments that the Holy Spirit makes for the one who walks in the Spirit.

Recently on an airplane I won a 90-year-old lady to Jesus. When we arrived at our destination she looked at me through tears and said, "God put you in that seat." Yes, God did, and God put her in her seat, for I had asked the Holy Spirit to lead me. He had made a divine appointment for me with the lady who needed Jesus.

Many such appointments are recorded in the Scriptures. In Acts 10 Peter was sent to the house of Cornelius. In John 4 Jesus met the woman at Sychar's well. These are beautiful illustrations of the appointments that God makes for the Christian who walks in the Spirit.

Sometimes the Holy Spirit will lead us positively. At other times, He will lead us negatively. **Acts 16:6, 7, "Now when they**

had gone throughout Phrygia and the region of Galatia, and were forbidden of the Holy Ghost to preach the word in Asia, After they were come to Mysia, they assayed to go into Bithynia: but the Spirit suffered them not." In these two verses we find two occasions where the Holy Spirit forbade His people to go to a certain place because He had other plans and appointments for them.

One day I was out soul winning. I was to visit a Mrs. Turner on Michigan Street. However, the next street from Michigan was Truman, and I got the words "Truman" and "Turner" mixed up, so I went to Truman Street to the same house number that I was supposed to visit on Michigan Street. A lady came to the door. I said, "Mrs. Turner?"

She said, "No, sir."

I said, "Is this a certain house number on Michigan Street?"

She said, "No, sir. This is Truman."

I said, "Oh, I'm so sorry. I made a mistake. I was going to visit a Mrs. Turner at this number on Michigan Street, and because her name and your street are similar, I got on the wrong street." I started to leave, and then I realized I should witness to this lady. I turned and said, "Ma'am, I'm Brother Hyles, Pastor of First Baptist Church of Hammond." The moment I said that, she burst into tears.

She said, "You won't believe this, mister, but just when you knocked on my door, I was on my knees asking God to send me a preacher to help me." Praise the Lord! In just a few minutes God had given her the help she needed and she trusted the Saviour.

One day I was out soul winning on the north side of Hammond. All of a sudden I felt impressed to go see a man on the south side of Hammond. However, he worked days, and I knew he would be at work. The Holy Spirit kept burning in my heart, "Go see him. Go see him."

I said to the Holy Spirit, "He works the day shift at the steel mill." I still felt impressed of the Spirit to go to the man's house. This I did. I walked up, knocked on the door, and would you believe it, he came to the door! I called him by name and said, "I've come to talk to you about Jesus."

He said, "I don't have time. I'm not supposed to be here, but I forgot something this morning and had to come back to get it so I came home to eat a bit of lunch."

I said, "Friend, let me tell you about Jesus." He was a harsh man and not in the least interested in the Gospel. He told me to leave and this I did. As I got into the car, I became overcome with emotion. I was crying uncontrollably. I went back to the man's door and knocked again. He opened the door and stared at me angrily! I fell to his feet and hugged his ankles and called him by name and said, "You've just got to get saved."

He looked down at me as I was hugging his feet and said, "Reverend, you really care, don't you?"

I said, "Sir, I'd rather see you saved today than anyone in the entire world."

He said, "I can do it when you cry." In a few moments he received Christ. That event took place about 15 years ago. Not many months ago that man went to Heaven. Thank God for divine appointments, and thank God that there is a Person Who knows all, Who is able to make those appointments for us.

The question comes, how does the Christian have the Holy Spirit make such appointments for him? The answer is in one word — yield! Every morning when I get up I bow beside my bed and yield myself to the Holy Spirit. After breakfast I do the same thing. At mid-morning, I do the same thing; after lunch, the same thing; mid-afternoon, the same thing; after the evening meal, the same thing; and then again before I go to bed, again I yield myself to the Holy Spirit. I do it seven times a day!

Oh, how many opportunities He has for us if we would only be available to Him and present ourselves for His use! Notice the sensitivity of deacon Philip to this leadership in **Acts 8:29, "Then the Spirit said unto Philip, Go near, and join thyself to this chariot."** Notice, the Holy Spirit led him specifically to the eunuch's chariot! Then when the eunuch was won to Christ, Philip was caught away by the Spirit to another place. Verse 39, **"And when they were come up out of the water, the Spirit of the Lord caught away Philip, that the eunuch saw him no more; and he went on his way rejoicing."**

Years ago when I was a lad there was one baseball player who was my hero. For years I checked his batting average every morning. Even after I became an adult and even a pastor, I continued following him with rabid enthusiasm. He is now in the Hall of Fame. Recently I was in Florida and looked up, and there he was! I had never met him. What an exciting time it was for me to shake his hand! Then the excitement intensified and increased when I told him the story of Jesus. With many people looking on, he bowed his head, prayed the sinner's prayer and trusted Christ as his personal Saviour.

Hallelujah for the Holy Spirit and the divine appointments He makes for those who will yield to Him and walk in Him and with Him!

14

Pleading for the Power
of the Holy Spirit

Luke 11:8, 13, "I say unto you, Though he will not rise and give him, because he is his friend, yet because of his importunity he will rise and give him as many as he needeth. If ye then, being evil, know how to give good gifts unto your children: how much more shall your Heavenly Father give the Holy Spirit to them that ask him?"

When a middle-easterner received guests into his home, it was the custom to set food before them. In the first 13 verses of Luke 11 we have a guest arriving at midnight. The embarrassed host had no bread to feed him, so he went to a friend at midnight and asked him if he would let him borrow three loaves of bread. The friend and his family were all asleep; consequently, he refused to be bothered. The embarrassed host, however, was unwilling to take "no" for an answer and continued to plead for bread. Though his friend would not give him the bread simply because of their friendship, verse 8 reveals that he did give him bread because of his importunity. The word "importunity" means "much begging." What he could not get just because of friendship, he could get by continuing to beg. Verse 13 teaches us that this represents the Christian begging for the power of the Holy Spirit. **"If ye then,**

being evil, know how to give good gifts unto your children: how much more shall your Heavenly Father give the Holy Spirit to them that ask him?" Note the word "ask" in verse 13. This is durative action. It means "continue to ask."

Notice verses 9 and 10, **"And I say unto you, Ask, and it shall be given you; seek, and ye shall find; knock, and it shall be opened unto you. For every one that asketh receiveth; and he that seeketh findeth; and to him that knocketh it shall be opened."** The words "ask," "seek" and "knock" are also durative action, which means that we are continually to ask for the power of the Holy Spirit!

Some would say that the power of the Holy Spirit is obtained as salvation is obtained, simply by faith. There is a basic truth that needs to be examined concerning which of the workings of the Holy Spirit are obtained instantaneously by faith and which are obtained by sincere supplication. The answer is determined by whether a certain work of the Spirit is TO us and FOR us or whether it is His working THROUGH us FOR others. Those works of His that are primarily FOR us such as salvation are given to us in response to our faith. However, when the Holy Spirit decides to work THROUGH us and to let us become partners with Him in working for others, it is a different matter! For these things He insists upon such sincerity that we demonstrate to Him our intense desire by paying a higher price than that of faith only.

If a person would come to the First Baptist Church of Hammond to be ministered TO, he simply walks in and we minister to him. If that same person is being considered for a staff position whereby he MINISTERS TO OTHERS, we would take extra care by investigating his past record; we would want references concerning his credit, his service for God, his character, etc. When we minister TO him, he simply presents himself; when we minister WITH him, he must pay a price and be the object of our intense scrutiny. When the Holy Spirit ministers TO us (as in salvation) we must simply come to Him in faith. When He ministers TO us by teaching us the Word, by leading us, by comforting us, etc., we simply come to Him by faith. If, however, we would desire to be used as an instrument OF His, there is a price that we must pay. This price, of course, includes personal separation and purity. It includes, among other things, a complete surrender to Christ. It also includes supplication, or begging for His power.

It is one thing for a son to ask his dad to drive him somewhere in the family car; it is another thing for that son to ask to USE the family car!

In the model prayer known usually as the Lord's Prayer, there are several things for which we are to ask. First, we are to ask for daily bread. The very fact that it is DAILY bread teaches that we simply ask for it and receive it. Then there is the prayer for forgiveness. God offers forgiveness to us by sincere request in faith. Then, we are to ask protection from temptation and deliverance from evil. This is received in response to our earnest request.

The lesson on prayer, however, does not end there with **Luke 11:1-4.** It goes on to the discussion of the aforementioned host who was embarrassed because he had no bread when his friend came to him at midnight. When one receives bread for himself, he may simply ask his father. When he works in the bakery, he must pay a great price of cleanliness, purity and supplication. God will not allow us to enter into His very work, and He will not impart to us the fulness of His Holy Spirit for the winning of others until we have proven our purity and our sincerity.

When our son David was a teenager he could receive his food at the table by simply saying, "Dad, pass the meat, please. Pass the bread, please." One day, however, he said to me, "Dad, could I have $20? I want to take my girlfriend out and buy her a steak." Now he got the $20, but not as easily as he got the meat and bread when he said, "Pass the food."

I said, "Twenty dollars? What are you going to do — buy that girlfriend a cow/"

He said, "Oh, come on, Dad. This is something special. Please let me have $20 so I can take my girlfriend out to eat and buy a steak."

I said, "When are you going? Where are you going? Why are you going? With whom are you going?" I then replied, "I've got to think about this, Son." He kept on begging and kept on pleading. Finally I realized how important it was to him, and I gave him the $20. It was simple for him to get bread for himself, but when I gave him that which he needed to feed another, it was another matter.

When we employ somebody to work on the staff of the First Baptist Church of Hammond, he is required to be clean. He is required to be faithful. He must share our beliefs. He must convince me of his intense desire to work with me and for me.

When God employs someone to work in His work, He also requires that one be clean, that he be faithful, that he agree with the true doctrines of the faith and that he be in agreement with what God has written in His Book.

This is why yielding and praying for His power is constantly necessary. When the Holy Spirit was ministering TO you, He did it in response to your simple faith. When He ministers WITH you, He requires that you pay a great price in your personal life and in your supplication.

15

The Mind of the Spirit

Romans 8:5-7, "For they that are after the flesh do mind the things of the flesh; but they that are after the Spirit the things of the Spirit. For to be carnally minded is death; but to be spiritually minded is life and peace. Because the carnal mind is enmity against God: for it is not subject to the law of God, neither indeed can be."

Philippians 2:5, "Let this mind be in you, which was also in Christ Jesus."

It is amazing and sad the way many people seek the leadership of God. An entire future is often based on something like opening the Bible and pointing to a verse. One man moved to the East because he pointed one day to the Scripture concerning the wise men which says, "We have seen his star in the east." Another went south because he saw the Scripture in Daniel, "The king of the south." Then there is the old story about the young man who went off to college to study to preach. He was asked why he was going to preach and he said, "God called me."

"What evidence do you have of that call," he was asked.

"Well, I was out plowing," he said, "and I saw letters written across the sky — GPC. I thought that must mean "Go preach Christ." Someone who heard him preach a while later thought it meant, "Go plow corn."

It is often difficult to find the will of God for one's life and to be sure that one is following the leadership of the Holy Spirit. One of the great secrets to being sensitive and knowledgeable concerning the will of God is to be spiritually minded. It is true that sometimes God gives wonderful revelations of His will. Such was the case when I became Pastor of the First Baptist Church of Hammond, Indiana, and such was the case when I became Pastor of the Grange Hall Baptist Church of Marshall, Texas. However, I was just as sure that God led me to the Marris Chapel Baptist Church near Bogata, Texas; to the Southside Baptist Church of Henderson, Texas; and to the Miller Road Baptist Church of Garland, Texas. However, the will of God was revealed to me in a more quiet and subtle way when I accepted these three pastorates. More often than not God uses our minds and leads them to make the right decisions. For example, I receive many times more speaking engagements than I can accept. I lay the engagements before me and ask the Holy Spirit to control my mind as I decide which ones to accept.

Sometimes God reveals in a spectacular way which sermon I am to preach, but most of the time I ask Him to control my mind as I seek the sermon He would have brought for a specific occasion.

If a decision must be made with which there is a deadline, I tell the Lord that if He will reveal to me in a special way what He wants me to do, I will do it. However, if when the deadline comes, He has not made such a revelation, I then ask Him to control my mind as I make the decision, and I believe that He does. Hence, I believe the decision is of Him.

Sometimes the Spirit leads His people in an obvious way, as in **Acts 8:29, "Then the Spirit said unto Philip, Go near, and join thyself to this chariot."** Most of the time, however, it is more like **Acts 15:28, "For it seemed good to the Holy Ghost, and to us, to lay upon you no greater burden than these necessary**

things." Notice especially the words, "It seemed good to the Holy Ghost, and to us."

A spiritually-minded person asking God to control his mind will come nearer finding the will of God and doing it than one who asks for a so-called "fleece." Entire lives have been changed by someone saying, "God, if You want me to do so-and-so, let there be three people from the east side of the auditorium saved tonight." This is dangerous and not nearly as spiritual as the decision made by one whose mind is that mind of Christ and who walks in the Spirit asking God to reveal to him His will, and who, if there is no definite revelation, gives his mind to the Holy Spirit in surrender, believing that the Holy Spirit will control his mind as he makes his decision.

'Tis blessed to read **Revelation 1:10, "I was in the Spirit on the Lord's day, and heard behind me a great voice, as of a trumpet."** Notice the words, "I was in the Spirit." This is the way to be in the will of God, letting the Holy Spirit control the mind, always being willing to follow a definite revelation, and yet always believing that the Holy Spirit will so control the mind that the decision will be His decision.

I counsel with over 150 people a week. Before a series of counseling sessions, I always kneel and say, "Holy Spirit, control my mind as I give advice to these Thy children today."

The staff members of the First Baptist Church of Hammond have often heard me pray, "Holy Spirit, control our minds and our thinking, and give us wisdom as we make the decisions that we face."

There are several things that should be done before making a decision in the Spirit.

1. *One must lose his own will.* I remember years ago when I was considering coming to Hammond, I called my dear old pastor, J. C. Sizemore, and asked his counsel. He said, "Son, the first thing you must do is lose your own will. You cannot make an intelligent, spiritual decision as long as you have a desire in the

matter."

2. *One should read the Bible excessively while seeking the will of God.* Psalm 119:105, "Thy word is a lamp unto my feet, and a light unto my path."

3. *One should spend much time alone pleading with God to reveal to him His will.*

4. *When the believer is saturated by the Word and walking with God and has lost his own will and no definite revelation of God's will has come, he should then, at the deadline, believe that God is leading him, surrendering his mind to the Holy Spirit, asking the Holy Spirit to make his decision for him and control his mind.*

5. *Then, in faith, he should make the decision; and once it is made, never doubt!*

When a young man who plans to enter into the ministry graduates from Hyles-Anderson College, he immediately begins to pray about where he should go. I advise him to ask God to lead him definitely to a place. Then I suggest that he set a reasonable deadline (perhaps 4-6 months) during which time he is to pray, live in the Word, and ask God to reveal His definite will. I often suggest to such a man that once the deadline has come, he should claim the mind of the Spirit, choose a place in faith and start a church. (There are more things involved than this, and this explanation is an oversimplified one.)

Note **Psalm 37:4, "Delight thyself also in the LORD; and he shall give thee the desires of thine heart."** Compare that with **John 15:7, "If ye abide in me, and my words abide in you, ye shall ask what ye will, and it shall be done unto you."** God is saying that there is a way He can trust us and give us what we want. It is possible for a child of God to walk in the Spirit, delighting himself in the Lord, abiding in His Word and in the Person of Christ so that he will become so in tune with God's wants that God can trust him to ask what he wants. God, in such cases, almost gives power of attorney or a blank check, for He comes to believe that some of His children are spiritually minded enough so that He can usually trust their decisions.

I often pray this prayer, "Holy Spirit, control my mind when I am choosing a route to work in the morning, or choosing an object to purchase, or choosing a seat on an airplane."

Oh, to be spiritually minded and to so walk in the Spirit until my wishes will be His wishes, my desires His desires, and my mind will be conformed to His!

16
The Liberty of the Spirit

Those who misunderstand law and grace often call those who have standards and strong convictions "legalists." In so doing, they reveal their misunderstanding of the Scriptures. A legalist is one who adds something to salvation apart from grace through faith. Legalism is adding good works, baptism, church member-ship, communion, confirmation, or confession, to faith. These sometimes sincere, but misguided ones, point us to **II Corinthians 3:17, "Now the Lord is that Spirit: and where the Spirit of the Lord is, there is liberty."** However, they do not understand its meaning. They would say that since the coming of the Holy Spirit during this age, rules are no longer important and that standards are of little value, but they misunderstand II Corinthians 3:17. They interpret the words, "Where the Spirit of the Lord is, there is liberty," to mean that where the Spirit of the Lord is, the Christian is at perfect liberty. All he must do is follow the leadership of the Holy Spirit, and this is the only law, rule or standard. They forget that the Spirit of the Lord WROTE the Book and that the Book IS Spirit! **John 6:63, "It is the spirit that quickeneth; the flesh profiteth nothing: the words that I speak unto you, they are spirit, and they are life."** Hence the Holy Spirit does not have to lead a person when He has already spoken. For example, it is very

123

plain in the Bible that the Holy Spirit wants ladies to wear modest clothing. **I Timothy 2:9, "In like manner also, that women adorn themselves in modest apparel, with shamefacedness and sobriety; not with broided hair, or gold, or pearls, or costly array."** It is likewise plain that a man is not to have long hair. **I Corinthians 11:14, "Doth not even nature itself teach you, that, if a man have long hair, it is a shame unto him?"** Now when the Spirit writes in His Book a standard or a rule, it is as much the Spirit's leading as if we ask Him in prayer to lead us in some intangible way.

These interpreters of the Bible also misunderstand the word "liberty." The liberty here is not talking about the liberty of the believer. God is not saying here that where the Spirit of the Lord is there is liberty for the believer to do as he wills. He is talking about where the Spirit of the Lord is there is liberty for the Holy Spirit to work and do as HE wills.

These students of the Bible also would lead us to believe that in this age all of the rules and standards have been broken down and that there has been a change now. They are right in one thing. There has been a change. They are wrong, however, in their teaching that God's expectations of us and from us are less than they were in the Old Testament. Notice **Romans 8:2, "For the law of the Spirit of life in Christ Jesus hath made me free from the law of sin and death."** This verse teaches us that on this side of Calvary we have moved to a new country. Hence, we are under a different law. We are now under the law of love. However, God expects more from us under the law of love than He did under the written law.

Notice **Matthew 5:17-22, "Think not that I am come to destroy the law, or the prophets: I am not come to destroy, but to fulfil. For verily I say unto you, Till heaven and earth pass, one jot or one tittle shall in no wise pass from the law, till all be fulfilled. Whosoever therefore shall break one of these least commandments, and shall teach men so, he shall be called the** least in the kingdom of heaven: but whosoever shall do and teach them, the same shall be called great in the kingdom of heaven. For I say unto you, That except your righteousness shall exceed the righteousness of the scribes and Pharisees, ye shall in no case enter into the kingdom of heaven. Ye have heard that it was said by them of old time, Thou shalt not kill; and whosoever shall kill shall be in danger of the judgment: But I say unto you, That whosoever is angry with his brother without a cause shall be in danger of the judgment: and whosoever shall say to his brother, Raca, shall be in danger of the council: but whosoever shall say, Thou fool, shall be in danger of hell fire."** Now, decide in your own mind during which age God expected the most. He tells us that under the old law man was not to kill, but under the new law a man that is angry or calls his brother a fool commits an equal sin.

Now notice **Matthew 5:27, 28, "Ye have heard that it was said by them of old time, Thou shalt not commit adultery: But I say unto you, That whosever looketh on a woman to lust after her hath already committed adultery with her already in his heart."** Under the old law man was not to commit adultery; under the new law he is not to look at a woman and lust after her in his heart. In which age does God expect the most?

Now notice **Matthew 5:31, 32, "It hath been said, Whosoever shall put away his wife, let him give her a writing of divorcement: But I say unto you, That whosoever shall put away his wife, saving for the cause of fornication, causeth her to commit adultery: and whosoever shall marry her that is divorced committeth adultery."** The old law said if a man puts away his wife, let him give her a writing of divorcement; the new law said that there is only one reason for this divorce.

Now read **Matthew 5:38-40, "Ye have heard that it hath been said, An eye for an eye, and a tooth for a tooth: But I say unto you, That ye resist not evil: but whosoever shall smite thee on thy right cheek, turn to him the other also. And if any**

man will sue thee at the law, and take away thy coat, let him have thy cloke also." Notice, the stricter law is the law of love.

Now read **Matthew 5:43, 44, "Ye have heard that it hath been said, Thou shalt love thy neighbour, and hate thine enemy. But I say unto you, Love your enemies, bless them that curse you, do good to them that hate you, and pray for them which despitefully use you, and persecute you."** Notice in how many cases our Lord reminds us that under the law of love we are to go beyond the law of the letter.

Now turn to **II Corinthians 3:6, "Who also hath made us able ministers of the new testament; not of the letter, but of the spirit: for the letter killeth, but the spirit giveth life."** These words teach us clearly that we are to do the same in this age of the law of love and the law of the spirit of life in Christ Jesus as we were to do under the law of sin and death. However, there is a DIFFERENT REASON for our actions. The letter killeth and has been pronounced guilty. Now the spirit has brought life. The law was never punished by spiritual death but by physical death. Hence, we keep it, not to avoid death but in order that we may realize the only way to receive life is through Jesus Christ. Basically, the difference between the old law and the new law is that we have just changed reasons for doing the same thing.

Here is a person who goes to work in a new job. He does his job because he has character. He doesn't particularly like his boss, but he realizes his responsibilities and fulfills them. For months he works under those conditions until one day it dawns on him that the boss is a nice person, and whereas he used to have a distaste for his boss, now he loves him. He still does the same responsibility under this newfound love that he did under his old legalism. He is doing the same thing he always did, maybe even a little more, but he has a new purpose and a new motive.

Here is a teenager who is made to iron her dad's shirts. She doesn't want to, but she has character and so she obeys the orders given to her by her parents. Then one day she gets married. Now she irons the same number of shirts that she ironed before, but she does it through love. She doesn't have the liberty to quit ironing shirts; she irons shirts just as she always did, but now she does it through love, not through the letter of the law. The same standard prevails, but there is a different reason and incentive.

The story is told of slaves who were emancipated by Abraham Lincoln and yet who chose to return to their masters and serve them as they always had. These were called bondslaves. Hence, should not we in this age have stricter standards and go beyond those of the letter of the law?

God has not changed His mind about right and wrong. What was wrong in the Old Testament is wrong in the New. What was wrong 3500 years ago is wrong today.

Now let us return to **II Corinthians 3:17, "Now the Lord is that Spirit: and where the Spirit of the Lord is, there is liberty."** We are not the ones who have that liberty mentioned in this verse; 'tis the Holy Spirit Who has the liberty to tell us what to do! This means, where the Spirit of the Lord is in a life, the Holy Spirit may feel free to have liberty to control us and to command us.

This is not our having liberty to work as we will, but the Holy Spirit having liberty to be able to work through us as HE wills.

Here is a dating couple. They think they like each other enough to go steady. The young man asks the young lady if she will give up all other young men and not go with anyone else. This she does. Then the day comes when he asks her to marry him. Now he is saying, "From now on, you go only with me." These are two ways of saying the same thing. Right and wrong have not changed, but the reason has changed.

It is necessary to begin with the law in the life of a child. We tell him he can't do this and he can't do that, and we chasten him if he disobeys. There comes a time in his life, however, when he can transfer his actions to love. He still does not do the wrong and he still does the right, but he does it because of love.

This is what the liberty of the Spirit means. When the Spirit of the Lord is present in a life, there is liberty. There is liberty for

Him to tell us what to do and what not to do. These may be things that we did not do before because of rules and standards, but in every case, the manner of behavior exceeds under the law of the Spirit of life in Christ Jesus that which was under the law of the letter.

17
The Holy Spirit, Our Comforter

John 16:7, 8, "Nevertheless I tell you the truth; It is expedient for you that I go away: for if I go not away, the Comforter will not come unto you; but if I depart, I will send him unto you. And when he is come, he will reprove the world of sin, and of righteousness, and of judgment."

One of the works of the Holy Spirit is to comfort the believer. The word "comforter" means "one to run to our side and picks us up." This is what Jesus had done while he was on the earth. **I John 2:1, "My little children, these things write I unto you, that ye sin not. And if any man sin, we have an advocate with the Father, Jesus Christ the righteous."** The word "advocate" is the same word as "comforter" in **John 16:7, 8.** Hence Jesus is our advocate, or comforter, or the one who runs to our side to pick us up. Especially was this true during His earthly life, but when He went back to Heaven, He sent us ANOTHER comforter. **John 14:16, 17 and 26, "And I will pray the Father, and he shall give you another Comforter, that he may abide with you for ever; Even the Spirit of truth; whom the world cannot receive, because it seeth him not, neither knoweth him: but ye know him; for he dwelleth with you, and shall be in you. But the Comforter, which is the Holy Ghost, whom the Father will send in my name, he shall teach you all things, and bring all things to your remembrance, whatsoever I have said unto**

you." In a sense, the Holy Spirit came to be the baby sitter for the Christians. Jesus was the One Who ran to our side; now He goes back to Heaven. He sends the Holy Spirit to do to all of us what He did when He was here.

Yet, according to **I John 2:1,** in a sense, Jesus is still our comforter, so the Holy Spirit is not exactly a substitute but an additional one to run to our side.

It is interesting to note that the word "comforter" was also used for legal aid or the counsel for the defense; so the Holy Spirit is that. Jesus is our aid at the right hand of the Father; the Holy Spirit is our aid on earth. Jesus is a positional advocate in Heaven; the Holy Spirit is a conditional advocate on earth.

Someone has described it this way. God made a will. When Jesus died, it became valid to those who trust Him. He went to Heaven as our attorney at the right hand of the Father. The Holy Spirit distributes that will for Jesus on earth. There are two things in this will. First, **Ephesians 1:7, "In whom we have redemption through his blood, the forgiveness of sins, according to the riches of his grace."** Notice the words, "The riches of His grace." This is salvation by grace through faith in the finished work of our Saviour on Calvary. Second, "the riches of His glory." **Ephesians 3:16, "That he would grant you, according to the riches of his glory, to be strengthened with might by his Spirit in the inner man."** This will come at the rapture when we see Him as He is.

Perhaps the reason Jesus had to return to Heaven was two-fold. First, He went to do His work. **Hebrews 7:25, "Wherefore he is able also to save them to the uttermost that come unto God by him, seeing he ever liveth to make intercession for them."** Second, He went to give the Holy Spirit HIS work to do.

As the comforter, there is another thing the Holy Spirit does. He helps our comforters. **John 14:18, "I will not leave you comfortless: I will come to you."** In other words, He uses human instruments to do His comforting. There are times when the Holy Spirit will comfort you Himself without human aid. There are other times when He will empower and strengthen OTHERS to say just the words you need and give you just the comfort you need. This does not mean the Holy Spirit is not doing the comforting. He is leading and strengthening someone and using him to comfort us and strengthen us in our time of need. At times He runs alongside to help and there is no human aid in sight. At other times, He leads someone to come to us to be our aid, our comforter, to pick us up. In either case, this is the work of the Spirit. He simply sometimes chooses not to use human help, and other times He chooses to do so.

In my own life there have been many times the Holy Spirit alone has been my comforter. When I paused at the casket of my unsaved father, I touched his face. It was cold and hard as a stone. Suddenly I felt a grip on my arm. I turned to see who it was, and there was no one there. I could definitely feel fingers touching my arm. It was the blessed Holy Spirit coming HIMSELF to give me comfort. Then this same Holy Spirit led the pastor to speak words of comfort to me; He led loving friends to encourage my heart. He was comforting and strengthening me both WITH and WITHOUT human instruments. The Christian should yield himself to the Holy Spirit in order that the Spirit may use him to comfort, strengthen and restore others. When the Christian writes a note of comfort, he should ask the Holy Spirit to deliver it for him and to use it as a strength and comfort. When a word of comfort or strength is spoken to a bereaved or weary friend, the power of the Holy Spirit should accompany that word. Hence, the Christian should speak to the Holy Spirit BEFORE he speaks the word of comfort, asking Him to speak words that he cannot speak and to leave impressions that he cannot leave in order that he may be used as a tool of the Holy Spirit to comfort and strengthen the discouraged, weak, lonely, bereaved or fallen brother. There is a wonderful truth in **John 14:26, "But the Comforter, which is the Holy Ghost, whom the Father will send in my name, he shall teach you all things, and bring all things to your remembrance, whatsoever I have said unto you."** Notice the words, "and bring all things to your remembrance." The Spirit-led and Spirit-filled Christian may so yield himself to the Holy Spirit that when he comforts, the Holy

Spirit will bring to mind what he ought to say. The Christian will enter into the very work of the Spirit Himself as a tool to be a comforter.

Thank God for those times the Holy Spirit Himself has come to lift me up and strengthen me and to comfort me. Thank the Lord for those times when He has touched a friend and spoken through him as a human instrument to comfort me and strengthen me and lift me up. And thank God for those times when He has used me as a tool to comfort others! Oh, Holy Spirit, use me again and again and again and again to strengthen the weak, lift up the fallen, encourage the discouraged, offer fellowship to the lonely, give a smile to the sad and comfort to the bereaved and weary.

It is interesting to note that in a sense Jesus had to leave in order for the Holy Spirit to come that the Christian might be benefitted to the fullest. For one thing, Jesus can serve us better in His glory and we can do greater works because the Holy Spirit came. **John 14:12, "Verily, verily, I say unto you, He that believeth on me, the works that I do shall he do also; and greater works than these shall he do; because I go unto my Father."** Jesus entered the very presence of the Father; at the Father's side He can help us and intercede for us. He knows our needs more. He felt them while He was here, so He can send the Holy Spirit to dispense the fulfillment of our needs. Hence, He helps the Father to know our needs. Though He doesn't have to persuade the Father to help us, He does remind Him of what we need.

When I was a young pastor, I did so many things I do not do now. I once filled the baptistery, prepared the communion cup, cooked the unleavened bread, cleaned the building, turned on the lights, built the fire, printed the church bulletin and even led the choir. However, with the passing of the years and the increasing of the church membership I have had to have others to do what I used to do. Though I miss the personal contact and many of these tasks, it is expedient for my people that I administrate so that greater works can be done than were once done when I did it all myself. I could say to my people, "It is expedient that I go to administrate, for I can send many others to do the work that I did and get more done."

There is a sense also in which the Lord Jesus can teach us better from the right hand of the Father. When He was on earth, for example, He was in the flesh. **Mark 13:32, "But of that day and that hour knoweth no man, no, not the angels which are in heaven, neither the Son, but the Father."** The word "neither" means "not yet." Jesus did not know the day nor hour of the Son of Man's coming; at least, not yet, but in His resurrection body, seated at the right hand of the Father, He would know. Consequently, from that position, He can teach us better than through His earthly body here with us.

In summary, our Lord was our comforter while He was here. Though in a sense He continues to comfort from the right hand of the Father, He has sent us the Holy Spirit to comfort us and through that Holy Spirit greater works can be done than were done when our Lord was here.

I am dictating this chapter from the Lucerne Conference Grounds in Lucerne, California. I am in my room. It is 1:30 a.m. If Jesus were in Jerusalem tonight, I would catch the first plane tomorrow morning and I would fly to see Him, but I may not get to see Him or talk to Him, for millions of others would be seeking the same privilege as I. If He were here on earth, it just may be I would never get to touch His hand, see His face or talk to Him personally, but now that He is gone and has sent the Holy Spirit, He is in this room with me in the wee hours of the morning, and I feel His presence. I can talk with Him. In this sense, it was expedient for me that He go away, for through the Holy Spirit, I can be with Jesus anywhere I am, even in the wee hours of the morning in a quiet hotel room in the mountains of northern California.

18
Spirit-Filled Listening

Much is said about Spirit-filled preaching. Many manuscripts have been written on the subject of the man of God preaching in the power of the Holy Spirit. The spiritual pastor goes to his prayer closet day after day pleading with God to give him the power of the Holy Spirit as he delivers God's message to the people. The layman in the pew prays for God to give his pastor power as he preaches. An unbelievable and justified amount of interest is shown toward this subject. The preacher prays as he enters the pulpit, "Oh, God, give me power! Give me power!" It is not unusual for us in the song service to sing, "Holy Spirit, breathe on me," or "The Comforter has come," or "Spirit of the living God, fall fresh on me." We pray, "Lord, hide our preacher behind the cross and may he preach in the power of the Holy Spirit today." Books are written, sermons are preached, lessons are taught, and publications are printed to deal with the importance of the preacher having the power of the Holy Spirit upon him as he delivers God's message.

'Tis sad but true, however, that few of us have ever heard a sermon or read a manuscript dealing with Spirit-filled listening. The Bible, however, does not neglect this subject. Great emphasis is placed on the Holy Spirit filling the listener as well as the speaker. There is an abundance of Scripture dealing with this truth.

Revelation 2:7, "HE THAT HATH AN EAR, LET HIM HEAR WHAT THE SPIRIT SAITH unto the churches; To him that overcometh will I give to eat of the tree of life, which is in the midst of the paradise of God."

Revelation 2:11, "HE THAT HATH AN EAR, LET HIM HEAR WHAT THE SPIRIT SAITH unto the churches; He that overcometh shall not be hurt of the second death."

Revelation 2:17, "HE THAT HATH AN EAR, LET HIM HEAR WHAT THE SPIRIT SAITH unto the churches; To him that overcometh will I give to eat of the hidden manna, and will give him a white stone, and in the stone a new name written, which no man knoweth saving he that receiveth it."

Revelation 2:29, "HE THAT HATH AN EAR, LET HIM HEAR WHAT THE SPIRIT SAITH unto the churches."

Revelation 3:6, "HE THAT HATH AN EAR, LET HIM HEAR WHAT THE SPIRIT SAITH unto the churches."

Revelation 3:13, "HE THAT HATH AN EAR, LET HIM HEAR WHAT THE SPIRIT SAITH unto the churches."

Revelation 3:22, "HE THAT HATH AN EAR, LET HIM HEAR WHAT THE SPIRIT SAITH unto the churches."

Note the emphasis given on the Holy Spirit and hearing in these passages. The person in the pew is just as obligated to be filled with the Spirit as he listens as is the man of God in the pulpit. For years it has been my policy to seek the Holy Spirit's power upon me as I listen to a sermon and as I listen to a special musical number. It is amazing how many times the Holy Spirit helps me understand what is being said. Then He often tells me things that are not being said. Perhaps a preacher will say something, and the Holy Spirit will remind me of another truth. He also gives me seed thoughts for sermons and Bible studies. He also applies the message to my own life, and so many times He will lift out one statement that the preacher makes that I need in a special way.

When I was a young college student, I received a call to pastor a nice church that gave me a unanimous call. Within a few days I received a call from another church asking me to be their pastor. This, however, was a call that I received by only one vote. The logical thing was to accept the church that wanted me and that extended to me a unanimous vote. For some reason, however, I felt led to wait a few days before I made the decision. I was sitting in college chapel. As I sat down I asked the Holy Spirit to give me ears to hear. While I was listening, the preacher made this statement: "Sometimes God wants us to do those things which are not logical." Immediately I knew that that was the Holy Spirit's message for me in that sermon. Immediately He told me that this was His way of letting me know that I was to go to the church where I was called by only one vote. Though the battles were many at this church, we had a wonderful ministry, and though it was a small country church, there are now 40 pastors and missionaries serving God across America and around the world who were called to preach while I was pastoring that country church. It is possible that I would not have accepted that pastorate had I not asked the Holy Spirit to fill me as I listened.

It would be a wonderful thing if God's people would plead as much for His power as they listen as the preacher pleads for the power of God as he preaches. It would be a wonderful thing if God's people would plead for the Holy Spirit to empower their listening during the congregational singing and as the special music is presented. It would be a wonderful thing if God's people would pray for the power of the Holy Spirit to be upon them as they hear the message from God's man. Think of it! A Spirit-filled preacher preaching in the power of the Holy Spirit to a Spirit-filled congregation listening in the power of the Holy Spirit — what a combination!

It is interesting to note that on the day of Pentecost it is recorded in **Acts 2:6, "Now when this was noised abroad, the multitude came together, and were confounded, because that every man heard them speak in his own language."** Notice the words, "Every man heard them speak in his own language." The emphasis here is placed on the hearing. Then in verse 8 we read, **"And how hear we every man in our own tongue, wherein we were born?"** Notice again, when these people had come together, many of them could not understand the language which was being spoken. God miraculously gave them the ability to hear the truth each in his own language. It is just as possible that the miracle was in the hearing as much or more than it was in the speaking.

A similar statement is made in **Acts 10:44, "While Peter yet spake these words, the Holy Ghost fell on all them which heard the word."** Notice the emphasis on Spirit-filled hearing.

A blessed statement is made in **Isaiah 50:4, "The Lord God hath given me the tongue of the learned, that I should know how to speak a word in season to him that is weary: HE WAKENETH MINE EAR TO HEAR AS THE LEARNED."** Notice the last statement, "He wakeneth mine ear to hear as the learned." So we find that the Holy Spirit can waken the ear to hear. We find the admonition that we are to have an ear to hear what the Spirit says. Throughout the Scriptures there is a definite emphasis placed on hearing in the Spirit, or Spirit-filled hearing.

In **I Corinthians 2:9,** the Apostle tells us, **"...Eye hath not seen, nor ear heard, neither have entered into the heart of man, the things which God hath prepared for them that love him."** Then in verse 10 so beautifully he says, **But God hath revealed them unto us by his Spirit,"** which means the Holy Spirit can let us see things that the eye cannot see and hear things that the ear cannot hear. The deep things of God come when our hearing is empowered by the Holy Spirit. How do we receive these things? This is answered explicitly in **I Corinthians 2:12, "Now we have received, not the spirit of the world, but the spirit which is of God; that we might know the things that are freely given to us of God."** Then in **I Corinthians 2:14,** we are reminded that **"the natural man receiveth not the things of the Spirit of God."** God is saying that the natural ear cannot hear all that God has for us; there is a spiritual ear and a spiritual hearing that God has for us. Oh, the things that God has to reveal to us if we would but hear!

A Christian's life could be transformed if he would enter the Sunday school class pleading for the Holy Spirit to fill him as he listens and if he would enter the preaching service likewise begging for the Holy Spirit to empower his hearing. The natural ear cannot hear all that God has for us in a spiritual song. The natural ear cannot hear all that God has for us when a Spirit-led pastor proclaims the truth of the Word of God. The natural ear cannot hear lessons that God has for us during a prelude or an offertory. There is no doubt that thousands of us have not known the will of God because we have not entered into this great blessing of listening in the Spirit. God has things for us that are beneath the surface of the spoken word. He has truths for us that cannot be comprehended by the natural ear. There is an entire new area of the Christian life awaiting that believer who will plead with God to give him ears to hear what the Spirit saith. There are unexplored depths of truth and heights of experience that God has for that believer who exchanges his casual indulgence in a spiritual service for a spiritual ear to hear what the Spirit saith as well as for the physical ear to hear what the preacher says. Such Spirit-filled listening would make baby Christians mature, prevent hundreds of church problems, prevent tragedy in the lives of God's people, and sweep thousands into the kingdom.

The word "heard" in **Acts 10:44** means "perceived." This perception is available for every believer who will plead with the Holy Spirit to give him "an ear to hear what the Spirit saith to the churches." This perception is not available to those who glibly talk to their neighbors during the offertory, thumb through the songbook during the preaching service, and lightly enjoy the surface of a special number.

The wise believer will resolve that he will ask for Holy Spirit power as he fellowships the next Lord's Day, as he participates in the congregational singing, as he quietly listens to the offertory, as he is blessed by the ministry of music, and especially as the man of God preaches God's message! Such Spirit-filled listening is life-transforming and life-changing. If, as the man of God enters the pulpit pleading for the power of the Holy Spirit as he preaches, the hearer is pleading for the power of the Holy Spirit as he listens, God can communicate to us and we can fellowship with Him in a manner maybe too unknown.

19
The Sensitivity of the Holy Spirit

Acts 8:9, 18-21, "But there was a certain man, called Simon, which beforetime in the same city used sorcery, and bewitched the people of Samaria, giving out that himself was some great one: And when Simon saw that through laying on of the apostles' hands the Holy Ghost was given, he offered them money, Saying, Give me also this power, that on whomsoever I lay hands, he may receive the Holy Ghost. But Peter said unto him, Thy money perish with thee, because thou hast thought that the gift of God may be purchased with money. Thou hast neither part nor lot in this matter: for thy heart is not right in the sight of God."

Simon the sorcerer sought to obtain the results of the Holy Spirit's power by purchasing it. The end that he sought was a noble one, but the means that he used to reach that end were carnal and wrong.

The Holy Spirit is a very sensitive person. If we try to do His work in our way, He will not do His work. He will not sing a duet; either He does the work that He is supposed to do or He quietly tiptoes away and lets us flounder with our own flimsy substitutes.

It is His job to comfort me. If I comfort myself, He will quietly tiptoe away. His departure is such a quiet one that Samson did not realize that the Holy Spirit had left him powerless. He "wist not" that the Spirit had departed from him. **(Judges 16:20)** If I comfort myself, I do it alone. If I pity myself, I do it alone. If I yield to Him for comfort, what sweet solace is the result!

It is the job of the Holy Spirit to strengthen me. If I strengthen myself, He will not do His work but will quietly tiptoe away. This does not mean that I should not stay in good health, exercise, eat right, get proper rest, etc. This is spiritual strength or spiritual power. If I supply my own power for preaching, then He will tiptoe away and quietly leave me to do it alone. If I go soul winning in my own strength, He will not argue with me or push Himself on me. He will, as a quiet peaceful dove, take His flight, leaving me to wallow in my own strength and to flounder toward failure.

He is my teacher. If I read the Bible and use my own human wisdom, He will not pursue me. He will gently take leave and allow me to study the Book alone. How foolish of me when the Author is desirous to teach me!

Many years ago Henry Ford was driving down a highway. Soon he noticed that a car had pulled off the road, that its hood was up, and its driver was attempting a repair job. Henry Ford noticed that it was a Ford car, so he thought he could help. He pulled his car behind the ill one, got out and asked the driver if he could help him. The driver, in anger, said something like this: "Old man, there's not anything that you could do that I can't do. You go your way; I'll take care of it myself." Very quietly, graciously and gently, Henry Ford got back in his car and drove off. Little did the driver realize that he had turned down the maker of the car! Certainly the maker could repair it.

The Holy Spirit comes to me and says, "I notice you are having some trouble with your life."

I say to Him, "I can make it by myself, thank You." He will very quietly and unobtrusively take His flight, and I will have turned down my Maker, certainly the only One Who can adequately do the repair!

When I teach in my own power, this sensitive One takes leave.

When I preach in my own power, He likewise departs. When I seek to make my own synthetic joy, I deprive myself of His joy. This is likewise true in teaching a Sunday school class, singing a special musical number, teaching in a Christian school, rearing a child, and in the doing of every endeavor of life pursued by the child of God.

The Holy Spirit must be invited to help. He must be invited every day. He must be invited for every task. He must have free course to do His work alone. He will not force His way to your side. He will simply tiptoe out unnoticed and will not help again unless invited. Be careful! Be careful! Do not offend Him! Do not insult Him. Invite Him into every area of your life. Depend on Him to do that which He has been ordained to do for you. Love Him, talk to Him, be friendly to Him, lest He quietly slip away and leave you to work in your own energy which is doomed to failure. Please notice **II Corinthians 3:5-7, "Not that we are sufficient of ourselves to think any thing as of ourselves; but our sufficiency is of God; Who also hath made us able ministers of the new testament; not of the letter, but of the spirit; for the letter killeth, but the spirit giveth life. But if the ministration of death, written and engraven in stones, was glorious, so that the children of Israel could not stedfastly behold the face of Moses for the glory of his countenance; which glory was to be done away."** Notice the words, "for the letter killeth, but the spirit giveth life," in verse 6. The word "letter" comes from the Greek word which means "something traced." Paul is comparing two ways of doing the same thing: first, with the Spirit; second, trying to trace it or copy it without the Spirit. It goes back to two witnesses in court. The Jewish law required two witnesses for a matter. One witness would kill the case; two witnesses held up. When we witness alone in our own energy, it actually hurts. The letter killeth. When we and the Holy Spirit witness together, it giveth life. When the Christian witnesses in the power of the Holy Spirit, conviction comes and with it comes conversion. Oftentimes the Christian who witnesses alone apart from the power of the Holy Spirit is simply used to harden the heart of the sinner. When the teacher of the Bible teaches with the Holy Spirit and His power, how exciting it is! How refreshing it is! How thrilling it becomes! Yet when the teacher of the Bible teaches in his own strength without the second witness, he becomes unbelievably boring, and the attitude is given that the Bible is boring.

When a Gospel singer sings and the Holy Spirit sings with him and through him, how heart warming, how life changing it is! But what is more formal and dead than to hear a singer just perform in his own flesh for his own glory without the Holy Spirit? There is no better example of the letter killing.

When the Holy Spirit leads us as we rear our children, what a challenge it is to them! They respond. They feel our love, our care and our concern. When the same rules are enforced by the letter and not by the Spirit, they became harsh, cruel and hard.

There is nothing more wonderful than to serve God when the Holy Spirit works through us and empowers us. There is nothing more laborious and difficult than to serve in our own strength. Every servant of God should be very, very careful to invite this dear, sensitive Holy Spirit into every endeavor of his life and should take extra care to prevent His quiet departure, leaving the Christian to serve in the letter, which killeth.

20

The Holy Spirit and the Opposite Sex

I Corinthians 6:19, 20, "What? know ye not that your body is the temple of the Holy Ghost which is in you, which ye have of God, and ye are not your own? For ye are bought with a price: therefore glorify God in your body, and in your spirit, which are God's."

I Corinthians 3:16, 17, "Know ye not that ye are the temple of God, and that the Spirit of God dwelleth in you? If any man defile the temple of God, him shall God destroy; for the temple of God is holy, which temple ye are."

II Corinthians 6:16, "And what agreement hath the temple of God with idols? for ye are the temple of the living God; as God hath said, I will dwell in them, and walk in them; and I will be their God, and they shall be my people."

The most sacred place on earth to the Jew was the temple. The most sacred place in the temple was the holy of holies. Now the building itself was not sacred. It was made so by something within the holy of holies. This was the Shekinah Glory, representing the presence of God with His people. This Glory hovered over the mercy seat.

This place was so sacred that no one could look upon it but one man. That one man was the high priest. He, on the seventh month and the tenth day of that month each year, could enter, and only then could he enter if he brought with him the blood of the sacrifice on the day of atonement. This man (the high priest) was chosen by God. Imagine how he felt! Imagine how sacred was his annual entrance through the veil into the very presence of God represented by the Shekinah Glory hovering over the mercy seat! Imagine how honored he felt! He alone was chosen by God to enter into this, the holiest place of all.

There is a New Testament temple. This is not a building made with hands. This is not a church building. So often the words, "The Lord is in His holy temple," are placed above the pulpit or at some other obvious place in the church auditorium signifying that the church is the temple and the Lord is in His holy temple; that is, the church. This is contrary to the teaching of the New Testament! God does not dwell in buildings made with hands. The New Testament temple is the body of the believer. The Samaritan woman told our Saviour, **"Our fathers worshipped in this mountain; and ye say, that in Jerusalem is the place where men ought to worship." (John 4:20)** Jesus answered her by saying, **Woman, believe me, the hour cometh, when ye shall neither in this mountain, nor yet at Jerusalem, worship the Father. Ye worship ye know not what: we know what we worship: for salvation is of the Jews. But the hour cometh, and now is, when the true worshippers shall worship the Father in spirit and in truth: for the Father seeketh such to worship him. God is a Spirit: and they that worship him must worship him in spirit and in truth." (John 4:21-24)**

Our Lord was teaching that since the veil of the temple was rent in twain from top to bottom upon the death of our Lord, no more does the Shekinah dwell in a building made with hands but that this Shekinah now dwells within the body of the believer.

So many have the concept that God lives in the church building and that the saints come for a visit every Sunday morning to that building where God lives. Because of this, the church is often erroneously decorated with worship centers, divided chancels, burning candles, etc. The church building is NOT a temple; it is what Spurgeon called "a meeting place." It is a building to protect us from the elements and to make it convenient for the temples to meet for fellowship, for strength, for teaching, for edification.

Since the body of the believer is the New Testament temple, it then becomes the most sacred thing on earth to the Christian. Hence, it should be kept clean, pure, healthy and yielded.

When I was just a little boy, my mother said to me, "Son, there is nothing on earth as sacred as the body of a girl." She would remind me that it was delicate; it was weaker than a man's body. She would teach me never to be rough with the body of a girl. Now I'm sure that I did not know why a little girl's body was so sacred and perhaps my mother did not know the full reason, though she did teach me as I got older that it was sacred because it was used of God miraculously to bring new life into the world, but I doubt if she knew about the holy of holies and the Shekinah Glory. I doubt if she knew anything about the day of atonement, the high priest, the mercy seat, the ark of the covenant, or of the cherubim made of beaten gold. She probably didn't even know about the veil of the temple that was rent in twain or the fact that the body of the believer is the New Testament temple, but she did, thank God, have enough knowledge, awareness and perhaps intuition to teach me that it was sacrilegious to misuse the body of a girl.

There are some parallels between the Old Testament temple and the sacred body of a girl.

1. *No one could look within the holy of holies except one man.* The same is true with the body of a lady. It is reserved for one man!

I am sure that many of the Jews would love to have taken a glimpse into the holy of holies. It would have been a never-to-be-forgotten experience for them. It would have been exciting and thrilling for them, but it would not have been for their best because God did not plan it so. It is also a natural thing for a young man to want to look upon the body of a young lady, but God has ordained it that young men should restrain themselves as they yield to the Holy Spirit, realizing that the body of a lady is so sacred that God has reserved it for one man.

Just as the veil of the holy of holies separated its furnishing for the eyes of the people, except for one man, even so should modest clothing separate the body of a lady from all but one man. This is why the apostle Paul wrote to Timothy instructing him that ladies wear modest apparel. **I Timothy 2:9, "In like manner also, that women adorn themselves in modest apparel, with shame-facedness and sobriety; not with broided hair, or gold, or pearls, or costly array."**

The basic difference between modest and immodest apparel in Timothy's day was that the immodest woman had a slit in the side of her long dress. As she would walk, her thigh would be revealed. This symbolized that she had something that she wanted to show; she advertised her immodesty. The modest lady did not reveal her thigh to the public. It was too holy. It was reserved for one man.

God also admonishes women not to wear men's clothing. **Deuteronomy 22:5, "The woman shall not wear that which pertaineth unto a man, neither shall a man put on a woman's garment: for all that do so are abomination unto the LORD thy God.** God is not for the unisex movement. Not only does He want the clothing of men and women to be different, but He is for a man to have short hair. **I Corinthians 11:14, "Doth not even nature itself teach you, that, if a man have long hair, it is a shame unto him?"** He is also for a woman to have long hair. **I Corinthians 11:15, "But if a woman have long hair, it is a glory to her: for her hair is given her for a covering."**

It would seem then that there should be a modesty and even somewhat a mystique concerning the human body. Wicked, modern educators speak through their ignorance of spiritual truth, and advise parents to let their children see Mom and Dad unclothed. These pseudo-scholars do not realize that such is forbidden by God. **Genesis 9:21-25, "And he drank of the wine, and was drunken; and he was uncovered within his tent. And Ham, the father of Canaan, saw the nakedness of his father, and told his two brethren without. And Shem and Japheth took a garment and laid it upon both their shoulders, and went backward, and covered the nakedness of their father; and their faces were backward, and they saw not their father's nakedness. And Noah awoke from his wine, and knew what his younger son had done unto him. And he said, Cursed be Canaan; a servant of servants shall he be unto his brethren."** There should be a modesty even within a family circle. Family members should not walk around the house in underclothing; especially is this true concerning young ladies. Their bodies are very sacred and should be reserved for that one man in all the world who is allowed to see something so sacred that it is compared to the holy of holies in the Bible.

2. *God chose that one man.* The one man that could see the holy of holies was the high priest. He was chosen by God for that specific task. The holy of holies of a young woman not only should be seen by just one man but God is the One to choose that man. For every young lady who is to marry, God has chosen the one man in all the world who is to have the right to look upon her and to love her. Because of this, a young lady should not choose her husband because he is cute, handsome, muscular, or athletic; or because he has a good personality; appeals to her physically, is educated, is wealthy or because he is talented! She is to go to her prayer closet and seek the will of God concerning her high priest, the one who is to share with her in that which is most sacred. To be sure, when God reveals to her the one who is allowed to enter into the holy of holies, He no doubt will create in her desires for him and a taste for him. Since God has created her for him and him for her, He certainly would choose someone who is pleasant to her eyes, someone whose personality would be pleasing to her and someone who would offer to her emotional, mental and

physical appeal.

The truth remains, however, that the final criterion for choosing a husband should be the will of God. From childhood a young person should pray for the Holy Spirit to lead him to the right mate, to that one person in all the world with whom he or she will become heirs together of the grace of life. **I Peter 3:7, "Likewise, ye husbands, dwell with them according to knowledge, giving honour unto the wife, as unto the weaker vessel, and as being heirs together of the grace of life; that your prayers be not hindered."**

The wise and spiritual young lady will wait until she finds the man whom God has chosen to be her high priest. She will not allow other men to see her body immodestly clothed. She will not dress to appeal to the sensuous nature of men but will rather keep her body reserved and veiled, as was the holy of holies, waiting for that one man in all the world who has been chosen by God for her.

Certainly this makes the chosen man honored and exalted. Fortunate is that woman whose high priest approaches her with all of the dignity, holiness, love and gratitude with which the high priest entered into the holy of holies. How sacred is this relationship! How beautiful it can be! How sad that wicked minds and mercenary motives have joined to commercialize something so sacred as a woman's body!

3. *Only one man was allowed to touch the furnishings of the holy of holies.* Only one man could enter; only one man could see, and only one man could touch! Uzzah was a man in the Bible who touched the sacred furnishings of the holy of holies and who immediately died because of his sin. **"And when they came to Nachon's threshingfloor, Uzzah put forth his hand to the ark of God, and took hold of it; for the oxen shook it. And the anger of the LORD was kindled against Uzzah; and God smote him there for his error; and there he died by the ark of God. And David was displeased, because the LORD had made**

a breach upon Uzzah: and he called the name of the place Perez-uzzah to this day." (II Samuel 6:6-8) Likewise the New Testament temple should be touched only by the one chosen as the one high priest. That sacred body of a lady is not only reserved for the eyes of one man and the presence of one man but for the touch of one man. Fortunate is that man who has such a temple that has been reserved for him, and fortunate is that lady who has a temple that has been reserved for her. This means that men should be very careful to be proper. "Hands off" should be the motto. Sometimes imprudent men carelessly touch the hand, arm or shoulder of a lady other than their own.

When our youngest daughter, Cindy, was married, she gave her dad quite a thrill. We were waiting just outside the door to walk the aisle. Her high priest was waiting at the altar. The music was being played. Cindy looked up and said, "Daddy, I have a wedding present to give to you."

I asked, "What is it, Puddin'?"

She said, "Daddy, in a few minutes I will become Mrs. Jack Schaap. After you pronounce us husband and wife, we will kiss. Now, Daddy, here is the wedding present: This will be the first time I have ever kissed a boy. I have wanted to, but I wanted more to give you this present." Tears filled the eyes of a happy and proud father who realized that here was a holy of holies that had been veiled from the eyes of lustful men and reserved for that chosen high priest that he alone may see, touch and enter.

A young lady came to our church during her high school years. She wanted to attend our Christian high school, but she was not allowed to do so. She did, however, vow that she would be true to Jesus as she attended a large public school in Hammond. True to Jesus she was. She carried her Bible to class. She dressed like a lady with modesty and propriety. The careless students called her "the Jesus girl." When she became a senior in high school, she was chosen as homecoming queen and was crowned as such at the homecoming football game. As she was crowned, the band played a song that they had chosen just for her to play at the homecoming game! It was "Amazing grace! how sweet the sound, that saved a wretch like me! I once was lost, but now am found; was blind, but now I see." Somehow this just seemed appropriate for "the Jesus girl."

This is just one of hundreds of examples of young ladies who have grown up in the First Baptist Church and who have believed the Pastor's teachings about the Holy Spirit and the opposite sex. These young ladies have dressed modestly. They have not worn the clothing of men. They have guarded their purity and their visibility even as God Himself guarded the holy of holies in the temple. They have realized that out yonder somewhere there was a chosen high priest who alone could see them, touch them and enter into the holy of holies. They waited for God's revelation of that chosen priest. One day God revealed to them His choice. How happy they are! How proud of them I am! How pleased the Saviour is! Their faces show true beauty. Their lives reveal the grace of God. Their husbands feel as important as Aaron felt when he approached the mercy seat inside the veil. Their pastor says, "It's all worthwhile!" Their parents feel a heavenly reward. One day these lovely, holy, young ladies can join hands with their high priest and train their children concerning the Holy Spirit and the opposite sex.

21
The Holy Spirit and Music

In the Old Testament the holy oil, representing the Holy Spirit, was poured and sprinkled on Aaron and his sons, **Exodus 30:30-33, "And thou shalt anoint Aaron and his sons, and consecrate them, that they may minister unto me in the priest's office. And thou shalt speak unto the children of Israel, saying, This shall be an holy anointing oil unto me throughout your generations. Upon man's flesh shall it not be poured, neither shall ye make any other like it, after the composition of it: it is holy, and it shall be holy unto you. Whosoever compoundeth any like it, or whosoever putteth any of it upon a stranger, shall even be cut off from his people."** No one else received this anointing. No one was allowed to make any other anointing oil, and the oil was not to be poured on a stranger. There were priests and Levites in the Old Testament chosen to minister.

Something wonderful was predicted in **Joel 2:28, 29, "And it shall come to pass afterward, that I will pour out my spirit upon all flesh; and your sons and your daughters shall prophesy, your old men shall dream dreams, your young men shall see visions: And also upon the servants and upon the handmaids in those days will I pour out my spirit."** Notice, the Holy Spirit's power is for young men and old men, for servants and handmaids. It is for all of us. As believers, we are all priests. We are all to minister.

One of the ministries of the Levites was that of singing and providing other forms of music. How sad it is when religious music depreciates and degenerates by the use of the rock beat! How sad when something so spiritual as music becomes nothing more than a concert appealing to the flesh for which tickets are sold! Can you imagine Spirit-filled New Testament believers placing a price on their music? Would God the church of the Lord Jesus Christ could return to **Colossians 3:16, "Let the word of Christ dwell in you richly in all wisdom; teaching and admonishing one another in psalms and hymns and spiritual songs, singing with grace in your hearts to the Lord."** Notice in this passage that we are to sing to each other. Singing is not just for those who have pleasant voices, and singing is not simply a display of some talent caused by the formation of a set of vocal cords.

As I grow older, I find myself bursting with song. The sad thing about it is, I am woefully lacking when it comes to singing! When I sing, David puts down his harp, Asaph resigns the choir of Heaven, the angels weep and Heaven's flag is flown at half-mast. In spite of this fact, when I am preaching I find myself unable to restrain a song. One day in a church service while I was preaching I just started to sing. Linda, our middle daughter who is married and a mother, leaned over to our youngest daughter, Cindy, who is likewise married and a mother, and said, "I just love to hear Dad sing. His voice is so . . . so . . . sincere." I am afraid that she voiced the only good quality that my voice possesses!

Note in **Colossians 3:16** the words, "teaching and admonishing." The words are important in music. It also means we are to use teaching songs in our services. Songs such as "He Leadeth Me," "Majestic Sweetness Sits Enthroned," "There Is a Fountain Filled with Blood," "The Old Account Was Settled Long Ago," and "Jesus Paid It All" teach us spiritual truths. What an improvement over the silly words that are found in the pitiful substitutes for music in this generation!

Then we are told to ADMONISH each other through our singing. This is done by such songs as "Our Best," "Tell It to Jesus," "Help Somebody Today," "Brighten the Corner Where You Are," "Rescue the Perishing," etc. The wise song leader would choose some of each of these types of songs for the church service. He could be careful to include at least one song that teaches and one song that admonishes in each service.

We are also taught concerning the use of music as it relates to the Holy Spirit in **Ephesians 5:19, "Speaking to yourselves in psalms and hymns and spiritual songs, singing and making melody in your heart to the Lord."** It is very interesting that this follows the statement in **Ephesians 5:18, "And be not drunk with wine, wherein is excess; but be filled with the Spirit."** We would be tempted to follow such a statement about Spirit-fulness with an activity such as preaching or soul winning, but the first statement that is made by the Holy Spirit after His fulness is mentioned is that of music!

Notice the three types of singing here. First, THE PSALM. There is no doubt but that the Christian should sing the Psalms. Many of them have been put to music. "In Shady Green Pastures So Rich and So Sweet, God Leads His Dear Children Along," "Surely Goodness and Mercy Shall Follow Me All the Days of My Life," and one of the verses in the song, "The Joy of the Lord Is My Strength" would be a few examples. A music director, or for that matter, a layman, could collect all of the psalms that he can find which have been put to music. They should be used.

I have found that it is easy to make up my own tune as I sing a psalm. I just make it up as I go along.

Now also notice that HYMNS are mentioned. These are songs of praise addressed to God. Songs such as "Saviour, More Than Life to Me," "Come, Thou Fount of Ev'ry Blessing," etc. These also should be a part of our musical repertoire.

We also find in **Ephesians 5:19** the mention of SPIRITUAL

SONGS. Songs like "Blessed Assurance," "At the Cross," "At Calvary," which are neither hymns nor psalms, can certainly be used with great blessing.

We have mentioned five types of songs: (1) songs that teach, (2) songs that admonish, (3) psalms, (4) hymns, and (5) spiritual songs. All of these should be included in the services of the church.

We are also told to sing to ourselves. How about singing in the bathtub, while doing the dishes, while walking, and while working! My favorite singer is me! Your favorite singer is you! I love to hear myself sing! You love to hear yourself sing!

When I get up in the morning, I always ask the Holy Spirit to give me a chorus or a song for the day. Then I hum it, whistle it and sing it throughout the day. Choruses such as "Everything's All Right in My Father's House," "Yesterday, Today, Forever, Jesus Is the Same," "Let's Talk About Jesus," "Isn't He Wonderful!" "Only Believe," etc. can be in the subconscious mind throughout the day as we hum, whistle and sing.

So many times my song or chorus for the day has been used by the Holy Spirit in a wonderful way. I had just boarded a plane in Knoxville, Tennessee. I was humming, whistling and singing, "I am so glad that my Father in Heaven tells of His love in the Book He has given. Wonderful things in the Bible I see; this is the dearest that Jesus loves me. I am so glad that Jesus loves me, Jesus loves me, Jesus loves me. I am so glad that Jesus loves me. Jesus loves even me." The stewardess approached me and said, "Mister, you sound happy."

I replied, "I certainly am."

She said, "What kind of music is that you are singing?"

Without a thought, I replied, "Rock music."

She said, "That doesn't sound like rock music. Sing some of it to me."

I sang, "ROCK of Ages, cleft for me, Let me hide myself in Thee." I also said, "It is rock and ROLL."

She said, "Where is the roll?"

I sang, "When the ROLL is called up yonder, I'll be there."

She laughed and laughed, and in a few minutes I was telling her the wonderful story of Jesus. Standing in the aisle of the plane she unashamedly bowed her head and prayed with tears moistening her eyes.

One time while I was waiting for my luggage at O'Hare Field in Chicago, I was whistling, "There's a land that is fairer than day, and by faith we can see it afar; for the Father waits over the way, to prepare us a dwelling-place there. In the sweet by and by...." An elderly man walked up to me and said, "Mister, I know that song, and what a blessing it is to hear you whistle it. You see," he said, "I have been serving as a foreign missionary for many years. My health has forced me to return home. I am in America for the first time in years, and I hunger for my field where I have served for most of my life. You have no idea what your song meant to me."

Another time I was being served in a cafeteria in Garland, Texas. I was alone, and as I pushed my tray along the counter I was whistling, "Oh, How I Love Jesus." An elderly lady who was serving my vegetables looked up, smiled and said, "I do too."

I replied, "You do what?"

She said, "I love Jesus too." I did not even know I was whistling!

Our church used to sing this little song: "Get the new look from the old Book; get the new look from the Bible. Get the new look from the old Book; get the new look from God's Word — the inward look, the outward look, the upward look, from the old, old Book. Get the new look from the old Book; get the new look from God's Word." When we would come to any word or words mentioning the Bible, such as "the old Book," we would hold our Bibles high and wave them. One day this was my song for the day. I was sitting in a restaurant in Decatur, Georgia, eating a bite and reading the newspaper. Upon finishing my meal, I folded the newspaper and began to walk back to my room. As I walked along the highway, I was humming the aforementioned song. Subconsciously, I raised the newspaper in the air every time I came to the word "Bible" or "Book." I was not even aware of it. A car stopped. The driver said, "Sir, are you trying to sell that newspaper?"

I laughed and told him our custom at our church, and then I told him of our Saviour. Beside the highway, he bowed his head and received Christ!

Recently I was on an airplane flying west. I was not aware of it, but I was humming some old songs of the faith. A well-to-do, middle-aged man sitting beside me looked over and said, "Those are the songs my mother used to sing."

I said, "Sir, do you have the faith your mother used to have?"

Through tears he said, "No, I do not."

I told him of that faith, and he received Christ on the airplane.

What a ministry music can be if we sing spiritual songs and sing them in the power of the Holy Spirit!

Spirit-filled singing played such a part in the Word of God. Of course, the Psalms formed the songbook for the Israelites. They were known as a singing people. When they were taken into captivity in Babylon, even the Babylonian people asked them to sing. **Psalm 137:3, "For there they that carried us away captive required of us a song; and they that wasted us required of us mirth, saying, Sing us one of the songs of Zion."** But, sad to say, the Israelites when they perhaps needed to sing the most hanged their harps on the willows. **Psalm 137:1, 2, "By the rivers of Babylon, there we sat down, yea, we wept, when we remembered Zion. We hanged our harps upon the willows in the midst thereof."** They refused to sing the Lord's song because they were in a strange land. **Psalm 137:4, "How shall we sing the LORD'S song in a strange land?"** Their deliverance from captivity returned their song. **Psalm 126:1, 2, "When the LORD turned again the captivity of Zion, we were like them that dream. Then was our mouth filled with laughter, and our tongue with singing: then said they among the heathen, The LORD hath done great things for them."**

When the Israelites crossed the Red Sea, they sang for joy. When God gave the victory to Barak and Deborah, the occasion was marked by singing. When our Lord observed the last supper with His apostles, the Holy Spirit reminds us, "when they had sung an hymn, they went out into the mount of Olives."

Spirit-filled music is vital to any endeavor for God. Let it not be forgotten that when the Apostle mentions being filled with the Spirit, he immediately mentions music!

22
The Holy Spirit and Oneness

II Corinthians 13:14, "The grace of the Lord Jesus Christ, and the love of God, and the communion of the Holy Ghost, be with you all. Amen."

The word "communion" in this passage means "having in common." This is the way that God has provided that Christians may live in harmony. They have something or some things in common. One of the most misunderstood passages in the Bible is **Matthew 18:19, "Again I say unto you, That if two of you shall agree on earth as touching any thing that they shall ask, it shall be done for them of my Father which is in heaven."** The word "agree" in this passage is the word from which we get our word "symphony." Basically, it implies that if two parties are in tune with the same object, they will be in tune with each other. Two violins will be in tune with each other when they are in tune with the same piano. When the believer is in tune with the Holy Spirit, he will be in tune with the other believers who are in tune with the Holy Spirit. Consequently, the believer should not be so much concerned about being in harmony with other Christians as much as he is about being harmony with the Holy Spirit. If the Holy Spirit Who leads me also leads you, we will walk together in agreement. If you and I are in tune with Him, we will be in tune with each other. If you and I have things in common with Him, we will be in common with each other.

It was said of the New Testament church that they had all things common. **Acts 2:44, "And all that believed were together, and had all things common." Acts 4:32, "And the multitude of them that believed were of one heart and of one soul: neither said any of them that ought of the things which he possessed was his own; but they had all things common."** This unity of spirit was caused because they were in tune with the same Holy Spirit. **Acts 2:46, "And they, continuing daily with one accord in the temple, and breaking bread from house to house, did eat their meat with gladness and singleness of heart."**

When Christians are all filled with the Holy Spirit, then they have a common bond and they have a third party to Whom they are tuned, making them in tune with each other. When they all go soul winning, it gives them something in common. When Christians walk in the Spirit and are in tune with Him, then they have many things that will keep them in tune with each other. When they love the same Book, delight and fellowship with the same God, walk in the same Spirit, sing the same songs, spread the same message and love the same Saviour, they find themselves in common or in communion with each other.

I John 1:7, "But if we walk in the light, as he is in the light, we have fellowship one with another, and the blood of Jesus Christ his Son cleanseth us from all sin." Notice that the first thing we are to do is walk in the light, and then as two of us walk in the same light, as a result, we have fellowship with each other.

I was born and reared in Texas. As I travel across the country, I often meet fellow-Texans. Immediately we are attracted to each other because we have something in common, a place we both love.

In World War II, I was a paratrooper. Quite often I meet ex-paratroopers in my travels. We love to sit and talk about the training, the 34-foot towers, the 300-foot towers, the 10-mile runs, the calisthenics pit, the suspension lines, the static cord, the flying boxcars and other things that we have in common. We do not simply get together and say, "Let's enjoy each other." We center our attention on something that will tune us to itself, and in the process, tune us to each other.

On my travels I meet hundreds of our graduates from Hyles-Anderson College. We don't get together and say, "Let's have communion." We get together and talk about the experiences that we have shared, the people that we both know and love, the same places that have grown dear to both of us, and in so doing, we are in communion because we have something in common.

This means that several times a day God's child should tune himself with the Holy Spirit. If every Christian would pause several times a day to get in tune with the Holy Spirit, we would not have unnecessary church splits. We would not have the gossip, the spreading of rumors, the critical natures and the slander that we have in our churches because each of us would be in tune with the same instrument.

I love a cappella music, but it does have a weakness. Even the best of singers will occasionally gradually leave the right key; whereas, if they have accompaniment, they are more likely to stay on key. The Holy Spirit is our accompaniment. He is our tuning fork.

Young couples getting married should resolve to keep in tune with the Holy Spirit so that they can keep in tune with each other. Brothers and sisters could avoid unnecessary fussing and fighting if they would stay in tune with the Holy Spirit, thereby keeping in tune with each other. Church members could love each other again. Church splits could be avoided if the church members would tune themselves with the Holy Spirit, thereby being in tune with each other. Troubles on a church staff could be prevented if each staff member would be sure that he is in tune with the Holy Spirit, making him in tune with the other staff members that are likewise in tune with the Holy Spirit. In any relationship of life, that relationship can be one of accord and peace if each of us would pause several times a day to yield to the Holy Spirit and to tune ourselves with Him.

Michelangelo said of sculpturing as he looked at a block, "It is in there; all I must do is chop off the outside." Peace, communion and oneness are in there for the child of God. All we have to do is chop off the outside. The outside is chopped off when two of us tune ourselves with the third party. This third party is the blessed Holy Spirit. As we walk in tune with Him, we keep in tune with each other.

This same method enables us to have fellowship with Jesus and with the Father. **I John 1:3, "That which we have seen and heard declare we unto you, that ye also may have fellowship with us: and truly our fellowship is with the Father, and with his Son Jesus Christ."** Since the Lord Jesus is the perfect example of being yielded to the Holy Spirit, when you and I are yielded to that same Holy Spirit, we then are in harmony and fellowship with the Lord Jesus.

23

The Holy Spirit and Fellowship Between Christians Who Are Apart

I John 1:3, 7, "That which we have seen and heard declare we unto you, that ye also may have fellowship with us: and truly our fellowship is with the Father, and with his Son Jesus Christ. But if we walk in the light, as he is in the light, we have fellowship one with another, and the blood of Jesus Christ his Son cleanseth us from all sin."

According to this passage, especially the words of verse 3, there appears to be a fellowship that believers can enjoy even though they are absent from the other. John is writing to some believers who are many miles away and he speaks in verse 3 the words, "that ye also may have fellowship with us." He implies there is a fellowship in the Spirit even across the miles. This same thing is implied in Philippians 1:3-5, "I thank my God upon every remembrance of you, Always in every prayer of mine for you all making request with joy, For your fellowship in the gospel from the first day until now." Notice in verse 5 the words, "For your fellowship in the gospel from the first day until NOW." Paul was several hundred miles from these people, and yet he said that they had fellowship continually from the first day until that very moment. Something is implied here, that if two people walk in the Spirit, they can have fellowship with each other across the miles.

Would a computer have more power than Christian fellowship? A person can punch a keyboard in a small city 2,000 miles from Chicago and get information from a central office in Chicago. Is it not possible for our Lord to give us a fellowship with each other even though we are separated by the miles? Again, I must confess that I do not completely understand this, but I do know that I feel extremely close to people that I seldom see. Some of the dearest friends that I have live hundreds of miles away and yet I feel that I know them very well. Perhaps this is the meaning of the words, "fellowship of the Spirit," found in **Philippians 2:1, "If there be therefore any consolation in Christ, if any comfort of love, if any fellowship of the Spirit, if any bowels and mercies."**

How then would this fellowship be available? First and foremost, it comes through prayer. **Hebrews 4:16, "Let us therefore come boldly unto the throne of grace, that we may obtain mercy, and find grace to help in time of need."** If I in Hammond, Indiana, come to the throne of God in prayer, and if a friend of mine on the west coast comes at the same moment to the throne of grace, are we not appearing at the same time at the throne of grace? We must understand that the Holy Spirit is everywhere, but when we pray, our spirit is carried by the Holy Spirit to the throne of grace where the Father sits, for the Father is NOT everywhere. So if two believers arrive at the throne of grace at the same time and fellowship with the same Father through the same Spirit, are they not extremely close together? When our spirit goes to the Father and is carried there by the Holy Spirit, we arrive at the throne of grace. **Hebrews 9:8, "The Holy Ghost this signifying, that the way into the holiest of all was not yet made manifest, while as the first tabernacle was yet standing."**

Perhaps there is something to this thing of two people agreeing to pray at the same time in order that they may feel closer to each other. Methinks it would not be sacrilege for a husband and wife who are separated by the miles to pray at the same time, thereby arriving at the throne of grace simultaneously. Perhaps a wife could say to the Heavenly Father at the appointed time, "Tell my husband that I love him." I think the Father would do that, don't you? The same could be true for families who have servicemen away from home, for parents who are many miles away from their children in college. It could even be a wonderful way of fellowship for young married couples, if the man works long hours or has to have two jobs in order to support the family.

Revelation 4:4, "And round about the throne were four and twenty seats: and upon the seats I saw four and twenty elders sitting, clothed in white raiment; and they had on their heads crowns of gold." This verse teaches us that our saved, departed loved ones are at the throne of God. Is there not then a sweet fellowship that we could have with them when we appear before that throne? Oh, 'tis true we cannot talk to them, and I'm not advocating such foolishness as having a séance, but there is, I think, some sweet kind of communion we can have with them and feel toward them because they are near the throne where the Holy Spirit carries us when we pray in the Spirit. There is a certain unity that we can have with believers on earth and believers in Heaven if we walk in the Spirit. **Ephesians 4:3, "Endeavouring to keep the unity of the Spirit in the bond of peace."** What a comfort and what a peace this can afford to those who are separated from loved ones who are on earth or who are in Heaven! Would it be wrong for a son to pray in the Spirit, and as the Spirit takes him to the throne of grace for him to say, "Father, tell my mother I love her." We sing the song, "Tell Mother I'll Be There." Certainly this does not do an injustice to the Scriptures.

Though no one has explored all there is to know about the subject, it nevertheless is true to some degree and in some way that people who are led by the Spirit, who pray in the Spirit and who work in the Spirit (especially those who do the same work) can know a fellowship that deepens their love for each other, even though they are separated by miles or space.

24

The Transfer of the Holy Spirit

Though it is a bit difficult to understand exactly all of the meanings involved, the patriarchs in the Bible often gathered their children and grandchildren before their death and imparted to them some kind of a blessing. This was the blessing that Jacob stole from his brother Esau when he deceived his father and received his brother's blessing.

There is also the story of Elisha receiving the mantle of Elijah before Elijah went to Heaven. Elisha told him that he wanted a double portion of his power. Elijah told Elisha that the Lord had sent him to Bethel, but Elisha would not leave him. **(II Kings 2:2)** Then Elijah announced that he was going to Jericho. Again Elisha said, **"As the LORD liveth, and as thy soul liveth, I will not leave thee." (II Kings 2:4)** Later Elijah announced that he was going to Jordan. Again Elisha said, **"As the LORD liveth, and as thy soul liveth, I will not leave thee." (II Kings 2:6)** When Elijah got to Jordan, he took his mantle, wrapped it together and smote the waters and they were divided. Elijah and Elisha went over on dry ground. When they walked over, Elijah said unto Elisha, **"Ask what I shall do for thee, before I be taken away from thee."** Elisha said, **"I pray thee, let a double portion of thy spirit be upon me."** Then Elijah said, **"...if thou see me when I am taken**

from thee, it shall be so unto thee; but if not, it shall not be so."
Consequently, Elisha stayed with Elijah until Elijah was taken into
Heaven. **II Kings 2:11-13, "And it came to pass, as they still
went on, and talked, that, behold, there appeared a chariot of
fire, and horses of fire, and parted them both asunder; and
Elijah went up by a whirlwind into heaven. And Elisha saw it,
and he cried, My father, my father, the chariot of Israel, and
the horsemen thereof. And he saw him no more: and he took
hold of his own clothes, and rent them in two pieces. He took
up also the mantle of Elijah that fell from him, and went back,
and stood by the bank of Jordan."** Then Elisha took the mantle
of Elijah that fell from him, and parted the same waters that Elijah
had parted. **II Kings 2:14, "And he took the mantle of Elijah
that fell from him, and smote the waters, and said, Where is
the LORD God of Elijah? and when he also had smitten the
waters, they parted hither and thither: and Elisha went over."**
It is a well-known fact that Elisha performed twice as many
miracles as did Elijah.

There is a similar statement at the call of Elisha in **I Kings
19:16, 19, "And Jehu the son of Nimshi shalt thou anoint to be
king over Israel: and Elisha the son of Shaphat of Abel-
meholah shalt thou anoint to be prophet in thy room. So he
departed thence, and found Elisha the son of Shaphat, who
was plowing with twelve yoke of oxen before him, and he with
the twelfth: and Elijah passed by him, and cast his mantle
upon him."**

It is not clear just exactly what happened, but there is a truth
here that should not be overlooked. There is certainly nothing
wrong when someone wants what someone else has that can be
used in service for God. Exactly what power it is that is
transferable is unclear, but it is clear that good men want to
receive some form of blessing from great men who precede them.

When Dr. Bob Jones, Sr. was in his last days, Becky, our
oldest daughter, and I went to Bob Jones University to see him.

We went in the room where he was spending his last days. We talked for a while and I asked him if he would place his hand on my head and pray that God would give me the kind of power that he had had. Oh, what a prayer as I knelt at his knees and as the dear old giant of God laid his hands on my head and prayed for God to impart to me a special blessing! I do not know exactly what happened. Maybe because of our hunger for a special blessing, God gives it to us. Perhaps we get more hungry in the presence of greatness.

When Dr. John Rice was coming toward the end of his life, again and again I would ask him to place his hand on my head and pray for me. How sacred were the hours that we spent when he was praying for God to bless me! Though I do not know exactly what happened, I do know that God blessed me. Was it because of my hunger and thirst after righteousness? Was God pouring water on him who was thirsty? I do not know, but I do believe that there is merit in a servant of God wanting to be touched by greatness so that in some way the power that rested upon an Elijah could also rest upon an Elisha.

This does not mean we are to ask God to make us like another. It does mean it is all right to ask for the power of another. Paul wrote young Timothy and told him to stir up the gift that was given him at the laying on of his hands. I am sure that the laying on of the hands had nothing to do with it, and yet there seems to be something about the touch of the man of God that God uses to bless people and oftentimes to save people and to heal people. Now the man of God does not do the saving or the healing or the blessing.

Whatever it is, let us look at those whom we admire — our pastors, our parents and other spiritual leaders and ask God to give to us the qualities that we see in them that would help us be better servants of our Lord. The wise preacher boy will watch his pastor and other great preachers carefully. The wise son will watch his father. The wise daughter will watch her mother. Even in the humblest of men and in the simplest of women there are admirable traits that should be desired by sons and daughters and sons of the prophets. As a minimum, let us hunger and thirst for the greatness that we see in others and ask God that in some way these traits of greatness and power be transferred or at least given to us.

25

What Happened at Pentecost?

Dwight L. Moody put it best when he said, "Pentecost was a specimen day." God was saying to the New Testament church, "Look, this is what you can have now." However, Pentecost has been so misunderstood, so exaggerated and so complicated that many dangerous doctrines have arisen. Let us see what the Bible says about Pentecost.

1. *Pentecost was not the founding of the church.* Note **Matthew 16:18, "And I say also unto thee, That thou art Peter, and upon this rock I will build my church; and the gates of hell shall not prevail against it."** The key word in this verse is "build." It is the Greek word that is used for building a house. To be sure, there must be a time when the house is BEGUN to be built, but it is not a house until the plans are completely made into reality. The word "build" is in a linear tense in the Greek, and our Lord is simply saying, "Upon this rock I will be building My church." The church spoken about here is not a church yet; it is a church that is BEING BUILT. Because of this, there is no such thing now as a universal church, and there is no such teaching that the body of Christ is now a church. The word "church" comes from the Greek word which means "a called-out assembly." Now since the body of Christ has not yet been called out and

assembled, it is not yet a church. Note **Hebrews 12:23, "To the general assembly and church of the firstborn, which are written in heaven, and to God the Judge of all, and to the spirits of just men made perfect."** The church of the firstborn will become exactly that when she is a called-out assembly. She becomes a called-out assembly at the rapture when all of the saved, both dead and alive, are called up in the air to assemble with Jesus. Then and then only do all believers become a church!

Much stress should be placed upon this because so many people bypass the local body of believers, which is the church of this age, or perhaps it should be said, which are the churches of this age.

The truth is that there is not one mention in the Bible of the church being founded at Pentecost. That local organization known as the New Testament church was founded sometime during the life of Jesus. **Matthew 18:15-17, "Moreover if thy brother shall trespass against thee, go and tell him his fault between thee and him alone: if he shall hear thee, thou hast gained thy brother. But if he will not hear thee, then take with thee one or two more, that in the mouth of two or three witnesses every word may be established. And if he shall neglect to hear them, tell it unto the church: but if he neglect to hear the church, let him be unto thee as an heathen man and a publican."** Here Jesus says, "Tell it unto the church." He does not say, "Tell it unto the future church"; He says, "Tell it unto the church." Hence, we know the church was in existence at the time of the writing of this chapter. Added light is given to this in **Acts 2:41, 47, "Then they that gladly received his word were baptized: and the same day there were added unto them about three thousand souls. Praising God, and having favour with all the people. And the Lord added to the church daily such as should be saved."** Note the words, "added to the church." It is impossible to add to something that is not in existence. The church was already in existence at Pentecost and people were added to it at that time. People often make light of the New Testament churches by saying they belong to the "big church" or the "church of the blood-washed," etc. These terms may be spiritual ones, but the truth is, nobody belongs to a church unless he has associated himself with a group of born-again believers such as our Lord started sometime during His earthly ministry.

The question comes, "When did He start the church?" The Bible does not say, but it is possible that in **Matthew 10** when He called His disciples and assembled them, He was starting the church at that time. It is unwise to be dogmatic about this, but it is not unwise to be dogmatic in emphasizing that the church was not started at Pentecost. It is important that this is seen because it takes away the attention from the real meaning of Pentecost — the fact that the church prayed and witnessed, 3,000 people were saved, and God gave us, as Moody said, "a specimen day."

2. *Pentecost is not the coming of the fulness of the Holy Spirit.* There are those who teach that the fulness of the Holy Spirit came for the first time at Pentecost. It is important that this error be refuted in order that we may strip away another of the distractions from what really happened at Pentecost. It is without question that the fulness of the Holy Spirit was known by many before the day of Pentecost.

John the Baptist was filled with the Holy Spirit from his mother's womb. **Luke 1:15, "For he shall be great in the sight of the Lord, and shall drink neither wine nor strong drink; and he shall be filled with the Holy Ghost, even from his mother's womb."**

Zacharias was filled with the Holy Spirit. **Luke 1:67, "And his father Zacharias was filled with the Holy Ghost, and prophesied, saying."**

Jesus was filled with the Holy Spirit. **Luke 4:1, "And Jesus being full of the Holy Ghost returned from Jordan, and was led by the Spirit into the wilderness."**

Bezaleel was filled with the Holy Spirit. **Exodus 35:30, 31,**

"And Moses said unto the children of Israel, See, the LORD hath called by name Bezaleel the son of Uri, the son of Hur, of the tribe of Judah; And he hath filled him with the Spirit of God, in wisdom, in understanding, and in knowledge, and in all manner of workmanship."

Hence, it is not difficult to see that Pentecost was not the day when Christians were first filled with the Holy Spirit.

There is no doubt that others in the Old Testament were filled with the Holy Spirit and that this fulness was simply described with other terms. In **Judges 6:34** we read that the Spirit of the Lord came upon Gideon. In **Judges 14:6** we read that the Spirit of the Lord came upon Samson. In **I Samuel 11:6** we read that the Spirit of God came upon Saul. In **I Samuel 16:13** we read that the Spirit of the Lord came upon David. All of these occasions were before Pentecost, so let us strip away another of the detractors of what really happened on Pentecost — that great specimen day when the church prayed and witnessed and 3,000 were saved.

3. *Pentecost was not the beginning of the indwelling of the Holy Spirit.* There was a time when the Holy Spirit did not indwell all believers. This coming of the Spirit to indwell God's people is taught by many to have happened at Pentecost. Yes, the Holy Spirit was promised by Jesus. **John 14:16, 17, "And I will pray the Father, and he shall give you another Comforter, that he may abide with you for ever; Even the Spirit of truth; whom the world cannot receive, because it seeth him not, neither knoweth him: but ye know him; for he dwelleth with you, and shall be in you."** He is said to indwell believers. **Romans 8:9, "But ye are not in the flesh, but in the Spirit, if so be that the Spirit of God dwell in you. Now if any man have not the Spirit of Christ, he is none of his." I Corinthians 6:19, 20, "What? know ye not that your body is the temple of the Holy Ghost which is in you, which ye have of God, and ye are not your own? For ye are bought with a price: therefore**

glorify God in your body, and in your spirit, which are God's."
This coming of the Holy Spirit to indwell believers did not,
however, happen at Pentecost. **John 7:37-39, "In the last day,
that great day of the feast, Jesus stood and cried, saying, If any
man thirst, let him come unto me, and drink. He that believeth
on me, as the scripture hath said, out of his belly shall flow
rivers of living water. (But this spake he of the Spirit, which
they that believe on him should receive: for the Holy Ghost
was not yet given; because that Jesus was not yet glorified.)"**
Notice, the Holy Spirit "was not yet given; BECAUSE THAT
JESUS WAS NOT YET GLORIFIED." In other words, the thing
that was necessary before the Holy Spirit could be given for
indwelling was that Jesus must be glorified. Hence, it was at the
resurrection of Jesus that the Holy Spirit came to indwell
believers, not at Pentecost!

Now examine **John 20:19-22, "Then the same day at
evening, being the first day of the week, when the doors were
shut where the disciples were assembled for fear of the Jews,
came Jesus and stood in the midst, and saith unto them, Peace
be unto you. And when he had so said, he shewed unto them
his hands and his side. Then were the disciples glad, when they
saw the Lord. Then said Jesus to them again, Peace be unto
you: as my Father hath sent me, even so send I you. And when
he had said this, he breathed on them, and saith unto them,
Receive ye the Holy Ghost."** Notice that Jesus came to the upper
room in His glorified body and said to His disciples, "Receive ye
the Holy Ghost," so the coming of the indwelling of the Holy
Spirit was not at Pentecost, but rather, when our Lord's body was
glorified. This may seem to the reader to be a trivial thing. It is,
however, made important by the fact that it removes another of
those things that would divert our attention from the great truth of
Pentecost, when the church prayed and witnessed and 3,000
people were saved, giving us a specimen day for the New
Testament church.

4. *Pentecost was not the beginning of a new dispensation.*

We will not enter into a dealing with the controversy over dispensationalism. This author believes, however, that it is a dangerous thing to speak of a dispensation of law and a dispensation of grace. This could lead some weak ones to believe that there was a time when men were under the law and now men are under grace. From the time that Adam and Eve offered a sacrifice which pointed to God's sacrifice of His Son that would someday come on Calvary, men have been SAVED BY GRACE.

The purpose of the law the day that it was given is STILL the purpose of the law today. The law is holy and good. **Romans 7:12, "Wherefore the law is holy, and the commandment holy, and just, and good."** The law was given in order that we may know sin. **Romans 7:7, "What shall we say then? Is the law sin? God forbid. Nay, I had not known sin, but by the law: for I had not known lust, except the law had said, Thou shalt not covet."** The law was given as a plumb line to reveal our true crookedness and as a mirror to reveal our true condition and inability to satisfy the righteousness of God. The law was given so that sin might appear to be sin. **Romans 7:13, "Was then that which is good made death unto me? God forbid. But sin, that it might appear sin, working death in me by that which is good; that sin by the commandment might become exceeding sinful."** Then we could say that though we are to attempt to keep the commandments of God, it is impossible to do so. Hence, the law was given to be broken rather than to be kept, not that God wanted us to break it, but that God knew that we were helpless to fulfill it. God, knowing that man likes to establish his own righteousness, gave us the law to reveal to us our unrighteousness and to cause us to realize that we cannot save ourselves and that in order to be saved we must come to Him Who fulfilled the law for us, even the Lord Jesus. This was the purpose of the law the day it was given, and it will be the purpose of the law until Jesus comes again.

Salvation was by grace when Adam trusted the coming Messiah by shedding the blood of an innocent substitute.

Salvation will be by grace until Jesus comes again. No one was ever saved by the keeping of the law. No one has ever kept the law. So then the law was given to show us that we could not meet the righteousness of God in ourselves, causing us to turn to Jesus Who met that righteousness for us. **Romans 10:2, 3, "For I bear them record that they have a zeal of God, but not according to knowledge. For they being ignorant of God's righteousness, and going about to establish their own righteousness, have not submitted themselves unto the righteousness of God."**

It is also a dangerous thing to talk about the seven Gospels. Though the theologian may understand what it means, the weak Christian may be deceived into thinking that there have been seven ways to be saved in the history of man. There has been only one Gospel, and there will never be another; that is, the good news that man, though he is a sinner, may be justified in the sight of God by faith in the finished work of Calvary, where our sin debt was paid by Jesus.

As was mentioned before, this is not an effort to argue the merits or demerits of dispensationalism. It is an emphatic statement that whatever dispensations there may or may not be in the Bible, no dispensation started at Pentecost! No Christian could sit down with JUST his Bible and come to that conclusion. Let us be reminded again that the issue here is not to become sidetracked on these doctrines but rather to remove those things which cloud the real meaning of Pentecost — the church prayed and witnessed and 3,000 souls were saved, giving us a specimen day for the church for this age.

5. *Pentecost was a sample day fulfilling the prophecy of Joel 2:28, 29.* **"And it shall come to pass afterward, that I will pour out my spirit upon all flesh; and your sons and your daughters shall prophesy, your old men shall dream dreams, your young men shall see visions: And also upon the servants and upon the handmaids in those days will I pour out my spirit."** This prophecy told of the age after the resurrection of our Lord when

the message of Christ would be carried to all the world and that the amazing power of the Holy Spirit would be available, not just for a Zacharias here and a John the Baptist there, but for all flesh. In other words, now all can be soul winners, all can do the work of Christ, and all are supposed to do so! **John 14:12, "Verily, verily, I say unto you, He that believeth on me, the works that I do shall he do also; and greater works than these shall he do; because I go unto my Father."** The mighty power of God became available to all. Pentecost was just the first time that this happened after the resurrection of Christ.

To conclude this discussion, it should be emphasized that the author's desire is not to divide believers concerning starting of the church, the time of the indwelling of the Spirit, etc. If differences along those lines persist, it will not destroy the spirit of the author. The intention of this discussion is to emphasize that whatever else Pentecost may or may not have been, it was, to say the least, a time of 3,000 people being saved and a time when God was saying to New Testament churches, "Look at Jerusalem on Pentecost, and you will see what is available for you during this entire age."

26
The Throne of the Holy Spirit

God the Father sits on His throne. **Psalm 11:4, "The LORD is in his holy temple, the LORD'S throne is in heaven: his eyes behold, his eyelids try, the children of men." Psalm 47:8, "God reigneth over the heathen: God sitteth upon the throne of his holiness."** God's throne is in Heaven and there He sits overseeing the universe and providing for His own people.

Jesus has a throne. **Hebrews 1:3, "Who being the brightness of his glory, and the express image of his person, and upholding all things by the word of his power, when he had by himself purged our sins, sat down on the right hand of the Majesty on high." Hebrews 8:1, "Now of the things which we have spoken this is the sum: We have such an high priest, who is set on the right hand of the throne of the Majesty in the heavens." Hebrews 10:12, "But this man, after he had offered one sacrifice for sins for ever, sat down on the right hand of God."** Notice especially the words, "sat down on the right hand of God." Much of the book of Hebrews reveals to us the priestly work of Christ as typified by the Old Testament priesthood. So as God the Father is sitting on His throne, even so, Jesus is sitting at the right hand of the Father.

The Holy Spirit has a throne. **I Corinthians 3:16, "Know ye**

not that ye are the temple of God, and that the Spirit of God dwelleth in you?" I Corinthians 6:19, "What? know ye not that your body is the temple of the Holy Ghost which is in you, which ye have of God, and ye are not your own?" The throne of the Holy Spirit is in the body of the believer.

A Christian is rightly disturbed when someone tries to sit on the throne of the Father. This is why we are admonished in **Matthew 23:9a, "And call no man your father upon the earth."** No man has a right to sit on God the Father's throne. Hence, the believer who addresses a clergyman as "father" is placing him upon a throne which he does not deserve and which is reserved only for God the Father. When such a clergyman uses such a title for himself or admonishes others to use that title toward him, he is usurping a throne which is not his. It is infinitely more sacrilegious when we choose one man in the world and call him Pope (Papa or Father). When we call him by these names, we are placing him on a throne that is not his. When we bow down before him, we are giving to him a throne which is reserved only for God the Father. When we address him as the Holy Father, we are giving to him a place reserved for no human being, but rather for our Father which is in Heaven. It is a wicked thing for one to usurp the throne of our Heavenly Father!

Likewise some have tried to sit on Jesus' throne. His position in this age is at the right hand of the Father as our priestly intercessor. **Hebrews 7:25, "Wherefore he is able also to save them to the uttermost that come unto God by him, seeing he ever liveth to make intercession for them." I Timothy 2:5, "For there is one God, and one mediator between God and men, the man Christ Jesus."** This means that our access to God is only through Jesus Christ. When we claim access to God through the virgin Mary, we are placing her on a throne that belongs only to Jesus. How sad that some have tried to put in a place reserved only for the dear Son of God this good woman who mothered the physical body of our Lord.

Likewise some attempt to find their access to God through a

clergyman. How foolish and how futile! **Hebrews 10:11, "And every priest standeth daily ministering and offering oftentimes the same sacrifices, which can never take away sins."**

A dear lady lay dying. She was a wonderful Christian. She called for her pastor to come and be with her at her Homegoing. Since he was not available, a friend called her pastor who was of a different theological persuasion. This pastor came to the bedside of the dying saint and asked her if he could absolve any of her sins before she died. With a look of Christ on her face she replied, "Yes, if you can qualify."

"What must I do to qualify?" the clergyman asked.

The little lady faintly said, "Let me see your right hand." The clergyman extended his right hand. Then she said, "Let me see your left hand." The clergyman extended his left hand. Very sweetly the dying saint said, "Sir, you cannot absolve my sins. My Saviour has scars in His hands."

A true believer abhors such an intrusion into the priestly work reserved only for our Saviour as He sits at the right hand of God.

The spiritual Christian rightly abhors another's intrusion on the throne of God the Father and another's intrusion to the position of our Saviour at the right hand of the Father. There is, however, another throne which is often usurped. This throne is that of the Holy Spirit. With righteous indignation we show our disfavor when one takes the throne of God the Father. With abhorrence we chaff when one takes the place reserved only for our Saviour, and yet multitudes of us commit a sin of equal significance when we usurp the throne of the Holy Spirit. It is the job of the blessed Spirit to lead us. **Romans 8:14, "For as many as are led by the Spirit of God, they are the sons of God."** When we lead ourselves, make our own decisions and go our own way, we are placing self at the place reserved for the Holy Spirit.

It is the work of the Holy Spirit to teach us. When we study and learn without His leading, we take a position reserved only for Him. When we sing in the flesh, preach in the flesh, teach in the flesh, pray in the flesh or witness in the flesh we are placing ourselves on His throne.

There are many other duties of the Holy Spirit. He convicts. **John 16:8, "And when he is come, he will reprove the world of sin, and of righteousness, and of judgment."** He strives. **Genesis 6:3, "And the LORD said, My spirit shall not always strive with man, for that he also is flesh: yet his days shall be an hundred and twenty years."** He regenerates. **Titus 3:5, "Not by works of righteousness which we have done, but according to his mercy he saved us, by the washing of regeneration, and renewing of the Holy Ghost."** He baptizes. **I Corinthians 12:13, "For by one Spirit are we all baptized into one body, whether we be Jews or Gentiles, whether we be bond or free; and have been all made to drink into one Spirit."** He indwells. **John 14:16, 17, "And I will pray the Father, and he shall give you another Comforter, that he may abide with you for ever; Even the Spirit of truth; whom the world cannot receive, because it seeth him not, neither knoweth him: but ye know him; for he dwelleth with you, and shall be in you."** He seals. **II Corinthians 1:21, 22, "Now he which stablisheth us with you in Christ, and hath anointed us, is God; Who hath also sealed us, and given the earnest of the Spirit in our hearts."** He assures. **Romans 8:16, "The Spirit itself beareth witness with our spirit, that we are the children of God."** He teaches. **John 16:12-14, "I have yet many things to say unto you, but ye cannot bear them now. Howbeit when he, the Spirit of truth, is come, HE WILL GUIDE YOU INTO ALL TRUTH: for he shall not speak of himself; but whatsoever he shall hear, that shall he speak: and he will shew you things to come. He shall glorify me: for he shall receive of mine, and shall shew it unto you."** He comforts. **John 14:16, 17, "And I will pray the Father, and he shall give you another Comforter, that he may abide with you for ever; Even the Spirit of truth; whom the world cannot receive, because it seeth him not, neither knoweth him: but ye know him; for he dwelleth with you, and shall be in you."** He gives gifts. **I Corinthians 12:28, "And God hath set some in the church, first apostles, secondarily prophets, thirdly teachers, after that miracles, then gifts of healings, helps, governments, diversities of tongues."** He bears fruit. **Galatians 5:22, 23, "But the fruit of the Spirit is love, joy, peace, longsuffering, gentleness, goodness, faith, Meekness, temperance: against such there is no law."** He fills. **Ephesians 5:18, "And be not drunk with wine, wherein is excess; but be filled with the Spirit."**

Hence, when the believer enters into any of these ministries reserved for the Holy Spirit, he places himself on a throne reserved for the dear Spirit of God. The believer SHOULD be concerned when the Pope or another sits on the throne of the Father. A Christian SHOULD be concerned when a clergyman sits on the throne of the Saviour. He should have EQUAL CONCERN when he himself sits on the throne of the Holy Spirit!

27
The Holy Spirit,
the Ultimate in Conviction

God is so good to us in helping us flee sin. Hence, He uses everything within His disposal to let us know that sin is wrong and is not for our own good. There are several things that God uses in a progressive way to keep us from sin and to convict us of evil.

1. *The conscience.* **Romans 2:15, 16, "Which shew the work of the law written in their hearts, their conscience also bearing witness, and their thoughts the mean while accusing or else excusing one another;) In the day when God shall judge the secrets of men by Jesus Christ according to my gospel."** The conscience is the kindergarten of conviction. It is that part of us that God has given that instinctively tells us what is wrong. It tells us what NOT to do. It is, in a sense, the accuser. When one is in a situation where he should not be, the conscience says, "You should not be here." You then obey the conscience and leave. Being the kindergarten of conviction, the conscience does not tell you where to go when you leave the undesirable place.

The conscience says, "You shouldn't do that," so you quit, but it does not tell you what you SHOULD do. The Bible teaches us that the conscience can become seared and depraved. **Hebrews**

9:14, "How much more shall the blood of Christ, who through the eternal Spirit offered himself without spot to God, purge your conscience from dead works to serve the living God?" Consequently, one should be very sensitive to his conscience and obey that righteous instinct not to do evil.

2. *The Bible.* **Romans 7:13, "Was then that which is good made death unto me? God forbid. But sin, that it might appear sin, working death in me by that which is good; that sin by the commandment might become exceeding sinful."** Conscience tells us what NOT to do; the Bible does THAT AND MORE. Not only does it tell us what NOT to do, but it reminds us of the exceeding sinfulness of sin. Then it adds WHAT to do and gives us prin-ciples and examples to tell us how to do good, the blessings of doing good and the consequences of doing evil. The conscience says, "You should not be here," and stops there. The Bible comes along and says, "You should not be here, but this is the TYPE PLACE you should be." Now the Bible does not give us the EXACT place, but it does give us the TYPE place that we should go. The conscience says, "You should not do this." The Bible comes along and says. "That's right. You should not do that, and this is the type thing you should do." It does, however, stop short of telling us EXACTLY what good thing to do and WHERE TO DO IT.

The conscience says, "You are in the wrong neighborhood." The Bible comes along and underlines the words of the conscience and goes farther and says, "Not only should you not be in this neighborhood, but this is the type neighborhood to which you should go." In a sense, the Bible then becomes the grade school of conviction.

3. *Jesus.* **Luke 2:34, 35, "And Simeon blessed them, and said unto Mary his mother, Behold, this child is set for the fall and rising again of many in Israel; and for a sign which shall be spoken against; (Yea, a sword shall pierce through thy own**

soul also,) that the thoughts of many hearts may be revealed."
The conscience told us what NOT to do. The Bible told us what
not to do and went a step farther to tell us WHAT TYPE of thing
we SHOULD do. Now Jesus comes along and convicts us by His
pattern. He shows us a model life with which we can compare
ours. As we compare our life to His, we become aware of our
weaknesses and failures and thereby are convicted of our wrong
and our lack of right. So in giving us a pattern of life of One Who
follows both the conscience and the Word of God, Jesus becomes,
in a sense, the high school of conviction.

4. *The Holy Spirit.* **John 16:8, "And when he is come, he
will reprove the world of sin, and of righteousness, and of
judgment."** We could call the Holy Spirit the university of
conviction. We have learned from the conscience what NOT to do
and from the Bible the type thing we are TO DO; in Jesus we see a
model of the above; now the Holy Spirit adds another dimension.
He comes to tell us that sin is wrong, but He tells us specifically
WHERE to go and WHAT good to do. When one by his
conscience has been convicted of his wrong and by the Bible has
been taught principles of what is right and sees both of them
combined in the perfect life of Christ, he then must come to the
Holy Spirit and ask what good he is supposed to do. The
conscience says, "You should not be here. You should leave." The
Bible comes along and tells you the type of area into which you
should go. The Holy Spirit then tells you into WHICH of the
desirable areas you should go.

A man is driving too fast on the highway. He does not know
the speed limit and his speedometer is not working, and yet
something tells him that he is driving too fast. This is the
conscience. He then sees a speed limit sign and his speedometer
begins to work, so he finds not only that he is driving too fast but
exactly how fast he is driving. The speed limit sign and the
speedometer symbolize the Word of God. He then notices another
driver who is driving carefully within the speed limit. This typifies

Jesus, the pattern of the Spirit-filled life. Then he asks the Holy Spirit to tell him WHERE to drive and EXACTLY HOW FAST to drive.

In summary, the conscience tells us what we should NOT do. The Bible comes along and verifies the conscience and adds the type thing we SHOULD do. Jesus comes along and shows us the perfect EXAMPLE. Then the Holy Spirit tells us WHICH good thing we should do and which acceptable area is God's place for our lives.

If one leaves out the Holy Spirit, he may drive properly in the wrong place. If one leaves out the Bible, he may drive improperly in the wrong place. If one leaves out the Bible and the Holy Spirit and trusts only his conscience, he may come out of the wrong place but not know where to go and will no doubt, sooner or later, return to the place where he should not be. Hence, the wise Christian will be careful to listen to his conscience concerning evil. He will examine the Scriptures to find Bible principles that tell him what not to do and what to do. He will study the life of Jesus and ask the Holy Spirit to help him become more and more fashioned in His likeness. Then day by day and moment by moment he will walk in the Spirit, asking the Holy Spirit that EXACT place that he should be and the exact thing that he should be doing.

This chapter is being written in the early hours of the morning. The sun is just coming up. I am sitting in a rented car on the top of a mountain overlooking Mary Lake near Lucerne, California. The handiwork of God is unbelievable. No one knows where I am. Not a person in the entire world knows exactly where I am at this moment, but I am sure that the Holy Spirit has led me to this very spot. My conscience and my Bible tell me some things that people are doing here that I should not do. I should not dress as many are dressed. I should not go into the taverns that are so popular. However, there are many places nearby that would be desirable for me to visit, so I asked the HOLY SPIRIT to lead me to the ONE SPOT where He wants me this morning so that I may fellowship with Him for a while. Here I am looking across at a mountain that He made, looking down at a beautiful lake that He formed, admiring gorgeous trees that He planted and nurtured and looking at a sunrise that He painted. I am in the will of God; He ordained it so. I have already yielded myself to the Holy Spirit and to His leadership today. Won't you join me now and bow your head. Promise God that you are going to flee that which the conscience says is evil and that you are going to live in the Word of God so that you may know what is evil and what is good. Then yield yourself to the Holy Spirit and walk with Him and in Him today so that you may know exactly into what good place you should go today and exactly what good you should do today. May your conscience convict you of wrong, the Bible convict you of the areas of right, and may the Holy Spirit lead you into that particular area that He has planned for you today!

28
The Body of the Holy Spirit

Luke 16:23, "And in hell he lift up his eyes, being in torments, and seeth Abraham afar off, and Lazarus in his bosom."

Emerson said, "Every man is carrying his own statue." He is saying that each of us has a body within a body. It is no secret that the flesh is the body of the soul. It is often unrecognized, however, that the soul is the body of the Spirit. Just as the soul lives in the flesh, the Spirit lives in the soul and the soul has a form (a body). This body cannot be recognized by the physical senses. Nevertheless, there is a body which is inhabited by the Spirit.

There are many real things that cannot be seen by the natural eye. **II Kings 6:17, "And Elisha prayed, and said, LORD, I pray thee, open his eyes, that he may see. And the LORD opened the eyes of the young man; and he saw: and, behold, the mountain was full of horses and chariots of fire round about Elisha."** Elisha was surrounded by the enemies of God. His servant came to him to report their predicament. Elisha did not seem to be disturbed. The servant could not understand it. The entire city of Dothan was surrounded by Elisha's enemies who were dedicated to his destruction. Elisha simply asked God to open the eyes of his servant to see that which was not visible to the human eye. This means that the soul is the real man. Your soul is the real you. Scientists say, "Matter is spiritual entity in manifestation." There is a manifestation of spiritual entity which is not visible to the human eye but which is, nevertheless, a real body which is the soul which is the habitation of the Spirit.

That soul body is being fashioned now. It is exactly what your personal character is. Emerson said, "You are carrying your own statue, and you are carving it day by day!" Just as the physical body is what one makes it by exercise, proper food, rest, etc., even so this soul body is what one makes it. Every thought is used to form this body. Every word that is read is used in the formation of this body. Every television program we watch and every song that we hear unite in the formation of this body.

This body is being prepared for Heaven. A Christian will enter Heaven at his spiritual maturity when he leaves the earth. Hence, the wise Christian will, through the use of proper spiritual diet, proper spiritual exercise, prayer, fellowship and meditation, build up that body which houses the Spirit.

I Corinthians 6:19, 20, "What? know ye not that your body is the temple of the Holy Ghost which is in you, which ye have of God, and ye are not your own? For ye are bought with a price: therefore glorify God in your body, and in your spirit, which are God's." I Corinthians 3:16, 17, "Know ye not that ye are the temple of God, and that the Spirit of God dwelleth in you? If any man defile the temple of God, him shall God destroy; for the temple of God is holy, which temple ye are." II Corinthians 6:16, "And what agreement hath the temple of God with idols? for ye are the temple of the living God; as God hath said, I will dwell in them, and walk in them; and I will be their God, and they shall be my people." We find from these passages that the body of the believer is the temple of the Holy Spirit.

The Old Testament temple was divided into two main parts. The second part, known as the Holy of Holies, was very sacred. The building itself was not sacred, but it was made so by something that was in it. This something was the Shekinah Glory, representing God's presence with His people. So sacred was this room that only one man could enter. So sacred was this room that that man was chosen by God and he could enter it only one time a year and only then, by bearing the blood of the atoning animal.

Likewise the temple of the New Testament has two rooms — an outer room which is visible — the body. The inner room which is not visible to the human eye is the soul. Just as the inner room of the tabernacle possessed the Shekinah Glory, even so the inner room of the New Testament tabernacle possesses the Spirit. How tragic it is when the Christian forms this habitation of the Spirit with bad literature, evil thoughts, sinful music, sensuous radio and television programs, etc. Wise is that Christian who feeds his soul the proper diet realizing that the soul is the body of the Spirit!

29
The Holy Spirit, Our Seal

Before an animal could be declared fit for sacrifice or for food, he had to be examined. This was required to receive the seal of approval. If, for example, the animal was to be offered for a sacrifice, he was examined and approved by the priest. If he was without blemish and qualified for sacrifice, a seal or branding was placed on him to signify his acceptance.

Jesus offered Himself as the perfect sacrifice. This is why He is called the LAMB OF GOD. **John 1:29, "The next day John seeth Jesus coming unto him, and saith, Behold the Lamb of God, which taketh away the sin of the world."** These were the words of John the Baptist, the forerunner of Christ, who introduced Him first as God's sacrifice. There are many passages which point to Jesus as the LAMB OF GOD. **Revelation 7:14, "And I said unto him, Sir, thou knowest. And he said to me, These are they which came out of great tribulation, and have washed their robes, and made them white in the blood of the LAMB." Revelation 13:8, "And all that dwell upon the earth shall worship him, whose names are not written in the book of life of the LAMB slain from the foundation of the world." Revelation 19:7, "Let us be glad and rejoice, and give honour to him: for the marriage of the LAMB is come, and his wife**

191

hath made herself ready." Revelation 21:9, 14, 27, "And there came unto me one of the seven angels which had the seven vials full of the seven last plagues, and talked with me, saying, Come hither, I will shew thee the bride, the LAMB'S wife. And the wall of the city had twelve foundations, and in them the names of the twelve apostles of the LAMB. And there shall in no wise enter into it any thing that defileth, neither whatsoever worketh abomination, or maketh a lie: but they which are written in the LAMB'S book of life."

Since Jesus was the Lamb of God, meaning that He was the complete, perfect sacrifice, He too must be examined and approved by God the Father. When man sinned, he was separated from God. God wanted that fellowship restored, but He could not do so unless His justice was satisfied. God's mercy said that He wanted to forgive man, but God's justice said that man could not be forgiven unless a suitable sacrifice was found. Christ offered Himself as that sacrifice, which means that the sacrifice of Christ as the Lamb of God was the only way that God could be merciful and just. It was the only way that God, within His righteousness, holiness and justice could receive man back to Himself. Since God wanted man's fellowship more than man wants God's fellowship, then Christ first died FOR GOD. It is often said that Christ died for us, but the main thing was that Christ died FOR GOD in order that God could accept us back, for Christ and Christ alone satisfied the righteous and holy demands of God!

God approved His Son for sacrifice. That approval must be followed by a seal. That seal was the Holy Spirit. John 6:27 "Labour not for the meat which perisheth, but for that meat which endureth unto everlasting life, which the Son of man shall give unto you: for him hath God the Father sealed."

God announced His approval in Matthew 3:17, "And lo a voice from heaven, saying, This is my beloved Son, in whom I am well pleased." It is interesting that at the same time that God announced His approval, the Holy Spirit was upon Jesus

Matthew 3:16, "And Jesus, when he was baptized, went up straightway out of the water: and, lo, the heavens were opened unto him, and he saw the Spirit of God descending like a dove, and lighting upon him." This simply fulfills the type that the sacrifice must be examined, approved and sealed. God accepted Christ as the perfect sacrifice. He declared His approval when He said, "This is my beloved Son, in whom I am well pleased." At the same time the Holy Spirit was upon Jesus in the form of a dove sealing Him as the only acceptable sacrifice for the sins of man.

It must be remembered that the lamb was approved by the priest for sacrifice AND for food. Ah, what a beautiful picture! Not only is Jesus the sacrifice that God accepts and upon Whom God has placed His approval and His seal, that is the Holy Spirit; but Jesus is acceptable by God as a feast! We feast on Him. Notice **John 6:27, "Labour not for the meat which perisheth, but for that meat which endureth unto everlasting life, which the Son of man shall give unto you: for him hath God the Father sealed."** Notice especially the stress on "meat that perisheth." This meat that perished had to be approved and sealed by the priest. This meat that does not perish, even our Saviour, was approved by God and sealed by the Holy Spirit.

When the passover lamb was slain, he was approved. He was examined for four days, from the tenth day of the first month to the fourteenth day of the first month, after which he was offered. Then for seven days after he was killed, the families feasted upon the sacrificial lambs. Hence, the lamb was approved for sacrifice and for food. Praise the Lord, our Saviour is the only acceptable sacrifice approved by God and sealed by the Holy Spirit. He also is the only approved One on Which we can feed in order that we might grow in grace.

We shall see that there is another sacrifice that has been approved by God and sealed by the Holy Spirit. When a person comes to Christ, he is accepted by the Father in Christ. His faith is counted for righteousness. **Romans 4:5, "But to him that worketh not, but believeth on him that justified the ungodly,**

his faith is counted for righteousness." God then sees the believer clothed in the righteousness of Christ, declares him blameless, without blemish. This is the doctrine of justification. God declares the believer as righteous as Jesus Christ, for He sees him clothed in Christ's righteousness, and his standing before God is just as if he had never sinned. This does not mean that the believer lives a life above sin; it means that he stands before God blameless because he has had the righteousness of Christ imputed to him in response to his faith in the finished work of Calvary.

This makes the believer fit for sacrifice, for he has been accepted. The believer's sacrifice, however, is not that of offering himself to die as did his Saviour, but rather offering himself to live for his Saviour! This is called a LIVING SACRIFICE. **Romans 12:1, "I beseech you therefore, brethren, by the mercies of God, that ye present your bodies a living sacrifice, holy, acceptable unto God, which is your reasonable service."** No one is fit to become this sacrifice until he has first become inspected and examined. This examination is done after the believer has put on Christ and is wearing His imputed righteousness. He immediately receives the seal, which is the Holy Spirit. **Ephesians 1:13, "In whom ye also trusted, after that ye heard the word of truth, the gospel of your salvation: in whom also after that ye believed, ye were sealed with that holy Spirit of promise." II Corinthians 1:21, "Now he which stablisheth us with you in Christ, and hath anointed us, is God."** Now that the believer has been examined and declared righteous, he is fit for sacrifice, and God will accept his living sacrifice as holy and acceptable by God. The Holy Spirit is this seal, and as such, is called the earnest of our salvation. **Ephesians 1:14, "Which is the earnest of our inheritance until the redemption of the purchased possession, unto the praise of his glory."** This word "earnest" means that the Holy Spirit seals us and becomes the down payment for our salvation. When a down payment is made, it is forfeited if the payment is not made in full, so when God allowed the Holy Spirit to seal us and become the earnest (down payment) for our salvation, He was risking the unity of the Godhead on the security that the believer has in Christ. If one justified person could lose his salvation, then the Godhead would lose His unity.

This seal of the Holy Spirit is for eternity. It remaineth even in the end time. **Revelation 9:4, "And it was commanded them that they should not hurt the grass of the earth, neither any green thing, neither any tree; but only those men which have not the seal of God in their foreheads."** The only ones that will be preserved will be those who have the seal.

In some amusement parks when a person pays for his ticket, he receives a mark on his hand that is not visible unless it is placed under a certain light. He wears this mark. When he presents himself for a ride or other entertainment, this mark, invisible unless it is under the light, is presented, which means the price has been paid for his admission. Thanks be to God, even when Jesus comes again, we will be sealed by Him. Though that seal is unseen by man, the seal (the Holy Spirit) is seen in the light of eternity, and we are declared as His! The seal of eternal divine ownership shall be worn by the believer for eternity! Hallelujah!

30

The Holy Spirit and Fire

So often in the Bible the Holy Spirit is associated with fire. This was so concerning John the Baptist. **Luke 3:16, "John answered, saying unto them all, I indeed baptize you with water; but one mightier than I cometh, the latchet of whose shoes I am not worthy to unloose: he shall baptize you with the Holy Ghost and with fire."** The Holy Spirit was likened unto fire at Pentecost. **Acts 2:3, "And there appeared unto them cloven tongues like as of fire, and it sat upon each of them."** The cleansing power of the Holy Spirit was symbolized by fire in **Isaiah 6:6,7, "Then flew one of the seraphims unto me, having a live coal in his hand, which he had taken with the tongs from off the altar: And he laid it upon my mouth, and said, Lo, this hath touched thy lips; and thine iniquity is taken away, and thy sin purged."** We find that His ministers are made a flame of fire. **Hebrews 1:7, "And of the angels he saith, Who maketh his angels spirits, and his ministers a flame of fire."** The Word of God was as fire in the bones of Jeremiah. **Jeremiah 20:9, "Then I said, I will not make mention of him, nor speak any more in his name. But his word was in mine heart as a burning fire shut up in my bones, and I was weary with forbearing, and I could not stay."** David said that while he was musing, the fire burned. **Psalm 39:3, "My heart was hot within me, while I was musing the fire burned: then spake I with my tongue,"**

Obviously then, the Holy Spirit appears by fire. When God accepted a sacrifice, He showed His pleasure by sending fire to consume the sacrifice. **I Chronicles 21:26, "And David built there an altar unto the LORD, and offered burnt-offerings and peace-offerings, and called upon the LORD; and he answered him from heaven by fire upon the altar of burnt-offering."** This is what happened to Cain and Abel. They knew that God accepted Abel's sacrifice because He consumed it by fire. This is why Elijah prayed for fire to consume the sacrifice on Mt. Carmel. This is no doubt the way that God showed His acceptance of the sacrifice on the day of atonement.

There was another fire in the Bible. This fire was provided by God. **Leviticus 6:12, "And the fire upon the altar shall be burning in it; it shall not be put out: and the priest shall burn wood on it every morning, and lay the burnt-offering in order upon it; and he shall burn thereon the fat of the peace-offerings."** It was the fire upon the altar in the courtyard of the tabernacle. It was always to burn. **Leviticus 6:13, "The fire shall ever be burning upon the altar; it shall never go out."**

Coals from this fire were taken to the altar of incense. **Leviticus 16:12, 13, "And he shall take a censer full of burning coals of fire from off the altar before the LORD, and his hands full of sweet incense beaten small, and bring it within the vail: And he shall put the incense upon the fire before the LORD, that the cloud of the incense may cover the mercy seat that is upon the testimony, that he die not."** The altar of incense was the last piece of furniture in the tabernacle before entering through the veil to the holy of holies. This incense sending its fragrance heavenward was a beautiful symbol of the prayer life of the child of God. Notice that this symbol of prayer must come from the burning coals of the altar where the lamb was slain. God is telling us that there is no way to come to Himself, even in prayer, unless we come through the Lamb of God, even Jesus, Who shed His blood for our sins.

There were two men in the Bible, Nadab and Abihu, who offered other fire on the altar of incense. **Leviticus 10:1, 2, "And Nadab and Abihu, the sons of Aaron, took either of them his censer, and put fire therein, and put incense thereon, and offered strange fire before the LORD, which he commanded them not. And there went out fire from the LORD, and devoured them, and they died before the LORD."** Now why was their fire unacceptable? It was unacceptable because it did not come from the brazen altar where the lamb was slain. There is no real fire unless the fire comes from the cross of Calvary and from our Lamb Who gave His life on that cross. Only bloody coals are allowed by God to send up fragrance to the throne of grace.

Bear in mind that the fire is a symbol of the Holy Spirit. Any work that the Holy Spirit does must be based on the vicarious sacrifice of Jesus Christ on the cross. The Holy Spirit did not even come in the manner that He works in this age until Jesus had been crucified and raised from the dead. Any kind of work the Holy Spirit does He does only for those who have been to Calvary, those who have been washed in the blood. Any other fire is false fire; any other so-called gifts of the Spirit are false gifts of the Spirit. There are those today all across America who claim to have the gifts of the Spirit, who believe in the apocrypha books, who pray to Mary, who believe in purgatory, and there are those who even do not believe in the vicarious death of Christ who claim to have gifts of the Spirit. This is foolishness and unscriptural. Nobody can have the real fire (Holy Spirit power) unless that fire comes from the cross of Calvary and is sprinkled by the precious blood of Jesus, our Saviour.

Because it is the Holy Spirit Who has been rejected by this age, He will be given the executioner's role in the tribulation period. So many of the judgments are made with fire. For example, look at **Revelation 8:1-6, "And when he had opened** the seventh seal, there was silence in heaven about the space of half an hour. And I saw the seven angels which stood before God; and to them were given seven trumpets. And another angel came and stood at the altar, having a golden censer; and there was given unto him much incense, that he should offer it with the prayers of all saints upon the golden altar which was before the throne. And the smoke of the incense, which came with the prayers of the saints, ascended up before God out of the angel's hand. And the angel took the censer, and filled it with fire of the altar, and cast it into the earth: and there were voices, and thunderings, and lightnings, and an earthquake. And the seven angels which had the seven trumpets prepared themselves to sound." Notice in the following verses that one-third of the trees will be burned with fire. All green grass will be burned with fire. There is a mountain burning with fire. There is a burning fire that makes one-third of the water bitter. One-third of the sun is darkened.

Then it is perfectly Scriptural to speak of one who is filled with the Holy Spirit as being "on fire for God." It certainly was in order when the Emmaus disciples spoke of their hearts burning when Jesus spoke with them. **Luke 24:32, "And they said one to another, Did not our heart burn within us, while he talked with us by the way, and while he opened to us the scriptures?** John Wesley used to say, "I just set myself on fire, and folks come to watch me as I burn."

Fire is chosen to symbolize the Holy Spirit, no doubt, because of what it does. Fire burns out the dross. Fire gives light. Fire gives warmth. Oh, to be on fire for God! May the fire fall for us as it did in Elijah's day! May people who hear us have burning hearts! May we be baptized with the Holy Ghost and with fire! May the Word of God burn in our hearts like unto fire!

31
Woman, the Holy Spirit of the Family

(A sermon preached to the nationwide Christian Womanhood convention at the First Baptist Church of Hammond, Indiana.)

Genesis 2:21-24, "And the LORD God caused a deep sleep to fall upon Adam, and he slept: and he took one of his ribs, and closed up the flesh instead thereof; And the rib, which the LORD God had taken from man, made he a woman, and brought her unto the man. And Adam said, This is now bone of my bones, and flesh of my flesh: she shall be called Woman, because she was taken out of Man. Therefore shall a man leave his father and his mother, and shall cleave unto his wife: and they shall be one flesh."

"Our Heavenly Father, we come to speak on this vital subject. I'd love to be a help and a blessing. I pray that for some ladies this will be life-changing. May we give our attention to this truth and to Thee. In Jesus' Name, Amen."

The Lord chose to compare a family with the Trinity. In so doing, He called the head of the family, the man, after His own name, Father. We pray, "Our Father, Which art in Heaven." Then He likened the son or children in the family to His own Son, the second-named Person in the Trinity. Hence, we have in the family a person who represents God the Father, and we have a person who represents God the Son. By process of elimination, we come to realize who represents the Holy Spirit in the family. There is only one person left, and that's the lady. That means that you — the woman, wife, mother — represent the Holy Spirit. If you would like to find your duties in life, just find in the Bible what the Holy Spirit is supposed to do. He comforts; so does Mother. He teaches; so does Mother. He instructs; so does Mother. He leads; so does Mother. Think of all the ministries the Holy Spirit has in the world. He's the unseen One; so is Mother. He is the one Who gives others attention; so does Mother. If you want to know what your duties are in the family, all you have to do is find out the duties of the Holy Spirit in the Trinity, for you are the Holy Spirit of the home.

The week of creation began. First came the light. After the light, God made the firmament. Then God lit the starry hosts of the nighttime in their constellations. Then God made the fishes of the sea and then all the tribes of the animal kingdom. Now creation's week is almost finished and all is prepared for God to make man. God did make man in His own image.

All that God had made before was made for man. The stars of the nighttime were placed in the heavens for the enjoyment of man. The herbs and grass of the field were placed there for the nurture and health of man. The water was placed there for the refreshment of man. The sun in the noontime and the moon in the nighttime were placed in the heavens for man. It was marvelous.

Every tree that grew was pleasant to the sight. Rivers flowed peaceably between verdant banks in Eden's garden. Every sound was a melody and every scene was a delight. There was no war to unrest the breast of man. There was no sickness to cause in his heart a fear of death. The leaf never withered. The wind never chilled. No perspiration moistened man's brow. There was no profanity to cause discomfort to his ears. There was no weariness, no heat, no cold. No blossoms were ever smitten by a tempest. Man had not yet learned to sigh and to weep. This was the Garden of Eden. God had made it and the entire universe for one person — man! No withering frost to chill the rose and no shadow of guilt was ever felt in the heart of man. For Adam there were choirs of birds to sing. Man had everything he would need, it seemed, in this Edenic bliss, and yet something was missing!

Adam needed someone to share with him these beauties. Adam needed someone to whom he could say, "Look at the stars! Aren't they pretty?" Adam needed someone with whom he could share the joys of the beautiful garden. He longed for communion with a kindred soul, one whose wants and joys were like his own. The virgin world was cold and blank. Adam needed somebody, and God made her; and here she comes dressed in all the beauty for a human being to possess.

Milton said of Eve, "She was adorned with all of heaven and earth that they could bestow upon her to make her amiable." Grace was in her steps. Heaven was in her eye, and every gesture possessed dignity, poise and love. Perfection was stamped on her. The sons of God shouted for joy, the morning stars sang together, and Eden was transformed. Now Adam has what he needed. Someone wrote, "The earth was sad, the Garden wild, the hermit sighed, till woman smiled." The work of Omnipotence was finished.

Notice, woman was not taken from man's head to lord over him, nor from his heel to be crushed by him, but this magnificent creation of Omnipotence was taken from man's rib, near his heart, so she could be loved and protected by him.

The winds are a thousand times more refreshing now that she is here. The flowers are a thousand times more fragrant now that she is here. The birds are a thousandfold more melodious, the trees are more beautiful, and the fruits are more delicious. The sun is brighter, the moon is more lovely, the stars are closer, the animals are tamer because she is here. There she is — Miss Universe! She was created because all of the perfection of the Garden of Eden did not give to Adam what he needed.

There she stands with the beauty of Sarah as she made

Abraham her lord, with the courage of Deborah as she stood beside Barak in the battle against the enemy, with the depth of Hannah as she prayed for and reared her son, with the devotion of Rizpah as she vowed to protect even the dead bodies of her own, with the royalty of Esther as she stood before the king and spared a nation. There she is with the grace of Lydia, the poise of Mary, the humility of Phebe, the friendship of Dorcas, the faith of Rhoda, the ambition of Salome, the worship of Mary, the care of Martha, and the praise of Mary Magdalene. There she stands, our Miss Universe, with the patience of Anna, the loveliness of Rachel, the love of Jochebed, the gentleness of Elisabeth and the spirit of Lois. Wrapped up in all these personalities is what you ought to be. Take all the good from all the good women of the Word of God and there, dear lady, is what God intended you to be.

Who could have guessed that in the midst of Eden's loveliness, innocence and peace where angels guarded the gates of the garden and where peace, love and joy prevailed, who could have looked at this magnificent creature of God's omnipotence and ever thought that evil could find an entrance! In the loveliness of this woman is also the potential for ugliness. In her joy is the potential for sadness. In her grace is the potential for selfishness. In her humility is the potential for pride. In her submission is the potential for rebellion. In her faith is the potential for doubt. Though she is lovely and though all the good qualities of all the women in the Bible are potentially hers, there is another potential that she possess. She bears in her breast the potential of Michal, who hated her husband and laughed at him because he got happy and shouted when the ark of the covenant came back to God's people. She can, if she chooses, possess the rebellion of Jezebel, who fell and with her took a nation. She owns the seed of the selfishness of Athaliah, who could kill her own grandchildren for her own rights and privileges.

It's difficult to imagine that this beautiful queen of the Garden of Eden, the one who filled every need of Adam, could possess in her breast the hatred of Herodias, who had John the Baptist's head served in a platter! It's hard to believe that she could be a soiled Rahab, who could sell her body to the hands and lusts of wicked men. It's hard to believe that this beautiful one has the potential so that her feet could carry her to Moab with Naomi. It's hard to believe that these lips could possess the potential of lying as did Sapphira. There behind her smile dwells the possibility of hatred and the disposition of Abigail.

Ladies, it is up to you, as it was to Eve, to decide, for there is in your breast all the loyalty of Sarah, the loveliness of Rachel, the tenderness of Mary, the servitude of Martha, the patience of the mother of Christ (His earthly mother), and the gentleness of Rebekah. There is also a bit of Jezebel, Athaliah, Michal, Abigail and the others. It is up to you to decide.

Whether it be good or bad, there is one thing that woman always does; she determines the spirit and the atmosphere of any place where she is present.

Woman was not made to till the soil, she was not made to build the house, she was not made to steer the crane, nor stack the brick, nor hew the stones, nor lead the church, nor reap the harvest.

It is woman's job to determine the atmosphere while the soil is being tilled. It is woman's job to determine the atmosphere while the house is being built. Though it is not her job to steer the crane, it is her job to make happy the one who steers the crane. It's not her job to stack the brick nor hew the stone; it's her job to make a wonderful spirit and atmosphere while the brick is being stacked and the stone is being hewn. It's not her job to build the road, nor head the state, nor lead the church, nor reap the harvest. Everywhere woman has ever been, it has been her job to provide the spirit of atmosphere while man does his work and changes the course of history.

Woman can make Eden a paradise if she so chooses, or she can curse everything in it, as she did. She can make an ark a lifeboat and the Nile River a nursery if she wants to, or she can curse her husband in Job's ash heap. It's her choice! She can ruin a nation as did Jezebel or she can change a house into a church as did Priscilla. She can make a preaching service great by giving all or ruin one by withholding some as did Sapphira. She can fill the house with Mary's ointment or she can fill it with Michal's hatred. She can save a nation as did Esther or she, like Jezebel, can destroy one.

Ladies, I don't think you understand completely how the atmosphere is determined by you.

Much of the atmosphere of Hyles-Anderson College is caused by the lovely young ladies who grace our hallways. Our college was made basically for God's men. When I was in Los Angeles, California, praying all night one night, God didn't give me a burden and say, "You need to start a college and turn out some young ladies." My burden was for God to send us some young men who could go across this country with the fire of God in their breast and change this country, build churches, call America back to God and fight evil, but we could not have done it had it not been for the marvelous spirit that permeates our campus caused by the sweetness of the "Holy Spirits" of our campus who make it so much sweeter.

We have some fine young men in our high school who play football and basketball, and who are the officers of the classes, but our high school this year has an amazing spirit. Do you know one reason? A group of young ladies determine what it's like.

Woman's spirit determines the tranquility of the home, the spirit of the office, the unity of the church, the reputation of the preacher, the health of her husband and the joy of her children. She's not the one whose name is put in the headlines of the paper. She's the one who makes man have a delightful place to be. 'Tis her spirit, her attitude, her disposition.

The little song is true: "Sometimes I'm happy, sometimes I'm blue; my disposition depends on you!" That's the way it is. You can make your church a marvelous place. You ladies can determine the spirit of your church more than menfolks can, for your spirit determines the spirit of the menfolks. I wonder how many preachers have gone to church and bawled the people out because of some discontent they received from their wives concerning the church while they were home. I wonder how many preachers have kept churches tranquil and serene because of the tranquility they received at home.

Any time a woman is present, she determines the spirit and the atmosphere many times more than does the man. Though she's not the head, she's the neck that determines which way the head looks. Though she's not the arm, she's the fuel that gives it strength. Though she's not the strong cedar of Lebanon, she's the myrrh that makes fragrant the atmosphere. Though she's not the pillar of the temple, she is the altar of incense that makes everything fragrant within its walls. Though she's not the harvest gatherer, she is the lily that makes the gathering of the harvest more beautiful as she graces herself in the field.

Woman is the flower on the communion table. She's the honey at the banquet table. She's the Holy Spirit in the home, the unseen power.

Man worked before woman came, but man worked harder after she came. Man ran before she came, but man ran faster after she came. Man jumped before she came, but man jumped higher after she came. Man was good before she came; man excelled after she came.

Some women are not listed in the Bible by name — the Shunammite woman, the little maid that pointed Naaman toward the man of God, the widow who gave two mites, the widow at Zarephath, the others. You see, the honest truth is, though you're not made to have your name in the headlines, break the records, win the wars and fight the battles, God made you for a specific purpose.

Jesus is the One we exalt in our preaching here, but the Holy Spirit gives us power to exalt Him. The Father is the One Who is the great omnipotent God, but the Holy Spirit is the One Who causes our attention to turn toward Him. The Gospel gets people saved, but the unseen power of the Holy Spirit is felt in the services; His power causes folks to walk the aisle; His power causes Jesus to be more lovely; His power causes God to look more omnipotent, omniscient and omnipresent; that power causes the church to go out and bring more folks to Christ and draw folks to Calvary; that power is the unseen One, the Holy Spirit! That's what you are! You're the determiner — the unseen one.

When I was a boy, my mother used to sing to me in some tune that you would not recognize, for she was possessed with the same musical talents with which I am obsessed! She used to rock me on her knee and sing, "Brighten the corner where you are! Brighten the corner where you are! Someone far from harbor you may guide across the bar. Brighten the corner where you are!" As she sang it, my father was probably out drunk. We lived in a little two-room shack. Light came from a kerosene lamp, and heat came from a wood stove which was too often empty because we had no wood to place in it.

Mother did not know the story behind the song, "Brighten the Corner." Years ago a little lady, Ina Duley Ogdon, was given a beautiful voice. Someone asked her to sing a concert tour around the world. She had anticipated the day when she could cover the globe and carry the bright light of Christ through her voice. She had signed the contract; the date had been set for her journey to begin. Just days before her departure, she found her father was taken seriously ill. No one else could care for him — only she! With some bitterness and much disappointment, she canceled her worldwide trip to use her voice to sing the praises of Christ and shine His light around the world!

Ina Duley Ogdon looked at her aged father and saw him as he was nearing death. She realized that she could not take her trip. Her bitterness changed to joy, her disappointment changed to gratitude as she sat down one day and began to write, "Brighten the corner where you are! Brighten the corner where you are! Someone far from harbor you may guide across the bar. Brighten the corner where you are!"

What the soloist could not do with her journey she did with her sweet spirit as it went from her heart to her mind, from her mind to her pen, from her pen to the paper, from the paper to the hymnbook, and from the hymnbook to the whole world! Not just in her lifetime did she brighten the world, but she will do so as long as the song is sung!

That's your job — brighten your corner! The atmosphere of the office is determined more by the spirit of the secretaries than that of the bosses. The atmosphere of the home is determined more by the mother and wife than by the father and the children.

Man looks to you first to see in what kind of mood you are now. Your husband comes home at night and one of the first things he wants to know is, "What kind of a mood is she in tonight?" His evening is brightened or saddened according to your mood! Why? Man doesn't determine the mood of the house; you do! You are the Holy Spirit of the home.

You won't get the praises man gets. You won't get your name in the paper like he does. You won't get your name honored like he does, and you won't be as big, as strong and as much of a leader. He is the Father, the children are the Son, but you are the Holy Spirit. The whole atmosphere wherever you are is determined by you.

Did you know that God has made it so that your spirit can overwhelm the spirit of man? He is stronger than you as far as your body is concerned. Your emotions could never do it, because there is more emotional stability in a man than in you, but there is one place where you can always overpower your guy or any guy and that is your attitude, the spirit, the atmosphere!

Sometimes your home is happy; sometimes it's blue. Its disposition depends on you.

Sometimes the place you work is happy; sometimes it's blue. Its disposition depends on you.

Sometimes your school is happy; sometimes it's blue. It disposition depends on you.

If your church doesn't have a good spirit, it's more your fault than the man's. I like this building. I helped to build it. I love it. I think it's the prettiest building in the whole world, and I wouldn't trade anyone's building for it. I love this pulpit. It's the same pulpit I had in the other building; we just put some new wood on the outside of the pulpit. When we meet here Sunday morning, it doesn't matter about the building, and all of my training and planning for the services doesn't matter if the Holy Spirit is not here! It doesn't matter what kind of a guy you've got or what kind of kids you have, if the Holy Spirit is not there.

That's what it's all about. It's your job to comfort. Dad's not a very good comforter; in fact, he's a weak comforter. Dad's a horrible spirit-determiner or atmosphere determiner. He waits on you.

Not many years ago, I think it was in the state of Georgia, a mother and a child fell into an open well. The mother was beneath the child. She held the child up above her and cried for help. For hours that mother was there, just holding her arms up, holding the child above her. When the rescuers came, they found the child was alive, but the mother was dead. They took the mother's body to the funeral home. The funeral director came to the family and asked, "How shall we bury her?"

The family said, "What do you mean?"

The director said, "What shall we do with her arms?"

They said, "What do you mean, 'do with her arms'?"

He said, "Her arms are locked in position above her head. We'll have to break the bones to put them across her breast."

The family said, "Bury her with her arms up." As the people came by to view her body at her service they looked at her face, but her arms were raised out of the casket, and that's how she was buried.

That's the way it ought to be. Lady, your job is to keep lifting up those who are yours. Your guy and all guys are symbols of the Father; your children are symbols of Jesus Christ; you are the unseen and often forgotten, overlooked, unpraised, but always necessary Holy Spirit!

Think about the songs we sing: "Holy Spirit, breathe on me."

"All is vain unless the Spirit of the Holy One comes down." Compare your purpose to the jobs of the Holy Spirit: teach, lead, comfort, encourage, strengthen, help.

I'll be honest with you. I think you ladies got the long end of the stick. Preachers get on their faces and say, "O God, give me the fulness of the Holy Spirit." I think I may get the men to demonstrate to God. We got short-changed in all of this. We're going to start our own men's ERA. We build the wall, but you decide whether we smile or frown while we build it. We build the city, but you decide whether we have normal blood pressure or high blood pressure while we build it. We are the ones who build the churches, but you are the ones who decide whether we have tranquility or frustration while we lead. It's up to you.

Why don't you say, "My church is going to have a new spirit because of me"? Some of you ought to meet your preacher before he walks out to the pulpit Sunday morning and encourage him. Do what some of our college girls did as they formed a little honor guard behind the platform and began to sing for me about loving the Preacher.

The next time you are prone to think, "I'm not very important; nobody appreciates me," remember that you are the one in the family that typifies the One in the Trinity that nobody appreciates either. His job is as the spotlight that is covered by the bushes or the ravine, but it shines upon the building so that all may see the building. 'Tis your job to be the unseen one, that comforter, that Holy Spirit.

Take your Bible, look up the term "Holy Spirit," and find all He does. Then resolve that you are going to do what He does. Get alone somewhere, bow your head, lift your heart to God, and say, "O God, I'm so thankful that You made man in the image of God the Father, and I'm so glad that our children symbolize God the Son, and I'm so glad that You made me a woman, something that the earth had to have, something that paradise could not replace, something that could not be satisfied by the breeze of Eden, the taste of the fruit, the fragrance of the flowers, nor the gentleness of the wind."

The earth had to have you, lady, just as the church has to have the Holy Spirit.

Get on your knees and say, "Dear God, I am satisfied with my lot in life. I am glad You made me a woman in the image of the Holy Spirit. I yield myself to promise You that everywhere I go the flowers will be a little prettier, their fragrance a little sweeter, the sun a little brighter, the wind a little more gentle, the smile a little broader, the shoulder a little straighter, and the arm a little stronger because I'm present."

You're somebody! You are God's Holy Spirit in the family. It matters not what else you do — that's your job. It matters not what else you accomplish. That is your job.

Mrs. Evans conducts these Christian Womanhood Spectaculars. To you she seems like a mighty strong-willed person. I don't see her that way. I see her as, "Whatever you say, Preacher." "Preacher, you know what's best." "Preacher, you're the wisest." "Preacher, I'm dumb compared to you." That's what it's really all about.

You carry with you two little dispensers. One dispenser is filled with the most marvelous fragrance and one is filled with a bad odor. You have the potential for making everything around you sweet or foul. We can't overbalance you. There is no way we can. You give me ten gossipy ladies in a church, and I'll chase off any preacher in America! Churches aren't split by men; they are split by women. Wounds in churches aren't healed by men; they are healed by women!

One day I was teaching a class in a college in Texas many years ago. I was driving down the highway coming home, and the cutest little "cat" came across my path. It was black and white. It was a polecat or a skunk, and I tried to miss him. I didn't! Not a bit of his Chanel No. 5 touched me, but do you know that for weeks everywhere I went people said, "Whew! My! What's that odor?" There was no way around it.

You have the potential. It's up to you.

The Russell Andersons and we were in Nassau, Bahamas. I was standing in a big department store and I heard something behind me going, "psst, psst, psst." I thought, "What is that — gas escaping?" Then I felt something trickling down my neck, and Russell Anderson had take a little sample perfume bottle and absolutely washed my hair in it. For weeks everywhere I went people said, "Ah!" My deacons said, "Ohhh!" You have both in your personality!

There Miss Universe stands with power enough to complete the perfection of the Garden of Eden or to let the serpent find his way into her heart and destroy and curse all in the garden.

You have that power too. It's up to you which one you choose. You are the mood-determiner, the atmosphere-determiner, the Holy Spirit of the family.

32

The Holy Spirit and Your Schedule

Every day is a microcosm of life, death and resurrection. Every day is a little life. We spend the youth of the morning, the mid-life of the noontime, the declining years toward sunset, and then we sleep. This is followed in the morning by the resurrection. In a sense, every day is a life of its own.

There are many things in the Bible that we are to do daily. We are to die daily. **Galatians 2:20, "I am crucified with Christ: nevertheless I live; yet not I, but Christ liveth in me: and the life which I now live in the flesh I live by the faith of the Son of God, who loved me, and gave himself for me." I Corin-thians 15:31, "I protest by your rejoicing which I have in Christ Jesus our Lord, I die daily."** We are resurrected daily. **Philippians 3:10, "That I may know him, and the power of his resurrection, and the fellowship of his sufferings, being made conformable unto his death." Romans 12:2, "And be not conformed to this world: but be ye transformed by the renewing of your mind, that ye may prove what is that good, and acceptable, and perfect, will of God."** Our daily desire should be to awake the next morning in the likeness of Christ. **Psalm 17:15, "As for me, I will behold thy face in righteousness: I shall be satisfied, when I awake, with thy**

likeness."

Now if the Christian is to live the Spirit-filled life, he must live a disciplined, scheduled life. There are some things he should do on a regular basis that have direct connection to the Holy Spirit.

1. *The Spirit-filled Christian should set times daily to yield to the Holy Spirit.* I have found it advisable to yield to the Holy Spirit upon rising in the morning, immediately after breakfast, at midmorning, after lunch, at midafternoon, after dinner and before retiring in the evening. This could be a very simple matter and yet life-changing. Simply drop to your knees, lift your heart to God and say, "Dear Holy Spirit, I yield myself to You today." Mean it with all your heart and believe that He will control you.

2. *Set times to ask Him to lead you to those who need help and to allow such people to cross your path to whom the Holy Spirit would have you minister.* This could be done at the same time you yield to the Holy Spirit, or it could be done in the morning once a day. My practice has been to do this at the beginning of every day. When I yield to the Holy Spirit early in the morning, I then ask Him to allow me to cross the paths of those who need me today and of those whom the Lord Jesus would help if He were in my shoes. Oh, the blessedness of such a life! I have made it a practice for many years to ask the Holy Spirit which way I should drive to work in the morning. A few days ago, after asking Him to lead me, I was driving past a corner and suddenly I felt I should back up and turn left. This I did. A few hundred yards down the street was a car that was stalled. A lady had raised the hood and was trying to get it started. The Holy Spirit seemed to say to me, "This is the reason I had you back up and turn left." I stopped and she told me she was going to the service department to have her car worked on and just did not make it there. I told her I would push her car. This I did. Though I pushed her car for four or five miles, it nevertheless gave

opportunity for a ready witness for the Saviour.

3. ***Pray for power on a regular basis.*** The Christian should constantly be praying for the power of God. Place some reminders to pray for power near places where you go the most. I have the words, "Pray for power," on my desk in my office, on the mirror where I shave, in the car I drive, inside every Bible I own, and in my briefcase. This means as I drive down the road, I am constantly praying for the power of the Holy Spirit. As I shave, I pray for His power. Hundreds of times a day I pray for the power of God upon my life and ministry. Have a reminder at the telephone, at the kitchen sink and the other places where you go the most so that you will be reminded to plead with God for His power on a regular basis.

4. ***Set a time to pray.*** Allow at least 15 minutes a day to pray in the Spirit. Get alone with God. Then ask the Holy Spirit to help you to know for what to pray. After you have asked Him, then with His guidance make a list of things for which you should pray. Then go to the Father and present your petitions one at a time. Ask the Holy Spirit to go with you to the Father to remind you and the Father of things that you may forget to ask. It maybe that you should walk while you pray. It is difficult to kneel for 15 minutes or more. I found it good to walk. Maybe you could take a walk outside in some private place or maybe pace the floor in the study or living room. Whatever you do, schedule at least 15 minutes a day when you pray in the Spirit.

5. ***Place in your schedule at least 15 minutes a day for Bible reading.*** I would recommend more than 15 minutes a day, but that could be a minimum. Adhere strictly to this schedule. Before you open the Bible, remember that the Holy Spirit wrote it. Ask Him to help you understand it and to be your teacher as you read His Book.

6. ***Set a time each week when you do nothing but plead for***

the power of the Holy Spirit. This is in addition to your 15 minutes of prayer each day. Perhaps it should be longer than 30 minutes, but make this a minimum. Do nothing but beg God for His power — power as you preach, power as you sing, power as you train your children, power as you seek to be a good Sunday school teacher. Get alone and plead for the power of the Spirit.

7. *Choose one 24-hour period a week when you fast and pray.* Maybe it could be from 6:00 one night until 6:00 the next night or from noon one day until noon the next day. During this time take every available moment when you are not at work or otherwise occupied and pray for the big needs of your life. This is the time to pray for a wayward son, for a lost husband, for a job, for a new church building. This is vital. **Mark 9:29, "And he said unto them, This kind can come forth by nothing, but by prayer and fasting."** Notice the two words, "this kind."

This is the story of a boy who was possessed of a devil. He would rip his clothes off of himself. He would wallow on the ground and foam at the mouth. Our Lord was with Peter, James and John communing with Moses and Elijah on the Mount of Transfiguration. The father of this boy came to the disciples and asked for help. They could not help. Jesus performed the miracle of healing the boy. The disciples then came privately and asked our Lord why they could not do it. Jesus answered, "This kind can come forth by nothing, but by prayer and fasting." This is the miraculous kind, the supernatural kind, the kind that cannot be gotten by talent or by man's effort. This is the kind when God must intervene, and there is no way to get this kind but by prayer and fasting. Please note the next chapter of this book is a sermon on the subject. Read it carefully. It will increase your faith and show you the miracles that can be received by prayer and fasting.

8. *Throughout the day ask the Holy Spirit to help you and lead you in your everyday tasks.* Ask Him to lead you when you go shopping so that you may find the bargains. Ask Him to lead

you in the way you should drive to work. Talk to Him. Get up in the morning and say, "Good morning, Holy Spirit." Before retiring, say, "Good night, Holy Spirit." Tell Him you love Him. Thank Him for His leadership.

Billy Sunday's wife (Ma Sunday) was a dear friend of mine, though I never met her husband. She used to tell me how Billy would be carrying on a conversation with her and with the Holy Spirit at the same time. It was difficult sometimes for her to know to whom he was talking. Time and time again during the many years I shared the pulpit with John R. Rice I have heard him in the car driving to the services mumbling to the Holy Spirit to give him power. Oh, to make the Holy Spirit a part of our everyday lives! Oh, to include Him in the schedule!

9. ***Every morning present yourself a living sacrifice.*** **Romans 12:1, "I beseech you therefore, brethren, by the mercies of God, that ye present your bodies a living sacrifice, holy, acceptable unto God, which is your reasonable service."** The word "present" means simply "to yield." Yield your mind to Him. **Romans 12:2, "And be not conformed to this world: but be ye transformed by the renewing of your mind, that ye may prove what is that good, and acceptable, and perfect, will of God."** Then believe that He is going to lead you. Reckon yourself to live the resurrection life. **Romans 6:11, "Likewise reckon ye also yourselves to be dead indeed unto sin, but alive unto God through Jesus Christ our Lord."**

Remember constantly that the Holy Spirit is a person. He has the qualities of a person. He can be vexed. **Isaiah 63:10, "But they rebelled, and vexed his holy Spirit; therefore he was turned to be their enemy, and he fought against them."** He grieves. **Ephesians 4:30, "And grieve not the holy Spirit of God, whereby ye are sealed unto the day of redemption."** Please note in **Ephesians 4:31** the things that grieve Him.

The Holy Spirit loves. **Romans 15:30, "Now I beseech you,** brethren, for the Lord Jesus Christ's sake, and for the love of the Spirit, that ye strive together with me in your prayers to God for me." He has a mind. **Romans 8:27, "And he that searcheth the hearts knoweth what is the mind of the Spirit, because he maketh intercession for the saints according to the will of God."** He possesses knowledge. **I Corinthians 2:11, "For what man knoweth the things of a man, save the spirit of man which is in him? even so the things of God knoweth no man, but the Spirit of God."** He can be insulted. **Hebrews 10:29, "Of how much sorer punishment, suppose ye, shall he be thought worthy, who hath trodden under foot the Son of God, and hath counted the blood of the covenant, wherewith he was sanctified, an unholy thing, and hath done despite unto the Spirit of grace?"** He can become your enemy. **Isaiah 63:10, "But they rebelled, and vexed his holy Spirit; therefore he was turned to be their enemy, and he fought against them."** He can instruct, remind and uncover truth and offer us stability. **Nehemiah 9:20, "Thou gavest also thy good spirit to instruct them, and withheldest not thy manna from their mouth, and gavest them water for their thirst."** We are to fellowship with Him and commune with Him. **II Corinthians 13:14, "The grace of the Lord Jesus Christ, and the love of God, and the communion of the Holy Ghost, be with you all. Amen."**

It is very interesting that we tell our Heavenly Father that we love Him, and we tell the Lord Jesus that we love Him. We sing, "My Jesus, I love Thee, I know Thou art mine. For Thee all the follies of sin I resign." Isn't it amazing then that we never tell the Holy Spirit that we love Him? We rejoice that God the Father loves us. We sing, "O love that wilt not let me go." We sing, "The love of God is greater far than tongue or pen can ever tell." We think of Jesus loving us. We sing, "Jesus loves me, this I know." We sing, "I am so glad that Jesus loves me." Yet, we never seem to dwell upon the fact that the Holy Spirit loves us too! He is as much a person as is God the Father and God the Son. Why then do we not dwell on His love? We praise the Father. We sometimes say, "Praise God!" and "Praise the Lord." We praise Jesus, and yet, did you ever hear anybody say, "Praise the Holy Spirit"? Isn't He deserving of our praise? We thank the Father for what He does for us. We thank Jesus for what He does for us. Why not thank the Holy Spirit? Oh, beloved, realize that He lives! He is a person like God the Father is a person, like God the Son is a person. He wants to be accepted as such. Begin a new day in your life by pausing now to love Him, to praise Him even as you would praise the Father and the Son.

33
This Kind

A Sermon by Dr. Jack Hyles

Mark 9:14-23, "And when he came to his disciples, he saw a great multitude about them, and the scribes questioning with them. And straightway all the people, when they beheld him, were greatly amazed, and running to him saluted him. And he asked the scribes, What question ye with them? And one of the multitude answered and said, Master, I have brought unto thee my son, which hath a dumb spirit (now that dumb spirit means that he could not speak, not that he was stupid); And wheresoever he taketh him, he teareth him: and he foameth, and gnasheth with his teeth, and pineth away: and I spake to thy disciples that they should cast him out; and they could not. He answered him, and saith, O faithless generation, how long shall I be with you? how long shall I suffer you? bring him unto me. And they brought him unto him: and when he saw him, straightway the spirit tare him; and he fell on the ground, and wallowed foaming. And he asked his father, How long is it ago since this came unto him? And he said, Of a child. And ofttimes it hath cast him into the fire, and into the waters, to destroy him: but if thou canst do any thing, have compassion on us, and help us. Jesus said unto him, If thou canst believe, all things are possible to him that believeth."

I like the Scriptures that speak of the limitless power of God. **"All things are possible!"** I like the Scriptures that say, **"...we are more than conquerors through him that loved us." (Romans 8:37) "I can do all things through Christ which strengtheneth me." (Philippians 4:13) "...and there is nothing too hard for Thee." (Jeremiah 32:17) "For with God nothing shall be impossible." (Luke 1:37)**

Mark 9:24-29, "And straightway the father of the child cried out, and said with tears, Lord, I believe; help thou mine unbelief. When Jesus saw that the people came running together, he rebuked the foul spirit, saying unto him, Thou dumb and deaf spirit, I charge thee, come out of him, and enter no more into him. And the spirit cried, and rent him sore, and came out of him: and he was as one dead; insomuch that many said, He is dead. But Jesus took him by the hand, and lifted him up; and he arose. And when he was come into the house, his disciples asked him privately, Why could not we cast him out? And he said unto them, This kind can come forth by nothing, but by prayer and fasting."

There is so much superficiality in our Christianity, so little that is real. I told the Lord years ago I was not going to be a preacher if I could not be real. I am not going to be a sham. I am not going to waste my life on something superficial.

I go a step further. I am not going to waste my life on something that is not miraculous. Our people have a right to expect the miraculous when they come to our churches.

The Bible says, **"This kind** (this miraculous kind that everybody knows God does) **can come forth by nothing, but by prayer and fasting."**

It doesn't come by education, though I am for education. It doesn't come by talent, though I am for talent. It doesn't come by human wisdom, though I am for human wisdom. This kind, where everybody knows that God does it — this miraculous kind — cometh forth by no other way except by prayer and fasting.

Our Lord had been up on the Mount of Transfiguration. (I think it was Mount Tabor. Some think it was Mount Hermon.) Peter, James and John had accompanied Him. There they had spoken with Moses and Elijah. Our Lord had had His body transfigured, likened to His glorified body, and had given them the foretaste of the coming kingdom.

Our Lord comes back from the transfiguration. As He returns, a man comes to Him and says, "My son has a dumb spirit. He wallows on the ground. He foams at the mouth. He pineth away. While You were gone, I went to the disciples and asked them if they could do something, but they could not."

After our Lord had cast out the devil, the disciples came to the Lord privately and asked Him, "Why couldn't we do it?"

Jesus answered, "The reason you could not is that this kind can come forth by nothing, but by prayer and fasting."

In **Psalm 35:13** the Psalmist said, "**...I humbled my soul with fasting: and my prayer returned into mine own bosom.**"

In **I Corinthians 7:5** the Apostle Paul admonished us to give ourselves to "**fasting and prayer.**"

In **Joel 1:14** the people were admonished to sanctify themselves.

Daniel 9:3, "And I set my face unto the LORD God, to seek by prayer and supplications, with fasting, and sackcloth, and ashes."

In **II Corinthians 11:27** the Apostle Paul was giving a little biography of his life and he said, "**in fastings often.**"

Something you don't hear much about anymore is "prayer and fasting."

It has been a way of life at our house. It was nothing unusual for our children when they were teenagers not to eat for a few days.

To this day, when Cindy has a heavy load or heavy burden or

some big decision to make or when she needs something big from God, it is not unusual for her not to eat anything for a day or two or three or more while she fasts and prays.

What I am trying to say is this: If we want the supernatural, we have to get back to God's methods and God's ways. You don't get this by having just a Sunday school contest, nor by simply having a degree from a college or seminary. You get this supernatural kind, this kind that happens where everybody in town knows God did it, by prayer and fasting. There is no way man could do it. This is a work of God.

Now, "this kind..." You can have pretty good meetings with just a good evangelist and a singer. You can have a special meeting. You can have a few children saved and few other folks saved along, but if you want a revival that will shake the whole town, it must come by prayer and fasting. If you want the drunkards, the harlots, the prostitutes saved, that comes by prayer and fasting. To get the town atheist saved, the town drunk saved — that comes by prayer and fasting.

I don't care how suave you are, how much personality you have, how big your reputation is, if you want God to work where everybody knows He did it, then you have to pray and fast.

I am talking about seasons of prayer, all night in prayer, begging and pleading with God.

I. THIS KIND OF MIRACLE

I was a very quiet introvert, the most timid boy in my class. No one ever suspected I would ever amount to anything. I failed public speaking, didn't go with girls, and couldn't make any kind of a mark when I was a kid.

I went off to college. In the first chapel service a Presbyterian spoke. I do not know what Scripture he used, nor the topic of his message. The one thing I do remember was this statement: "Young people, be a miracle! Be a miracle! I challenge you to be a miracle!"

I went alone and prayed, "Dear God, if I ever amount to anything, it will be a miracle! But if You will help me, I am going to be a miracle!"

A long time after you have forgotten the name of this speaker and the title of this sermon, I would like for you to hear those words ringing in your ears: **BE A MIRACLE! BE A MIRACLE! BE A MIRACLE!**

I call your attention to **Judges 6:12, 13.** The angel of God came to a young man, Gideon, who likewise was a timid fellow, an introvert. We read:

"And the angel of the LORD appeared unto him, and said unto him, The LORD is with thee, thou mighty man of valour. And Gideon said unto him, Oh my Lord, if the LORD be with us, why then is all this befallen us? and where be all his miracles which our fathers told us of, saying, did not the LORD bring us up from Egypt? but now the LORD hath forsaken us, and delivered us into the hands of the Midianites."

I want to call your attention to that little question Gideon asked the Lord, "Where be all His miracles?"

Elijah prayed it would not rain, and it didn't! And he was a man of like passions as I. Elijah prayed it would rain, and it did! And he was a man of like passions as I.

Years ago at a conference at the Bill Rice Ranch, Dr. John R. Rice was preaching. Suddenly it began to rain. Dr. Rice stopped and prayed, "Lord, stop the rain." I saw it stop raining right around that tabernacle while it rained all over the county. And as soon as John Rice finished preaching, it started raining again.

On May 16 this year we had over 170,000 people attend our services in places all around the Chicago area — in outdoor services, in football stadiums, in parks, etc. Our people worked as I have never seen folks work. We just couldn't have rain!

All day Saturday — an avalanche of rain! All night Saturday

night — torrential rain! And the weather forecaster said it was to rain throughout the weekend. Well, I prayed, "Dear God, You stopped the rain for Elijah. You stopped the rain for John Rice. Now, do it for Jack Hyles tomorrow. I claim a dry, beautiful day tomorrow — Sunday." We had the most beautiful Sunday we had had all year long! On the news report that night, the weather man said that something unusual had happened. He reported that there had been all day Sunday a solid mass of rain, clouds and torrential rain storms all over the Midwest from Iowa to Ohio except for a little spot over Hammond. He then said, "Folks, it is like a miracle." **AMEN!**

Now, you listen! We DO have a mighty omnipotent, omniscient, omnipresent God Who still stops the rain and starts it for His people. Where be all the miracles?

Am I talking to somebody whose body is eaten up with cancer, or has a baby with a tumor, or who has a building half built and you cannot finance it, or has a son in a distant city on dope, or has a daughter who has run off with the hippie crowd and is on narcotics? Am I talking to somebody who needs a new auditorium? Am I talking to a man whose wife is unsaved, or a woman whose husband is seemingly hopelessly lost? Oh, go back home with a new faith in the omnipotent God of Heaven and say, "I am going to be a miracle for Jesus Christ."

One Sunday morning we were having services in the Civic Center, downtown Hammond, while we were enlarging our auditorium. I preached and gave the invitation. A man who had been blind many, many years, with the nerves in his eyes gone, came running down the aisle saying, "Pastor, Pastor! I can see! I can see!" He hugged me and hugged the song leader. "I can see! I can see! I can see!"

I was preaching on a Sunday night in Hammond. I stopped in the middle of my sermon and said, "God is going to do a miracle right now." (I have never said that in my life before or since.) I said, "Tonight something miraculous is going on in this room. I don't know what it is."

I got a letter the next week from a Moody Bible Institute student who was in our services. She said, "I have an eye that I have never seen with. When you said that last Sunday night, I saw through that eye!"

Now, how does one get that? You get that when you come to know God, when you walk with God, spend time with God, and beg and pray, and sometimes fast.

People often say, "I want to go see what this fellow looks like who pastors the largest church in the world." They come. They say, "Well, is THAT Jack Hyles? There is nothing unusual about him!" No, but he spends a lot of time with Somebody Who is pretty unusual! This kind, I mean this kind of miracle where folks in town know that God does something down there, comes by nothing but by prayer and fasting.

Years ago in Texas, one of our fine ladies called me on the phone. She was weeping. "Pastor, my little girl is four years old. She has cancer in a kidney and we have to have a kidney removed."

They went to the hospital. The doctors removed the kidney eaten up with cancer.

It was only a few weeks until this same lady called again. She was beside herself. "Pastor, she has cancer in the other kidney and the doctor says there is no hope. Pastor, doesn't the Bible say something about anointing with oil and praying and fasting?"

I was in Texas just a few months ago and a beautiful young lady walked up. "Dr. Hyles, do you know me?"

"No, I don't."

"I am 22 years of age. Do you know me now?"

"No I don't."

"I have just one kidney. Do you know me now?"

I said, "You are not the little girl we anointed who had the kidney cancer?"

"Yes, I am." She said, "I am going to get married in a few

weeks. Brother Hyles, I have been well now all these years."

A dad lay in the hospital dead. His death certificate had been made out. The funeral service was announced in the church service. He had been dead for hours. A deaf young man walked inside that room and he had some things he wanted to say to his daddy before his daddy died. He pulled the sheet back off his daddy's dead body and said as best as he could, "Daddy! Daddy! Daddy!" Those dead eyes opened, that dead mouth spoke, and that dead body lived for another day so that boy could tell his dad some things he wanted to tell him. The man died. The boy had some things he wanted to tell his daddy. The fellow had been dead for a while. The son walked back in and talked to his daddy who had been declared dead twice and whose service had been announced in church again to be the next day. The night before the service was to be conducted, that man who had been lying dead for hours and hours with a sheet pulled over his head — that son, who is a deaf lad about 22 or 23 years old, said, "Daddy! Daddy! Daddy!"

And the Lord in Heaven seemed to say, "Make up your mind when you are through talking to your dad." The Lord said to the dad, "Go back down there for a while; John wants to talk to you." And his eyes opened and his voice spoke and his lips moved, and God proved again He can do anything but fail.

"This kind can come forth by nothing, but by prayer and fasting."

We had a lady in our church with a tumor on the brain. The doctor had shown me the x-ray several days before. I went to the hospital the morning she was to have surgery. (The doctor said it would be a five to seven-hour surgery.)

I took a bottle of olive oil. I put a little on her forehead and prayed, "O God, heal this lady and show that doctor there is a God in Heaven Who still can perform miracles."

They rolled her up to surgery. I was waiting out in the hall. In less than an hour they rolled her back. The doctor was beside her.

I said, "Doctor, is surgery over?"

"She didn't have surgery."

"Why?"

"The tumor is gone!"

You don't get this because you have a D.D. You don't get this because you have been to college and seminary. You don't get this because you have taken Strong's theology. You get this because you realize there is nothing in the world you can do, and you throw yourself at the mercy of God Almighty and say, "O my God, You have to do something!"

Two weeks ago I was in a certain city. Folks brought a little three-year-old chid to me. They said, "Dr. Hyles, the doctor said both of us are sterile and could not have a baby, and a few years ago out East you took a little bottle of olive oil and anointed my wife's head and mine. You prayed for God to open her womb and give life to my seed. Brother Hyles, within a year's time we had a baby and we want to show you the baby."

What we need in our Baptist churches are some preachers who know God, walk with God and can say, "I spend time in prayer, I fast, I beg and I plead. Night after night I walk with God and day after day I walk with God."

"This kind can come forth by nothing, but by prayer and fasting." This kind of miracle!

I prayed for 12 months for God to give us the beautiful Hyles-Anderson College campus we have right now.

I had said to the Catholic priest, "We would like to buy your campus."

He said, "It is not for sale." For a year I fasted and prayed for a day and a night each month.

I got a call from the Catholic priest twelve months later. "We have only nine students now. Do you want to buy it?"

"Yes, I sure do."

You get that by all-night prayer meetings. You get that by fasting and praying. You get that by walking with God. This old country needs some men of God to stand up before the pulpits and let the people know they have been with God.

I decided years ago that my people might not have the best preacher in town, and they might not have the smartest preacher in town, but members of the First Baptist Church of Hammond were going to have a man on Sunday preaching to them who has walked with God for six days during the week.

I was in New York. The pastor there had had his third heart attack. The doctor said he could not live very long. I asked the pastor to come up on the platform. I put my hand on his head. We had a sincere prayer meeting. I fasted and prayed during the whole conference and begged God to give back that pastor. I prayed for God to give him the victory and to heal him. He has been healthy for many years.

I could stand here and bless God over and over again and tell you the might power of God Almighty in answer to prayer and fasting. This kind! This kind of miracle!

What is it you need? Is there some son who has gone away on dope and narcotics and you can't sleep at night and your heart is broken? Is there some daughter who is breaking your heart? You carried her in your own body and gave birth to her and fed her when she couldn't feed herself; you loved her before she even knew who she was and gave her the name she bears — has she broken your heart? Is there some problem in the home? Is there some problem in the church? Is there a church that is languishing in mediocrity? Is there some disease? Does a little child of yours have leukemia? What is it? "This kind can come forth by nothing, but by prayer and fasting."

II. THIS KIND OF CONVERSION

Where be all the miracles concerning conversions? Where are

the old-fashioned conversions we used to know? Where are the drunkards who used to get saved because we prayed all night for them? Where are the harlots, the prostitutes? Where are they? I will tell you where they are. They are still going to Hell because of preachers and Christian laymen who know nothing about the power of the Holy Spirit.

I was preaching in Pennsylvania on "This Kind Cometh Forth by Nothing, But by Prayer and Fasting." I gave the invitation. I said, "If there is something tonight you are going to claim, something supernatural, God is going to have to do it. The preacher cannot do it, you cannot do it, your husband cannot do it, your wife cannot do it, your mother cannot do it, your father cannot do it, the church cannot do it; whatever is done, God is going to have to do it supernaturally." I said, "Come down this aisle tonight and you tell the pastor or me what it is and we will have a prayer, and you dedicate yourselves to go home and fast and pray until the victory comes and the miracle takes place."

The aisles were filled. One young man came and said, "I have a tumor on the brain. I believe God can heal it. I am going to pray He will." He knelt to pray.

One lady came and said, "My son is in Canada, a draft dodger with the hippie crowd, on dope. I am going to pray and claim the victory and fast and pray until he comes back."

One little young lady came and said, "Pastor, my husband loves me, but he is a wicked man. He hates the church. He hates preachers. Everybody has given upon him. Preacher, I am going to fast and pray until my husband gets born again."

I turned to the next person. "Sir, what are you going to claim for God?"

He said, "I want to get saved."

I said, "I did not say anything about getting saved tonight. Who are you?"

He said, "Her husband."

I said, "She did not even know you were in church tonight!"

He said, "I was not in church tonight. I drive my wife to church and come back and get her. Tonight I waited and waited. "But," he said, "all of a sudden they began to sing the invitation. Then my car door opened on its own. The handle went down and nobody was there but me, and I was not touching it; and Reverend, a hand grabbed my arm. It pulled me out of the car, pulled me inside and all the folks were coming forward and I thought, I have never been in a church before, and I may never come again, so I had better get saved while I am in here!"

What are you going to do about it? There are thousands of broken hearts in this room tonight. There are people in this room who know there lurks in their own bodies a disease that is incurable by human science. There are wives in this room who have husbands who have been visited and visited and visited by everything but an old-fashioned visitation of Holy Ghost revival. There are young people who cannot see their way to go to college. There are husbands and fathers who are heartbroken because of sons or daughters they have loved, reared, fed and clothed and who have taken their hearts and broken them.

Say, I believe God could help along there, somewhere! I believe God could do something about that daughter. I believe God knows where that son is. I believe God is powerful enough to save that old drunkard husband of yours. God could raise your church budget for you. I expect God might could build that building you need.

I was out soul winning one day in Hammond. I knocked on a door. A big tall fellow came to the door.

"I am Brother Hyles, Pastor of the First Baptist Church."

The fellow, about six feet, four, said, "Yeah, I know who you are. You are the biggest fake in town!"

I said, "Sir, I am not much of a preacher, but I am not a fake. I am sincere from the crown of my head to the sole of my feet. God knows it and I know it, and I'll bet you know it, too, if you will just admit it."

He said, "You are the biggest fake in town." He turned around and said, "Hey, folks, old Hyles is here." (He had thirteen people in his living room.) "Old Hyles is here from First Baptist Church, the biggest fake in town."

"Sir, I don't think you ought to say that any more."

"Are you trying to scare me?"

"No, I am not trying to scare you, but if you say it one more time, we are going to find out whether I am a fake or not."

He said, "What do you mean?"

I said, "There are thirteen people in there who need to know I am a man of God. Now, you said I am a fake. If you say it one more time, I am going to put my hand on your head and pray for God to kill you. And if God doesn't kill you, I will admit I am a fake."

He said, "You are not going to scare me."

I said, "I don't aim to scare you. I aim to pray for God to kill you."

I had never done this before and, to be quite frank with you, I was scared. I thought, "What in the world have I said?" I never had said it before and never have said it since!

He said, "Hey, folks, old Hyles is going to pray for God to kill me! Hyles, you are a fake!"

That did it! I put my hand upon his head and I said, "Dear God, You know I'm not a fake and I know I'm not a fake, but there are thirteen people in here who need to know. I pray, God, show this man I am not a fake. Show these people I am not a fake. I pray that right now, in the name of the God of Isaac and Jacob, and the God Who sent fire on Mount Carmel, the God Who caused the sun to stand still, the God Who parted the Red Sea, the God Who caused the axe head to swim — I pray in the name of Jesus right now that You would cause this man..."

He said, "Hold it, Reverend! Hold it! Hold it!" You ain't no fake! You ain't no fake!"

We had a revival break out in that room that day!

Listen, every city and village and town and neighborhood in America ought to have one person who walks with God so much that everybody in town can know he is God's man, everybody in town can know the power of God is on him, and they can know that God works when that man works.

III. THIS KIND OF REVIVAL

I have learned years ago what you have to do to have real revival. I don't mean "sign a banana to be one of the bunch." I am not against that. We have signed everything there is to sign. I don't mean, "Sign up, be a white sheep instead of a black sheep." I don't mean that. I don't mean campaigns or promotions, though I am certainly not against that. Brother, when you get people there because they signed a sheet, it is not going to do one bit of good unless the power of God falls on the place.

I decided to have a revival in Texas in the church I was pastoring. I called it "The Home Folks' Revival." Bill Harvey was my song leader. I said, "We are going to have revival, Bill. I am going to preach it. You are going to lead the singing. We are not going to have any guests in, or any kind of promotion. I am not against that, but we are just going to have revival. I am going to go to the motel down the road toward Dallas and rent a room. I am not going to eat all week. I am going to spend my time preaching and then staying on my face in that motel room."

The meeting lasted eight days. It started Sunday morning and lasted until the following Sunday night. Not one bit of food went in this mouth during that revival. I would go outside the motel room only to preach; then I would go back to the room to pray and beg God. I prayed for God to show my people there is a God in Heaven Who can send miracles.

I won't tell you all about that revival, but it was the best I have ever seen. There are eleven pastors in America who were saved in that one revival campaign of eight days.

Preachers, I am not preaching to you; I am trying to help you. What you need is to get to know God. What you need is to pray while others are playing. I don't play very much. I like to play. I like to have fun. I like to tell funny stories. I love sports. I love to go to ball games. I never go to a ball game. I love to play golf. I have an expensive set of golf clubs in my basement I have never used; my staff gave them to me. I have bowled about one time in the last ten years.

You say, "Don't you like to bowl?" I love to bowl. "Don't you like to go to ball games?" We have a high school basketball team. I seldom see a game. We have a high school football team. I seldom go see a game. I love it. I follow it. I pull for the Dallas Cowboys. I am saying, if you are going to have "this kind," you have to pray while others play. You have to be alone while others are having fun. You can't do a lot of things if you are going to have this kind of revival!

I was in a town conducting a revival meeting. They had more bootleggers in that county than in any county in Texas. I preached at the First Baptist Church in that little town when I was a young preacher. On Sunday night nothing happened. The pastor said this was the meanest bunch of people. I preached against liquor. The bootleggers heard about it, and they would come by and shoot guns up in the air while I was preaching. Sunday night nothing happened! Monday night nothing happened! Tuesday night nothing happened! Wednesday night nothing happened! Thursday night nothing happened!

I decided to pray all night Thursday night. I got in the room while people were outside shooting guns up in the air, driving by and calling me dirty names, threatening to kill me. I said, "Dear Lord, I'm not going to sleep or eat until You give revival!" I prayed all night. I got the idea that if I could get the head bootlegger saved, maybe we would have revival in that town.

I went to the pastor, woke him up, and said, "Pastor, who is the meanest man in town?"

He gave me the man's name. He said, "He is as mean as the Devil. He will kill you on sight. He is in charge of all the bootleggers in this whole county."

I said, "Let's go see him."

We got in the car and drove down a winding country trail to a little one-room shack. This man was out in the yard with a fire. He had eggs and bacon and coffee cooking in the yard on a summer morning.

I got out of the car and walked up. This big tall fellow looked down at me.

I said, "I understand you are the meanest man in town."

"Who told you that?"

I said, "Never mind. God Almighty is going to judge you, and your Hell is going to be hotter than anybody else's in this town. You are breaking homes, robbing wives of their husbands, wrecking little children's lives, and sending wives to premature graves. You are the cause of the trouble in this town. I am going to pray God's judgment on you. God is going to judge you!"

To make a long story short, before we left, he had gotten saved!

Word spread all over town that he had "gotten religion" and was going to "join the church" that night.

He went with me that afternoon and bought the first suit he had ever owned, the first tie he had ever owned, the first white shirt he had ever owned. That night he was at church.

Bootleggers came. They were outside looking in; some were sitting in their cars listening. We had hundreds of people in church that night in a building which seated two hundred people, in a town of two hundred population. The county came! Bootleggers came out of those woods like groundhogs out of their holes.

I preached that night! I announced I was going to preach on, "Will There Be Any Drunkards in Heaven?" Invitation time came. The old bootlegger stood up, stepped out in the aisle, and walked down the aisle. When he stepped out and walked down the aisle, the cars outside began to honk and folks began to holler and shout. Eleven bootleggers who were not even inside that building got out of their cars and came inside the church and came down the aisle and got converted! A revival broke out. We had more people saved in the next three days than lived in that town. Why? A little scared preacher prayed and fasted and said, "We are going to have revival!"

You live your life in a dead kind of ministry if you want to; you go ahead if you want to and let nothing ever happen; you go ahead and say that miracles are not for this age; go ahead and die and face God someday with the blood of sinners on your hands who could have been saved and a nation that could have been spared if you had spent some time with God. "This kind can come forth by nothing, but by prayer and fasting."

I am going to tell you now the sweetest story I know.

When I was in my early twenties I was asked to go to a southeast Texas town for a revival. The pastor didn't want me. The young people chose the evangelist once a year and they chose me to come preach a revival sponsored by the young people. It was on the north side of town. I drove down on a Sunday afternoon. The pastor took me off to the side and said, "Now, Brother Hyles, I am 72 years of age — 50 years older than you. I want to tell you before the revival starts that I did not want you and do not want you to preach this revival. You are not my kind of preacher, but we told the young people they could vote. They voted for you. That is why we have you here. We have some rules! In the first place, nobody ever hollers in this pulpit or hits the pulpit while he preaches. Nobody ever shouts and screams. Nobody ever cries. Nobody ever says, "Amen." We are a dignified group. We have a wealthy membership. We don't have any display of emotion. Now, you can preach, but you can't holler and scream and you can't cry and you can't tell a bunch of funny stories. You have to be dignified."

I stayed in a little parlor room out on the side of his home. I never spent a more lonesome week in my life. I preached Sunday night. Not one person walked down the aisle. I preached Monday night. Not one person walked down the aisle. I preached Tuesday night. Not one person walked down the aisle. I preached Wednesday night. Not one person walked down the aisle.

I went to my room that night and prayed, "Lord, I am not going to be a powerless preacher. I am not! I am not!" I said, "Lord, I promise You something. I am going to pray all night long every night. I am not going to eat a bite of food. I am going to fast and pray until revival comes to this church."

I have never seen a prettier church building. It seated about 1,000 people. It had beautifully padded pews with upholstered arms. It had carpet — you would have a hard time seeing your shoe when you walked down the aisle, the carpet was so thick and plush!

The choir was up in a balcony like an opera balcony. Then you had to go outside to the hallway to get down to the audience from the choir. I never have seen a church like it.

I prayed all night. I can't explain this, but the Lord put His hand on my shoulder and said, "I am going to give you revival tonight." I knew revival was coming. Have you ever prayed until you knew the answer came? I knew revival was coming.

I got up off my knees. I preached that night. Well, since revival was going to come, I thought I would preach my best sermon. I preached on "The Prodigal Son." When I preach on the prodigal son, I act it out. I always call the prodigal son Bill and call his brother who stayed home John. I always act it out.

I began talking about the early events of the parable and got to the point of naming the prodigal son, but to save me I could not think of the name Bill. I backed off and started over again. When I got to the naming of the prodigal son, again the name escaped me. The third time I tried. Again and again I tried. Finally I called the prodigal son by his brother's name, John, thinking by the time I got to the brother I could give him the name of the prodigal son, but still I couldn't think of Bill. I had already given Bill John's name and I was trying to think of Bill so I could give that name to John. I backed up and tried again but still could not think of the name Bill. Again and again I tried and failed. Finally in desperation I said, "The brother didn't have a name. They called him Little Bud for short." So there I was calling Bill John and John Little Bud. Did I ever get confused! The sermon seemed to be in every way a failure; in fact, some folks, realizing my predicament, were snickering.

When I finished the sermon, I could hardly wait to get out of the auditorium and away from my embarrassment. During the invitation, however, a young man in the back on my left started toward the aisle. To be quite frank, I was surprised that anyone would come to the aisle after my message. When he arrived at the aisle, however, he turned and went toward the back door. Again, to be frank, I could hardly blame the fellow for walking out. However, when he got to the back row he stopped and put his arm around a lady, and she began to praise the Lord. Then the two of them ran down the aisle and threw themselves at the altar. Seeing this, the chairman of the deacon board who was sitting in the front row jumped in the altar and began praising God with them. Soon the pastor who had told me that no emotion was allowed was on his knees at the altar joining in the praise. The choir began to weep and could not sing. The music director could not see to lead the singing. Numbers of other people joined the happy altar scene, and real revival broke out. I had no idea what had happened, but I knew I liked it!

Finally the pastor gained enough composure to ask me to lead the closing prayer, after which I walked toward the side door. Just as I arrived at the door, the church secretary took me by the shoulder and turned me around. With tears and emotion she asked, "Who told you?"

I replied, "Who told me what?"

She said, "Who told you to preach on the prodigal son? You

see, the young man who came forward tonight was the son of the deacon chairman. He was a prodigal son who ran away from home one year ago. He is now twenty. No one knew he was within a thousand miles of this place tonight. We were all stunned to see him in the service as we walked in. Then when you announced that you were preaching on the prodigal son, we knew you must have been told of his presence. He came home tonight, got saved, and is going back to his parents. That is what happened at the altar tonight."

I felt praise swelling in my own heart and turned to walk out the door.

The church secretary then asked, "But who told you his name was John?"

I could hardly believe my ears. 'Twas the Holy Spirit Who kept me from remembering the prodigal son's name. It was the Holy Spirit who led me to call the prodigal son John instead of Bill.

The church secretary had still another question. "Who told you he has a brother whose nickname is Little Bud?" By that time I was about to shout! 'Twas the Holy Spirit Who would not let me think of the name Bill and who led me to call the prodigal son John and his brother Little Bud.

This young preacher went to his room that night and stayed on his knees most of the night in praise, prayer and thanksgiving that there is a living God Who leads His preachers who pay the price of waiting on Him.

There is a God in Heaven. Oh, we Baptist preachers need to find out about it. This kind — this kind of revival, this kind of old-fashioned, Holy Spirit power, this kind of miracle. "This kind can come forth by nothing, but by prayer and fasting."

IV. THIS KIND OF CHURCH

The first full-time church I ever pastored was a great church. I was called by a vote of 27 to 26. One adult and 26 young people voted for me. One lady named Mrs. Lambert; her daughter, Jean the pianist; and she rounded up all the kids — they voted for me. I prayed all night, night after night, in the pine thickets of East Texas. I was afraid to walk in the pulpit Sunday after Sunday. God gave us a great church! Over forty pastors in America right now came from that little church.

I went to Garland, Texas, to pastor. The church grew faster than I could handle it. I won't go into it, but the church became a great church one New Year's Eve night when I prayed all night long.

I went to Hammond. The same thing is true in Hammond. There is a little apartment at the Bill Rice Ranch now that has my name on it and it has some concrete out in front with my hand print, my footprint, and my signature because that was where this happened. I was going to resign the First Baptist Church.

I went down to the Bill Rice Ranch and one Friday night there, after I had preached all week, I said, "Lord, I am going to leave First Baptist Church of Hammond! I am not going to stay!"

I went to bed and couldn't sleep. I tried and couldn't. I finally figured I should pray. I prayed all night there in Room 11 of Widner Inn at the Bill Rice Ranch.

About sunup the dear Lord Jesus said to me, "I need somebody to take a great big American Baptist church and turn it upside down and fight the battle and prove that churches can be transformed."

After all night prayer, First Baptist Church of Hammond was born.

"This kind" of revival, "this kind" of miracle, "this kind" of church, and "this kind" of conversion can come forth by nothing, but by prayer and fasting. I am hungry for the old-fashioned kind.

A fellow came and got saved the other day. He said, "I spent all night last night in a house of prostitution. I want to get saved."

The next week a lady came to see me. She said, "I am a

prostitute in Calumet City; I have been for several years. I want to get saved. One of my customers came back to me this week just to tell me what happened to him last Sunday, and I want to get the same thing."

She now goes to our church and is regular and faithful, never missing a Sunday morning or Sunday night or Wednesday night. This kind!

What you really need is a new breath, a new unction, a new heavenly breath upon your ministry! This kind!

Don't you think you ought to learn how to pray and fast? What is it that you need? Do you have a wayward son? Is there some disease lurking in your body and you don't know what it is? Is there a little child not well? Is it a husband who is an alcoholic and a drunk? Are you tired of getting beaten for going to church? Is it a dead church, languishing in failure? This kind! This kind! This kind! This kind where God does it, and God has to do it, can come forth by nothing, but by prayer and fasting!

34

The Holy Spirit and the End Time

II Thessalonians 2:1-12, "Now we beseech you, brethren, by the coming of our Lord Jesus Christ, and by our gathering together unto him, That ye be not soon shaken in mind, or be troubled, neither by spirit, nor by word, not by letter as from us, as that the day of Christ is at hand. Let no man deceive you by any means: for that day shall not come, except there come a falling away first, and that man of sin be revealed, the son of perdition; Who opposeth and exalteth himself above all that is called God, or that is worshipped; so that he as God sitteth in the temple of God, shewing himself that he is God. Remember ye not, that, when I was yet with you, I told you these things? And now ye know what withholdeth that he might be revealed in his time. For the mystery of iniquity doth already work: only he who now letteth will let, until he be taken out of the way. And then shall that Wicked be revealed, whom the Lord shall consume with the spirit of his mouth, and shall destroy with the brightness of his coming: Even him, whose coming is after the working of Satan with all power and signs and lying wonders, And with all deceivableness of unrighteousness in them that perish; because they received not the love of the truth, that they might be saved. And for this cause God shall

send them strong delusion, that they should believe a lie: That they all might be damned who believed not the truth, but had pleasure in unrighteousness."

There are three main comings of our Lord to the earth. He came TO His own. **John 1:11, "He came unto his own, and his own received him not."**

He is coming FOR His own in the air. **I Thessalonians 4:13-18, "But I would not have you to be ignorant, brethren, concerning them which are asleep, that ye sorrow not, even as others which have no hope. For if we believe that Jesus died and rose again, even so them also which sleep in Jesus will God bring with him. For this we say unto you by the word of the Lord, that we which are alive and remain unto the coming of the Lord shall not prevent them which are asleep. For the Lord himself shall descend from heaven with a shout, with the voice of the archangel, and with the trump of God: and the dead in Christ shall rise first: Then we which are alive and remain shall be caught up together with them in the clouds, to meet the Lord in the air: and so shall we ever be with the Lord. Wherefore comfort one another with these words."**

He is coming WITH His own at the end of the seven-year tribulation period to put down the Antichrist and establish His kingdom. **II Thessalonians 2:8, "And then shall that Wicked be revealed, whom the Lord shall consume with the spirit of his mouth, and shall destroy with the brightness of his coming."**

To understand the Holy Spirit's part in the end time, one must understand the purposes behind the writing of the books of I and II Thessalonians. The apostle Paul had started the church in Thessalonica. He especially imparted to this church the truths concerning the coming of our Lord. They had become excited about the rapture and our Lord's returning FOR them. However, something unforeseen happened. One of their members passed away. They were not prepared for this, so they wrote the Apostle asking what would happen to their departed member when Jesus came FOR His own. This book of I Thessalonians is a letter from the Apostle to the church at Thessalonica explaining to them what would happen to the dead when Jesus comes.

Soon trials came to the church, trials that were so great that the members began to wonder if they were already in the tribulation period. They wrote to the Apostle inquiring concerning this matter. The book of II Thessalonians is a letter from Paul to the church at Thessalonica reminding them that they were not in the tribulation period and teaching them of things that must transpire before the tribulation could come and teaching them in general concerning the order of events of the end time. Following is that order:

1. *The mystery of iniquity (that is, sin) will continue.* That is, sin will continue to abound. **II Thessalonians 2:7a, "For the mystery of iniquity doth already work."**

2. *The rapture of the saints must take place.* **II Thessalonians 2:7b, "...only he who now letteth will let, until he be taken out of the way."** The word "let" here means "to hinder." There seems to be someone hindering the mystery of iniquity. This someone, of course, is the Holy Spirit. He does this hindering through His people who are the salt of the earth. Now notice the words in verse 7, "until he be taken out of the way." This means the Holy Spirit will continue to hinder the mystery of iniquity until that day comes when He is taken out of the way. Since He hinders the mystery of iniquity through His people, then His people will be taken out of the way. This is the rapture when God's people are caught up to meet the Lord in the air; the dead will rise first, followed by those of us who are alive and remain. Now notice in **II Thessalonians 2:1** the words, "by our gathering together unto him," which speak of the same event — the rapture. Read further in **II Thessalonians 2:2, 3.** The Apostle says that that day, that is, the tribulation period, cannot come "except there come a falling away first." The term "falling away" means "departure." This, no

doubt, speaks of the rapture.

3. *The Antichrist will then be revealed.* II Thessalonians 2:8, "And then shall that Wicked (wicked one) be revealed." Also note in verse 3, "and that man of sin be revealed, the son of perdition." In other words, the tribulation period will not come until the rapture has taken place and the man of sin is on the scene. This man of sin is the Antichrist, who will be the main character of the tribulation period.

4. *The tribulation itself will take place.* This is that seven-year period when the saints are in the air with Jesus enjoying the marriage of the Lamb, the marriage supper, and appearing before the judgment seat of Christ. The tribulation period is divided into two parts. During the first 3½ years the Antichrist is a peaceable person, deceiving the world by his flatteries. In the middle of the tribulation period the Antichrist becomes Satan incarnate, just as Jesus was God incarnate during His earthly ministry. The last half of the tribulation period, hence, will be the working of Satan incarnate for a period of time about the same as the period of time when our Lord ministered as God incarnate (3½ years).

5. *Then we have the coming of Christ WITH His own.* II Thessalonians 2:8, "And then shall that Wicked be revealed, WHOM THE LORD SHALL CONSUME WITH THE SPIRIT OF HIS MOUTH, AND SHALL DESTROY WITH THE BRIGHTNESS OF HIS COMING." This is the time when Jesus comes back to earth with His saints to establish His kingdom of righteousness which shall last for 1,000 years. This is the time when the wolf shall lie down with the lamb, the little child shall lead the wild animals and play at the hole of the cockatrice den. This is the time when men shall beat their swords into plowshares and their spears into pruning hooks. This is the time when the knowledge of the Lord shall cover the earth as the waters cover the sea. This is the time when God's people shall be kings and priests of God and shall rule and reign with Him for 1,000 years.

6. *The millennium itself will take place.* This is the afore-mentioned 1,000-year reign of Christ upon the earth.

Now let us trace the activities of the Holy Spirit during this time.

1. *He is taken out of the way at the rapture.* **II Thessalonians 2:7, "For the mystery of iniquity doth already work: only he who now letteth will let, until he be taken out of the way."** This does not mean that He will not work at all on the earth. This does mean the end of His ministry as the church age has known it.

2. *He will still convict sinners, and people will be saved during the tribulation period.* **Revelation 7:9, 14, "After this I beheld, and, lo, a great multitude, which no man could number, of all nations, and kindreds, and people, and tongues, stood before the throne, and before the Lamb, clothed with white robes, and palms in their hands. And I said unto him, Sir, thou knowest. And he said to me, These are they which came out of great tribulation, and have washed their robes, and made them white in the blood of the Lamb."** These people are those who received Christ during the tribulation period. There will be multitudes of them. Of course, they must be convicted by the Holy Spirit in order to be saved. These converts are probably those who had never heard the message of salvation. The Bible seems to teach that those who have heard the message of salvation and refused it shall be sent delusions during the tribulation period and will not be saved. **II Thessalonians 2:9-12, "Even him, whose coming is after the working of Satan with all power and signs and lying wonders, And with all deceivableness of unrighteousness in them that perish; because they received not the love of the truth, that they might be saved. And for this cause God shall send them strong delusion, that they should believe a lie: That they all might be damned who believed not**

the truth, but had pleasure in unrighteousness."

3. *The Holy Spirit will work in mighty power during the millennium.* Isaiah 11:1, 2, **"And there shall come forth a rod out of the stem of Jesse, and a Branch shall grow out of his roots: And the spirit of the LORD shall rest upon him, the spirit of wisdom and understanding, the spirit of counsel and might, the spirit of knowledge and of the fear of the LORD."** Here we have a summary of the work the Holy Spirit shall do during the kingdom age. It is He Who will lead us as we rule and reign on the earth. It will be His wisdom by which we rule and His power through which we rule.

Before this discussion is concluded, mention should be made of the counterfeit work that shall be done by Satan in the end time. This work will be manifested by the workings of miracles. When the Antichrist and the false prophet shall come, they shall come performing miracles. See Revelation 13. Satan, you see, has a trinity. Satan himself is the opposite of God the Father. The Antichrist, who shall head the political end-time confederation, is the opposite of God the Son. The false prophet, who will head up the ecclesiastical confederation in the end time is the opposite of God the Holy Spirit. Hence, in these three we have Satan's trinity. **Revelation 13:1, 11, "And I stood upon the sand of the sea, and saw a beast rise up out of the sea, having seven heads and ten horns, and upon his horns ten crowns, and upon his heads the name of blasphemy. And I beheld another beast coming up out of the earth; and he had two horns like a lamb, and he spake as a dragon."**
Notice also that this second beast (false prophet) will do great wonders and even call fire from the heavens. **Revelation 13:13, "And he doeth great wonders, so that he maketh fire come down from heaven on the earth in the sight of men."**
Also notice that he will do miracles and by them will deceive

the nations. **Revelation 13:14, "And deceiveth them that dwell on the earth by the means of those miracles which he had power to do in the sight of the beast; saying to them that dwell on the earth, that they should make an image to the beast, which had the wound by a sword, and did live."** Now notice that he even makes an image, that is, a man-made replica of the first beast (Antichrist) and actually gives to that image life and the ability to speak! **Revelation 13:15, "And he had power to give life unto the image of the beast, that the image of the beast should both speak, and cause that as many as would not worship tie image of the beast should be killed."**

Be not deceived, beloved, when those who are in error concerning the great doctrines of the faith suddenly perform miracles, for in the end time the performance of these miracles will not at all confirm that God is working. If a man comes to town and you see tumors disappear before your very eyes, this does not necessarily mean that he is of God. There are people today who no doubt are seeing physical miracles take place who do not believe in the virgin birth, who pray to the virgin Mary, and who do not believe in the verbal inspiration of the Bible and other foundational truths. This doing of miracles is in no way an evidence of being genuine. Christians should not be deceived; there is a supernatural which is not of God. There are miracles which are not of God and these miracles of the Antichrist and false prophet will intensify as we see the day approaching. Many will be deceived; do not be among them!

35
The Holy Spirit in Heaven

The subject at hand should not be characterized by dogmatism, but it does warrant a brief investigation. Will the Holy Spirit be in Heaven? Will He have a body? What form will that body take? Will we see three in Heaven or one? These are questions that force their way into our minds. Their answers should certainly should not divide fundamental believers, but the very presence of the questions would warrant a brief investigation into the subject.

Occasionally in the Scriptures we get a glimpse into Heaven of the Father and the Son. We do know that there was a fellowship between the Father and the Son before the foundation of the world. **John 17:5, "And now, O Father, glorify thou me with thine own self with the glory which I had with thee before the world was."**

We get the same teaching from **John 1:1, "In the beginning was the Word, and the Word was with God, and the Word was God."** Note especially the words, "and the Word was with God." This could be worded, "and the Word was toward God," or "the Word was facing toward God." This implies a fellowship enjoyed by the Father and the Son in the beginning and from the beginning.

When Stephen died, he looked up into Heaven and saw the

glory of God, and Jesus standing on the right hand of God. This implies that the Father is visible in Heaven and that the Son, likewise, is visible in Heaven. **Acts 7:55, "But he, being full of the Holy Ghost, looked up stedfastly into heaven, and saw the glory of God, and Jesus standing on the right hand of God."**

We also find from the writer of the book of Hebrews that Christ appears in the presence of God for us. This leads to the conclusion that the presence of the Father and the presence of the Son in Heaven are different. **Hebrews 9:23, 24, "It was therefore necessary that the patterns of things in the heavens should be purified with these; but the heavenly things themselves with better sacrifices than these. For Christ is not entered into the holy places made with hands, which are the figures of the true; but into heaven itself, now to appear in the presence of God for us."**

Now that we have established that the Father and the Son have a presence in Heaven, we turn our attention toward the Holy Spirit.

First, the Scriptures seem to teach that He is in Heaven. **I John 5:7, "For there are three that bear record in heaven, the Father, the Word, and the Holy Ghost: and these three are one."** Though no one can explain the trinity, we do know that they are three different personalities and yet there is one God. All attempts to explain this truth accurately have failed. Oh, it could be said that the trinity is like the egg — the white, the yellow and the shell — three parts of one egg. Or it could be explained that it is like H_2O — vapor, water and ice. Some try to explain it comparing it to fruit — that is, peeling, seed and meat. However, all of these attempts fail completely to explain the trinity. We simply believe that there are three persons in one Godhead and that all three will be in Heaven.

Second, the question comes, "What does the Holy Spirit do in Heaven?" Note **Psalm 139:7, 8, "Whither shall I go from thy spirit? or whither shall I flee from thy presence? If I ascend up**

into heaven, thou art there: if I make my bed in hell, behold, thou are there." Again we find that the Holy Spirit is in Heaven. Though the Scripture is not as clear on this subject as on others, it would seem that the Holy Spirit basically will do His work in Heaven much as He does on earth. Some light is shed on this in **Isaiah 11:1, 2, "And there shall come forth a rod out of the stem of Jesse, and a Branch shall grow out of his roots: And the spirit of the LORD shall rest upon him, the spirit of wisdom and understanding, the spirit of counsel and might, the spirit of knowledge and of the fear of the LORD."** Now these verses deal with the work of the Holy Spirit during the millennium. Bear in mind that the saved person will have his glorified body then. It appears that the Holy Spirit continues to work even through the glorified body. He will give us the spirit of wisdom and understanding, the spirit of counsel and might, the spirit of knowledge and of the fear of the Lord. Perhaps this working of the Spirit in the millennium, when the Christian possesses the body that he will have in the New Jerusalem, will continue in eternity.

Will the Holy Spirit have a body in Heaven? Once again we come to a question for which the answer is not as clear as for some Bible questions, but perhaps some light may be shed on this subject in **I Corinthians 15:44, "It is sown a natural body; it is raised a spiritual body. There is a natural body, and there is a spiritual body."** Notice the words, "there is a spiritual body." In another chapter we deal with the body of the Spirit and we find that just as the physical body is the habitation of the soul, even so the soul is the habitation of the Spirit. We could assume then that since there is a spiritual body, the Holy Spirit will have some form of body in Heaven. This body is not recognizable by fleshly eyes any more than the soul (which is the body of the Spirit) is recognized by physical eyes. Again we must avoid dogmatism, but there seems to be some evidence that since there is a spiritual body, we will with our spiritual bodies be able to recognize the spiritual body of the Holy Spirit in Heaven.

We then find that the Holy Spirit will someday present us to Jesus. **Jude 20, 24, "But ye, beloved, building up yourselves on your most holy faith, praying in the Holy Ghost. Now unto him that is able to keep you from falling, and to present you faultless before the presence of his glory with exceeding joy."** It appears that the Holy Spirit Who has been our guide, comforter, helper and companion will someday present us to the Lord Jesus Christ. He Who knows us best will present us to Him Who died for us, and then the Holy Spirit will open our eyes and we shall see Jesus as He is!

These words are being written shortly after the death of my beloved friend, Dr. John R. Rice, with whom I preached for nearly a quarter of a century. Over 2200 times I have sat on the same platform to preach with this servant of God. He walked in the Spirit. He was anointed for his task. He was filled with the Holy Spirit. Recently he went to Heaven. The Holy Spirit, Who knew him so well and Whose leadership he followed so beautifully and Whose power he had known so often, opened his eyes and introduced him in a visible way to the blessed Saviour, and he who had walked in the Spirit for so many years perhaps even now is seeing through spiritual eyes the Holy Spirit. To say the least, he is seeing Jesus to Whom the Holy Spirit pointed him when He was saved as a lad, to Whom the Holy Spirit pointed him as he preached His Gospel for so many years and to Whom the Holy Spirit pointed him when he breathed his last physical breath and entered into the presence of his Saviour.